Julie Isard-Brown

The Mason's Wife

novum ◢ pro

This book is also available as e-book.

www.novum-publishing.co.uk

© 2016 novum publishing

ISBN 978-3-99048-116-5
Editor: Arun Natarajan
Cover photos: Robert McLeish, Anna Yakimova | Dreamstime.com
Cover design, layout & typesetting: novum publishing
Illustrations: P. 6, 48, 49, 117, 235, 236, 320, 321, 322, 323, 400, 401, 402, 403 © Julie Isard-Brown; P. 177 © Robert McLeish

www.novum-publishing.co.uk

Preface

This story is based in fact. My grandfather knew nothing of his family as he lost both his parents shortly after he turned four. He was taken into the workhouse and adopted out by the Aspley Guise Committee to a family in Bow Brickhill. His sister, Lily was also sent out to Bow Brickhill but she was never adopted, just in service. Their brother, Walter Alexander Brown stayed in the workhouse as he was much older. He soon enlisted in the army and became a musician in the 1st battalion of the Royal West Kent Regiment. Walter was the only one of the three siblings to never marry and died with my grandfather at his side in 1961.

After my grandfather and father died I took it upon myself to find out what I could about their and my other ancestors. It was this line of my family, however, that interested me most.

I have spent many years researching the family and visited Scotland frequently. There were many more records for the family in Scotland than I ever found in the English archives. I have built the story up around these facts and interspersed it with events of the time.

Over the years I feel I have come to know this family almost like they were alive and living with me.

I dedicate this story to my father, Reginald James Brown, and my grandfather, James Lumbard Brown. I know they would have loved to have been alive when I found out the details.

James Brown, my grandfather,
me and Reginald Brown, my father

CHAPTER 1

Starting out

Young Walter turned to his grandmother, and asked, "Granny, where were you born?"

It was Friday, 21 July 1865 and Walter and his granny, Sarah McWilliam, were in her kitchen, in a two roomed cottage in Lesmahagow. The inside of the cottage was basic. The bricks on the inside had been whitewashed and you could see up into the low roof arch. The roof supports were clearly visible, however, the cottage was divided into two at the roof apex, so half of the supports were in one room and the other half were in the other room. The cottage had a stone floor made up of tiles. They were nearly always cold, even in the summer.

There was a big open fireplace in the centre of the wall adjoining the next cottage and there was a range of sorts in the centre of the fireplace. In reality, it was a metal frame following the shape of the fireplace, which reached up to almost head-height, from which chains with hooks dangled for pots to be hung from for cooking. There was also a small metal stove at one end of the fireplace – a modern contraption, which was used more often than the original construction.

A cupboard stood against the wall to the other room, furthest away from the window. It held the crockery on its shelves and cups hanging from hooks. A table and chairs were next. They weren't fancy, but adequate for the family's needs. On the table was a vase of flowers, to add a bit of colour to the room. A well-used rocking chair, that had seen better days, was over by the window, and it was here that Sarah was sitting.

Two beds were built into the wall in the front room, by the front door. Makeshift curtain frames had been put around them to distance them from the main living area, so they looked like primitive four-poster beds, without the wooden frame. Both of the beds had been made up with simple patterned blankets, although one appeared more used than the other.

Sarah was 52 years old, and looked tired. She looked about 7 years older than her age, and had grey hair that was once mousey brown, tied back in a bun. She stood about 5 feet 4 inches tall and was slightly plump, almost the image of her mother at that age. She had a jovial face, but one that looked like it had seen much misery. She wore a simple black dress with long, straight sleeves and a high neck line with a small white collar that buttoned at the front. The dress had a natural waist and came down to just below her ankles. It was flatter at the front but had a bit of a bustle at the back. She wore a pair of neat black lace up shoes.

Three boys of varying ages sat at the table; Sarah's son, Nathaniel, whose tenth birthday was that day, sat quietly reading. To his left, his nephew, Walter, who had turned 6 years old just three weeks earlier, was carefully learning his letters, whilst Alexander, Walter's younger brother at 2½ years, happily scribbled a picture. As it was Nathaniel's birthday, Sarah was taking some time out to sit with the boys. The two older boys were dressed in a cream shirt and grey trousers with long socks and the youngest one was in a navy check dress of the period, with mid length sleeves and coming to just below the knees, from which protruded pantalettes of the same colour. All the clothes were less than new, and in the case of the children, most of them were hand-me-downs.

Sarah looked at Walter and smiled. She replied, "Hmm, now tha's somethin' I've no' been asked for a while. It almost seems a lifetime away now. Do you really want tae know?"

"Aye, Granny," replied Walter, then, turning to his uncle, he asked, "Do you know the story?"

Nathaniel stopped what he was doing and looked at Walter. "I knew ma' was from England," he replied, "but I've no' really asked." Turning to his mother he said, "Aye, I'd like tae know as well."

Sarah looked at the boys. "Well, if you must, and as it's your birthday, Nat..."

Sarah began to relate the story. "I was born in a wee village called Tranmere, in Cheshire. Tranmere sits on the river Mersey and my father was a ferryman, travelling back and forth across the river. His name was Thomas, and my mother was Mary. I was one of eight bairns – I had three sisters and four brothers. Hannah was two years older than me, John was three years younger than me, then came Mary two years later, Robert one year after that, Jane nine years later, and then came Thomas five years later. There was also another, Joseph, born two years after Thomas, but he only survived a few months. Father made sure we learned to read and write. He taught us in his few days off, and made sure we kept it up.

"I never thought I'd move sae far away way back then, hmm, s'funny how life changes." Sarah stopped talking, and recalled in her mind the days of her youth. She woke out of her reverie and continued.

"I had lots of friends my own age, too – all wee ones of the boatmen. There were six farms – I knew the families on three o' them." She smiled as she thought of them. "There was also a butcher, a brewer, a couple o' blacksmiths and a couple o' carpenters. And then there were three ale houses and two shops.

"My childhood was nothing different. The fun started a few years later, when I was in my teens. Things started to get a wee bit busy. There were people coming in to build the new houses in Birkenhead, just a wee bit up from Tranmere. There was space in some o' the cottages, so the villagers took in incomers before they found somewhere in the new town.

"That's where I met Robert and his wife Agnes –"

Walter suddenly interrupted her. "You mean gran'fer? He was a'ready married?"

Sarah nodded and continued.

"Aye, well he was then. They came tae the village when I was about 23. They had their two bairns, Agnes and William – your Uncle and Auntie, and Agnes was expecting another. She was nearly due tae have the bairn when they came tae the village. There was an empty cottage on the French's farm, up in Holt Hill, so they rented that for a while."

"I dinnae remember Agnes and William," said Nathaniel, surprised.

"They didnae come tae Scotland wi' us," answered Sarah. Her eyes glazed over as she thought fondly of the last time she ever saw either of them.

Walter and Nathaniel had stopped what they were doing and sat enthralled as Sarah continued to relate the story. Alexander had gotten bored with his scribbling, and was now sitting on the floor, playing with his wooden farm animals, looking up from time to time, but not really listening.

"I was helping my ma' wi' her job. She was the local midwife and was teaching me how tae help her. We'd just come from the Reverend Martindale's house – they'd just had a wee daughter born, and I'd been really excited, because ma had let me deliver the bairn by myself. I'd been working with her a while, and I'd watched, and helped, but this was the first one I'd done alone. It was so easy and I thought I was doin' sae well. Ma had said that it was the first one, but I was still learning. How right she was, too…"

It was Friday, 7 July 1837. The day dawned warm and fair. The sun was shining and there were a few clouds in the sky, with a gentle breeze. Mother and daughter left a house on the west side of Church Road, in a plot on Garner's Field, almost in Holt Hill. The mother, Mary Foulkes, was 51 years old, but energetic. She looked about 5 years older than her age, and had greying hair that was once mousey brown, tied back in a bun. She stood about 5 feet 4 inches tall and was slightly plump. The daughter, Sarah, was 23 years old. She had mousey brown hair, also, and looked very much like a younger version of Mary. She stood about 5 feet 7 inches tall and was very slim by comparison. They both wore similar clothes – drab colours, long sleeved, high neck dresses, with a natural waistline that buttoned up at the back, finishing just below the ankles, but not so close to the ground that they dragged. Mary's dress was grey, whilst Sarah's dress was mid brown. They both wore caps, shawls and well-worn black lace up shoes. Mary carried a wicker basket with a lid which held the women's aprons and other birthing equipment.

Sarah was talking excitedly to her mother as they hurried away from the Manse. Agnes McWilliam had just gone into labour – her next door neighbour had come there to tell them that Agnes was in great pain, and she had called in to see her, asking what to do. Susanna Martin, the neighbour, had told Agnes to go back home and wait. Susanna then went to the Foulkes cottage and Hannah, the eldest daughter, had told her where her mother was. Susanna had knocked at the big house and asked to see the pair. Sarah listened to what Susanna had to say and she told Susanna they would come as soon as they were able. Mary had heard them talking and joined her daughter. Mary told Susanna they'd be there presently, so she asked for Susanna to go back and stay with Agnes until they arrived – about a half hour.

Mother and daughter turned left along the road and up towards the junction. There were fields as far as the eye could see, interspersed with cottages. They took the left fork in the road, to Holt Hill, and walked along to the third cottage on the left. Mary knocked on the door and after a moment Susanna opened it. She let them in and they immediately saw poor Agnes, a heavily pregnant woman, who was struggling to stand upright. She was wearing a similar brown-coloured dress, but ill-fitting, due to her condition.

Agnes was a very pretty woman – would have been tall and slender, had it not been for her current predicament – with dark brown hair, tied back in a bun. There were two small children standing at her skirt. The children were both in dresses, the older one wearing cream and the younger one wearing brown. They were both similar to the adults' dresses, except that they finished just below the knee, with pantalettes. The older child was a girl, aged 3½ years, and her dark brown hair hung loose, coming down to be just about shoulder-length. The younger child was a boy, aged 2 years, and his hair was black, about 2 inches long.

Mary explained, "I'm the midwife, come to help you. How far gone are you?"

Agnes told her that she was in a lot of pain. She'd been in labour for what seemed an eternity, so Mary told her they would see what needed to be done. This was a two roomed cottage, stone built with a thatched roof. The brick walls looked the same inside as they did on the outside, and the thatch was visible from the inside, too. The room to the road was the kitchen-cum-living-room and it was full of both living and cooking furniture.

There was a large fireplace with an open fire, with a metal frame to hold the hooks for the pots to hang from. A large pot was hanging from one of the hooks and water was bubbling away in it. Against the wall was a table and four chairs that were well used. In a corner, away from the cooking area was a rocking chair, which appeared to be the only new item of furniture in the room. The stone floor had some grass matting on it, which made it warmer to walk on and for the children to sit on.

Susanna helped Agnes through to the bedroom, which was through a door off the kitchen. There were two beds in this room, one for the parents and one for the children. The children's bed was tucked away in a recess and was made up so the children slept at opposite ends to each other. The other bed was free-standing and by its side was a simple wooden cradle.

Susanna sat Agnes down on the bed and said, "Now the midwife is here, I'll be going." Agnes nodded. Mary turned to Susanna. "Thank you kindly for staying with Agnes until we could get here. She'll be fine, now." Susanna nodded and left the cottage. Mother and daughter prepared for the birth.

Agnes lay down on the bed and Mary felt her belly. "So, Agnes, is your husband at work?" Mary asked.

"Aye," replied Agnes. He's a stonemason, working in Birkenhead."

"Does he know you're in labour?" Mary asked.

"I'd no' bothered tae tell him," Agnes replied. "Mind, this time seems worse than the others."

"You'll be fine," replied Mary. She then turned to her daughter, and in a quiet voice, so as not to worry Agnes, she said, "You need to go fetch Annie Prieson. I'm thinking we're going to need the doctor, and she's got a cart we can use to fetch him. I've a feeling something's not quite right. I'll make a start here while you go and get her."

"Right, ma'," replied Sarah. She walked out of the house, trying not to appear nervous, turned right and ran back down the road, in the direction they had just come, to a cottage opposite the church, part of one of the local farms. Five minutes later she knocked on the door and a woman, dressed in a green skirt and yellow blouse, appeared at the door.

"Mrs. Prieson, ma' wants you to come."

"Why Sarah," Annie started, "Whatever's the matter?"

"It's the new lady – she's in labour, and ma's worried about her." Sarah replied.

"Right, give me a few minutes to get myself sorted and I'll be with you," Annie answered, turning to go back into her house. Sarah waited on the doorstep until Annie re-emerged a few minutes later with a cap and a shawl on. "Let's go get the horse and cart," she said.

They went to a barn further down the farmyard and Annie brought out a simple cart. She then brought out a bay horse and harnessed it to the cart. Both women jumped up on the cart and they galloped off back up the road to Agnes' cottage. Annie stopped outside and she and Sarah jumped off. Annie tied the horse to the post outside, and they went indoors.

Agnes was lying on the bed. Her contractions were coming thick and fast, but the baby was not. With each contraction Agnes was getting more and more agitated and her screams could be clearly heard outside of the cottage. Once inside, Annie stood beside Agnes to offer her support. She wasn't a proper midwife, like Mary was.

Mary called to her, "Agnes, the baby is coming, so you have to push now."

As she tried to push, Agnes said, "I'm pushing as hard as I can. There's something wrong. I know it. My other two bairns weren't this hard."

Mary tried to reassure her. "You're doing grand." Inside, Mary knew Agnes was right.

Mary told Agnes she could see the baby's head. "Come on Agnes, you can do it," she added.

Sarah began to panic. She'd never seen a difficult birth. She knew the waters had to break before the baby was born but she'd never seen bleeding before the baby had been born. "Ma'," said Sarah, in a whisper, "she's bleeding really bad. What's wrong?" "Shush Sarah," said Annie Prieson, "we don't want Agnes to panic."

Mary called out, "Here it comes!" The baby slithered out but not very far. "Oh, but the cord is around its neck," said Mary. "Where are those scissors? We need to get it cut as quickly as we can." Sarah handed them to her. The older women tied off both ends of the cord with twine and Mary cut the cord.

"Done!" said Mary. She gently cleared the cord from around the baby's neck and pulled it free of Agnes' body. "Here, Sarah, you see to baby while we try to help Agnes." Mary handed the baby to Sarah and as she did so the baby made a cry. Sarah took the baby into the other room and began to clean the blood off it.

Agnes, barely conscious, asked, "What is it?"

"It's a girl Mrs. McWilliam", said Annie, as she tried to make the woman more comfortable. "Sarah's just taken her to clean her up. She'll be back in a minute."

"It's you we've to concern ourselves with at the moment," added Mary.

As she said this, Sarah came back into the room and handed the crying baby to Agnes, who was very pale and still, but she managed to take the baby from Sarah. Agnes looked lovingly at the baby. "Jane. Tell Robert. Jane."

"You can tell him yourself Mrs. McWilliam. He'll be home soon," said Sarah. But, Agnes was very weak from her labour and she lost consciousness, so Sarah took the baby back. "Ma'," Sarah asked, "what's happening?"

"She's lost a lot of blood, Sarah," said her mother. "They don't normally happen like this. It won't stop."

Annie had been waiting for the final stage to be over. She now came over to Mary, who had cleaned up and was checking on the baby. "I've got the afterbirth," said Annie. "She should stop bleeding in a bit. Just look at it – see how it's torn..." Mary looked at it and nodded. "That's why there's so much bleeding. Annie, you'll have to go get the doctor. I don't know what else to do."

"Good job you sent for me", said Annie. "I'll not be long." Annie wiped her hands and rushed out of the cottage, leaving Mary and Sarah to tend to their patients. They listened as the horse and cart disappeared down the road to Bebington to go for help.

Mary had found some baby things to dress the infant in and had taken them in the kitchen. Sarah began to dress the infant as she sat in the kitchen, unsure of what else to do. The children stood around Sarah looking at the baby. Agnes, the older child, said "She's so tiny..."

"You were that size once", said Sarah, smiling. She was glad of the children's company at that moment. It took her mind of the difficult childbirth she had just witnessed. Agnes asked, "Can I touch her?"

"Yes, but gently," Sarah replied. Agnes stroked her arm for a moment.

In the other room, Mary tried frantically to stem the bleeding, but without success. Agnes became paler and more lifeless by the minute. An hour passed. Mary was beginning to think the doctor would never come but then she heard the horse and cart pull up outside and the door opened. Annie ran in, closely followed by Doctor Williams. He was 55 years old and slightly balding. He had a ruddy complexion and was well filled out, wearing a grey suit with a waistcoat, and a John Bull hat. He carried a bag with his equipment.

He called out as he entered the house, "Mrs. Foulkes, I'm here!" He went over to Sarah, holding the baby. She was the first thing he had seen as he walked in the door. He looked at the baby. "Well, she seems fine enough," he said. He then went into the bedroom and over to Agnes as he asked, "So how's Mrs. McWilliam?"

"I can't stop the bleeding, doctor," said Mary. "What should we do? Look at the afterbirth..." She showed him the torn placenta. He took one look at it and said, "Oh my... That's not good. Where's the husband?"

"He's out at work, doctor," replied Mary. "He's a stonemason working in Birkenhead. He doesn't know. He left for work before Agnes went into labour. He should be home soon."

Doctor Williams looked concerned. "Well, he needs to be here." He turned to Annie. "Annie, I think we should go fetch Martha. Mary, watch Agnes while we've gone." Both Annie and Mary replied almost simultaneously. "Yes, Doctor." Back in the kitchen, Dr. Williams stopped beside Sarah. "I think you should put her into the cradle, now," he said.

Annie and the doctor left the cottage and once again the sound of the horse and cart departing filled the room.

Sarah sat with the children, still holding the baby. She was almost in shock. She had finished dressing baby Jane and she was ready to be put in the cradle, as the doctor had instructed. Sarah sat there, thinking about what had happened. Giving birth had always been so easy. She felt, up until this time, that she was ready to be a midwife, but clearly, after today she needed to think again. Sarah stood up holding the baby and took her into the bedroom.

Sarah laid the baby in her cradle. "Ma'," she asked, "who is Martha?"

"Martha Lidsome," replied her mother. "She's a wet nurse. Agnes is too ill to feed Jane, so somebody has to do it, and that's why they've gone for Martha."

16

Sarah began to understand how serious the situation was, now. It hadn't occurred to her there would be a problem with feeding the baby.

Mary sat watching Agnes, who was laying there, deathly white in bed. It seemed like hours had passed, but in reality it was only an hour. The front door opened and in ran Robert McWilliam.

He was a handsome man, 5 feet 9 inches tall, well built and very muscular, with a shock of bushy black hair. He also had a black moustache and a few whiskers on his chin. He was wearing standard working man's clothes, brown trousers with a belt, cream shirt with no collar, on top of which he wore a matching jacket. On his feet were large work-boots and he had a cap on his head, which he pulled off as he rushed in through the door.

He was distraught. He rushed into the bedroom and up to the bed where Agnes was lying. He knelt down beside her and gently wiped her brow and kissed her hand. "Agnes, Agnes!" he called out, desperately hoping she would answer.

Mary stood up as he rushed to Agnes' bedside. "She's still alive, Mr. McWilliam, but only barely."

Clinging on to Agnes' pale and lifeless hand he asked, "What happened? Where's the baby? Is it a'right?"

"The baby's fine," Mary replied. "She's here in her cradle." Robert glanced over at the cradle, but his main concern was for his wife.

"We came as soon as we could," began Mary, "but there were problems with the birth right from the start. The baby didn't want to come out, and when she did the cord was wrapped around her neck." Robert listened, horrified.

"She had a bad night, last night," he said. "I didnae want tae leave her, but she insisted." He looked down at Agnes as he spoke. He shook his head as he continued, "Why did you make me go?" he asked his unconscious wife. "I should never have gone tae work!"

Mary tried to put Robert at ease. "You could never have known what was going to happen," she said. "We managed to save her – and the baby. My daughter Sarah is with your chil-

17

dren right now in the kitchen. Agnes was bleeding badly before she even gave birth, and we couldn't stop it. We'd sent for Annie Prieson and she came with her cart, so we were able to get the doctor here fast, but even he couldn't stop the bleeding. She passed out soon after she saw the baby."

"Did Agnes say anything before she passed out?"

"She said to call her Jane."

Robert looked around the room. "Agnes, William," he called out.

Sarah heard Robert talking and came in from the kitchen with the two little ones. They pushed past Sarah and went up to hug their father, one on each leg. Sarah went round to the cradle and fetched out baby Jane. She walked round to the other side of the bed and Robert took the baby from Sarah.

Robert stood there, looking down at the tiny infant in his arms. "She's a bonny wee thing." He looked down at Agnes, lying there, unconscious. A sudden thought gripped him as he looked at the baby. "What's tae be done wi' the bairn? How am I going tae feed her?"

"The baby will be fine," said Mary. "Martha Lidsome is able to wet nurse her until Agnes can feed more easily. Annie and the doctor have gone to fetch her."

Robert relaxed a little. "You seem tae have everything well in hand, tha's for sure," he answered.

"Mr. McWilliam –" Mary started, but was interrupted by Robert. "My name's Robert. Please ca' me by my first name. You've earned my respect today, tha's for sure. But who's tae look after my other bairns? I have tae work, for I'm no' asking for charity."

"If Martha's acceptable as wet nurse," Mary said, "I'm certain she'll look after the little ones."

"Aye, that'd be grand," Robert replied. "She'll be paid, o' course – you'll ask her for me?"

"For sure I will."

A few minutes later Robert and Mary heard the horse and cart pull up outside. Sarah took baby Jane from him as she knew he must have much to ask the doctor. She laid her back in her cradle and covered her with a blanket. The door opened and the doctor, Annie Prieson and Martha Lidsome rushed in.

Martha was not so drably dressed. The style of dress was the same, but the dress was a light blue colour. Her hair was mousey blond and was curled in ringlets. She wore the customary cap. Martha was a very slight young woman, only about 5ft tall. She had a very small frame and looked no bigger than a girl in her teens. She carried a small valise with her containing a few belongings, which she put down on the floor just inside the door.

The doctor saw Robert standing there. "Good evening, Mr. McWilliam. Glad to see you back – and not a moment too soon!"

"If I'd known I'd never have gone tae work this morning," said Robert, tritely.

"You could never have known," replied the doctor. Turning to Mary, the doctor asked, "How is she? Mary."

"She's not well, doctor," replied Mary. "The bleeding's stopped, though."

"Well, that's something," the doctor replied. He went over and started to examine Agnes.

Martha went over to Robert and introduced herself. "Good evening, Mr. McWilliam. I'm Martha Lidsome. I'll be your wet nurse, if you're willing."

Robert looked at Martha. She was young and pretty. "Thank you kindly, ma'am," Robert replied. "I'll pay for your services."

Martha looked around the room. "Where is the baby?"

"She's in the cradle, there," he said, pointing in its direction. He looked at Sarah. "Will you pass Jane over tae this lassie?" he asked Sarah. She came forward and gave the baby to Martha. He looked down at the baby as she screwed up her face, getting ready to cry. He said, "Here she is, Martha. She must be very hungry. Would you mind taking her now?"

"Of course – that's why I'm here. Do you have somewhere private I can sit?"

"If you'll come with me, Martha," said Mary, "there's a suitable corner in the other room." Mary notioned to her to follow, and they went out of the bedroom and into the kitchen. Mary showed Martha to the rocking chair and Sarah took the two children outside to play for a while so that Martha could have some privacy. Martha began to feed the infant.

After a few minutes the doctor finished his examination of Agnes and turned to speak with Robert, who was now sitting beside the bed, holding Agnes' hand. "Robert, I'm afraid there's nothing more we can do for your wife," he said. "The birth caused her to bleed very badly. I think there was a problem with the afterbirth – it looks like it wasn't where it should be and it tore, which is one of the reasons why there were problems with the baby being born."

Robert looked at the doctor, not believing what he had just heard. 'How can this be?' he thought. 'When I left the house this morning she was a fine, healthy woman.' He was interrupted from his thoughts by Martha, as she came back in from the kitchen. "Mr. McWilliam, I've fed Jane her first feed. She was very hungry, but I've not overfed her. Shall I lay her back down in the cradle?"

Robert just sat there, holding his wife's hand. He nodded submissively and then stood up. He went over to the doctor, who was in discussion with Mary. "So, doctor," said Robert, "what's going tae happen now?"

As Robert was talking, Agnes woke up and began to murmur. Robert rushed back over to her, sat down on the bed beside her and took hold of her hand. "Agnes, it's me, Robert."

Agnes wearily opened her eyes and looked at Robert. She could barely see him, but she knew the sound of his voice. Weakly, she began to talk to him. "Robert, you came home. Have you seen her? Wee, baby Jane? She's bonny, is she not?"

Robert leant in closer, to hear her better. He said, "Aye, I know. I've held her. She's the image of you." Agnes smiled at him. "I havenae any strength," she murmured. "How am I goin' tae look after her?"

Robert brushed a stray wisp of hair out of Agnes' face. "Dinnae worry yoursel'," he said to her. "It's all in hand. The doctor's fetched us a wet nurse, so you can concentrate on getting better."

The doctor tapped Robert on the shoulder and Robert turned to look at him. "Robert, I'll take my leave of you now. I'll be back in the morning to see how Agnes and the baby are doing. It is only a matter of time, I'm afraid."

"Are you sure? She's awake now, and talking to me," Robert replied in disbelief. He stood up and moved away from Agnes. "I think she'll be fine now – all she needed was some sleep."

The doctor shook his head. "She's lost so much blood. It needs a miracle. I'll see you tomorrow." He turned to Annie. "Annie, will you take me home, please?"

"Certainly, doctor," said Annie. She then turned to Mary. "I need to get back to my family, Mary, so I'll take my leave of you."

"That's fine," Mary replied. "You were a great help today."

Martha went up to Robert before he sat down with Agnes again. "Mr. McWilliam, Mrs. Foulkes has asked if I'd look after your other children as well. I've not looked after that age but I'll take them on for you." Robert looked at Martha and nodded in appreciation.

Martha picked up her bag and asked where she should sleep. There were only the two beds in the bedroom, and Martha wanted some privacy if she was to be feeding the baby.

After a moment's thought Robert spoke. "There's a spare mattress under the wee ones' bed. Perhaps we could make that up for you in the living room, for now, and I can work out something more permanent in a couple o' days."

It was a little primitive, Martha thought, but considering the family had never imagined this would happen it was understandable they were ill prepared, so she accepted his proposal.

The doctor and Annie left the cottage. Robert went back to sit with Agnes, who had, once again, lost consciousness. Mary went over to him. "Robert, do you want me to get you anything? Are you hungry?" Robert just sat there. His mind was conscious of only one thing. The woman he loved was lying before him asleep, but everybody around him was telling him she was dying. 'It's just no' possible' he thought. 'It cannae happen.'

Mary tapped him gently on the shoulder. "Robert, you need to eat – to keep your strength up – for Agnes' and the baby's sake."

This woke him up from his reverie. "Aye, Mary – you're right."

"What shall I get you?" she asked. After a few moment's thought he replied, "I'll just have a sandwich – there'll be some cheese in the kitchen, for sure."

Mary went into the kitchen and prepared him a sandwich. While she did this, Sarah came to her. "Shall I go home, ma', and prepare us some food?" "Yes, Sarah," her mother replied, nodding. "We have mouths of our own to feed. Tell Robert you'll be taking your leave, and I'll join you presently." Sarah went over to Robert and told him she was leaving. He barely moved. Mary finished preparing the sandwich and took it and a glass of beer to where Robert sat. "Here you are, Robert," she said, "and I've taken the liberty of drawing you a glass of beer. She held the plate and glass out to him and he took them both. He put the glass of beer down and ate the sandwich. 'Yes,' he thought, 'I was hungry – I was just so wrapped up in looking at Agnes that I didnae realise!' Mary told him that she would have to go now, but would be back next day and he nodded. With that, she collected her things together and left for home.

Next morning, Mary and Sarah went back to see how Robert was coping, and if Agnes had shown any signs of recovery. Robert had been up all night and looked tired. Agnes lay there in bed, pale and still. Mary stood there and watched her. 'Yes', she thought, 'I can see her breathing, but barely.' Sarah went to see Martha and the baby. Martha sat in the rocking chair, having just fed Jane, and she was settling her back down before returning her to the cradle.

"Did you have a good night with her?" Sarah asked.

Martha shook her head. "She cried most of the night," she said. "She just wouldn't settle.

The little ones, Agnes and William, came over to Sarah. They had been somewhat ignored and wanted attention. Sarah took them to one side and sat down in a chair with them. William held his arms out to be lifted from the floor. Sarah picked him up and Agnes climbed on her lap.

Mary went over to Robert. "Has there been any improvement?" She walked over and looked at Agnes' face. She was so pale.

"No, she just lays there sleeping," he replied, not taking his eyes off Agnes. He stroked her face.

"Did you get any sleep yourself?" Mary asked.

Robert shook his head. "The bairn was crying all night, so I just sat here, watching her," he replied. "She looks so peaceful. I'm sure she'll wake up – she's just got tae!"

"Have you had any food?" Mary asked the question, but she knew what the answer was going to be.

"I'm no' hungry, but thanks anyway."

There was a knock at the door so Mary went to answer it. "Morning, doctor," she said. "Come in."

Doctor Williams came in with his bag, took his coat and hat off and looked over at Agnes. He spoke quietly to Mary. "How is she?"

"She hasn't woken since last evening. It doesn't look good, does it?" Mary replied.

Doctor Williams shook his head and went over to Robert and Agnes. Robert stood up and went over to meet him. "She's no' woken up this morning," he said. "She seems so peaceful. But she's so pale."

"I was afraid this would happen," the doctor replied, putting down his bag. "At least you had some time with her last night."

As the two men stood there talking Agnes began to convulse. She was in the last throes of her fight for life. Both doctor and Robert rushed to her side. The convulsions stopped and the breaths of a dying woman could clearly be heard. She took her last breath and was gone. Robert sat down on the edge of the bed and cradled Agnes in his arms. He looked, hopefully, at the doctor, who was checking Agnes for signs of life. The doctor returned the look but he shook his head. Robert gave in to the knowledge that Agnes was finally gone. He sobbed and he clutched her lifeless body to him.

"I'm so sorry Robert," the doctor said, moving away from the bed. "There was nothing else we could have done."

"No! She cannae be dead! It's no' possible!" Robert wailed.

Dr. Williams walked round the bed to Robert, and he put his hands on Robert's shoulders, making Robert look at him. "She lost too much blood, man. What with giving birth as well, it was just too much for her body to take. Do you understand?"

Robert relaxed his rigid body as he realised that everything he had been told was a reality. He relaxed his hold on Agnes and carefully laid her back down on the bed. "Aye, I do," he nodded his head as he said this. He continued, slowly, "It's just hard tae take in," he said, shaking his head. "What am I goin' tae do?" He paused for a moment, then he continued. "Thank you so much for all your help. My mind's in a turmoil."

The doctor let go of Robert. "It will be for a while yet, but you've got the three children. They need you now, more than ever," the doctor answered. "I'll take my leave of you now, Robert. If you want, I'll let the vicar know so you can make arrangements."

Robert nodded and turned to face the doctor. He nodded, realising that there was only one way forward, now. "Aye, I'll have need of his services. Thank you doctor – for everything," Robert replied. He was just about to turn back to sit with Agnes when he realised he ought to pay the doctor. "How much do I owe you?"

"I've done very little, Robert. It's these women have done all the work. Two shillings will be more than enough – but not just now. If you give it to Mary or Sarah they'll give it to me in the week. Goodbye."

The doctor went to say his goodbye to Mary. "It's a sad day when a baby's born and loses its mother at the same time."

"Yes, doctor," she replied. "We all tried our best. Sarah and I will stay here awhile and see if there's anything we can do to help."

The doctor nodded and put on his coat and hat, picked up his bag and left the cottage. Robert went back to sit with Agnes. He was lost, and in a world of his own.

Little Agnes, sitting with Sarah, said "Why is my papa so sad?" Sarah looked at her mother. This was the first time she had ever seen a childbed death, and it had upset her deeply. Mary came over to them and picked up Agnes.

"Your ma' has gone to be with the angels," she said. "She won't wake up again."

"I want to hold her hand," Agnes replied, understanding. "Are you sure?" Mary asked, surprised. "Aye," Agnes replied, in a very grown up manner. Agnes struggled to get down, so Mary put her on the floor. Agnes walked proudly over to her father and wriggled in front of him so she could be next to her mother. She laid her head on her mother's arm. Robert, woken out of his sadness and reverie, gave his daughter a hug. He lifted her onto the bed so she could be closer to her mother. "I love you, mama," she said. "God will look after you now."

The vicar, the Reverend Robert Martindale, arrived that afternoon. He gave his condolences to Robert and they sat down to make the funeral arrangements. He told Robert that he could bury Agnes on Monday morning. Robert agreed to this and left all the other arrangements to the vicar.

Monday, 10 July 1837 was another beautifully sunny day. There were clouds in the sky and a gentle breeze. Robert and his family were at the church of St. Andrew, in Bebington, to bury Agnes. There were only a few people there – Robert had only recently moved to the area and didn't know many people.

Present at the funeral were Robert McWilliam and his two children, all dressed in black. Robert, in true Scottish tradition was wearing a frock coat and tall hat. He looked even more handsome as he stood there, thought Sarah, standing there with her mother. They were both dressed in subdued colours. Also present was Martha Lidsome, dressed in more suitable colours, holding baby. There was a short ceremony in the church. Robert had chosen 'Abide with Me' and 'The Lord's My Shepherd' to be sung at the service. Afterwards, the group moved into the churchyard to be at the graveside for the interment. Robert stood there, holding his daughter's hand, whilst William was held by Sarah. In the few days that Sarah had known the family the children had become very fond of her.

After the service, Robert and Martha turned to go back to the cottage. Sarah offered to walk back with William, and Robert accepted. "It's very kind o' you," he said. Sarah and Robert walked side by side while Martha walked behind with the baby. Once inside the cottage Sarah turned to Robert. "I'll be going back home now," she said, "but I can come back another day, if you would like." "That'd be grand," Robert replied.

Next evening there was a knock at the door of Robert's cottage. Martha answered it to see Sarah standing there. "Come in," Martha said to Sarah, so Sarah entered the cottage carrying a basket. Robert was there with his children. He was sitting alone while the children played on the floor with their wooden toys. Sarah took a dish out of the basket. "Good evening Mr. McWilliam, Martha," said Sarah. "Ma' thought you'd like it if she cooked for you, and I wanted to bring it, to see how you and the children all were."

Robert stood up to greet Sarah. Martha took the dish from Sarah as Robert replied, "Coping. Gie your mother my thanks for the meal. We've no' got into a routine as yet. Jane is poorly and Martha spends all her time looking after her. She's no time for Agnes and William, or anything else, come to that."

Martha quietly went over to the table with the dish without saying a word. Sarah looked concerned. "Would you mind if I came along and helped with them? I've had plenty of experience with my younger brothers and sisters, and could teach them things. It would give Martha more time to spend with the baby."

"Are you sure?" replied Robert. "I wouldnae want tae impose on you, but it'd be a great help. What do you say, Martha?"

Martha finally spoke. "It would make it easier for me to look after Jane, and it would also mean that the children would be occupied doing something." Martha looked quite relieved as she said this. She wasn't used to looking after children, only newborns.

"Then it's settled," said Robert. "I'll pay you – it'll no' be a grand sum, but it'll make it worth your while."

"That's fine. I'll be back in the morning," Sarah replied. She turned to go and Robert opened the door to let her out. "Till tomorrow, then," he added. He watched as Sarah walked off down the road. It was a chilly evening, despite it having been a warm day, and the cool air made Robert feel better.

Next morning, exactly as promised, Sarah arrived. Robert was getting ready to go to work and Martha was dressing the baby. "You're bright and early," he said, his face brightening. "It's good tae see you again. I know the bairns like it when you come." Robert let Sarah in through the door as he was getting ready to leave. "I'm just away tae work," he continued, carrying on out of the cottage and walked down the road and out of sight.

Sarah closed the door and went over to Martha. "Morning," said Martha. "Anything I can do to help?" Sarah asked. "I'm getting on just fine with the baby," Martha replied. "Will you see to the children's breakfasts?"

Sarah nodded and went into the bedroom to get the children up. They were overjoyed to see her there. They jumped out of bed and hugged her. "What do you want for breakfast?" Sarah asked. "Porridge!" shouted Agnes. "I've never made porridge," lied Sarah, with a twinkle in her eye. "Will you show me?" Agnes grabbed Sarah's hand and took her out to the kitchen. Between them they prepared breakfast for Agnes and William.

After breakfast Sarah sat down with the children in the main room of the cottage and watched them play. Agnes had a rag doll which she caressed, lovingly. William had some bricks that he played with and Martha was feeding Jane. Sarah watched the children playing and thought how sad it must be for them not to have their mother with them. Sarah could see Agnes was troubled by recent events. Neither child was as happy as she had seen them the day they first arrived to help.

Martha broke the silence. "I lost my own baby in December. It was a bit of a blessing really, looking back. I should never have gotten into that situation, but at least I now can work. Robert's baby is the second one I've wet nursed. I looked after one in Barnston. They were a well-to-do couple and the wife wouldn't have anything to do with the feeding. Their little one is weaned off the breast, now, so this came along just at the right time. But I've no experience with the older ones..."

"Did you not have any brothers or sisters?" asked Sarah. Martha replied, "Aye, I do, but I'm the youngest, so it was them bringing me up!"

"Ah," replied Sarah, understanding. "I'm one of eight. I've four younger brothers – one died soon after he was born, one older sister and two younger ones, so Hannah and I were helping ma' with them while I grew up."

"That's why it's so easy for you, then," replied Martha.

Sarah nodded. "There's a way to do it," she continued. "I've always loved being with children. That's why, when ma' suggested I help her out with the birthing I thought it was a good idea."

As the day wore on the two women realised they worked well together. They enjoyed talking and the children loved having Sarah around. Martha looked after Jane beautifully, and before they knew it, Robert was home from work. Sarah had cooked them all a decent meal, and she served it up for them before she left for home.

"It's been a real good day having you here with me, Sarah," said Martha, as she let Sarah out. "I'd like to think we've become friends," replied Sarah.

"Aye," added Robert, "we'll be seeing you in the morning."

"For sure," replied Sarah. She walked off out of the cottage and down the road to her home.

The household was beginning to get back to some form of normality. Robert was back at work, and although the woman he planned to spend his life with was no longer there, he had carers for his children, whom he got along with and he liked. He thought Sarah was very beautiful and intelligent, and a perfect role model for his older children.

The next few days passed much as the one just finished. Friday, 4 August 1837, however, got off to a bumpy start.

Robert was up having breakfast, and Martha was getting ready to feed the baby. "She's quiet this morning," she muttered, as she walked over to the cradle. "Jane, Jane!" she called out. She went to pick her up but her body was cold and lifeless. "Robert," she screamed, "Robert, there's something wrong with the baby. She's cold!"

Robert ran in from the kitchen. "No," he moaned, "this cannae be happening!" He shook his head in sorrow. "I've just buried Agnes. No' again!" He took the baby from Martha and sat down, hugging her, sobbing.

There was a knock at the door. Martha opened it and Sarah walked in. "The baby," stuttered Martha, "The baby... I did everything right... I just don't understand what can have happened..." Martha put her hand to her mouth as if to stifle a sob, but nothing came.

Sarah looked around the room in shock. She saw Robert hugging the lifeless baby. She had no idea what to do. "Do you want me to go and get ma'?" Robert nodded and Sarah, hurriedly, left the cottage.

A short while later Mary arrived. "I've sent Sarah to fetch the doctor," she said. "These new-fangled laws mean that even though we know the little one is dead he has to come and write a death certificate."

"Aye. It's no' like that in Scotland, but I expect they'll bring it in eventually," Robert replied.

Mary took the baby from Robert and put her back in the cradle. A while later the doctor and Sarah arrived.

"I'm sorry to be back, Robert," said Doctor Williams. "So little Jane didn't make it then?" Robert shook his head. "She's in the cradle."

Sarah went to sit with the children. Agnes was visibly upset, but William took little notice. The doctor examined the baby. "Do you know what she died of?" asked Robert. The doctor looked up. "It's not apparent," the doctor replied. "It appears she just didn't thrive. It happens sometimes." He put his medical equipment away and continued. "She did find it difficult to come into the world – perhaps it took more out of her than we realised."

The funeral for baby Jane took place two days later. The weather was still warm but there were a lot of clouds in the sky. The sun shone when it could break through the clouds. Robert and his family were at the church to bury baby Jane. Along with Robert McWilliam, all dressed in black, as before, and his two children, were Sarah Foulkes and her mother Mary, both dressed in subdued colours. Also, Martha was there. The burial, this time, was performed by the Curate, Mr. Thomas Fisher Redhead, as the Vicar was away performing other duties for the Bishop. Once again it was a simple ceremony in the church, with 'Amazing Grace' and 'The Lord's My Shepherd' being sung and then outside for the interment. Jane McWilliam was buried with her mother.

After the funeral, Martha approached Robert. "It's time for me to leave your service now," she said. "You've no need of me, and the doctor tells me there's another family out of town with need of a wet nurse."

"Aye, you're right," replied Robert. "Well, thank you for all you did for us. Dinnae blame yoursel' for anything. There was nothing anybody could have done." After a pause, Robert said, "I'll pay you when we get back tae the cottage so you can be on your way."

"Thank you," Martha answered. Robert then turned to look at Sarah. "Will you be staying on tae help wi' the bairns?" he asked.

Sarah looked shocked. "And who would be looking after them if I didn't help?" she replied. Her manner softened as she replied, "Of course I will, Robert. Do you need me to live in?" Robert thought for a moment or two. "It might be a good idea tae," he replied. "There's space now that Martha's leaving."

Sarah went over to her mother. "Robert's asked if I'll be his full time nanny. Do you think I should?"

Mary looked at Sarah. "Is it what you want to do?" Without hesitation, Sarah replied, "Yes, ma'."

"Then you should do it," answered Mary. "There'll be other babies to deliver when they're older."

The days passed. Sarah became fonder of Robert's children, as they did of her. They began to regain some of their childlike sparkle, but they were more aloof, now.

Robert became fonder of Sarah as time went by. By mid-October both Robert and Sarah had become close enough for Robert to propose. Sarah wanted time to think about her answer, so she decided to go to see her mother. Mary was a good listener and always gave sound advice.

On Friday, 13 October, Sarah went to speak with her mother. Outside it was raining, so Sarah wrapped herself and the children up warmly and braved the weather. They quickly walked up to her parents' cottage and Mary let them in.

The cottage that the Foulkes lived in was similar in style and build to the McWilliam cottage, but it was larger and had an extra room. The kitchen-cum-living room was off the front door, but on either side of it was another room. Both of these rooms were bedrooms – the Foulkes had a large family. Mary and her daughter were sitting around the table, talking in the kitchen. The two children were playing with Sarah's sister, Hannah.

"Are you sure this is what you want?" Mary asked. "Ma', I couldn't be more sure," Sarah replied. "The children adore me, and Robert relies on me."

Mary looked concerned. "But does he love you?" she asked. "It's all well and good that he relies on you, but will it be enough?" Sarah, without hesitation, said, "He says he loves me, and I love him. I know he relies on me, but there's more than that between us!"

Mary was not convinced, and it showed in her expression. Sarah continued, "Anyway, Robert wants to come and speak with you and da', after work tomorrow. It's what I want."

Mary took a moment to answer. "I'm not so sure," she said. "Agnes is not long in the ground. It isn't wise to rush. Robert's much older than you – and there are the two children. You'll be taking on a lot."

"Are you saying I'll not be able to cope?" Sarah angrily retorted.

"Of course not," said her mother. "I know you. You always do well at whatever you do. It's not that at all. I just think you're taking on too much, too soon."

Sarah thought for a moment. "So what? Are you wanting us to wait? Is that it?"

"Waiting would be better," replied Mary. "I know your father will not be too keen just now. See how you go, and maybe have Robert come over in a couple of weeks."

Sarah relaxed. "If you think that's best, ma'. But I do want to marry him."

The rain began to come down heavily, so Sarah and the children waited a while. Eventually, the rain stopped and Sarah and the children left for home. Mary watched them go. She was worried about her daughter. Afraid she had bitten off more than she could manage. She would talk about it to Thomas when he got home from work.

Two weeks later, on 27 October, Robert and Sarah were sitting down to their evening meal after Robert had returned home from work. It had been another rainy day and the cold weather was beginning to set in. Inside the cottage at Holt Hill there was a fire burning in the hearth and it made the cottage feel more cosy than usual. The children were in bed and Robert and Sarah had just finished their evening meal. They were sitting in silence when Robert took hold of Sarah's hand. He said, "Do you love me?"

Sarah looked down at her hand and then into Robert's eyes. "You know I do, Robert," she replied.

"So when am I tae go and ask your father for your hand in marriage? You keep putting it off." He sat there, looking at Sarah, motionless.

"I spoke to ma' the other day – she thinks it's too soon," Sarah began. "She said she didn't think it was proper love." Sarah paused for a moment. "You do love me, don't you Robert?"

"Of course I do," he replied. I'm wanting so much tae be your husband." Robert lifted Sarah's hand to his mouth and kissed it.

Sarah contemplated what she should say next. She looked into his eyes and knew what they were doing was right. She said, "Then you should go and see them. Ma' will always say it's too soon. Just do it."

Robert replied, "I'll speak tae your father on Sunday, then."

At church, Thomas sat with Mary and their children. Thomas was a thick set man, but tall. He had a swarthy skin, from working on the ferries. He had a short grey beard and his grey hair, with streaks of black running through it, was balding on top. He was fit for his age – 48 years. Of his children, John, Jane and Thomas looked more like their father, whilst Hannah, Sarah, Mary and Robert favoured their mother. All the children had brown hair, although young Thomas' hair was more blond than brown.

Hannah, despite being the oldest child, was only just five feet tall. Sarah was the tallest at 5 feet 7 inches, and Mary about two inches taller than Hannah. Jane was a couple of inches shorter than Hannah, and little Thomas was about three feet tall.

Robert politely asked Thomas in church if he could call to speak with him later in the day. Thomas agreed, "Come back with us to the house straight after the service," he told him.

Sitting there in the pew, Thomas turned to Mary. "Robert's asked to speak to me. What do you think to it? Is Sarah doing the right thing?" Mary looked over at her daughter. She saw the way that Sarah and Robert looked at each other, and she smiled to herself. She then turned to Thomas. "They'll do fine together. I had my doubts in the beginning, but just look at them there…"

After church everybody returned to the Foulkes cottage, where Robert formally asked Thomas if he could marry Sarah.

"Is it what you want, Sarah?" asked Thomas. "Yes, da', it is," she replied.

He looked quizzically at Sarah. "Do you love him?" "Yes, da', I do," she said, nodding her head.

"Hmph!" Thomas turned to Robert. "Do you truly love her?" Thomas asked. "This better not be a marriage of convenience."

Robert looked surprised and hurt to even think Thomas should consider that and replied, "I would never think such a thing. O' course I love her. I just want tae make an honest woman of her so she can truly be a mother tae my bairns, and tae have bairns wi' her so she's a mother hersel'."

Thomas thought for a few minutes. "Hmm," he said, slowly, "well, I'm not totally convinced this is for the right reason, despite what mother thinks, but since your minds are both made up, I'll let it be. You just make sure you treat her right!"

"You can be sure o' that – I'll no' let you down Mr. Foulkes," replied a very relieved Robert.

"I'll hold you to that," replied Thomas.

Sarah went up to her father and gave him a loving kiss on his cheek. "Thank you, da'."

Just over a month later, on Sunday, 3 December 1837, on a breezy, cloudy, cold day, a little over freezing, Sarah got married to Robert in the afternoon. Robert, Sarah and the children were lodging in rooms in Scotland Road, and had been there for the last three weeks, in order for the reading of the Banns. The whole family had gone to Liverpool for the wedding in St. Peter's church. Robert had chosen it, despite Sarah's parents' protestations. They would have preferred she had got married in the new church, St. Catherine's, in Tranmere, but Robert wanted the wedding to take place in a big church. Mary and Thomas were not happy, despite what both Robert and Sarah had told them about being in love. Thomas and Mary were going to be there for her, all the same.

The whole family from Tranmere came to the wedding together in a large cart and horses. Thomas sat up front with Mary and everybody else sat in back. There were Sarah's siblings, Hannah, aged 26, John, aged 21, Mary, aged 19, Robert, aged 18, Jane, aged 9 and Thomas, aged 4.

Robert, Thomas' youngest brother by five years, had also travelled with them. He brought his wife, also called Mary, and their six children. They had a younger family. Mary, their eldest, was only 19 years and she was the only girl. Then there came John, aged 14, Edward, aged 12, Robert, aged 6, Thomas, aged 4, and William, aged 1.

The other Foulkes brother, William, two years younger than Thomas, already lived in Liverpool, so the journey for him to get to the church was much shorter. They had only two children, John, aged 6, and Annie, aged 2, but William's wife, Ann was heavily pregnant. They joined the group as everybody else arrived at the church. They didn't plan on staying long past the service, since, in her condition, Ann was easily tired.

Both Thomas' brothers looked like Thomas in many ways. William was marginally taller and Robert was the same height. Their wives were both a fraction shorter than their husbands. Robert's wife had auburn coloured hair and William's wife had blond hair. William's children were blond while Robert's were brown haired.

Although Sarah had a large family, sadly, the same could not be said of Robert McWilliam's family, as, apart from his two children, all his family were still in Scotland, such as were still alive. There were one or two of Robert's friends from work there with them, however, and some friends from the village.

Thomas refused to be a witness, so her uncle Robert agreed, along with Sarah's friend, Anne Morely. The ceremony was performed by the curate, the Reverend Thomas Halton.

All the guests were sitting in the church, waiting. Robert was wearing his smart black suit – he had only one – without the hat, this time, which he kept for special occasions, with a cream shirt and blue cravat – to match Sarah's dress.

Thomas and Sarah arrived on time, with Agnes and William. Once inside the church, Sarah took off her thick black winter coat to reveal a cream and blue dress for the wedding. Thomas looked at Sarah, beaming.

"You look lovely," he said. Thomas was wearing his brown suit. It fitted, but not well.

"You look alright, too," Sarah replied.

He smiled at Sarah as she took his arm. Sarah squeezed his arm as she lay hers down upon it. "I know what I'm doing, da'," she said. The organist started up playing 'The Trumpet Voluntary' and the congregation all stood up in anticipation.

Sarah and her father walked up the aisle together, towards Robert, as he stood there with his best friend, George Hogg. Agnes and William walked behind Sarah in their best outfits. Agnes wore a plain blue dress and William wore a boy's dress in the same colour. Brother and sister held hands as they followed

Sarah and her father up the aisle. The vicar welcomed everybody and the service began with 'Love Divine, All Loves Excelling'

The service was perfect. The final hymn was 'The Voice that breathed o'er Eden' and then the couple left the church to the sound of 'The Trumpet Voluntary', once again. All the families and friends left the church and all stood talking for a while, wishing the newly-weds good luck. Being so cold, nobody really wanted to be outside, and as it was dark now it was decided the families should say their goodbyes and depart to their various homes.

Robert and Sarah returned to their lodgings with Agnes and William. The street contained a long row of terraced houses on a hill. Robert and Sarah, Agnes holding Sarah's hand, and William asleep in Robert's arms, turned the corner into the street and walked about halfway up to it. They opened the front door and looked at each other.

"If I had a free hand, Mrs. McWilliam, I'd carry you over the threshold," Robert said, kissing Sarah on the cheek. "I know you would. It doesn't matter. I love you, husband," she replied, smiling to herself as she called him husband. Together, they all walked into the house and upstairs to the two rooms that they now called home. Robert lay William down on his bed, but the action of laying him down woke him up. He sat up and looked at them, then got off the bed and went to play with his sister Agnes. Robert watched the two children as they played. They were happy now – for the first time since their mother had died.

Robert and Sarah went in the front of the two rooms on the first floor. There were two armchairs, a table, four chairs and a desk. The room was small, but adequate, if not a little dark. Sarah had her arms around Robert and they were dancing around the room, Sarah was humming a tune. Robert made her stand still. "I promise you this, Sarah," he said, "as soon as I can afford it we will have our own home, with our own front door on tae the street."

"You've given me everything," she replied. "I am so happy. I wouldn't care if we stayed here for ever." "But I would," Robert replied. "This place is so dreary, so built up, and the houses are all on top of each other. I hate it. Your village was lovely. I'd love tae show you mine."

Agnes came rushing in the room, closely followed by William. Sternly, Robert looked at them and stood still. "Haud yer wheesht!" he said, in a voice as stern as his stare. Sarah didn't know what Robert was talking about but Agnes and William obviously did, because they stood stock still and silent in front of him. "What's so important you forget house rules? Calm down. You should know better than this, young miss. You'll be running into something and breaking it. You're setting a bad example for your brother!"

"Sorry, papa," said Agnes, straightening herself up. "We're just so happy now we have a new mama."

Robert tried to keep the stern look on his face, but couldn't hold back a smile. "Sarah, I think it's time you put our children tae bed. They've had a busy day and it's getting close tae their bedtime." "Yes, husband," she replied, smiling. Sarah gave Robert a peck on the cheek, picked up William and took Agnes' hand. She took them into the next room and put them to bed. Agnes lay there, looking at Sarah. "You're no' going tae leave us, are you?" she asked.

Sarah looked at Agnes and smiled. "Of course I shan't," replied Sarah.

"That's good. We want you tae stay for ever!" answered Agnes.

Sarah tucked both children in and gave each of them a kiss on the forehead. "Night night," she said, then turned and left the room, turning out the lamp on the way.

For the next few months they lived in this property in Scotland Road. Robert had given up the cottage in Holt Hill. It held too many unhappy memories. He was starting out in a new marriage so he was adamant that they should live in a new home. Besides, most of the work was in Liverpool and Birkenhead at that time, and it seemed sensible to live close to the work.

But these were nasty houses. They had been built very cheaply and badly. They had no damp courses, so Robert and Sarah were lucky to be on the first floor. There was no bathroom in the whole of the house – and no running water either. Water was collected from a pump at the end of the street. The toilet was a cesspit at the rear of the house – and it wasn't just for their house, they had to share it with the house opposite. They could hear the night men clearing up from the back yards most nights.

Sarah took it upon herself to start to teach Agnes to read. Thomas Foulkes had given Sarah a good grounding in education and she felt it wise to pass on her knowledge. Agnes was a quick learner, despite being so young. Sarah was pleased she could help her step-daughter.

Finally, by March, they had managed to find another property to rent in Birkenhead. Monday, 12 March 1838 dawned a dry day. The weather was a little warmer now. There were clouds in the sky and if you looked at them you could see them rolling fast towards the horizon. It was very windy. Robert and his family stood outside a little terrace of two storey houses that were round the corner from the park on Hamilton Square. This was Hamilton Terrace and the number on the door was number 8. They still shared their house with another family, but this time they had the downstairs rooms, which were marginally bigger. Most of the furniture came with the property, which they rented, however they had brought the rocking chair with them. All their belongings were on a cart and two horses that Robert had rented.

"Well, this is it," said Robert. "We've come back tae the other side o' the Mersey. Closer tae your family." He gave Sarah a hug. Sarah's red skirt billowed out due to the wind, and Agnes and William, dressed in their Sunday best, clung tight to their father's legs. "It's no' such a slum as the other place. The houses are no' sae close together and there's a wee bit of open ground round the back, so I think things are beginning tae look up," said Robert. "Oh, Robert, it's wonderful," Sarah replied. "It looks like we've come home!" Sarah gave Robert a peck on the cheek and they went inside.

Through the front door was a hallway, with stairs leading up against the party wall and a long corridor beside it leading to the kitchen. Leading off the hall were two large rooms, one at the front and the other at the back. They carried in their belongings bit by bit. It didn't take long and soon everybody and everything was indoors. Robert told Sarah he would return the cart and horses and would be back as soon as he could. As he left Sarah and the children were unpacking everything and putting the things away.

Robert was gone about an hour and in that time they had got everything away, neat and tidy. There was only one bed, though, so Robert decided he would buy one as soon as he could. That night, they all slept in the one bed. It was cosy – a bit too cosy, so Sarah told Robert she would see if she could get a bed the next day – and a second mattress to replace the one on their bed because it was uncomfortable.

The next night they all slept better. A new bed and two mattresses arrived that afternoon, that Sarah had bought from Daniel Corkbill in Argyle Street that morning, and it had been delivered by afternoon. Sarah enjoyed going shopping for furniture, and she decided that it was now time to buy her own things to make this place look just the way she wanted. She put the old mattress from the original bed underneath it for when they finally moved away. They couldn't leave the bed with no mattress for whoever moved in after them!

The first month went by in a haze, with Sarah and Robert enjoying their time closer to Tranmere. Bit by bit she bought small items of furniture and tat to make the place look more homely. At last, Sarah had begun to put her imprint on the small dwelling. She looked around and smiled. 'This time last year,' she thought, 'who would have guessed I'd be married!' She was happy, and the children were also happy. Agnes was now 4½ and William was one month short of turning 3. Robert was working hard to keep the family safe.

By the time April came around, the weather was getting warmer. But this particular day outside a storm was brewing and the clouds were getting darker. Sarah looked out the window and shivered. She hoped that Robert would be home soon or he would be soaked to the skin.

Sarah went back to getting the food ready for when Robert came home. She heard the front door open and close. "I'm home!" called Robert. He came into the back room, which doubled as a dining room and living room. The table was set for two people – the children had already eaten and were ready for bed. He walked up to Sarah. She turned to him. "You made it before the rain started," she said. "Dinner's almost ready, so sit yourself down and I'll get you a drink." Robert sat down and Sarah got him a glass of beer. The children came up to him to say goodnight and Sarah took them to bed.

When she returned without them, a few minutes later, she went back to the evening meal. Robert started to chat to her as she continued to cook. "The work's getting well underway on the railway now," he said, taking a sip of his beer. "There's a bit of an argument about the track running through Lord Stanley's estate, so we've got a bit of a hiccup, there, but I'm sure it'll all get sorted out. When it's all done you'll be able tae catch a train to go home tae see your parents."

Sarah stopped and looked at him. "That'll make everything so much easier. I do miss the village. Tell me about your village. I love to hear you talk about your home."

Robert smiled as he thought of his life when he was younger. "Kirkmaiden parish covers most of the Galloway head. As you go down tae the point there's barely one mile of land atween the sea on either side. From the lighthouse you can see miles of ocean, and the Isle of Man and England in the distance. My parents lived in Portnessock, halfway up on the west side. It's also called Port Logan, and my mother's family have lived there for generations. For Scotland, unusually, the land there is flat, once you get up the cliffs, which is why Portnessock was so important, for it's one the bays, and you're on the right side for Ireland. It's farming country."

Sarah had finished cooking lobscouse and served it up as Robert was talking. She put his plate down in front of him and then sat down opposite him. They both started to eat their meal. "It sounds so wonderful. I always used to think there was nowhere better than Tranmere, but I'd love to visit your village." "Maybe we will, one day," he answered.

As the year passed by the weather began to warm up. It was a beautiful spring day. The sun was shining but there wasn't too much heat in it. There was a gentle breeze, which would help with drying. It was now Monday, 14 May, and Sarah was outside in the yard talking to her new neighbour. Margaret Cowan. They lived in the upstairs rooms at number 8. Her husband was an engineer, working on the railway. They had come down from Scotland in June 1837 solely for the work. Margaret had her baby in February, since moving south, and they now had four children. Margaret's sister Mary was living with them.

Mary was indoors with the baby and their daughter Janet, aged 7, but Margaret and their little boys, Robert and Thomas, aged 4 and 3 years, respectively, were in the yard, such as it was. It was about three yards long with an out-house at the bottom for a toilet. There was a gate at the end on to an alleyway that ran along between the two rows of houses. Both of them wore dark coloured dresses and pantalettes. Sarah had brought Agnes and William out there with her, so the four children were playing together in the yard while the women talked. The women were doing their washing.

Margaret was a tall, slender woman. She had vivid blue eyes and blond hair, and the hair was reflected in her children, all of whom were blond. She wore a navy skirt and white blouse with the sleeves rolled up so they didn't get wet.

"Morning," said Margaret, who had met Sarah soon after she and Robert moved in. "What a beautiful day it is." "Indeed it is," replied Sarah. "Good washing weather!"

"I saw your Robert the other day. I'd no idea he was Scottish" added Margaret. "So what part of Scotland is he from?"

"Robert's from Wigtownshire, Portnessock," Sarah replied.

"We're from Dreghorn, in Ayrshire," said Margaret. "It's right at the top of the county, but Wigtownshire is the next county down from Ayrshire. I thought the accent was local. How long have yous been married?"

Sarah replied, "We were married in December. I'm Robert's second wife."

"I thought you'd been married longer than that," answered Margaret. "So the bairns are no' yours?"

"Well, I treat them as if they were," said Sarah, "But no. Agnes is 5 in October and William will be 3 next week. So what does your husband do?"

"He's an engineer, working on the railway," said Margaret.

Sarah said, "My Robert's working for the railway, too – he's a stonemason."

Margaret nodded, "They're a big employer round here."

"Yes, that's for sure," agreed Sarah. After a moment's thought she added, "It must be hard for you, living so far away from home."

"Aye," replied Margaret, nodding, "But I'm getting used tae it." Margaret paused for a moment as she took a sheet out of her basket and hung it on the washing line. "We're hoping tae move soon," she continued. "These two rooms are just no' big enough now that we have the new bairn. I think the families next door are goin' tae move soon, so William's asked the landlord if we can have first refusal on the whole building."

Sarah looked disappointed. "You're the only people I've got to know yet, so I hope you can get it. Then we can still be neighbours, especially since you're from Scotland. Your husband will be good company for Robert."

The women continued on with their washing. Sarah was the first to finish. "Well, that's me done for today," she said. "No doubt, I'll be seeing you tomorrow."

"Aye, no doubt you will", replied Margaret. Sarah cleared away her washing gear and she and the children went inside.

Another week on, the weather hadn't started to warm up yet, but it was still a sunny day. On Saturday, 26 May, two doors up there was a dreadful commotion. Sarah and Margaret went outside to see what was going on. They looked out of their front door and there were police outside, banging on their neighbour's door. As the noise continued, more and more neighbours looked outside. Finally, the door opened and the police could be seen talking to somebody. A few minutes later two of them went inside and all was silent – for five minutes, at least.

Then, once again, the door opened and the police emerged, dragging with them a man who they had never seen before. They dragged him off up the road and all was quiet once more. That Monday following, Robert looked through the newspaper to find out if there was anything in it about their neighbour. Apparently, he had been part of a gang stealing from down on the docks. The story was the talk of the street.

That week, the rest of his family moved out. They were there on the Tuesday, but when people got up on the Wednesday the downstairs rooms were empty, save for lots of rubbish on the floor and a few old chairs and that were upturned and broken in the front room.

The remaining occupants of the street waited to see who the new people would be. They didn't have long to wait. On Monday, 4 June a new family moved in. Sarah made it her business to speak to the wife. She looked a similar age to herself and there weren't too many of Sarah's age in the few houses near number 8. It would be lovely to make another friend.

That Wednesday, Sarah was going with the children to the market, which was on Hamilton Square. As she walked along the road she saw her new neighbour, from two doors up, also leaving her house, and walking in the same direction. She was a well-built woman, as tall as Sarah, and heavily pregnant. Sarah caught up with her and struck up a conversation with her new neighbour, as they all walked up the road.

"Good morning," said Sarah. "I'm Sarah McWilliam, and I live just two doors up from you. When's the baby due?"

"Hello. I'm Elizabeth – Elizabeth Cross," her neighbour replied. "Baby's due very soon. It's my second – I lost my first when he was only 2 months old, so I really hope this one will be fine."

"We saw you move in," added Sarah.

"Yes, we were lucky to get this place," continued Elizabeth. My older sister's come to help me, so we've rented a larger place than we had before. We've just the downstairs rooms, but they're plenty big enough for us for now. Mind, they were in a right state when we got here. It's taking us a while to get it round to being decent."

Sarah smiled. "The last family there did a moonlight flit. The father got arrested for stealing, and I suppose they couldn't afford to pay the rent. Here one day, gone the next. I can imagine the mess you found, from what we saw in the front room."

"Oh," replied Elizabeth. We did wonder. Have you been here long?"

"We moved in mid-March," said Sarah. We got married in December in Liverpool. We spent a few months in rooms in Liverpool but then this place came up, and Robert knew how much I wanted to be back this side of the river. So here we are."

"We got married in Liverpool, too," replied Elizabeth, intrigued. Where were you married?"

Sarah said, "St. Peter's."

"So were we!" exclaimed Elizabeth. How strange is that!"

Sarah gasped in surprise. She continued, "Back home my mother was the local village midwife, and she was training me before I got married, so if you need any advice just ask."

"Why, thanks," replied Elizabeth. "I might just hold you to that!"

The women walked along a little further, then Elizabeth asked, "So whose are the children?"

"My husband's by his first wife", said Sarah. "She died a while back." Sarah finally gave in to her thoughts. She had been trying not to say anything until she had spoken with Robert, but she could hold her tongue no longer.

"I think I may be expecting," Sarah said.

"Does your husband know?" Elizabeth asked.

"Not yet," replied Sarah. "I'm planning on telling him, but seeing you like this, it's made me so excited."

"Good luck to you, then," added Elizabeth. The women continued along the road on the way to do their shopping.

Soon, the weather started to get much hotter. With the longer evenings and better weather, Robert and Sarah had started taking the children out on a Sunday, the one day of the week that Robert got to spend with his family.

The family was getting ready to go out for an evening stroll. It was one of the summer treats. The day had been hot, and still had some of the heat left. The sun was shining and there was hardly any wind. Sarah was getting the children ready. She was just beginning to show that she was expecting. Robert had been sitting watching Sarah busying herself. He sat there, smiling, "Sarah, are you puttin' on weight? Or is there somethin' you've neglected tae tell me?"

Sarah gave him a coy smile. "I think I might have news for you," she said. "I wasn't sure before, but I do believe we're going to have a baby. I'm so excited." She paused for a moment, and then continued, "You know I love your two as if they were my own."

"Aye, Sarah, I know you do," said Robert. "But I also know that you've been desperate tae have one of your own. Do you have an idea as to when it's tae be born?"

"From what my ma' has taught me," Sarah replied, "it should be born about January or February time."

"Enough time tae get things together, then. Come here!" Robert grabbed Sarah's hand and pulled her towards him.

Sarah was taken pleasantly by surprise, but she said, "Mind – the children are watching!" She turned to Agnes and William, and then back to Robert. "Come on. We're all ready. Let's go for that walk on this gloriously sunny evening."

"I hear tell," said Robert, now positively beaming, "that there's tae be fireworks this evening – from a steamer that's moored off Woodside-bank. Shall we go tae watch?"

"That sounds exciting," replied Sarah. "I'd love to see them." "Come on then, let's go," said Robert. The family went out into the street, and headed down towards the docks for a wonderful free evening of entertainment.

A few days later, Robert and Sarah were sitting in their parlour, relaxing. They had settled the children down in bed for the evening when there came a knock at the door. Robert got up to answer it. He opened the door and found Elizabeth Cross outside.

"Good evening Mr. McWilliam" she said, a strained look on her face. "Could I please have a word with your wife?" Robert beckoned her in.

"Come in and sit yoursel' down," he said. "Sarah, you've a visitor."

"Why, Elizabeth, whatever is the matter?" Sarah asked, knowingly, "Is it time?"

Elizabeth nodded. "I think so. Will you help me?"

"Of course I will," replied Sarah. "Let's get you back indoors. Is your husband there?"

"He's had to go out," said Elizabeth. "He's a coachman. He'll only be out a couple of hours. Mary's gone out for some air, but she won't be long, I'm sure."

Sarah looked at Robert. "Do you mind if go with Elizabeth? It'll just be until Mary or her husband get home."

Robert smiled. "Like mother, like daughter, is it?" He chuckled. "The bairns are asleep. I'll be going nowhere, now. Off with you, woman. Look after her!" With nothing more needed to be said, Sarah took Elizabeth back home. Sarah stayed with Elizabeth for two hours that evening. Mary had returned within the first hour, but Sarah felt she had to stay, just to make sure everything seemed to be progressing smoothly.

She had asked Elizabeth if she had a midwife to help her, and Elizabeth told her she did and would send for her now that Mary was back. Sarah told Mary to go and she would wait with Elizabeth until Mary got back with the midwife. Mary dutifully went to fetch her.

After a couple of hours Sarah returned home. "Mary's fetched their midwife, and her husband came home soon after, so she has all her family around her now. She'll be fine, so I took my leave."

They went to bed and Sarah lay there, whispering to Robert. "It was so strange, being there with Elizabeth," she said. "It was almost like I had been transported back to before I met you. It all came back to me as if it was only yesterday I last helped deliver a baby."

"Do you miss it?" Robert asked.

"No, not a bit," she replied.

Next day dawned, bright and sunny. You could feel the heat from the sun even with all the windows open. Robert was just getting ready to go to work and Sarah was doing the dishes after breakfast. Robert stood up, ready to leave for work.

"So when do you think she'll have the baby?" Robert asked, putting his work boots on.

"I shouldn't be at all surprised if it's already been born," Sarah replied. "Her contractions were close together when I left. It's her second baby, and they don't take so long to be born."

Sarah dried her hands so she could say goodbye to Robert. "Just think," she added, "in a few months' time it'll be me having a baby!"

Robert smiled at her and kissed her on her forehead. "You'll do just fine. Well, I'm away tae work now." He put his coat and left for work, and Sarah continued to clean up before the children got up.

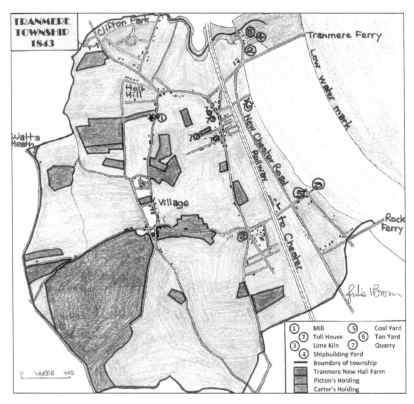

Tranmere Township map 1843

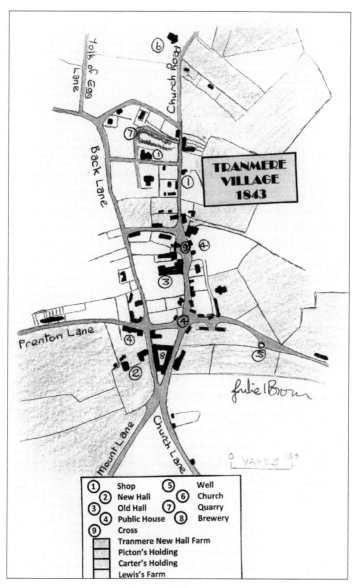

Tranmere Village map

CHAPTER 2

Family life

The months flew by and first summer, then autumn, and finally winter arrived. Saturday, 23 February 1839 dawned, and with it came the wintry weather. Snow had fallen but the sun now shone over the settled snow, making it look a brilliant white. By now Sarah, almost ready to have her baby, was still busying herself around the house. She was cooking the dinner in expectation of Robert coming home from work and she had almost finished dishing up the meals for the children.

Agnes was growing fast. She was now 5½ years old and becoming quite a charmer. She was tall for her age and tried to help Sarah as much as possible. William was nearly 4 years old and just losing his puppy fat. He was fast out-growing his baby clothes and Sarah was considering breeching him.

Sarah felt her first contraction, but she wasn't totally sure about it. 'It was all well and good delivering other people's babies,' she thought, 'but whatever you might tell them about what's happening to them, you don't really know what they're feeling until you go through it yourself!' By the time Robert came home from work she knew they were, most definitely, contractions. The children had finished their dinners by the time Robert came home and were ready for bed, just waiting for him to say goodnight to them before they got into their bed. He walked in to the kitchen and saw Sarah in the middle of one such contraction. "So it's started then, Sarah?" Robert asked.

Sarah grimaced, as she replied, "Yes. I'd just started cooking when I had the first one."

Robert smiled. "Well, your timing couldnae be better. It's my day off tomorrow."

Contraction over, Sarah straightened up. "I'm aware of that," she said. After a brief pause, she continued, "After you've put the children to bed, will you go next door and tell Margaret Cowan. She said she'd help when the time came."

"Does she know what she's doing, then?" asked Robert.

"She's not a proper midwife," replied Sarah, "but she's helped deliver some of her sisters' babies, and with what I know we'll get by."

Robert looked at the food she was preparing. "Is the food ready? Would it be wise tae wait until we've had dinner?"

"Well, you can eat, if you like," she retorted, "but I've lost the desire for food just now. I was just dishing up when you came in."

Robert softened as he realised that Sarah wanted sympathy. He said, "You go and sit down, then. I'll have my food and then I'll go and get Margaret."

Sarah smiled, finished putting Robert's meal on his plate and went to sit down. The contractions continued to come, faster now, and more intense. Baby was definitely on the way! Robert took Agnes and William to bed and then he sat down to eat.

After dinner Robert went next door. He knocked at the door and William Cowan answered it. He was about the same size as Robert, but he had brown hair and brown eyes. He was similarly dressed to Robert but you could tell he was better off.

"Is Margaret there?" Robert asked.

"Margaret!" William called out, "Robert from next door is here. He's wanting tae see you."

Margaret came to the door. She had just finished the washing up after dinner and her sleeves were all rolled up. "Robert," she began, as she dried her hands on her apron, "Has it started?" Robert nodded. "I thought it might, from the things Sarah was saying at lunch time. I've a couple o' things tae finish off but then I'll be round tae be wi' Sarah. You go back tae her now – she'll be needin' you."

Robert thanked her and returned to Sarah. A while later there was a knock at the door. Robert answered it to see Margaret Cowan, as promised, now come round to see how Sarah was doing. Robert let Margaret into the living room, where Sarah was sitting.

"How's it going, Sarah?" Margaret asked.

"I wish things would hurry up! Strange being on the other side of having a baby," Sarah replied.

Margaret checked out the situation. "How far apart are your contractions?" she asked.

"There's about ten minutes between them still," replied Sarah, sighing. She knew, only too well, that there was still hours to go.

"You've a while tae go yet, then," she said. "Those contractions are still way too far apart yet."

Sarah nodded in agreement. "I suppose I just wanted somebody else to tell me what I already knew. This waiting is the hard part."

Margaret chuckled. "You just settle back there," she said. "Your bairn will come in its own time." Margaret told Robert what he needed to have ready for the delivery. Then, turning to Sarah, she continued, "And, being your first, as you well know, this could take quite a while."

Sarah nodded. She had seen a great many first time mothers and heard her mother tell them exactly the same. Margaret said she would go home for now, since it would be while yet. She told Robert to go and fetch her when the contractions were coming really close together. She would be there, waiting.

Robert let Margaret out and he sat back down with Sarah. She tried to relax, but it wasn't easy. Robert timed the contractions with his pocket watch, but they were still way too far apart. They went to bed, but Sarah got very little sleep. Then, just before dawn, next morning, the waters broke, and Sarah and Robert jumped out of bed with a start. They had to take the mattress off the bed to dry it out. Robert lit the fire in the living room and rested the mattress against it so it could dry out. He put the old mattress back on the bed and Sarah made it up.

Afterwards, Sarah sat in the rocking chair and Robert busied himself reading the newspaper from the day before. "What shall we call this baby?" Sarah asked.

Robert put the newspaper down and looked at her. "What name would you pick?" he asked.

"One from the family, I suppose," Sarah answered, without a second thought.

"In Scotland we name the babies after our parents first and then ourselves," replied Robert. "So, if it's a boy he'd be named after my father – John and if it's a girl she'd be named after your mother – Mary."

Sarah smiled and added, "That takes all the trouble out of finding a name, doesn't it?" Robert nodded in agreement.

"Then that's what we'll do," she continued.

The children woke up and Robert saw to them. He gave them their breakfast, which was unusual for normally Sarah did everything. "Is baby coming?" asked Agnes. Robert nodded. "It should be here today," he said. "Are you excited?"

"Yes," answered Agnes. "I want a sister to play with."

"We cannae guarantee you'll get what you want, hinny," Robert replied, with a smile, "but whatever it is, you'll no' be able tae play wi' them for a while."

"Aw!" answered Agnes, sadly.

Finally, the contractions were close together and Robert went to tell Margaret it was time. He returned with Margaret and she was pleased to confirm that baby was finally on its way. But there was still a long wait before it made its debut into the world. At about 4 o'clock that afternoon, after a very long labour, Sarah's first child arrived.

The baby took its first breath just as it was born. Sarah felt the breath just before the baby left her body. The placenta came out without any problems. Sarah was so relieved. At least this birth was nothing like the last one she had witnessed. Margaret tidied Sarah up and handed a clean, well wrapped little baby to her mother.

"I'll be away, then, Sarah," said Margaret. "I'll let that man o' yours in tae see yous both. Rest now."

Margaret opened the door. "You can come in now, Robert," she called. Robert didn't need telling again. He was in like a rocket, and so proud to see Sarah and her new baby.

"Well, Sarah, I'll be taking my leave of you now," Margaret said. She turned to speak to Robert. "She's a fine bairn, no mistake."

"Thank you so much," he replied.

"Nae bother, Robert," replied Margaret. You and Sarah have been fine friends tae us. It was the least I could do."

Margaret left Robert and Sarah with their new baby. They both looked at her. She was so tiny. She lay there in Sarah's arms, looking up at her mother. Sarah began to cry tears of joy. "Oh, you are beautiful," she whispered to her. She kissed her on her forehead and then looked up.

"Margaret said 'She'," said Robert, as he stroked the baby's face.

"Yes," replied Sarah, "a very healthy bonny baby girl."

Agnes and William looked round the door into the room. Sarah motioned for them to come in and they both crept into the room. Robert moved over so they could see the new baby. They both looked at her, in awe.

"Say hello to your sister, Mary," Sarah told them. She then turned to Robert. "Will you send a wire to ma' tomorrow telling her she has a granddaughter?"

"Aye, Sarah, I'll send it first thing on my way tae work tomorrow. Are you sure you'll be a'right?"

"I'll be fine," said Sarah. "Margaret will call in from time to time; Agnes is old enough to help – she's going to be 6 in October."

"Aye, well… I'm sure you know best."

Sarah looked at Robert. For the first time since her labour had started she realised how worried Robert had been, and still was.

"Trust me, Robert," she said, "everything is going to be fine. There wasn't any problem. It's not like before." Robert was looking at Agnes and William. "Look at me," said Sarah, but Robert could not bring himself to look her in the eye. "Look at me!" Sarah said, sternly.

Robert looked at Sarah directly. "I didnae mean tae let you see how worried I was," he said, guiltily.

"Why should you be worried? Our baby is perfect," said Sarah. "She had a perfect birth. There weren't any problems. Everything was where it was supposed to be, and happened exactly the way it was meant to. Do you believe me?"

Robert nodded. "Aye, Sarah. I do believe you. You're right. I was just being foolish."

A tear rolled down Sarah's cheek as she realised for the first time that Robert had been transported back almost two years to the day that Agnes gave birth. "Not foolish, Robert," she said. "After everything that's happened, I would never call you foolish – just concerned. And I promise you, there's no reason to be concerned."

Robert wiped the tear from Sarah's cheek. "I do believe you. It just reminds me, that's all."

Sarah began, "I would never want you to forget them, Robert. Don't ever think that." She stroked his face. "Just move forward, and embrace the present."

Robert sat down on the bed so that all four of them could look at baby Mary. Sarah handed her to Robert and he took her. He looked lovingly down at her in his arms. "I love you, Mrs. McWilliam, and you, dear baby Mary," he said.

Next day Robert sent a telegram to Sarah's parents telling them of the birth. He walked to work with almost a skip in his step. He suddenly realised that grief he didn't know he had was lifted from him, and life felt good. He couldn't wait to get back home to his family that evening.

When he got home he saw that Sarah and baby Mary were doing well. Margaret had been in to see they were alright and Agnes had been an absolute angel to them. William had played on the floor in the room with Sarah watching over him.

A week later, Sunday, 3 March 1839, the McWilliam family had an afternoon visit from Sarah's parents. Despite the heavy snow everywhere, they came from Tranmere en masse, by cart. Mary and Thomas brought Sarah's sisters, Hannah, Mary and Jane, and little brother Thomas. The older boys were out and had no interest in babies – at least for the moment.

In just over a year Sarah's younger sisters were growing fast. Hannah, the eldest, had not changed. She was, by now 27 years old, but still childlike. She had always been slow growing up and although she could cope very well around the house, was very shy and immature. But Mary and Jane were developing normally. They had both grown taller. Mary was now 16 years old and had blossomed into a beautiful young woman, a good two inches taller than when we first saw her. Jane was 10 years old and was having a growth spurt. She was beginning to lose her child-like features.

Sarah was sitting in the rocking chair holding baby Mary, and her parents and sisters sat on what furniture there was available. Robert was out with William Cowan but was expected back shortly. Agnes and William were playing on the floor with Thomas.

"She's a fine one. She looks just like you," said Sarah's mother.

"Thank you, ma'," answered Sarah. "What do you think, da'?"

Thomas replied, "Your ma's right. She's a beauty." He paused for a moment, then said, "Are you happy?"

Sarah looked at her father and smiled. "Happy? Oh, da'! You've no need to worry. We're so happy here. Robert makes me happy. We love each other."

Mary looked at Thomas and then she spoke for both herself and her husband. "We can see that you're happy. You're positively glowing. It wasn't that we thought he wasn't right for you; we just wanted you to wait long enough to be sure."

Thomas nodded in agreement. "Exactly," he said.

Sarah replied, "We were always sure." She turned to her sisters. "And what do you think of your niece, Hannah? Mary? Jane?"

Mary was the first sister to speak. "I think she's adorable. Can I come to stay for a while? To help out?"

Before Sarah had a chance to answer, first, Jane joined in with "Can I come?" and Hannah with "Can I hold her?"

"Not so fast!" Sarah said. She turned to Jane. "Well, Mary did ask first, and she is a bit older than you, so she'll be more help. Maybe you can help out when Mary's a bit older."

Jane looked disappointed. Sarah continued, turning to Mary. "Mary, it's a wonderful idea! While baby Mary's so tiny you'd be such a godsend. My next door neighbour's been doing a bit of shopping for me this week, but I can't keep asking, so I was wondering how I'd get out and about to do the shopping."

Mary's face lit up and she cast a bit of a smirk at her sister. Sarah turned her attention next to Hannah. "Come sit by me, here and you can hold her – but be careful."

Hannah, despite being the oldest of the sisters, was not so capable. Hannah came over and sat with Sarah as she had been told. Sarah passed the baby to her but watched her like a hawk.

"Oh, she is beautiful," Hannah said. She sighed. "I wish I could have a baby…"

Mrs. Foulkes tried to ignore Hannah's comment, but it saddened her, knowing it was highly unlikely that it would ever happen. Instead, she turned to her daughter. "Oh, Mary, you are a good girl! We can sort you out with a few bits and pieces when we get home, and you can come back tomorrow. Will that be soon enough, Sarah?"

Sarah replied, "Yes, ma. I've enough in for now. I was hoping to get shopping at the market on Wednesday, so tomorrow will be just fine."

"Oh, thank you!" called out Mary to her mother and sister.

"That's settled, then," mother added.

Just at that moment, the door opened and in walked Robert. As he walked in he kicked his shoes against the step to knock the snow off them. He closed the door, took off his coat and hung it up. "Afternoon to you," he said. "Apologies for not being here when yous arrived, but I was out wi' William, next door helping him wi' an errand. Mary's a bonny wee thing, is she not?"

"That she is, Robert," said Thomas. "You must both be so proud of her."

"Aye, that we are." Robert sat down. He relaxed into his chair and looked over at the newspaper that was lying on the floor beside him. "Did you hear about the big race at Aintree in the week?"

Sarah joined in. Turning to Thomas she said, "Aye, da', Robert was telling me all about it. It's because of the new railway station at Liverpool – there were thousands of people went by train.

They'd never seen so many people there. The horses have to jump over these fences on the course." Sarah paused and looked at Robert, realising she didn't remember everything he had told her. "What were the fences, Robert?"

Robert continued. "It was in the Liverpool Mercury. The horses had tae jump a series of hedges, fences and brooks, including a stone wall, cross a stretch of ploughed land and finish over two hurdles. It was called "The Grand Liverpool Steeplechase." As I understand it, there were 18 horses covered the course and the winner was called Lottery."

Sarah's mother was amazed. "The poor beasts! Did any of them get hurt?"

"I read that one had to be put down after it fell at one of the fences," answered Robert.

"Oh how shocking!" Mary retorted. "I don't think it's somewhere I would want to go, myself."

"Not that we could afford to, mother," added Thomas.

"Well, that's true," she replied. We have to make do with entertaining ourselves at home, with perhaps a day out on May Day."

"Aye, mother," said Thomas.

"Will yous join me wi' a wee dram o' whisky?" asked Robert. The women shook their heads. "Lemonade?" added Robert. They all nodded.

"That I will," replied Thomas. Robert got up and went over to fetch two glasses and the bottle of whisky. He poured out enough whisky for Thomas and himself and lemonade for the others. He passed the glasses round and they raised a toast to the new arrival.

Thomas looked out of the window. The daylight was beginning to fade and he didn't want to be driving home in the dark. He turned to speak to his wife. "Well, I believe it's time we were going. Look after yourselves, Robert, Sarah."

"Yes, da'," replied Sarah, "and yourselves."

"Mary will come back tomorrow," said mother, "and I shall come over, when I can, to visit. Come along, girls. Get your coat on, Thomas!"

Everybody got their warm clothes back on, ready for the journey home. When everybody was properly dressed Robert opened the door and the family disappeared, leaving the house a whole lot quieter than it had been for a while.

The journey back to Tranmere was filled with talk of Sarah's baby. Young Mary was so excited about going back the next day to stay for a while. Such things she was going to do helping Sarah. Jane and sister Hannah were both envious of Mary. Jane declared that next time Sarah had a baby it would be her turn to stay with her sister.

Mary struggled to sleep that night. She started packing as soon as she had gotten indoors. Her mother had insisted she go to bed, and Mary did for about ten minutes, but she was so excited, sleep wouldn't come. Finally, Mary had packed all she could think of to take with her, and she sat down on the bed. She thought, "I'll just lie down for a few minutes, to make sure I haven't forgotten anything..." She lay her head down on the pillow and within a couple of minutes she was asleep.

Monday, 4 March dawned fair but cool. The temperature didn't rise above 50° Fahrenheit all day. Young Mary Foulkes was up with the dawn. She had breakfast and was ready to go. Annie Prieson had offered to take Mary into Birkenhead as she was going there late morning for some supplies. So all Mary could do, in the meantime, was wait. Finally, at 11 o'clock, Annie pulled up outside the cottage and Mary put her coat and hat on, took her bag and said goodbye to her mother. She then went outside and got on the cart. They were on their way.

Shortly after 1 o'clock Annie arrived in Hamilton Terrace. Mary thanked her kindly and got off. She put her bag down outside the front door of number 8 and knocked. It seemed like ages before anybody got near to the door, but it finally opened, and Sarah stood there, with baby Mary in her arms.

"Come in, come in," Sarah said. She then noticed Annie on the cart outside. "Annie! How are you doing? Come see my baby."

Annie didn't need asking twice. She got off the cart, tethering the horse to the nearest post, and came over to the house.

"Isn't she beautiful," Annie remarked. "You are so lucky. I have to say, if I hadn't already been married, I think I'd have snapped Robert up before you'd had the chance!" Annie laughed as she thought about it. "Well," she added, "I have to go – I've to get some supplies for the farm. It's been lovely to see you – look after yourself." She hugged Sarah and the baby, and then turned to go. "Bye!"

"Bye!" Sarah replied. Then she turned to her sister. "Come on in – you'll be catching your death out here."

Mary picked up her bag and walked inside. She put her bag down and took her coat and hat off. "What do you want me to do?" she asked. Sarah gave the baby to her sister. Mary looked down at her, lovingly, and then back to Sarah, suddenly afraid the baby might break.

Sarah turned to her sister. "Well, you'll have to get used to holding her, so now's as good a time as any. I've one or two things I need to do, so sit down with her and try to get her to sleep for me."

Mary sat down and Sarah busied herself around the house for a while. Meantime, Mary got the baby off to sleep, and sat there with her until Sarah came back. Sarah then showed Mary how to put the baby in the cradle beside the rocking chair without waking her.

The planned trip out on Wednesday was delayed due to heavy snow fall, but, a day later, the sun came out, making the fallen snow look beautiful. There was, however, no warmth in the sun. The temperature was just below freezing. Sarah and her sister Mary were going to the market on the corner of Hamilton Square and they were all wrapped up for the cold weather. They took all the children with them. Agnes held William's hand, Sarah carried the baby, snuggled inside the shawl around Sarah's shoulders, and Mary walked alongside watching all of them in case one of them needed catching on the slippery snow.

They had just set off into Hamilton Terrace when they bumped into a few of their neighbours. Margaret Cowan was also going to market – she saw Sarah ahead of her and caught up to her. She had brought her sister, Mary, and youngest children, Robert, Thomas and John. Robert, the eldest of the three, was walking with John, just a year old, who had just started walking and was defiantly refusing to allow anybody to pick him up. Thomas, now aged 4, walked with his Aunt Mary.

Sarah said, "Good morning, Margaret, Mary," and Margaret replied likewise. She had already met Sarah's sister, but she was still shy and didn't speak, just bobbed a curtsey.

"How's your Janet?" asked Sarah. "She's not with you today?"

"No, she's got a wee bit o' cold, so she's staying home," replied Margaret, referring to her 9 year old daughter. "She's got a good constitution, so it'll no' be long afore she's over it."

Elizabeth Cross was just returning from market. She carried baby Phoebe, similarly wrapped up in her mother's shawl, and her sister Mary had a basket of foodstuffs. They all stopped, together, one door away from Elizabeth's house. Elizabeth was the first to speak.

"Good morning, Sarah, Margaret, Mary. It's a beautiful day, is it not?"

Almost as one, all the ladies replied, "Good morning, too."

Margaret then spoke independently. "It is a beautiful day, but a wee bit windy."

"Sarah, I don't believe I've met – is it your sister?" Elizabeth asked. "You both look so alike!"

"Yes," replied Sarah, "this is my younger sister Mary. She has come to stay with me for a while to help with baby."

"Pleased to meet you," Mary said, as she bobbed a curtsey.

Margaret turned to Sarah. "Mind you're not out too long, and make sure that wee one stays well wrapped up."

Sarah nodded. "We're not going far, and, yes, little Mary is well dressed, and will stay so."

"Good tae hear," continued Margaret. "How's the feeding going?"

"She's feeding well, thank you, Margaret," Sarah replied, "but it's very hard work."

"You're so wise, to have your sister stay," added Elizabeth. "My sister has been with us since we had Phoebe, and I'm certain I'd not have coped without her. Don't you agree, Margaret?"

"Oh, indeed, I do," Margaret agreed. "Although, my sister came tae stay wi' us out o' necessity, for my parents were a wee bit too frail tae look after her, and she'd have been on her own wi' them. It wasnae fair on any o' them for her tae stay behind."

"Well, ladies," said Elizabeth, "I'll take my leave of you. I know you have places to go, and I need to get my shopping indoors."

"Indeed," replied Sarah, "we have our shopping to do, too."

Elizabeth and her sister, carrying the shopping, moved along and entered their house. Sarah, Margaret and their entourages continued on towards the market.

Over the next few weeks the family made several such trips to the market. There was still a lot of snow about, but by the end of March heavy rain had washed away most of the snow. On 27 March it was a dull, but dry day, not very warm.

Sarah, Mary and the children were just returning from the market, round about noon, with their shopping. The next door neighbour on the other side of the Cowan family, Janet Youds, was walking towards them, on her way home, when she stumbled and fell. This happened near the Cross house, four houses away from the Youds house.

Sarah watched, horrified as Janet fell down. Instinctively, she gave baby Mary to her sister. Mary put down the shopping so she could hold her. Sarah rushed over to Janet Youds and knelt down beside her. "Mrs. Youds – Janet – are you alright?" Sarah called to her. As she spoke Janet started to gather her thoughts.

"Oh my…" she began, "I don't know quite what happened there. I think I must have just lost my footing." Janet tried to get up so Sarah offered her arm.

"Do you have anyone at home?" Sarah asked.

"Margaret and David are indoors," Janet replied, "but William is out at work."

As Margaret stood up she swayed unsteadily. Sarah held her tightly. "Let's get you back home," she said. Just at that moment a man driving a horse and carriage stopped beside them. The driver jumped down to offer assistance. He asked, "do you need some help, ladies?"

Sarah quickly responded. "Why, thank you sir. If you could just help me get Janet back to her house that would be grand."

"No problem," he said. "You take one side and I'll take the other. We'll get you home in no time, missus."

Together, they slowly walked Janet back to number 4. Sarah knocked at the door and then she opened it. Carefully, they took Janet inside. The carriage driver helped Janet to a seat before he turned and went back to his carriage. Janet thanked him profusely. Margaret, Janet's 12 year old daughter, was hovering over her mother as Sarah explained what had happened.

"I have to go back to my own family, now," Sarah added. Will you be alright until your father gets home?"

"I'll do. You get back to your children," said Margaret. "I can look after ma' for now."

"Well, we're only at number 8 if you need us," added Sarah. Margaret nodded as Sarah turned and left the house. It seemed like hours had passed, but in reality it was only about ten minutes.

When Sarah got back outside the street was deserted. She went back to her house and opened the door. Mary had taken everybody and the shopping indoors.

"Well, it seemed the sensible thing to do," Mary said to her sister. "How is Mrs. Youds?"

"I think she has a bit of a fever," replied Sarah. "I'm glad she wasn't far from her door when she fainted." Sarah took her coat off and sat down. "I hope Janet will be alright."

Later that evening, the story had just been told to Robert when there was a knock at the door. "I'll go answer it," said Robert. He opened the door and William Youds was there.

"Good evening," said William. "I hope I'm not disturbing you."

"Of course not," replied Robert. "Come in. How's the wife?"

"She's not well," William answered. "I'd like to thank your wife for helping this morning."

Sarah came over to William. "Think nothing of it, Mr. Youds. I couldn't just leave her there. I'm sorry to hear she's no better. What's the problem, do you think?"

"She seems to have a fever," he said. "That must be why she fell over – she was just feeling weak. Do you have any idea what I can do to help her?"

Robert asked, "Have you fetched her a doctor?"

Sarah said, "I can come to see Janet, but I think Robert's right. You need to have her seen by a doctor. Would you like me to sit with her while you go to fetch him?"

"That'd be much appreciated, Mrs. McWilliam," William replied.

"Just give me a few moments," Sarah said. She got her shoes on and then fetched her coat. "I'm ready, now," she said. With that, Robert opened the door and Sarah and William left the house.

William opened the door to his house. "I'm so grateful for you doing this," he said. "Janet's in there. He pointed to the rear room so Sarah went in. Janet Youds was in bed. She was clearly very unwell and was sweating profusely. Sarah sat down on a chair beside the bed.

"I'll just go for the doctor," said William. "I really appreciate this," he added. "I'll be as quick as I can." With that he disappeared, leaving Sarah with his sick wife. Margaret appeared in the doorway in her nightdress. "How is ma'?" She asked.

"She's poorly," replied Sarah.

William returned with the doctor a while later. Sarah introduced herself, as she was sitting with Janet. She told him of the incident that morning and he then examined Janet. After the doctor left she returned home.

Robert was waiting for her as she walked back indoors. "Well? What did the doctor say?" he asked.

"Oh, Robert, that poor man! Poor Janet. The doctor said she's very ill. He thinks it might be influenza." Sarah was visibly upset as she explained while taking her coat and shoes off.

"So what can he do for her?" Robert asked.

"They've just to keep her cool and hope for the best," she answered. "The doctor said he'll call back tomorrow. There's nothing else they can do for her. Apparently, there's a lot of it about just now."

"Oh my...," said Robert, concerned, "and they've two children..."

"Well, two at home," replied Sarah, sitting down at last. "I understand they have two others off working for families. Margaret and David still live at home, but she's 12 and he's 9. I hear influenza can be bad."

"We'll just have to hope she pulls through, then," added Robert.

Janet Youds hung on to life as hard as she could, but influenza could be a killer, and Janet just wasn't strong enough to beat it. Seven days later, Wednesday, 3 April 1839, Janet died as the day dawned. Sarah had been called for by the doctor to comfort William and his children. Mary stayed at home with the children while Sarah helped William come to terms with his loss. Sarah stayed with Margaret and David while he went off to see about a funeral, and to tell his other children and Janet's family the sad news. When he returned home about four in the afternoon Sarah asked if he minded that she return to her family. He told her to go, and thanked her for all she had done for him.

Back home, later that evening, after they had eaten, Sarah told the sad tale to Robert and her sister.

"It was so sad, Robert. Those children didn't understand. Poor Mr. Youds was just walking round like he was in a trance."

"How old was she?" Mary asked.

"She was 50, three years younger than her husband. I don't know what he's going to do...," she said, starting to cry.

"Well, if I know you, you'll be there giving him support. You're a good woman," Robert added. He stood up and held Sarah in his arms. She laid her head on his shoulders and he stroked her hair. It had a soothing effect on Sarah. She regained her composure and sat down.

Mary looked puzzled. "It was influenza," she began. "I didn't think it would kill her."

"It doesn't always," replied Sarah. But this year's been a bad one. If you're not strong enough, it can kill you."

Mary wasn't convinced, but just replied, "Oh."

"I can't see people in distress," said Sarah. It upsets me. I have to do something…"

"Aye," said Robert, "I know. It's just your nature. Has the funeral been arranged?"

Sarah shook her head. "The vicar will be round tomorrow to make the arrangements," she said.

Robert looked at Sarah. She had worked so hard today, under exceptional circumstances. He could see she was tired even if she refused to admit it to him. "Well, I think it's time you were away tae your bed, woman. You look exhausted!"

"You'll get no argument there," Sarah replied. With that, she stood up and they all went to bed.

The funeral of Janet Youds was on the next Saturday, 6 April. Besides Janet's children there were a great many from Janet's side of the family. As the cortege wound its way down Hamilton Terrace to the church all the neighbours stood in silent respect. It was something that all of them knew, only too well, how it could just have easily been them in that situation.

William Youds and his children went to stay with his in-laws for a few days after the funeral. The next time Sarah saw him was three weeks later.

The day had dawned much brighter after the last, which had been full of rain. It was a bright day still with a bit of a chill to it. More rain looked like it was on the way, but not just yet. Sarah, Mary and the children were heading for Hamilton Square, to go to the park in the square. As they walked up the road they saw William Youds coming towards them. He had another woman with him, whom Sarah recognised from the funeral procession. They stopped as they came level.

"Good morning ladies," began William. "May I introduce you to my wife's cousin – Ann Prentice."

Sarah began to nod as she realised she was right. Both she and Mary said, "Good morning." Then Sarah continued, "Has Ann come to help you with the children?"

"She has, indeed," replied William. "I have no relations who could come to help – me being that bit older – but after Janet's funeral Ann offered to help out. She's not married, so it seemed the right thing to do." He then spoke to his companion. "Ann, this is Sarah McWilliam and this is her sister Mary. They live two doors up from us." Ann bobbed a curtsey to Sarah and Mary.

"I'm very pleased to meet you, Ann," said Sarah. "I'm sure we shall see a lot of each other."

"Thank you," Ann replied.

Pleasantries over, both parties separated and went their different ways.

Life passed by uneventfully for a few months. Mary went back home now that Sarah was more able to cope, but she still called round often to visit – when Annie Prieson was after supplies. About 25 August, four months later, Sarah was at home talking with Robert.

"There's more going on at the Youds than her just being there to help with the children and the house," she began.

"How can you be sure o' that?" Robert asked.

Certain in her own mind that she knew what was happening, Sarah replied, "Why Robert, she's putting on weight – fast. That can mean only one thing!"

Exasperated, Robert replied, "Why can you no' leave them alone tae get on wi' it? You're just putting two and two together!"

"Well, maybe I am," she retorted. "We'll just have to wait and see, won't we!"

Robert shook his head as he realised he would not hear the end of this conversation. Sarah was, most like correct, but he did so like to goad her. He loved it when she got worked up about something. There was such a fire in her eyes.

The autumn weather was approaching fast, and with it, the colds and chills that come at that time of year. Mid-September little Thomas caught a particularly bad cold, but it was a cold, and they usually passed unceremoniously.

Monday, 16 September 1839 was a day like any other. Robert and Sarah were finishing up after their evening meal. The children and baby were all in bed, and Robert and Sarah were just about to sit down for a while before bed themselves. Unexpectedly, there was a knock at the door. Robert and Sarah looked at each other.

"Who could that be at this time of night?" Sarah asked.

"I'll go and find out," answered Robert. He stood up, walked over to the door and opened it.

"Why Robert, come in. I'd no' expected it tae be you. It's your brother, Sarah."

"Thanks," replied Robert, stepping in through the door. "Though I wish it could be better circumstances."

Sarah came over to greet her brother. "Why, Robert, whatever do you mean?"

"It's little Thomas. You know he's had a bit of a cold this past week?" Robert continued, as he took his coat off.

Sarah nodded. "Yes," she said, "but I thought he was getting better?" She began to have a nagging feeling in the pit of her stomach. He wouldn't have come to tell her about a cold – not at this time of night.

"So did we all, but it went on to his chest the last couple of days," her brother added, trying to keep his composure.

Sarah looked at her husband. Robert could see she was beginning to panic. He turned to his brother-in-law. "It's bad, isn't it?"

Robert Foulkes nodded and said, "It is. We didn't realise just how bad until today. It was pneumonia." He paused for a moment, to let them take in the news. He looked directly at Sarah. "I'm sorry, sis, if we'd known…"

Sarah stumbled as she felt for a chair. Her husband understood her pain and guided her backwards until she was in the right position. He gently let her down into the chair. Sarah was horrified as the realisation began to set in of what her brother was about to say.

Robert continued, "You know we'd have sent for you, but it all happened so quickly. He died this afternoon. Doctor Williams was with him, but there was nothing he could do."

"NO!!!!!!!!!!!!" Sarah buried her face in her hands and began to cry. Her husband knelt down beside her and held her.

Two days later the family gathered at St. Andrew's church, Bebington, for the funeral of little Thomas. The service was performed by the Curate, Harry Ovenden Wrench. All of the Foulkes families from Tranmere were there. It was a fair day for the time of year. The temperature was in the 50s and there was little in the way of wind. It was a short service, with 'The Lord's My Shepherd' and 'Abide with Me', followed by interment in the graveyard. His mother, Mary, was devastated at her loss and she was unable to control her emotions. Thomas, on the other hand, was stoical, but you could see in his face the strain that this event had wrought on him.

After the funeral Thomas and Mary made it clear that they were going to move out of the village. There was a house in William Street vacant, and they had managed to rent it. It wasn't much better than Robert and Sarah's back-to-back dwelling, but it was in the town. Anywhere except Tranmere. Thomas was going to work down at Woodside docks – on the ferry, and the girls would all be able to get some domestic employment. And, they would now all be so much closer to Sarah and her family. By the end of October all the repairs that had been needed on the two up, two down, property were done and Thomas and his family moved in.

The last Sunday in October the weather was beginning to get noticeably cooler. The sun was out, but there was little warmth to it. Clouds were beginning to build in the sky. Thomas and Mary had organised most of their possessions and it was looking a cosy little place. Robert, Sarah and the children all came to see them. Mary was still sorting a few things out from the last boxes. Daughters Hannah, Mary and Jane were playing with the children, supervised by doting mum Sarah. Thomas and Robert were sitting down talking.

"It's grand," said Robert. "And it will be so easy now tae come and visit."

"There's so much more room than in our old cottage," replied Thomas. "We were all on top of each other. It seems a world away now – and mother didn't want to stay there any longer, not after we lost Tommy."

"Aye," said Robert, "it must be hard wi'out him – he was such a happy lad." Robert looked at the size of the room. "These houses gie you so much more room. I'm guessing you'll no' know what tae do wi' all this space!"

"That's for sure," added Thomas. "Robert's out walking a lass at the moment, so I don't know how long he'll be with us here, but the girls seem to be homebirds. Perhaps now we're in the town they can get a job. That'd be helpful."

"There's a good amount o' work tae be had here, for sure," said Robert. "The railway's kept me busy since I've been here. There's tae be a Chapel built down the end of our street, so the work's there. Did you manage tae get signed on with the ferry?"

"That I did. I've the experience, what with Tranmere ferry, so they were quick to hire me. It'll be enough to keep us going."

Mary finished sorting through the things and sat down at the opposite end of the room from the men. She called out to her daughter. "Sarah, come sit with me. Let me see my namesake."

Sarah went over to her mother and sat down bedside her. She handed baby Mary to her grandma but Mary really wanted to be on the floor, so she wriggled about as Sarah passed her over. "Here she is, ma. She's doing so well."

"Oh, yes," replied Mary. "Three generations all in the same house. I was beginning to think this day would never come. And you're keeping well, that's plain to see."

"Indeed I am, ma'," replied Sarah. "It's only when you have a baby that you realise how much hard work they really are – especially now she's ready to start crawling."

"That's only to be expected!" Mary said. "Well, Thomas, do you think the baby's grown?"

"I do indeed, mother," replied Thomas.

Sarah and Robert had brought a meal with them for the family as there was far too much going on for Mary to be able to cook for her brood, and since all the unpacking was done, Sarah said, "Can you look after Mary for me while I get the tea ready?"

"Of course I can," replied Mary. So, with that, Sarah got up and went into the kitchen. After dinner Sarah, Robert and the children got their coats on and went back home. They had been very busy that day, but were so pleased that the family was back together.

A few days later it was easy to tell that the cold autumn weather was beginning to set in. The temperature on this Wednesday, 13 November, was a few degrees above freezing and it was a cloudy, windy day. Everybody was out doing their shopping. Sarah was talking with Margaret Cowan. Neither woman had brought their families out with them.

"Have you heard?" Margaret asked. "About William Youds?"

"Heard what?" Sarah asked. "I know she's pregnant."

"He only went and married her last week!" Margaret told her.

Sarah looked pleased with the news. She crossed her arms as she stood there, and chuckled. "Did he, now? Well, at least he's doing the decent thing by her. But it's been seven months now since Janet died."

"Aye," said Margaret, "but she's so much younger than him... There's twenty five years atween 'em. When do you think baby is due?"

Sarah thought for a moment. "By my reckoning," she said, "it should be due about April time." Margaret nodded in agreement.

The days soon rolled on into Christmas. Sunday, 22 December was a stormy day and there was a chill in the air. Inside the house in William Street, the whole family was gathered. There were Thomas and his wife Mary, their three unmarried daughters, Hannah, Mary and Jane, sons Robert, and John, who had come home on his day off from his employers in Liverpool, and finally, Robert, Sarah and their family. This was the only day that the whole family could be together to celebrate Christmas because John had to work on Christmas Day. Agnes and William were playing and baby Mary was asleep. Christmas dinner was over and the adults were talking amongst themselves.

Robert McWilliam was talking. "We're taking on the whole of the house now. It's been about nine months since the Cowan's moved next door, and naebody else has moved in the upstairs. I spoke tae the landlord and he said we could have the whole house for a wee bit more than we're paying at the moment. We're getting tight for space, so I think it's the way tae go."

Mother looked at Sarah. "Is there something you're not telling us Sarah?" she asked.

"No, ma'," Sarah replied, chuckling. "We just thought we should make a move on the upstairs before anybody else moved in. But we have the three children now, and with Mary coming to stay from time to time, we do need the space. Who knows when anything might change?"

In an effort to change the subject away from babies, Thomas said, "So what do you think about this idea of the "Four Penny Post"?"

"Aye," said Robert McWilliam. "I've heard about it. If it works it'll be cheaper than the telegraph."

Thomas added, "Well, it can't be any worse that the postal companies that we have now. It's already cheaper – if you're sending a very small packet."

"Well, time will tell," added Robert McWilliam. He turned to John. "So what work are you doing in Liverpool?"

"Well," John began, "I'm a groom, but we live down dockside, and I do love watching the ships come in and out. It's a good job where I am, but I'd like to visit other countries. I've a mind to sign up with a merchantman."

Thomas looked at him. "A merchantman? Don't tell your mother or she'll never let you hear the end of it, lad!"

His brother Robert sniggered but Thomas stared hard at him, so he shut up.

"And what about you, brother," John began, "I hear you're out walking a lass?"

"We've only seen each other a couple of times," Robert Foulkes replied, blushing.

Meantime, Hannah, Mary and Jane had managed to draw Sarah away so they could talk amongst themselves. Mary had started working as a servant for a local family and she wanted to tell her sister about what she was doing.

"I have to work my way up," Mary started. "I'm scullery maid at the moment, but you'll see – I'll be a ladies maid before long!"

"I'm sure you will," replied Sarah. "You've shown me what a good worker you are. Strikes me, you should try to work with children."

"Do you think so?" Mary asked.

"For sure," replied Sarah.

Suddenly, Mary stood up from where she was sitting – beside her husband. "I've something special for us all today. I saved up for this. I'll just go and get it."

Mary went off to the kitchen. Everybody sat there, watching her go, looking puzzled. Sarah was the first to speak.

"What's ma' talking about? Do you know, da'?"

"I'm not sure," Thomas replied, "but your ma' has been a bit secretive the last few days."

Mary came back in the room with a large pot and some mugs on a wooden tray. She put everything down on the table, without saying a word.

"So what's this you've brought in for us?" Sarah asked.

"For the first time since it's been imported," their mother began, "tea is now affordable to the likes of us. So, I thought I'd treat us all this Christmas." Mary poured the tea into eight mugs and handed them round. Everybody took a drink from their cup.

"Well," began Thomas, "it has a different taste. Seems strange to be having a hot drink."

"It's no' a bit like beer," added Robert McWilliam. "I suppose I could get used tae it, mind."

"Not sure about it," said Robert Foulkes.

"Me either," added John.

"Well, I like it, ma'," said Sarah. "How do you make it?"

The other sisters just giggled and looked at each other as they drank it. Sarah stood up and went over to the table as her mother began. "It comes as leaves, which you spoon in a pot. You then pour boiling water on it and give it a stir. Mind you don't swallow the leaves – there'll be some at the bottom of the mug."

"Well, mother, you never cease to amaze me," said Thomas. "How do you find out about all this stuff?"

Mary just smiled at him.

As the day wore on, Robert, Sarah and baby Mary went home. They had really enjoyed this Christmas, even if it was a few days early.

A month later, at the end of January 1840, Robert's landlord told him they could have the use of the whole house. The rent was reasonable. They had been paying £2.0.0 a week for the two rooms and a share of the kitchen, but for the whole house they were being charged £3.0.0.

For a while daily life continued much the same, but early in February the country was talking about their new Queen and her husband-to-be. Finally, on 10 February 1840 they married. For those fortunate to be able to travel to London they could go to see them marry at St. James Palace. Robert and Sarah, however, had to wait until it made the newspaper. Robert brought the Friday evening newspaper home with him. He had started telling her about the day as she was preparing the dinner. After dinner, and when the children were in bed Sarah asked him to read the rest of the details of the day to her.

He continued "A cupid sat writing in a volume expanded on his knees the date of the day of the marriage, with various other cupids bearing emblems of the United Kingdom. On the top surface of the cake were numerous bouquets of Orange Blossoms and Myrtle entwined; similar sprigs were placed loose as presents tae the guests at the nuptial breakfast. The elegant Royal Wedding Cake, a symbol of the celebrations of marriage, was placed on the breakfast table of the Queen at Buckingham palace, at the breakfast which is to succeed the ceremonies in the chapel royal. From the Times"

Sarah sat there, enthralled. "Oh, Robert, it sounds so wonderful. I wish we could have been there. It's a shame we had to wait from Monday to today to read about it."

"Aye," he replied, "it would be grand tae be able to go tae London. Perhaps one day we'll get tae go."

Two weeks later, 24 February, was Mary's first birthday. Sarah could not believe how fast this past year had gone. Such a lot had happened in that time, and now she felt fulfilled as a woman. Mary was almost ready to start walking and she was loved by all.

But daily life continued unabated. Ann Youds had her baby that April, as Sarah had predicted. Margaret and her family continued to live next door to Robert and Sarah, and Elizabeth and her family on the other side.

Sunday, 10 May, Robert and Sarah were at home with the children. Agnes was playing with William, and Mary was trying to join in. There was a knock at the door, so Robert answered it. His brother-in-law, Robert, was there.

"Why, Robert… Come in man. Sarah," Robert called out, "it's your brother."

Sarah came to the door to greet Robert as he entered the house. He looked flustered.

Sarah was concerned. "Robert – whatever's the matter?"

"It's my girl – Jane – who I'm walking out with…," he began.

"What about her?" Sarah asked, once again afraid, remembering the last time he called round unexpectedly. "Come on Robert – you can talk to me."

"Well…," he continued, "I don't know what ma' is going to say… But, Jane and me – we're expecting a baby."

Sarah let out a sigh of relief. "Is that it?" she said, almost annoyed. "Well, you've work – you're a stonemason. You work with my Robert. You'll be fine." She gave him a hug and then stood back. "You'll marry her, of course?" she added.

"I will. I know. I want to – I just wasn't expecting this," he replied. "I'm not ready yet."

"Robert, you'll do grand!" Robert McWilliam added, patting him on the back. "When are you going tae tell your ma' and da'?"

"I'm taking Jane round to see them tonight. We'll tell them then."

"Well, ma' and da' will be fine about it. They were expecting Hannah when they got married, weren't they," added Sarah in an effort to calm Robert's nerves.

"I didn't think of that," added her brother.

"Have you made plans for a wedding?" Sarah asked.

"Jane lives in Liverpool with her family in Scotland Place," he replied, "so we thought we'd get married at St. Peter's, like you did."

After a while Robert had calmed down, so he left to tell his parents the news. He was glad he had called round to see his sister. She always talked sense.

The next day Sarah's mother came round to see Sarah and to tell her about Robert bringing Jane to see them.

"She's so pretty," Mary said. "She's already got a little boy, though. You'd think she'd be more careful to let something like this happen."

"Ma' – you were expecting Hannah when you got married!"

"Yes, but she was our first," Mary replied, indignantly. I didn't have a child already."

"Oh, that's harsh," replied Sarah. Do you know how she got the first?"

"No," answered Mary. "I don't. Why do you?"

Sarah shook her head. Maybe one day they would find out.

A few weeks later Robert told everybody the date of the wedding. As he had predicted, it was to take place in St. Peter's Church, Liverpool, at 2 o'clock in the afternoon on Monday, 6 July 1840. Jane's parents wanted it to be sooner, but it was only just over a month away. Jane worked as a servant for a dressmaker and her employer had kindly offered to make her a wedding dress.

The wedding day dawned cloudy but warm. It looked like it would rain, so everybody hoped they could get the wedding over beforehand.

The family gathered, once again, at the church of St. Peter, for the marriage of Robert Foulkes to Jane Salisbury. All the Foulkes family members were there, as were the Salisbury family. Jane tried to conceal her bump with a high waisted, 17th century-style wedding dress in beige. Curate Thomas Halton conducted the ceremony. The wedding went off without a hitch and afterwards Robert and Jane went back to the Foulkes' house in

William Street, where they were going to live until they could get somewhere of their own.

The long awaited railway line was coming to fruition. The Official Opening of the line at Grange Lane was on Tuesday, 22 September 1840. Both Roberts worked on the railway, both being stonemasons, and they were proud to take their families to see the event. The day before the line opened to the public saw dignitaries take the inaugural journey from Grange Lane to Brook Street, Chester.

The directors and their friends took a preliminary trip from Birkenhead to Chester and back again that morning. For this purpose a first class train was prepared, and the start was to take place at 2 o'clock, by which time Mr. Yarrow, one of the principal engineers, had all things in readiness, with one exception. The train.

A train had gone out in the morning with a considerable number of persons whom the directors had gratified with a trip, and several persons connected with the railway had accompanied it. As it was necessary to await the return of this train there was a considerable delay as a result. The train arrived back in Birkenhead about an hour later.

The day was somewhat changeable, alternating between showers and sunshine, rousing alternate hopes and apprehensions in those who looked forward to the journey with interest. However as the hour of departure approached, it became reasonably fine, though an occasional sprinkling still dampened the proceedings.

Robert McWilliam took Sarah and his children to watch as the events of the day unfolded, along with a large proportion of the town of Birkenhead. Sarah carried Mary while Robert held Agnes and William's hands.

The constable and officers of the company were kept fully employed in maintaining order, as some of the classes of spectators were not of the most easily managed quality.

"Well, Sarah," said Robert, "what do you think of it, now it's done?"

"I think it's a wonderful thing," she replied. "Now, at least, we have a railway like Liverpool does."

"Well, not quite as grand as Lime street, but we are on the map now." As he spoke he saw Thomas and Mary in the distance. "Look – there's your ma' and da' over there, with the girls."

"Yes," replied Sarah, "And, see over there, on the other side – there is Robert and Jane."

Each group made their way to meet up with Robert and Sarah, who were standing in the middle. Robert and Jane were the first to meet up. Sarah could see how close it was for Jane. She said, "How are you keeping, Jane? You must surely be near your time, now?"

"Indeed I am," she replied. "And the sooner the better, if you ask me. I didn't expect to see so many people here today. It's quite frightening to be surrounded like this. I'm holding tight to Willie's hand, I can tell you!"

Sarah looked down at the little boy. At 3 years old he was almost as tall as their William, who was two years older.

"I'll keep you safe, Jane," Robert said. He bent down and picked up Willie so he could see better. Just then, Thomas and Mary reached them with all three daughters.

"I hoped we'd see you here," began Thomas, "although when I saw how many people there were I began to wonder if we'd spot you! It's a grand day for the town."

Sarah's mother kissed her on the cheek and picked up William while Thomas picked up Agnes. Thomas continued. "So, now it's finished what will you be doing for work, Robert?"

"There's work going on in Liverpool now, so I've signed up for that," said Robert McWilliam. "What about you, Robert? Where are you working?"

"I've not found anything just yet. Is there much going on over there?" Robert Foulkes asked.

"There's a fair bit," answered Robert McWilliam. "You'll be well advised tae go over on the ferry and look around. I'm working on the Great George Street Chapel. The work's just started – you're bound tae get something."

"I'll do that!" Robert Foulkes replied.

Suddenly, the men were brought back to the moment at 20 minutes to 4 o'clock, when Mary, senior, called out, "Look! Look! The train's pulling out from the station!"

The train was of enormous length and excessively loaded. It was being pulled by two engines, bearing the names of Touchstone and Zillah. It was set in motion, amidst the cheers of the multitude, accompanied by a couple of reports from two pieces of ordnance, which were stationed on a neighbouring eminence.

As the two guns let off their charges all the family members jumped and the children started to cry out of shock. Sarah and Jane comforted them as best they could, and they stopped crying. As the train disappeared into the distance the crowds began to disperse. The Foulkes and the McWilliams said their goodbyes to each other and left to go to their separate homes.

Just short of a month later, Robert and Jane had their baby. The baby was born in the evening of 15 October 1840. The birth was completely straightforward and the baby was healthy. Jane suffered no complications, either.

Sarah came to visit her mother most Friday afternoons, and this week was no exception. As she walked in the front door she could hear the baby crying. Sarah turned to her mother. "When was the baby born, ma'?"

"She came yesterday evening. Jane was in labour a good while, but she's doing fine now. Go upstairs and see them – she won't mind."

Sarah went upstairs and into the bedroom. Jane was in bed holding baby Sarah. Sarah walked over to her sister-in-law and sat down on the edge of the bed.

"She is beautiful," Sarah said. "So, what will you be naming her?"

"We're calling her Sarah," replied Jane. "We're having her christened on Sunday at St. Mary's. Would you be her godmother?"

"That's kind of you to think of me," replied Sarah. "That'd be lovely. Who else are you having?"

"My sister Margaret and my brother Thomas," answered Jane. "Your ma' is putting on a spread afterwards. Do you want to hold her?"

"I would love to," replied Sarah. Jane held the baby out to Sarah and she took her from Jane. Sarah continued talking. "It will be great to have another baby about."

As Jane watched Sarah with the baby, she spotted something. "And from the look of it, you've also got one on the way!" Jane added.

Sarah sat there and chuckled. "You're right, I have. It'll be another winter baby!"

That Sunday, at St. Mary's church, the Christening went off smoothly under the auspices of the Curate Charles James Hamilton. The weather was cold but it was a dry day. All the families squeezed themselves into the Foulkes home for afternoon tea. A good time was had by all.

The weather was growing colder as the days moved into November. Friday, 13 November was a particularly windy day. Sarah and her children were off to go shopping when they saw Margaret Cowan. She was also going shopping, but this particular day she was on her own. Sarah hurried to catch Margaret up.

As they walked along Sarah started talking. "Morning, Margaret. Everything alright? I see you've not brought the family with you today."

"No, Sarah," Margaret replied. "Everything is not alright. The little ones have gone down wi' a fever. I've left them indoors wi' my sister so they dinnae have tae come out in this cold."

"Oh dear," answered Sarah. "Have you called the doctor?"

"No' yet," said Margaret. "I'll wait and see if I can get the fever tae break. It may no' last long. That's why I've kept them indoors."

"Well, let me know if I can do anything to help," added Sarah.

"Aye, I'll do tha'. Thank you kindly," said Margaret, Now, if you'll excuse me, I need tae hurry on so I can get back tae my family."

With that, Margaret hurried off into the distance and Sarah continued about her business. Sarah thought about poor Margaret all day, but she heard no more from her, so she assumed that the children were fine.

By Sunday evening, 15 November, however, it became clear that things were not alright.

Sarah and Robert were just tidying up after putting the children to bed when there was a knock at the door. Robert answered it and William Cowan was standing there, looking visibly upset.

"Why Bill," said Robert, "whatever's the matter? Come in, man, come in."

William entered the house and stood there wringing his hands, not knowing what to do or say.

Sarah spoke first. She said, "Is it the children? Is Margaret alright?"

Finally, William managed to speak. "It's my boy, Thomas... They had a fever this week..."

"Margaret said," replied Sarah. "Are they no better?"

"Thomas...," William began, "we've just lost him... We didnae call out the doctor until yesterday. Perhaps if we'd called him sooner it'd have been alright..."

"Oh no!" Sarah replied, thinking back a few months to her poor brother. "He was such a healthy lad. What about the others?"

"They seem tae be over the worst of it. It's just Thomas..."

Robert pulled up a chair for William. "Sit down, man," he said. "Do you need anything?"

William shook his head as he sat down. "It's Margaret," he said. "It's hit her real bad. I dinnae ken what tae do or say... She just keeps crying..."

Sarah brought a chair up beside William and sat down with him. "She just needs you there to support her, William. Just take each day as it comes," she said. "You'll get through it. You'll see... I know what it was like to lose my baby brother a few months back, but that's not like losing your child." Sarah thought for a moment, and then she said, "I might have a word with Elizabeth, just up the other way... I understand she lost her first baby when he was a few months old. She might be able to help Margaret more than I can do. I'll speak with her in the morning."

"That'd be much appreciated," William said after a moment to compose himself. "Well, I suppose I'd better be getting back tae her now. I just thought, since you're close, you'd want tae know."

"Indeed I do," said Sarah, "and I'm glad you chose to come and tell me. You'll get through this – just wait and see…"

William stood up and went to the door. He seemed to have aged overnight. Robert opened the door for him. As William stood in the doorway, Robert said, "Just remember, Bill – we're only next door. If ever you need anything…"

"Aye, I know. Thanks." William paused, then added, "and tae you, Sarah." He nodded to Sarah and then went back outside. Robert shut the door and turned to Sarah.

"It takes me back, Sarah, it takes me back…," he said. Sarah walked over to him and touched him on the arm. "Hey, hey…," she began, "we've been lucky this time. This influenza's brutal. You just don't know when it's going to get you."

"You're right, and no mistake!" Robert agreed.

The next few days were stormy and this day was no exception. It was Wednesday 18 November 1840 and the day of the Cowan's son's funeral. The cortege left the family home as the child's coffin was brought out and laid inside the horse-drawn hearse waiting in the street outside. The family were all dressed in black, William dressed in the Scottish tradition, wearing the same as Robert had three years earlier. He was supporting his wife Margaret, followed by her sister Mary holding the hand of 2 year old John, and behind them, children, Janet and Robert. The neighbours who stood outside all watched, sadly, on, knowing that this could have happened to any of their children instead.

Sarah and Elizabeth had both been asked to attend the funeral, so they fell in behind the party as the cortege passed. Sarah's children stood with Mary Price, Elizabeth's sister, who was holding Elizabeth's new, 2 month old, baby John in her arms and daughter Phoebe at her side. Mary Foulkes had come to help with Sarah's children, while Sarah was absent. The procession walked up the street and turned right at the corner to go to St. Mary's church.

The saddest days are always tempered, however, and less than a month later Sarah was blessed with a son. He was born on Thursday, 10 December 1840. The other children were all in bed and Robert was home from work. Sarah's mother helped with the birth.

"Well," said Mary, "he's a small baby, but he's beautiful, all the same. You took us all by surprise, this time. I didn't think he was due until after Christmas. What a birthday present for you, Sarah!"

"Nor was he supposed to be born yet," Sarah said with a smile. "That's why he's smaller than Mary was. I just hope he'll thrive."

"Knowing you, he'll do just fine…," said her mother.

"It was just as well you were here visiting Mrs. Foulkes," said Robert. He turned to Sarah. "What shall we call him?" he asked, hoping that Sarah would remember their conversation from the year previously.

Sarah thought for a few seconds and then said, "Well, we called Mary after my ma, so we'll call him after your da', in the Scottish tradition."

Robert's face lit up. "John it is, then!" Robert cradled the baby in his arms and turned to Mary. "Granny, say hello tae John McWilliam…"

"Hello, my dear little John…," said Mary. "I wonder what the world has in store for you?"

"A good, long, healthy, life, I hope!" Sarah replied.

"Won't the bairns be surprised in the morning when they get up!" Robert exclaimed.

"Indeed they will," Sarah replied.

Two weeks passed and Christmas Day came round again.

The day dawned bright and sunny, but very cold – a few degrees below freezing. Sarah, Robert and family were at the Foulkes house so the family could all be together on Christmas Day. Around the house could be seen the holly, ivy and mistletoe adorning the walls and doors. Roast beef was cooking in the kitchen and mother Mary, along with daughter Hannah, were out there preparing the vegetables. Sarah was sitting, nursing her newborn son and was talking to Jane, who was sitting with her 3 month old baby. Both women were comparing their babies.

Little Agnes and Mary were sitting on the floor playing with Sarah's sister Jane. The two Williams were also sitting on the floor, playing with toy soldiers. The three men were all sitting together talking about work and the world.

The large table in the room was decorated with holly rings containing red candles and set for six people, while there was a smaller table, without the decoration, for the four children, Agnes, William, and Mary McWilliam and William Salisbury. John and Mary Foulkes were conspicuous by their absence. John had done what he wanted, and gone to sea, much to his mother's despair, and Mary had gone into service with John Fell, a local book-keeper, whose wife had a year old daughter.

Thomas was talking to the two Roberts. "So how's your work doing?"

Robert McWilliam was first to answer. "No' so bad. We're getting on with the reconstruction o' the Great George Street Chapel, after it burned down in that fire in February. The new design is by Joseph Franklin, the Liverpool town architect. Should keep us busy for the next six months – or thereabouts – eh, Robert?"

"For sure it will," added Robert Foulkes. "But there's plenty of work about. I understand they're building a festival hall on the site of the old Liverpool Infirmary – to be called St. George's Hall. Harvey Elmes has designed it. There's a commemorative stone already laid and they're just drawing up the final plans, so they should be after tradesmen soon. What about you da'? Is your work alright?"

"Ferry runs fine most of the time – it's just when we get really bad weather and it can't cross the river," he said.

Sarah, at the other end of the room was deep in conversation with Jane. Sarah was saying, "He's so small, though… I was sure he wasn't going to be born until about January, February time. It's been a struggle these last two weeks, but he's starting to put on weight now. How's your Sarah doing?"

"Sarah's really growing," Jane answered. "She's sleeping well, too. William's such a good boy with her. I wish we could get a place of our own, though."

"You will… Give it time," Sarah said. "Robert's a good man – you can see how much he loves you. Before you know it you'll have your own place, even if it is only a couple of rooms to start with. That's what we first had."

"I know," Jane nodded. "Your ma' and da' are wonderful. They've given up a whole room for us so we can make it our own."

"Well, with Mary away in service now," said Sarah, "there's only Jane and Hannah, and they can share a room, easy.

At that moment, Mary and Hannah came in from the kitchen to the waiting table. Mary carried the roast beef and Hannah carried the various vegetables to accompany the meal. This was a big meal. The three families had combined to spend money on a big Christmas Day. It would be a real treat for everybody.

"Dinner's ready," said Mary. "Let's sit down to eat."

The adults sat at the main table while the children sat at a smaller table. Mary put the children's food on their plates, and then Hannah passed them down in front of them as they sat down. Thomas carved the joint, put it on everybody's plate in turn, and then everybody took a selection of vegetables. All the adults had a glass of beer and the children had lemonade.

Thomas stood up. "A toast…," he said. "Thinking of absent family, and hoping that the new year will be good one!"

All the adults raised their glasses to the toast, and the family sat there, laughing and chatting as they ate their Christmas lunch.

CHAPTER 3

Matchmaking

Sarah was interrupted from her reverie by her grandson, Walter. "So you were all in Birkenhead when my ma' and uncle John were born, then?"

"Aye, Walter," his grandmother replied. "Those were happy times. The work was good; the family was all together." She paused again, and a few minutes later she continued. "By 1846 Robert and Jane had three children – William, who came with Jane when they married, and Sarah, as I just told you, but they also had Mariah in 1843. They were getting to be almost as big a family as we were!" Sarah chuckled.

She continued, "Then, the landlord where we lived sold out so we had tae move. We went from our little house that was just us tae a brand new estate, only just built. There was a mix of sizes of houses, most with two floors each. In each floor was a self-contained flat, with a living room, two bedrooms and a scullery. There were a few that had four storeys, wi' one flat on each floor. 18 Back Beckwith Street, was ours. It was a block of three four storey houses. We had the 2nd floor. Dismal, it was, looking back, but we'd had tae move. I'd just had Jane when we moved. I hated it."

Saturday 24 January 1846 was a chilly, cloudy day. The temperature was 49° Fahrenheit. The family were moving to a flat and they were in the middle of packing all their possessions ready for

the move. A lot of the furniture came with the property when they moved in, but there were some pieces of furniture they were taking with them. The rocking chair was still their pride and joy. They had also bought two more beds. They had to leave one behind, for that was in the house when they arrived, and with the four children and Hannah, they had needed an extra bed, which they had bought three years earlier.

So, the week before the move Sarah had gone shopping to Corkbills again, and ordered a bed to be delivered that morning, ready for removal. Good as his word, the bed arrived promptly, ready to go straight into Thomas' cart.

Sarah and Agnes were busy putting things into boxes while Hannah was looking after baby Jane, who was born 21 November the year previously. Robert was out at work but Thomas, her father, was carrying the possessions out from the house to the large cart and horses that was waiting outside. It was his day off, which is why he was able to help. Sarah was recovering from influenza. Thankfully, in her case, it wasn't fatal.

Sarah stopped as she filled a box. "I hate leaving this little house," she said. "There are so many happy memories."

Agnes, now 12 years old, turned to her step-mother. "But ma', where we're going is all brand new... We'll be fine, just wait and see."

Thomas came back in from the street. "Well, that's the last of the big stuff loaded," he said. "How're we doing with the packing?"

"We're almost done da'," replied Sarah. "There's a load of boxes over there that can be packed. I've just to check through the house to make sure we've not forgotten anything, and that should be it."

"Grand!" Thomas said, and he began to take the boxes outside as Sarah left the room to go looking round the house for anything missed.

Finally, with everything on board that the family were taking, Thomas lifted Sarah up on the cart. He then passed baby Jane to her and lifted first Hannah and then the other four children up to sit in the cart, in an area that he had prepared for them to sit in safety, with Hannah watching over them.

With everybody on board he untethered the horses, jumped up and they set off. The journey took about 10 minutes through the streets. Finally, they pulled up outside the block of flats containing their address. Thomas jumped down from the cart and tethered the horses. Sarah passed baby Jane down to him and then she climbed down herself. She took the baby from Thomas and he took the key out of his pocket. He passed the key to Sarah and she walked off to the property. Thomas got Hannah and the remaining children down and took them to their new home. Agnes thought it was very exciting.

Sarah walked up the four half-flights of stairs to their 2nd floor flat. The stairwell was cold and uninviting. She shivered, then hurried on. Finally, she arrived outside her new front door. She put the key in the lock, turned it, then opened the door. She stood in a small lobby, with a door to her left, a door in front of her and a door to her right. She opened the door to her left and found a water closet. This was something new. In their house in Hamilton Terrace the family had to use an outside toilet. Being on the 2nd floor, though, she thought, it made sense to have one nearby. She opened the door in front of her and walked into the kitchen. This was a modern kitchen by comparison to the house in Hamilton Terrace. She opened the remaining door and walked into the main living room. It was a large room – much larger than any of the rooms in their house in Hamilton Terrace.

Sarah looked to her right, where there were two more doors, one in front of her and one leading off to the right, each leading to a bedroom. Just as well, now she had four children and the baby. To her left, Sarah could see a window out to the street, and tucked in the corner, next to the wall to the kitchen, was a fireplace. Sarah went over to the bedrooms and peeked inside. They were both good sized rooms, although one was a good deal larger than the other. She closed the doors as she heard running on the stairs.

At that moment, Agnes burst in through the door, swiftly followed by William. They were squealing, loving the echoey sounds their voices made. Mary followed soon after, with Hannah and John. Sarah went back into the living room. "Well?" She said, "What do you think?"

"It's big!" Hannah replied, looking around the room in awe. "Where's our bedroom?" Agnes asked.

"It will be one of these rooms through here," Sarah began. "Let's see which is biggest."

William opened the door on the right while Agnes opened the door on the left. "This one has a fireplace in the corner," called Agnes. "This is big, too!"

"It's only big because it's empty," Sarah added, as she walked in to join Agnes. "Once we've got our furniture in it won't look half as big." Sarah compared the two bedrooms. "This one is the big one," she said, "so this will be yours. We can get your two double beds in here, easy."

"So, we'll still be sleeping wi' Auntie Hannah, then?" Agnes asked. Sarah nodded.

Thomas brought the first of the boxes up. "Phew!" He said. This is going to be a long, hard job. Will you help me?" he asked William. "Aye, granddad!" William replied. "Come on, then, son," Thomas said, and William rushed out, down the stairs. Thomas chuckled as he followed him.

Sarah and Agnes began unpacking as fast as Thomas and William could bring the things inside. Hannah walked round the flat, looking after baby Jane and little Mary found a few toys and played with her brother John.

Sarah put the rocking chair in the front room, along with four chairs and a small table that Thomas had acquired for them. There were boxes of possessions on the floor in all the rooms. Sarah was beginning to get tired. Breathlessly, she said, "I need to sit down, Agnes. This is hard work…"

Sarah sat down in the rocking chair and looked around her at the room and the mess. There were tears in her eyes.

"What's the matter ma'?" asked Agnes. "You feeling poorly again?"

Sarah shook her head. "No… It's just… It doesn't feel like home yet… I wish we hadn't had to move…" Sarah wiped a tear from her eye. "Hannah, bring me Jane over. If I'm sitting down I'll give her a cuddle and you can help with the unpacking."

Hannah walked over to Sarah and handed Jane to her. Instantly, Sarah began to feel better as she looked into the baby's face.

Agnes took control. "We'll be fine, ma'," she said. "We're getting older and we can help more. You sit there and nurse Jane."

Sarah smiled, then she started to feel low again. "O, I wish your father was home…"

"Sit there for a while, ma'," she said. "Me and Auntie Hannah will empty the boxes. You just tell us where everything has to go."

They carried on like that – Hannah and Agnes busying themselves with sorting out the boxes while Thomas and William finished bringing in the furniture.

"Right, lass," he said, "that's the last of it. You'll be fine now – Robert will be home soon." He stood there and looked at Sarah. The influenza had hit her hard. Sarah was usually such a healthy person, but then again, there hadn't been an outbreak like this for a long while. As he was leaving, Robert returned home from work.

"It's all in," said Thomas to Robert as they met on the stairs. "You've not too much left to do. It was all a bit too much for your Sarah, but we all mucked in and got it done."

"Thanks, Thomas," said Robert, you've been a great help today."

"Your boy William's done you proud, and no mistake," added Thomas. "He's been carrying with me up and down the stairs all day!"

With that they carried on walking – Thomas downstairs and Robert upstairs.

Robert walked in the door of his new home, jubilant, for a change. He had managed to secure work on the new docks as some of the workers had left. This meant that he wouldn't have to travel to Liverpool every day. All the children were in bed and Sarah was sitting in her rocking chair.

"Good news! Sarah," he began. He suddenly realised that Sarah was crying, softly, so that she could not be heard, but the glistening tears on her face gave it all away. "What's the matter, hinny?"

Sarah tried to compose herself. "It's nothing... I'm just tired."

"I can see it's no' nothing!" Robert exclaimed. "It's coming here, isn't it? I've failed you."

"Don't you ever say that to me, Robert McWilliam," said Sarah, composing herself. "You've not failed me. You've always done your best. I couldn't ask for more. It's me just being silly." She then realised she had heard what Robert had said as he walked into the room. "What's the news?"

Robert came and knelt down in front of her. "Some o' the masons have left the dockyard and it's no' finished yet, so I've got mysel' work there. It means I willnae have to cross the Mersey every day. Everybody's feeling the pinch now, so I'm pleased tae have found it."

This made Sarah feel better. "That is good. I'll be glad to be seeing more of you." She wiped her face dry, then she looked around the room. "This place is so empty," she added.

"We'll do fine...," said Robert. "Just wait and see."

Two days later, Sarah was taking the children to be registered at the new school. It was very close by, so the children would have no problems getting there. Sarah brought Agnes, William, Mary and John out of their flat on the 2nd floor and she met their neighbours in the hallway, also taking children to school. Not all the flats were occupied yet, so there were only two other families in number 18.

In the ground floor flat lived the Millward family, James and Mary, with their three children, John, aged 7, Ann, aged 5, and Mary, aged 3. Their mother, Mary, was also taking the children to school.

Up on the 1st floor was the Beech family, Arne and Sarah, with their four children, William, aged 13, Ann, aged 11, Sarah, aged 4, and Joseph, aged 2. Daughter, Ann, was taking her sister, Sarah, to school.

Mary Millward was the first to speak. "Morning," she said to Sarah," you moved in at the weekend, didn't you? I'm Mary Millward. We live on the ground floor. We moved in last week."

"Yes, we came Saturday," replied Sarah. "My name's Sarah. Sarah McWilliam, and these are my children, Agnes, William, Mary and John. I'm just taking them to school to get them registered."

"Did I see you with a new baby?" Mary asked.

"You did," replied Sarah. "She was born in November. She turned two months, last week, on the 21st. My sister's looking after her just now. I didn't think she needed to be dragged out for this journey."

Mary nodded in agreement. Just then, Ann and Sarah Beech came down the stairs. Mary turned to talk to Ann.

"Your mother not with you today, Ann?"

"No," replied Ann. "I said I'd take Sarah to school. Ma's not feeling too good today. I think it was baby kept her awake all night."

"Ann," said Mary, "this is Sarah McWilliam. They moved in at the weekend."

"Pleased to meet you," said Ann, bobbing a curtsey.

Sarah introduced her children and they all set off.

Outside in the main street it was raining, although fairly warm for the time of year. Everybody was well dressed for the weather. Sarah had recently bought brand new Mackintoshes for all the family and they kept them all dry. She'd first come across them in the newspaper advertisement declaring them to be better than the vulcanised rubber ones, and she went straight out to buy one for each of her children. When she saw what she was buying she bought one for herself as well. Outside the front door they turned right and walked to the end of the alley into Back Beckwith Street proper.

Mary broke the silence. "So, Sarah, what about your husband? Who is he, what does he do?"

"Robert's my husband. He's a mason," Sarah answered. "He's working down at the docks just now. What about yours?"

"James is a wheelwright," Mary replied. "He works down at the joiner's yard. Where've you come from? You sound local."

"We've been down in Hamilton Terrace – near Hamilton Square – up till now," answered Sarah. "The landlord sold the buildings, so we had to move. I'm from Tranmere, originally, but Robert is from Scotland."

The families walked to the end of Back Beckwith Street. All the children were getting to know each other and Sarah and Mary continued to talk.

Mary continued, "I'm from Derby. James, my husband, was born in Tetbury – in Staffordshire – but he moved to Derby when he was apprenticed. We lived there for a couple of years after we married but then he wanted to come here because of all the new work. So, here we are."

Sarah looked around her at the new buildings, some occupied, some empty.

"It seems strange with hardly anybody living here, just now," she said.

"I know," replied Mary. "Best to make the most of it. I hear the potatoes failed again in Ireland, last summer, and that's why there's so many Irish over here right now. Likely to be many more before the year's over."

"I'd noticed there were more than usual about...," said Sarah. "D'you suppose they'll come here?"

"Where else are they going?" Mary answered. "The tenements down by the docks aren't ready yet and they have to live somewhere. It'll make getting work that much harder..."

"It's as well that our menfolk are already in work, then..."

Ahead of the mothers, the children were all laughing and joking together. Agnes, the eldest, was walking with Ann Beech, who, in turn, was walking along holding the hand of her sister Sarah. William and John Millward were together and John was watching over his sister Ann, whilst holding the hand of his sister Mary. Mary McWilliam was watching over her brother John.

As the children got to know each other more they split into different groups. Agnes fell back to the rear of the group as she talked with Ann Beech; William and John Millward walked ahead of the group; in the middle walked the other children, Sarah Beech, Ann and Mary Millward, Mary and John McWilliam.

They turned into Victoria Street *(between 1851 and 1861 Victoria Street became Vittoria Street)* and the two mothers watched the children rearrange themselves.

Mary said, "See that? It's grand the children are getting on so well…"

"Oh yes," replied Sarah, with a grin on her face. "You'd think they been friends for ages."

"You've a big family," added Mary. "Have you been married long?"

"Agnes and William are from Robert's first marriage," continued Sarah. "Agnes will be 13 come the autumn and William will be 11 soon. I brought them with me so they could all see the area where we living now, even though I know Agnes is too old for school, and there's not much chance of William going to school now."

"Did his wife die then?" asked Mary.

Sarah nodded. "She had a bad birth and died soon after. Her baby only lasted a few days more." Sarah sighed as she remembered.

"That's tragic," added Mary.

"Yes," continued Sarah, "my ma' was the local midwife at the time, and I was helping her. That's how I met Robert – I helped him bring them up. I taught them to read and write when they were little, and they know their sums, though. Do you have any older ones?"

"No," answered Mary, "just the three. So is Agnes to go into service soon? She'll be old enough."

"It's only a matter of time before she goes," replied Sarah. "Now we've moved in here we'll find who needs servants or maids. William will be taking up a trade, soon, too. Robert's taking care of all of that."

They turned left at the next corner, into Beckwith Street and on towards the school.

As Sarah suspected, Agnes was too old for school but William could do at least one year in the oldest class. Sarah had taught him well, so he was able to fit in with the boys his age. Mary went into the same class as John Millward, and John was put in the same class as Ann Millward and Sarah Beech.

Robert came home from work and found a happy Sarah, which pleased him beyond measure. He had been worrying about how the move had affected her. After dinner they sat and talked about how the children's first school day had gone. Sarah also asked

Robert if he would try to find some domestic work for Agnes. He told her he would.

A few days later Robert came home with news that he had managed to find a position for Agnes. She and William were still up, so he called her to him. As she stood before him he began.

"Well, Agnes, you're old enough tae be out working now."

"Yes, da'." She'd been expecting something like this since they moved in.

"There's a scullery maid needed at the Bull Inn on the corner of Beckwith Street," he continued. "You know where that is?"

"Yes, da'," she replied.

"You're tae start there on Monday. Mary Bullman is the landlady. She's expecting you for 10 o'clock in the morning."

"Thank you, da'," said Agnes.

Sarah had sat beside in her rocking chair, listening. When Robert had finished she said to Agnes, "You'll be coming home at nights for the time being, but once you turn 13 it's agreed for you tae live in."

"Yes ma'," Agnes said to Sarah.

"Come sit by me for a while, Agnes," Sarah said, beckoning her to sit at her side in a chair that Sarah had pulled up beside the rocking chair.

Robert then called out to William, who dutifully took his sister's place in front of Robert.

"William," Robert began, "You're old enough tae be apprenticed now, son. Have you any idea what trade you might want tae do?"

"I want to be a soldier, father," William replied.

Robert smiled but Sarah did not. Robert continued, "You're way too young for that yet, me lad. I'll soon start to make enquiries tae see who needs an apprentice round here."

Robert looked at Sarah, who looked as if she was asking him something. Robert understood. "You can spend the next few months going tae school – it'll do you good. Come spring I shall find you an apprenticeship. Wi' all the building going on there'll no' be a shortage tae pick from."

"Thank you, da'."

"Right then, that's settled," said Robert. "Say goodnight tae your ma' and away tae bed wi' yous both."

"Yes, da'," brother and sister said as one. Both Agnes and William said goodnight to both parents, and they both acknowledged in turn.

Sarah spoke for both herself and Robert. "Goodnight Agnes, William…"

The two children disappeared off to bed, leaving just Robert and Sarah in the room.

Robert turned to Sarah. "Well, hinny, that wasnae so bad, was it?"

"I know," said Sarah. "It seems so strange. I've seen them grow from almost babies, and loved them so much." She paused and reflected on the many memories they had acquired over the years. "Time flies," she continued, shaking her head, "doesn't seem possible they're ready to fly the nest. They're still so young."

"Aye, that they are," agreed Robert. "But there are others out there that age working. Come on, hinny, let's away tae bed."

Robert stood up and held his hand out to Sarah. She took it and stood up. He led her to their bedroom.

Sarah's mother came to visit a week or so later. The place looked much more homely, and Sarah was doing her washing. Agnes was at work and the other children were at school. Sarah let Mary in.

"Sit down, ma'," she said. I'll just finish this bit of washing I'm doing and I'll be out to talk." Five minutes later she was done, and she came to join her mother. Hannah was sitting, reading and the baby was asleep in her cradle.

"Well, Sarah," Mary began, "it's way different from your other place, that's for sure. Are you settling in?"

"Yes, ma'," replied Sarah. "It was harder coming here, especially with the baby, but we're managing. Agnes has started work now, but she was a godsend, helping me unpack. William was a great help, too, what with lifting things. Hannah's been wonderful with the baby."

"I'm glad moving in was easy," said Mary. "Your da' was full of how William had helped with all the carrying. He reckoned he'd not have finished before Robert came home if he'd been on his own."

"Yes, William was so excited at being asked, mind, he was straight off to sleep that night!" Sarah added, laughing.

Hannah put her book down. "Do you want tea, ma'?" she asked. "That'd be grand," replied Mary. "Shall I make you one, Sarah?" Hannah asked. "Please," replied Sarah. Hannah got up and went out to the kitchen to make them all a drink.

"Hannah's been missed at home, that's for sure," said Mary. "Don't get me wrong, it's good to have her out, doing something, but the house is so quiet." Mary paused for a moment to reflect, then she smiled. "Agnes and William are good children – I knew they'd help with the move... So Agnes is working now? How's she getting on?"

"She's doing grand – she's at the Bull, round the corner, ma'," Sarah replied. "She's not afraid of hard work. I miss her round the house during the day, though. She gets home mid-evening and is so tired she just goes to bed – but she has to be up early. After her birthday she'll live there." Sarah sighed. "I shall miss her when she goes." Sarah paused for a moment, as if to think of what to say next. Then she continued. "Any sign of Robert and Jane getting a place of their own?"

"They're still looking," Mary said. "Robert's hoping to get one of the flats they're building down by the docks. They'll soon be finished..." Mary smiled to herself. "We're managing. With both Mary and Jane in service, there's more room. Me and your da' are downstairs in the back room, Robert, Jane and the three children are upstairs in the front, and Hannah's room is upstairs in the back. It's not perfect, but we make do."

Hannah came out after a few minutes with a milk jug and three cups and saucers, which she put on the table in readiness for the tea. "Tea's just brewing," she said. She went back out to the kitchen to finish making the tea.

"What time are the children home?" Mary asked.

"William finishes about 4 o'clock and the younger ones finish about 1 o'clock," replied Sarah. "Ann Beech, the daughter of the family downstairs takes them, some days, and brings them home for me – her mother's just had a baby girl, too, and Ann helps her out, so she offered with mine."

"I take them some days, too," started Hannah, as she walked in with the pot of tea. She carried on to the table and poured three cups of tea. She handed them out to her mother and sister, and then took her own and went and sat back down.

"Do they like their school?" Mary asked.

"They're settling in. Robert's trying to get William apprenticed with someone, so he'll be off before the summer."

"What does he want to do?" Mary asked.

"He wants to join the army," said Sarah, "but we told him he was far too young for that still. He'll do whatever Robert finds for him."

"Well, the army's no bad thing, I suppose," said Mary. She continued, picking up the basket she had brought with her, "I've brought some lunch. I thought it'd be grand to have food ready prepared for you for a change. I made some sandwiches, and I've baked a cake."

"Oh, ma'!" Sarah exclaimed, "You shouldn't have."

"Well, I have, so let's get it ready for when the little'uns get back." Mary stood up and walked over to the table while Sarah went to the kitchen to fetch some plates. She put the basket on one of the chairs next to the table and began to empty it. The food was soon laid out on the table.

There was a knock at the door. "It's just Ann with the little ones," Ann Beech called through the door. Sarah was already on her feet, so she walked over and opened the door.

"Thanks, Ann," she said. She turned to the children, "Guess who's come to visit?"

"GRANNY!!!!!!!!!!" called out Mary and John, almost together.

They ran to their grandmother, Mary, and she gave them a hug. "There are sandwiches ready for you to eat. Come sit at the table," she said.

Mary and Hannah were already sitting at the table. The two children rushed for the remaining seats. Mary got there first, so she got the choice to sit next to her grandma' or her aunt. John sat on the remaining chair. Sarah remained in the rocking chair. Mary looked at Sarah. She had a pained expression on her face.

"Sarah? You alright?" Mary asked her daughter, looking concerned.

"Yes, ma'," Sarah replied, "I think so. It's just the influenza fair knocked me for six. I get tired easy, still."

"You're on the mend – you'll soon pick up now the move is over," Mary said. "What time does Robert get home?"

"I know I'm on the mend. At least I beat it!" Sarah smiled, thinking of the neighbours she knew that weren't strong enough. "Robert gets in about 5 o'clock when it's dark early."

"Well, when he does," Mary added, "I'll go back to mine."

"So, when are you moving, ma'?" Sarah asked, feeling a bit brighter. Mary picked some sandwiches up and put them on a plate for Sarah.

"Here, take this," she said. "Eat what you fancy – it'll do you good."

Sarah took the plate from her mother and began to pick at the sandwiches, eating a little, here and there.

"We've just had confirmation," Mary continued, "so we'll be moving into Albert Terrace at the end of the month. Now that Robert and Jane's family is getting bigger, we need more room."

"Well, there's plenty of you to move everything!" Sarah chuckled as she said it. "That's near where we used to live, isn't it?"

Mary nodded as she spoke, "Just round the corner."

A few hours later William arrived home from school and was pleased to see his grandmother. She talked with him about wanting to join the army at length. Then Robert arrived home. Sarah had, by now, prepared their evening meal. She put their plates down on the table. Mary stood up to go. Sarah walked with her to the door and opened it.

"William will be fine in the army, you know," Mary whispered to her daughter. "He's got a lot of common sense."

"I know, ma'," replied Sarah, unconvinced. "Safe journey home."

With that, Mary turned and walked off down the stairs.

A week later, Sarah was sitting nursing baby Jane in the rocking chair. The little ones were home from school and William was expected home in the next 30 minutes. Agnes was working at the Bull Inn, round the corner. Hannah was helping Sarah look after the children and do some of the chores. At that moment, she was hanging baby clothes and nappies on the clothes-horse to dry. Mary and John were playing with their toys.

Hannah looked at Sarah feeding baby Jane. "I wish I had a baby," she mused. "She is beautiful…"

"She's hard work, Hannah, that's the truth," said Sarah looking up at her. "It doesn't get any easier. Just be happy as you are."

"You're so clever. I wish I was married. But nobody wants me…" Hannah started to look sad as she said this. Sarah was cross.

"Don't you ever say that!" Sarah retorted. "You are special. We all want you, and love you. These last few months, I don't know how I would've managed with the chores and children if you hadn't been here. It just takes you a while longer to do things, but you manage. Agnes, William, Mary and John love you."

"I know they do," Hannah replied, "but I feel empty inside sometimes…"

Little Mary has been listening to the grown-ups' conversation. "Auntie Hannah, can I help you?" Mary asked.

"You can pass me the clothes from the basket if you like," answered Hannah. "Then I can hang them up."

Mary began to help her Auntie Hannah. She passed a nappy to her and then hugged her. "I love you, Auntie," she said.

By now, John has got the gist of the conversation and joined in. "I'll marry you!!!!" John shouted. Hannah laughed.

"Why thank you, kind sir." Hannah curtseyed to him as she spoke.

"See, Hannah," said Sarah, "don't you ever say that again. Don't ever say you aren't loved. One day, you will find somebody. Somebody who loves you just as much as we do."

"Oh, Sarah... I do hope you are right..."

Saturday, 28 February 1846 was a rainy, but average day. The temperature was 60° Fahrenheit. Sarah, Hannah and the family were out, shopping. Sarah was proudly pushing her baby in a new, three wheeled pram, a very early type. It had to be three wheels, as anything with more was not allowed on the pavement. Hannah was walking with the other children. They had walked down Victoria Street to Conway Street and turned left to go to the new market down by the docks. They were not far from the market when Sarah spoke.

"I wonder if we'll see ma' down here. She's always finding bargains."

"I love going shopping," said Hannah. "You see so many people in their lovely clothes... I wish I could wear them... Wish I had somewhere to go."

"Why are you so melancholy of late?" Sarah asked. She had never known her sister to be like this before. It was most concerning.

"Everybody seems to be moving on while I stay at home," Hannah mused. "I want to be able to meet someone... Do something."

At last Sarah really understood. It must be hard, she thought. First I got married, and now her sisters were away working as servants. Her brother Robert was married with children, and yet, here was Hannah, still alone. It was sad. But poor Hannah couldn't cope out on her own. At least, Sarah suddenly thought, nobody had given her a chance to prove herself. Sarah spoke.

"I expect you must be lonely now. I hadn't thought of that. You see us all getting married, having children. We shall have to see what we can do."

Hannah replied, "You are so sweet, Sarah." Then, in the next breath, as if she hadn't been thinking how sad she was, she shouted, "Look, we're nearly there."

Hannah rushed on ahead while Sarah smiled. Maybe Hannah would never be ready. Only one way to find out, she thought.

They crossed the road and went into the market. The market had only been open a few months and was a magnificent affair, not that you could see until you got inside.

From the outside it was a large brick building, looking like several separate buildings. Once inside, though, you could see the marvellous construction. It was a huge interior, held up by wrought iron pillars. The roof was semi-opaque, allowing in lots of light. The market traders' barrows lined the sides of the walls and there was a fountain in the centre. That, too, was magnificent. It was tall, with a bowl halfway up and a spout coming out from the top falling down into the bowl beneath. If you walked all the way through the covered section of the market there were doors leading outside to a further open air section.

Inside, the market was very busy. There were lots of stalls and lots of people. Hannah came back and walked with Sarah, so that Sarah could do her food shopping. As they got further inside they saw people they knew and said a quick hello to them before moving on. Sarah soon saw her mother and sister-in-law, Jane, with her children, William, Sarah and Mariah. They were facing away from them. William was looking round, though, and saw Sarah and the others walking towards them. He tapped his mother's arm.

"Ma'," he said, "it's Auntie Sarah."

Jane and Mary turned round and greeted Sarah and Hannah. The children all came together in a group and chatted amongst themselves.

"Oh, Sarah," said her mother, "have you heard? About the woman on the ferry?"

"No, ma'," replied Sarah, puzzled. "What about her?"

"Your father was full of it last night when he got home," continued Mary.

"Oh, ma'... Do tell!" Sarah exclaimed.

"Well," said Mary, "he was working on the ferry till late last night. He said that as the half past 8 o'clock boat set off for Liverpool he noticed this woman in a state. As the boat pulled out into the channel – and the tide was running fast – well, she does

102

no more, but stands on one of the end seats, and before he could get to her to tell her to sit down, she jumped!"

"Oh no!" Sarah and Hannah cried out together. "Oh, ma', how dreadful! Is da' alright?"

"Well, he was a bit shaken, I can tell you," replied Mary, "but he seems to be fine now. They tried to find the woman, but the tide was so strong they fear her body's gone for good. Apparently there's a reward of two pounds for anybody who finds her."

"Oh my – I bet there'll be a few looking out to find her body then!" Sarah added. "So, how are you settling in to the new house, ma'?"

"Well enough," Mary replied. "It's a little bigger than the old house."

"That's grand!" Sarah answered. "We'll have to come around and see as soon as you've settled properly."

"Yes, you must," replied Mary.

The families dispersed and Sarah and Hannah continued doing their shopping.

Later that evening, Mary and John were in bed, Agnes was working at the Bull, and William was out doing some part-time work that his father had organised for him. Sarah sat in the rocking chair holding baby Jane. Robert sat in a chair beside her. Sarah looked puzzled.

"So tell me again, Robert, the tradesmen are stopping working?" Sarah asked.

"Aye, hinny," he replied. "The joiners have gone on "strike". It means they dinnae intend to work until the masters gie them an increase in wages. It's expected that other trades will join in."

"So what about you? Will the masons join this – this – "strike"?"

"It's highly likely," Robert said. "We've tae have a meeting about it in the week."

"But if you don't work, you'll not get paid," said Sarah, now horrified.

"Aye, that's it exactly," replied Robert, nodding his head. "It's no' what I planned, but I cannae go against my fellow workers.

It's as well I've been careful wi' my wages so far. We'll no' suffer, hinny, o' that you can be sure."

"So how much is this all about?" Sarah asked.

"Well, the joiners are earning 23 shillings a week, and they're after a rise o' 3 shillings," Robert explained. "I get 24 shillings a week, which is similar. If they can get a raise I dinnae see why they'll no' gie it tae the masons and other trades."

"But what if they don't get it?" Sarah asked. "Will they go back to work? It can't last long, can it?"

"I hope not," said Robert. "We'll just have tae wait and see. We'll be fine. Dinnae bother ye'sen!"

"That's easy for you to say, Robert," said Sarah, angry at his comment. "How can I be anything but bothered!"

Sarah stood up and took baby Jane to her cradle. She lay her down in it and sat on the bed beside her. "Oh, Janey," she muttered to her daughter, "what are we going to do?"

Robert came through to the bedroom. He was more subdued than he had been before. He hadn't expected Sarah to be so upset about him not working, but the more she had talked with him the more he began to understand the wider picture. He was normally not such a religious man that he prayed at home, but this night he made a silent prayer to God that the strike should be short-lived.

The following Tuesday, 3 March, Sarah had just returned from collecting the children from school and they were sitting down having some sandwiches for lunch. Robert returned, unexpectedly. As he walked in through the door the children jumped down from their seats and ran over to him. Sarah looked worried.

"Robert? What's the matter?" Sarah asked.

"We've had a meeting," he said, sadly. "I was afraid it'd come tae this… We're on strike."

Sarah looked desolate. "Until when?" she asked.

"I have no idea…" Robert replied, reluctantly.

Sarah was beginning to panic. "What do you mean?" She retorted. "Surely you know when you'll be back at work?"

"No, hinny. We're out until the masters gie in tae our demands."

"So where's the money coming from to pay our bills?" She demanded, standing up.

As she waited for him to answer she realised this normally proud, confident, man was a shadow of his former self. Finally, he said, "I've a wee bit saved up. It'll have tae do."

Reluctantly, Sarah replied, "Well, we can cut down on what we spend, but we still have to pay the rent."

Robert walked over to Sarah, who was looking down. He touched her by the chin and gently raised her head so she was looking at him. "We'll manage, hinny," he said. "I dinnae want tae be out o' work either. There's a few of us feel the same. We'll do!"

Hannah was listening to the whole conversation. Finally, she voiced what she knew would be said over the next few days. "Sarah, I should go back home. I am an extra mouth that you have to feed, and it isn't fair on you now."

Sarah looked surprised. "Hannah, you don't have to go," she said.

"Don't be silly," she replied. "I can go back home to ma' and da'. Da' is not on strike, so it makes sense for me to go. Jane is not so tiny now, so you can manage. I have made up my mind. I shall pack today and go home tomorrow."

Sarah was visibly moved. Not only was she going to miss her sister, but it seemed that Hannah was much more adult in her thinking than she had ever seen her before. A tear trickled down Sarah's face.

Next morning, Robert was getting ready to go out. Sarah stopped getting the children's outdoor clothes on and looked at him. "So what are you doing this morning, Robert?" She asked. Sarah gave Mary's coat to Hannah so that she could put it on Mary. Sarah turned and looked at Robert.

"I cannae sit here doing nothing," Robert replied. "I shall go out and see if there's anything tae be done anywhere. Even if I can bring in only a few shillings, it'll help."

Agnes, who had overheard some of a conversation the previous evening, said, "You can have all my wages to help, ma', I know it's not much."

Sarah looked disapprovingly at Agnes. "Oh, Agnes," she replied. "I can't do that."

Hannah had, by now, put all the coats on the children. William and Agnes were waiting to go out with them.

"I mean it, ma'," said Agnes, defiantly. "It's only right I pay my way."

Robert finished putting his coat and boots on. He looked at his family, proudly, realising that things were not as bad as he had feared.

"Well, I'll be away," he said. "I intend tae find some form of work tae do. I'm no' about to live on charity."

As he said this, he reached into his pocket and took out 5 shillings. He gave it to Sarah.

"Here," he said, "Take this to buy what you need – but be sparing, for I'll no' be able tae keep it up for long."

"I don't expect you to," Sarah replied. "When I've taken the children to school I shall see if anybody needs any laundry doing round at the big houses. That'll bring in some money. We'll do… We'll do."

Robert went out of the door and closed it behind him. Agnes looked at Sarah.

"Don't worry, ma'," she said. "We'll do fine."

"I know, pet, I know," Sarah replied.

Sarah opened the door and everybody went out, Sarah closing and locking the door behind her.

Sarah did, indeed, manage to take in laundry from a few of the larger houses. Agnes spoke with Mary Bullman, landlady at the Bull and she gladly gave some laundry for Sarah to do. It wouldn't pay much, but anything she could get would be a help.

The days turned into weeks, though, and Sarah and Robert had visions of this lasting far longer than they could afford. Sarah kept doing laundry for the Bull, and Mary Bullman recommended her to other people, so washing kept coming in. Sarah had never been so busy. An advantage, though, was that Robert got to spend more time with his children, in between him going out doing odd jobs for people.

Almost two weeks into the strike, Thomas and Mary invited Robert and Sarah for dinner. Thomas was worried, and Mary more so.

"They can't have any money," she said to her husband. "I know how hard it is for poor Robert, but at least they are living with us."

"Agreed," Thomas replied. So, Sunday, 15 March Robert, Sarah and family all turned up at the Foulkes new home. The only absentee was Agnes, who was working at the Bull, as usual. It was the first time they had been there.

"So, what do you think of the new place?" Thomas asked.

"I think it's lovely," replied Sarah. "It's certainly bigger."

"Brighter, too," added Robert. "I appreciate what you're doing here, for us, I really do."

"Why you're family, man!" Thomas answered, understanding Robert's reluctance. "Don't talk like that. We've invited you to show you our new home – besides, it's the least we can do. You've looked after Hannah these past few weeks for us, now we're returning the favour."

They all sat down. The men, including William, who now felt far too old to stay with the children, sat together, talking; the children all went off to play and the women, taking their babies with them, all went into the kitchen.

Robert McWilliam was the first to speak. "Robert... How's it for you? Have you found any work at all?"

"I go out every day," Robert Foulkes replied. "I make a few shillings here and there... We're looking into getting William apprenticed. How's your William getting on?"

"He's only doing after school and at weekends just now," replied Robert McWilliam, "but he's doing fine, aren't you, boy?" Robert added, patting William on the shoulder.

William nodded and Robert continued. "It's no' what he wants tae do, mind. He's wi' McKean, Perkes & Co – the brass foundry in Cathcart Street. When he finished school in a couple o' months he'll live in wi' the family. They've another apprentice a couple o' years older than William there, so he'll have company of his own age."

"So what do you think of the job then?" Thomas asked William.

"It's hard work," replied William.

"Am I right you want to join the army?" Thomas asked him.

Robert interjected, "Well, he's another few years tae go afore they let him in, but, aye, that's what he wants tae do."

"It's all that talk about war that does it," added Thomas. "We're out in India just now – have you been following it?"

"Well, I've more time on my hands, now," said Robert McWilliam. "You mean the Anglo-Sikh war? I hear they beat them at the battle of Sobraon last month. I dinnae ken why we're out there, tae be honest."

At that moment the women came in with the food, so everybody took their place at table. Both Williams sat beside their fathers at the big table, while the younger children sat at their own special table. Mary was the last one to enter, carrying a joint of beef. Everybody had a hearty meal and afterwards the men continued their conversations as the women cleared away.

The strike continued, and Robert's savings were soon all gone. By Thursday, 23 April 1846 he was at his wits end. Sarah was busy doing washing for the Bull, bringing in a bit of money, but it just wasn't enough. This particular morning, Sarah was busy doing her washing, baby Jane was asleep and the children were at school. Agnes was, as usual, at work. Sarah was deep in thought, standing at the kitchen sink, when, suddenly, the front door burst open and in came Robert.

"I've had enough o' this fecking strike. I cannae be idle," he began.

"Why, whatever's up, Robert?" Sarah asked. "What do you mean?"

"Some o' the men and me – we've been talking," he continued. "This strike was never our idea, and we didnae vote for it, either. So, we went back tae the docks to see… Well, we're back at work tomorrow!"

Sarah looked at him, disbelieving. "So, it's over?" She asked.

"Well, no," he replied, "but it's over for us. Some are still out, and maybe they'll stay out for a while longer. But for us, it's over."

"Oh, thank the Lord for that!" Sarah exclaimed. "But what about Robert? Do you think he's still out?"

"I have no idea, hinny," her husband replied.

Sarah dried her hands and went over to Robert. He sensed what she needed, and he held her.

"Robert," Sarah began, "I've been thinking a lot about Hannah since she went back home. She's so lonely. I know you must think I'm being silly, but I'd like to take her somewhere she could be with people. Make friends, you know."

"Take her where, hinny?" Robert asked.

"I'll have to think about it," said Sarah, "but now you're going back to work there'll be a bit more money again. Do you know if there is anything happening here or in Liverpool?"

"I'll have a look when I get the next Mercury on Friday," answered Robert. "There'll most likely be something on in Liverpool. But what about the bairns?"

Sarah stopped and thought about it for a moment.

"I'll ask ma' if she'll help," said Sarah. "You find something for us to take Hannah to and I'll see to the rest."

"Fine," answered Robert, puzzled. "I'll see what I can do."

Robert got his work gear back out. "Are you going to work now?" Sarah asked.

"Nae, hinny, there'll no' be time now. But first thing tomorrow morning – and I tell you this, I cannae wait tae get there!"

Robert was back at work the next day, along with many of his peers. It felt strange crossing the picket line, but he knew he was right to do it. He wasn't alone, and he hoped the strike wouldn't last for too much longer. True to his word, he kept scanning through the newspaper to see if there was anything that might be suitable for Hannah. He understood exactly why Sarah wanted to do it. He, too, had been influenced by Hannah's melancholy.

Finally, Friday, 1 May, he saw exactly the right thing.

That evening, Agnes was home early, on an evening off. She didn't get many, but this was one of those times. Robert excitedly came in through the front door as his wife and daughter were talking.

"Sarah," he said, waving the newspaper in his hand. "I've found something. In the paper, but it's in Liverpool."

Sarah stopped talking to Agnes immediately. "What have you found? Show me!" Sarah replied.

Robert turned to the front page of the main part of the newspaper and he laid it down on the table so that everybody could see. In the first column was a notice of a concert by Henry Phillips. He read aloud:

"Henry Phillips, Esq, will, for the first time in Liverpool, give his new vocal entertainment, consisting of the second part of his adventures in America and the Canadas, at the Concert Hall, Lord Nelson Street, on Monday Evening next, the 4th instant, when he will introduce the following Songs: The Song of the Hudson, The Cot near the Wood, The Huron's Prayer, The Philosopher, My Mother, Celebrated Nigger Melody, The Factory Girl, The Opossum Finder, The Meeting of the Waters, Ernst Mein, The Groves of Blarney, The best of all, Good Company. Tae commence at 8 o'clock. Body 6d, Gallery 1s, Reserved seats 2s."

"Oh, Robert!" Sarah agreed, "that's perfect! I'll go see ma' tomorrow."

Agnes looked confused. "What are you two doing?" She asked.

"It's for Hannah," Sarah replied. "She's very melancholy of late... Lonely. With all of us leaving and starting our own lives, she's feeling left out. I hate to see her that way, so I asked your father to look out for something we could take her to."

"So what's this, then?" Agnes asked.

"It's a music concert," said Sarah. "Next week... In Liverpool."

"Oh, ma'," said Agnes, almost excited already for Hannah. "She'll love it... What about Jane and the little ones? Who's to look after them? What day is it? I'd love to look after them!"

"It's on Monday at 8 o'clock," answered Sarah, "so I would need to leave here by half past 5 o'clock at the latest. That should give me enough time to get to ma's, pick up Hannah, get to the ferry for the 7 o'clock. We should be there in plenty of time."

"I shall go directly to the Bull," said Agnes, jumping up from her seat, "and ask Mrs. Bullman if it would be possible for me to take the time off on Monday for you. It's a wonderful idea and I know Hannah will love it."

With that, Agnes went out of the door, before either Sarah or Robert could say anything else. They both looked at each other. Sarah was the first to speak.

"Well, I didn't expect it to be so easy to find somebody to look after the little ones."

"Hannah will love it," added Robert.

Next day, Sarah and the children turned up at her mother's unexpectedly. Hannah was sitting reading and her mother was putting her shopping away.

"What are you doing here on a Saturday morning?" Mary asked.

"Well," began Sarah slowly, "Robert and I have a surprise for Hannah – as a thank you for staying with us, looking after the children."

Hannah stopped reading instantly she heard her name mentioned. "What?"

Mary stopped what she was doing and came to sit down in the parlour. "Go on," she said.

"Well," began Sarah, "there's a concert on in Liverpool on Monday and we thought we would take Hannah. That's all."

"All? Oh, Sarah!" Hannah exclaimed. "Oh, how wonderful! What shall I wear?"

Mary tried to calm her down, but she could see it was a pointless exercise. "Come up to your room, then, Hannah," she said. "We'll see what you have."

"Thank you, so much," said Hannah to Sarah. Hannah stood up and kissed her sister on the cheek.

"We shall come for you at about 5 o'clock," added Sarah. "I must go, now," she added, "I've my own shopping to do. Bye!"

Sarah left her mother's house, smiling to herself. She would make this a night for Hannah to remember.

The weekend flew by. Hannah was so excited, she almost made herself ill. Her mother had found one of her own dresses that no longer fitted her and she had adjusted it to fit Hannah. This was a pretty light blue dress that Mary had worn when she was single. It had been a long time since it had come out, but Mary was so pleased she had kept it. It didn't need much taking in for it to fit Hannah. It had some white lace around the neckline, which dipped both at the front and the back. It also had a bustle, so it didn't look out of place. It looked beautiful on Hannah.

Monday evening soon arrived, and as promised, Sarah arrived at her mother's at 5 o'clock. Agnes was busy playing with the children when Sarah left. Hannah was nearly ready before Sarah arrived. It took all Mary could do to make Hannah wait until almost time to go before putting her dress on. Sarah explained that Robert was to join them as soon as he was able.

Mary had prepared a light tea for them to eat before they left, so Sarah insisted that Hannah eat before changing. Reluctantly, she waited.

Food eaten, Hannah began to get ready.

"I'm so excited!" Hannah said. "What time will Robert be here?"

"Robert will be here about half past 6 o'clock," answered Sarah, "in time, so we can make our way to the ferry."

"Your da' is working tonight," added Mary, "so it might be him on the ferry with you." Mary finished dressing Hannah. "There, you'll do."

Sarah couldn't believe the transformation in her sister. "Oh, Hannah, you look lovely!"

There was a knock at the door. Mary rushed out of the room to answer it. She returned a few minutes later. "Robert has arrived," she said. "He's looking very smart, too. Well, you're ready, so downstairs, both of you. It's time you were going."

Both sisters left the room, Hannah giggling as she did so. Mary followed on behind, smiling. She thought to herself, 'Well, Sarah, you never cease to amaze me.'

Robert had to do a double-take when the women walked in the room. "Is that really Hannah, there?" He asked.

Hannah was still giggling with excitement. "Come on," Robert continued, "it's time we were off."

They made it quickly down to the ferry, and, sure enough, Thomas Foulkes was working on their ferry. He couldn't believe this was Hannah he was looking at. He was so proud. The journey on the ferry was over quickly and the party soon arrived at the concert hall in Lord Nelson Street. It was a large white brick building, taller than all the others on either side of it. There were several doors that led into the foyer.

The hall was opened as 'The Hall of Science' (in 1840). It was a spacious building with a gallery on three sides, and had a seating capacity of 2,700 persons. The hall, which at one time was called the Nelson Assembly Rooms (from 1843), was one of the most popular places in town for concerts in general, for the holding of public meetings and the delivery of lectures. The Saturday evening concerts were very successful, the attendance being uniformly large.

There was a large room beneath the hall in which, occasionally, public meetings were held. It was here the Parliamentary Debating Society (a mimic embodiment of the Parliament of St. Stephen's), held its meetings.

Once inside, Robert paid for the tickets and they went into the auditorium and took their seats. Sarah sat between her husband and her sister. Next to Hannah was a vacant seat, but it was very quickly filled by a gentleman who had come on his own. As soon as he sat down he introduced himself to Hannah and it seemed that Hannah thought this was an invitation for her to strike up a conversation with him.

Sarah was so taken completely by surprise. No longer was Hannah a shy little girl, but she was showing herself off to be a confident young woman. But the man was happy to talk with Hannah, and they were soon in deep conversation.

Sarah nudged Robert on the arm. She whispered to him, "Look, Robert, Hannah has found somebody to talk to."

"Well," he quietly replied, "she is pretty enough. I thought this was part of the reason we brought her out – tae get her to meet people."

"Yes," Sarah answered, "but I didn't think it would be this easy, though!"

It was 8 o'clock, and as she spoke the lights went down and the curtain came up. Henry Phillips was introduced and he came out. He began to sing. His first song was entitled The Song of the Hudson and it was met with rapturous applause. At the end of the song he began to talk about his adventures in Canada. Everybody was enthralled.

The story of his travels was interspersed with several songs. The Cot near the Wood, The Huron's Prayer, The Philosopher, My Mother, and many more. During the interval they all got up from their seats and went to get refreshments. As they walked out to the bar Sarah moved close up to Hannah. "Well, Hannah," she said, "are you going to introduce us?"

"Yes, yes, of course," Hannah stuttered, suddenly brought back to earth, "John, this is my sister Sarah and her husband Robert."

Sarah turned to John. "Pleased to meet you," she said.

Robert shook his hand. "Same here," he said.

"Sarah, Robert, this is John Corless," Hannah continued. "He's a greengrocer and has just come to Birkenhead from New Brighton. He's intending on setting up a shop this side of town."

"I understand it was your idea to bring Hannah out this evening," said John. "I'm indebted to you. I decided to move into the town after my wife died. She's been gone a year now."

"I'm so sorry to hear that," said Sarah.

"Well," said John, "life must go on. I saw you two ladies sitting together when I came in and wondered if one of you was alone, so I thought I would come and sit by you to find out. I was so pleased to be sitting with Hannah. She is adorable."

Hannah began to blush. "Oh, don't," she said, coyly.

"Whereabouts in Birkenhead are you staying?" Sarah asked.

"Now here's the strange thing," John replied. "I'm living with my cousins, who moved about five years ago. We're living down at William Street, near where your family used to live!"

"A remarkable coincidence, indeed!" Robert added.

At that moment the bell rang to announce the end of the interval, so everybody returned to their seats. The performance continued with songs like, The Factory Girl, The Opossum Finder, The Meeting of the Waters, and more. Too soon it was the end of the performance and everybody called out for an encore. Henry obliged by reprising The Huron's Prayer.

As the lights came back up after Henry had finally left the stage John asked Sarah if he might see her sister again. Hannah looked, hopefully, at Sarah. Sarah couldn't be happier and told John that he was perfectly welcome to meet Hannah another time. As they were going in the same direction John walked back to the ferry with them. Back in Birkenhead, they said their goodbyes.

Hannah couldn't wait to get back home and tell her parents how the night went. Robert and Sarah could barely keep up with her as she rushed home. They took her to the front door and Mary let her in. Robert and Sarah had to get straight off back home as it was late.

Meanwhile, in Hannah's bedroom Mary was learning of the events of the evening. Hannah could barely get her words out, she was so excited.

"It was magical, ma'. And this man came and sat in the seat next to me. He was on his own – he's a widower – and you'll never believe where he lives," she said.

"Not around here?" Mary asked.

"He is living at the end of our old street!" Hannah replied. "His name is John. John Corless. He's a greengrocer and he's staying with his cousins. He wants to get to know me, so he's asked if he can call on me!"

Mary had finished undressing her daughter and was folding up the dress to put it carefully away for another time. Mary looked happy. "That is wonderful news," she said. "Now, calm down and get into bed. It's very late and you need to get some sleep. I expect we'll hear more about him from you tomorrow."

"Yes, ma', though I fear I shan't sleep a wink tonight!" She chuckled. "Night, ma'."

Hannah climbed into bed and Mary left the room to go to bed herself.

"Well, Thomas," she said as she got into bed, "I know Sarah arranged this so Hannah could get out to meet people, but I never expected anything to come of it!"

"We'll get her married off, yet!" Thomas replied. "Night, mother."

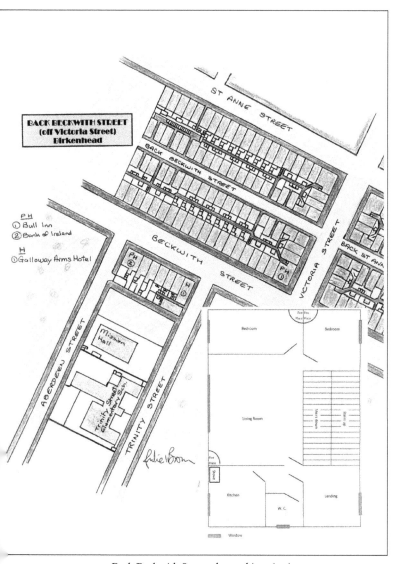

Back Beckwith Street plan and interior inset

CHAPTER 4

Tragedy of Youth

Sarah and Robert invited Hannah and John to lunch on Sunday, 17 May 1846. Sarah wanted to find out how their relationship was progressing. The table was set for six people: Robert, Sarah, Hannah, John, and children Mary and John, but they had not yet sat down to eat.

Hannah was with Sarah in the kitchen, helping as Sarah finished getting their meal ready. John was talking with Robert in the living room. Mary and John were sitting, playing with their toys.

The two men were sitting down with a glass of beer each. John was explaining, "She's such a wonderful girl... I can't believe my luck," he said.

"Aye, she's a heart of gold, that one," answered Robert. "She took a bit longer tae get tae where she is now, but she's so good with the children, an' all. Have you heard any more about getting a shop?"

"No, I've not found anywhere yet," said John. "To be quite honest, I'm so taken with Hannah, that the last week I've not thought about it. I had looked before we met, but I think I'm best off with my shop in New Brighton."

"So, do you have anybody looking after it for you at the moment?" Robert asked.

"Well," replied John, "I run it with my brother, James, so he's back in New Brighton at the moment. I thought about branching out, which is why I came here. I've been going back and forth ever since I got here. I want to take Hannah with me for a few days, so she can meet my family. I know they're going to love her."

Meanwhile, in the kitchen, the food was almost ready for serving. Sarah was talking to Hannah whilst at the same time preparing the food, ready to take to table.

Hannah said, "John is such a gentleman… Oh, thank you so much for taking me to the concert – I'd never have met him…"

"He is wonderful," replied Sarah, nodding in agreement. "I'm glad you've finally found somebody, mind I never expected anything to happen quite so quick!"

Hannah continued, "He's taking me to meet his family this week… In New Brighton… I'm so excited!"

Sarah looked cautious. "Be careful," she said. "I know John is marvellous news for you, but please be careful… Remember, you're a grown woman now, so act with a little decorum."

"I will, I will," replied Hannah, slightly annoyed that Sarah had misgivings.

"I know you will," said Sarah, handing a dish of vegetables to Hannah. "Can you take this in, and put it on the table for me please? Let everybody know it's time to get to table, then come back for the gravy."

"Yes, Sarah," answered Hannah, taking the dish from her sister. "I will."

Hannah took the dish into the living room and put it in the centre of the table. "Food's ready," she said. She then turned round and went back out to the kitchen. Sarah was just putting the side of roast beef on a plate. She gave the jug of gravy to Hannah and they both walked in together. Everybody was seated at the table. Sarah put the joint of beef in front of Robert, and he stood up to carve it. The plates were stacked next to the roast, so as a plate had the meat put on it, it was then passed to each person in turn so they could add their vegetables to it.

The meal was eaten with gusto. John kept looking at Hannah almost as much as Hannah was looking at John. Robert, at the head of the table smiled at Sarah. As always, she had been wise enough to know that Hannah was ready for the big wide world.

After dinner the men continued talking while the women cleared away the dishes. Sarah and Hannah were talking about the next month's celebration. It was Mary Foulkes' 60th birthday, and all her children were determined it should be a very special day. Sarah had written to her brother John, in the Merchant Navy, and he had sent her a reply that he was unable to attend, but he wanted to be included in whatever the family did. Hannah had suggested they buy an armchair for their mother. She was getting old now, and the furniture they had brought with them was worn. Mary needed a comfortable chair. Sarah thought it was a wonderful idea and would mention it to the other siblings.

Finally, John and Hannah said their goodbyes and left to go back to the Foulkes house. During the week Sarah managed to speak with Mary, Jane and Robert. They all agreed with her that they should do something for their mother and Hannah's idea was considered to be a wonderful one, and they couldn't believe it was she who had suggested it. They all pooled their money together and found a chair which they thought was ideal for Mary. It was a mahogany bergere in beige leather. It was expensive, but they considered it was money well spent.

Sunday 21 June was the closest day the family could get to celebrate Mary Foulkes' 60th birthday. It was really two days later, but everybody would be at work, so the celebration had to be on the Sunday. Thomas was in on the plan, and he took Mary out for a walk in the morning. It was a very hot, sunny, day without a cloud in the sky.

"I should be at home cooking the dinner!" Mary said, in exasperation. "The food will never be ready on time!"

"It won't hurt, for once, for the food to be late," Thomas said. "This is a special day!"

All the family, with one exception, had gathered there that day. John was away at sea, but was there in spirit, if nothing else. Agnes was only there for the dinner, since she had to go to work. Her brother, William, was there, too. It would be his last family event before he took up his apprenticeship with the brass foundry in Cathcart Street. Also there were Robert and Jane Foulkes with their children, Robert and Sarah McWilliam with their children, Hannah Foulkes and John Corless, and the other unmarried sisters, Mary and Jane Foulkes.

So, while Thomas and Mary were out everybody else carried the new chair in and put it down in place of the chair that Mary usually sat on. Then they got a blanket and covered it over. Not long after the chair was hidden, Thomas and Mary returned.

"We could have stayed out a bit longer," Thomas was heard to say.

"Well, I've far too much to do to be out wandering the streets!" Mary replied, annoyed.

They walked into the room and Mary stood stock still. She pointed at the object hidden by the blanket. "What is that?" she asked.

As she said that, everybody, who had been hiding in the back room, came in. They all called out, "Happy birthday, ma'!"

"Have a look under the blanket," called Hannah.

Mary just stood there. How had everybody managed to surprise her?

"Come on Granny," said her granddaughter, Mary. She took her grandmother's hand and pulled her towards the object. Finally, Mary could wait no longer, and she pulled the blanket off. She couldn't believe her eyes, and stood there, stroking the chair. She walked round it, taking it all in.

"This is beautiful!" She exclaimed. "You are so clever! All of you." Mary motioned for everybody to come to her and as they did she gave them all a hug. Each one of them, in turn, wished her a happy birthday. Mary stood so long looking at the chair they were afraid she was not going to sit in it.

"Are you going to sit in it, then?" asked Hannah, eventually.

"Well," she said, "I will just have a feel of it." She sat down in it. "Oh, it is lovely! What a wonderful idea from all of you."

"It was something you needed," said Sarah.

"For sure," said Mary, "but I should get on with the dinner, now." She stood up and went to go out to the kitchen. She got as far as the hallway.

"Where do you think you're going?" Sarah asked her mother, stopping her in her tracks. "I've a meal to cook," Mary replied.

"Oh, no, you don't!" Sarah said. "You go and sit down – in your new chair."

"Yes," said Jane, "If you were my own ma' I'd be saying the same. You gave up a room in your house so Robert and me, with our family, could live with you. It's about time I took over the reins for one day at least."

Sarah's sisters, Jane and Mary came out into the hallway to find out what was going on. Sarah turned to them. "Take ma' in the other room and make sure she sits down on her chair. We will be cooking the dinner."

The two girls took Mary back into the other room and the two married women continued on into the kitchen and cooked the meal. As they busied themselves they chatted.

"How are you coping?" Sarah asked her sister-in-law.

"Better, now all the rest of the masons have gone back to work," Jane replied. "It's grand to think they got what they were asking for."

"But it wasn't only money, was it?" said Sarah. "Robert says that Walkers the Builders met with a deputation of masons and agreed a raise of two shillings with forty minutes for breakfast, as well."

"Indeed, they did. Robert was full of it when he came home on Tuesday, after the meeting."

Finally, the meal was ready and the whole family sat down to eat. Afterwards, Agnes said she must go back to work, so she gave Mary a gift of a bottle of stout and a kiss on the cheek. She then left the rest of the family to enjoy the remainder of the day.

The younger children had all prepared presents for their grandmother and they had wrapped them up in brown paper for her. They now, one by one, came up and gave them to her. They were only small presents, but Mary loved every one of them. Some brought her a piece of fruit each; some brought an item they had made. There were scribbled pictures, but William surprised them all. During his short time he had been working at the brass foundry he had found the time to make her a small brass ornament. It was a plaque in the shape of a thistle and a claymore crossed.

Mary loved them all. With the presents opened, the men gathered into a huddle, at the opposite end of the room from Mary, and they began to talk.

Robert Foulkes was the first to speak. "It doesn't seem possible that ma' is sixty this week."

"Don't remind me," announced Thomas, "It's only another four years and it will be my turn!"

"My mother would've been 60 years old, two years ago," Robert McWilliam interjected, "had she survived. She died over ten years before Agnes and I moved down from Scotland. My father had already died two years earlier."

"So, you've no brothers or sisters?" John Corless asked him.

Robert McWilliam looked sad for a moment. "I have no idea. There were five of us tae begin wi'. My brother James was eldest, then me, then my sister Elizabeth, brother John and sister Susan." He stood there, quietly thinking of times past.

"Never mind," Thomas said, interrupting the awkward silence, "you've a big family here."

Robert McWilliam nodded.

The three unmarried sisters sat talking in a group. Hannah was talking about her new lifestyle and Mary and Jane asked her lots of questions.

"So, whose idea was it to go to the concert?" Jane asked.

"I think it was Sarah's," answered Hannah, "She was the one told ma', anyway."

"Well," replied Jane, "Well, I think it was a marvellous idea! How often do you see John?"

"He has to go back to running his family greengrocer shop," answered Hannah, "so he comes back to walk out with me at weekends."

Meanwhile, the men were talking to John, Hannah's beau.

"So, tell me John, what do you think of Birkenhead?" asked Thomas.

"Well," replied John, "it's a bit expensive, but nothing as expensive as Liverpool!"

"That's true," added Thomas. "But you don't notice the prices when you live here. I remember, when we were back in Tranmere we used to think everything was expensive, but we were shocked when we got to Birkenhead."

By now, the evening was upon them. It was mid-summer, so there was a while to go before it began to get dark, but being Sunday everybody had to get ready for the week to come. So, one by one, people started to leave to go to their own homes. Mary and Jane were the first to leave. They had to be back at their place of work, ready for bed. They said their goodbyes first to their mother, then to their father, and to their sisters and brother and their families. Then they opened the door and were gone.

"Well," said John, next, "I think I should be going now. I thank you heartily for your welcome here today."

"Think of yourself as good as family," said Thomas, as he shook his hand and patted him on the back.

John went over to Hannah. "I shall write to you when I get home," he said. "We will set a date for you to come visit my family."

"I shall look forward to your letter, and next weekend," said Hannah, "when I shall see you again." She gave John a hug and he brushed a wisp of hair off her forehead so he could kiss her there. "I must go," he said, breaking away from her embrace. She opened the door for him and he left, calling out "Goodbye!" and waving as he went.

Robert looked at Sarah. "We should get home, too," he said. Sarah nodded. Jane was fast asleep in her grandmother's arms, but Mary and John were playing happily with Sarah and Mariah, their cousins.

"Time to go," said Sarah to Mary and John. William stood up and kissed his grandmother, then he helped get Mary and John ready for the walk back home. Sarah plucked Jane from her mother's arms and put her in the baby carriage. When everybody was ready they, too, left for home.

Thomas and Mary sat back down. Robert picked up Sarah and Mariah and took them upstairs to their own room and Jane soon followed, after tidying up the toys that had been left on the floor.

The days went back to normal. There was no birthday to be planned, so the family felt at a loose end. They had enjoyed the excitement and wanted something else to concentrate their minds. Thankfully, something came along.

For the next month the whole of Birkenhead and Liverpool were buzzing. It had been a long time in the planning, but finally everything was set for the visit of Prince Albert to open the Prince Albert Dock in Liverpool. Robert came home with his newspaper on 24 July 1846.

"It's all in the paper," he said as he came home from work that Friday evening. "Have you made the arrangements for Thursday?"

"We have a plan of sorts," replied Sarah. "We were waiting for the final details – they've changed so much since we first heard the Prince was coming."

"Aye, that they have!" Robert opened the newspaper. "The Mercury has the intended timings," he said. "The royal train is due tae arrive at Lime Street Station about half past 11 o'clock. The Prince goes from there tae the Judges' Lodgings in St. Anne's Street till about half past 12 o'clock. From there they go tae the Town Hall by about a quarter to 1 o'clock. There's a short address at the Town Hall before they go tae Egremont Pier where the Prince joins the Royal Yacht, Fairy, for about half past the hour. The Yacht is due tae sail first tae New Brighton, then down tae Rock Ferry and back, arriving at the Albert Quay at about half past 2 o'clock. By 3 o'clock it will be all over for that's when he goes into the pavilion for their festivities. The day is due tae finish with fireworks."

"So where do you think would be best to stand?" Sarah asked him. Robert thought for a few moments.

"Well, as the yacht is coming all the way down from New Brighton, I think we could stand anywhere down by the docks," he said. Perhaps we could go down as far the Priory – stand waterside just there."

"I'll suggest that to ma' when I see her tomorrow, and see what she says," said Sarah.

Thomas and Mary agreed that it was just as good a spot to wait as any.

Finally, 30 July 1846 arrived. It was declared a public holiday so as many people who wanted to go were able. Everybody got up early that day. John Corless was the first to arrive at the Foulkes home. Hannah was ready and waiting, so she let him in. Thomas and Mary had already left to secure a spot.

"We're going," said Hannah to her brother Robert, "because we want to walk slowly and spend a bit of time on our own before everybody else arrives. You can catch us up."

"We're not leaving too early," said Robert. "The children will be restless if they have too long to wait to see anything."

With that, Hannah opened the front door and she and John walked off. It was a gloriously sunny day and everybody had dressed up for the occasion. Scores of people were walking to the river.

"Where do you think the Prince is now?" Hannah asked John.

"Well, I'm sure the train must have left London early," he replied. "I would think they have left Birmingham by now."

The train appointed by the directors of the London and North Western Railway (late the London and Birmingham and Grand Junction Railways) to carry his Royal Highness to Liverpool, had, indeed, left Euston station, London, that morning at 6 o'clock. The Prince travelled in the carriage, which was furnished by the London and Birmingham Company, expressly for the accommodation of her Majesty the Queen, when she travelled on that line. This vehicle looked splendid. It was elegantly lined with blue satin, with a canopied top on which was emblazoned the Royal Arms. There were couches in it, upon which the royal traveller could lounge during the journey and, at the same time, could have an excellent view of the surrounding scenery through the glass windows.

The exterior of the carriage was of a chocolate colour, richly gilt, and had both inside and out a chaste and elegant appearance. George Carr Glynn, the chairman of the company, and Richard Creed, the company secretary, accompanied the train; and the orders of the directors were, that everything on the line should give way to the royal train. The engine from London to

Birmingham was driven by Edward Burry, the locomotive superintendent of the southern division of the line. On arrival at Birmingham, Captain Huish joined the train.

Ready, too, to enjoy the celebration, were Robert and Sarah. Agnes had come home for the morning, at least, and she and Sarah were making sure the family had everything before they left home. Mary and Jane, in domestic service, were also going to the celebration, but they would stay with their respective households.

Agnes had finished dressing John when she announced, "That's it! We're all ready. Can we go now?"

Robert looked around him. Sarah had a hamper with her. "Are we feeding the five thousand, woman?" He asked.

"No, just the family. But I've packed enough to last us all day," Sarah replied.

"Well, gie it tae me," he said. "I shall carry that, it'll be quicker. You make sure everybody keeps up – we dinnae want tae leave anybody behind!"

With that, Robert, Sarah, who was pushing baby Jane in her carriage, Agnes, William and the little ones left for the Priory.

Meanwhile, back to the train, which had now arrived in Birmingham; the six-wheeled engine of the late London and Birmingham line had been changed for a four wheeled one of the Grand Junction Company, and Francis Trevithick, the Locomotive Superintendent of the Northern Division of the Line took charge of the engine, and conducted the train to Edgehill Station. The management of the arrangements at the London station was entrusted to Richard Creed; at Birmingham to Captain Huish; and at the Liverpool end to Messrs Booth and Poole.

Back in Birkenhead, as Robert McWilliam and Sarah were leaving Back Beckwith Street, Robert Foulkes, Jane and their brood were just arriving at the spot Thomas and Mary had secured.

"You've got a grand spot, da'," said Robert. "It's a perfect view." Jane secured her baby carriage and William and the girls ran up to their grandparents and gave them a hug.

Indeed the view was perfect. They were sitting on a blanket on a grassy bank at the edge of the Priory, with a clear view up and down the river. Opposite were all the docks, and just up river from them, on the opposite bank, was the new dock, and the hundreds of people gathering to watch. Also, a gentle breeze had just picked up, and all the ensigns were animated. Mary pulled her shawl around her to keep warm. She was getting older, now, and she felt the cold more.

The river Mersey was awash with colour. The river was filled with vessels that had been decorated for several days in readiness for the visit. The view from the river, shortly before the Prince's arrival, was one of surpassing beauty. Looking northward and southward, were vessels decorated with union jacks and other marks of loyalty. The various pendants streaming, and flags flying, as they were alternately acted upon by the gentle breeze which was blowing at the time, blended with the masts, spars and rigging of the vessels, presented the appearance of a vast forest, which seemed to have no limit and was bounded only by the extent of vision.

The piers skirting the river, crowded with spectators, occupying, as it were, the foreground, completed the panorama. The Cheshire shore was also covered with masses of human beings, more and more arriving all the time, from the Rock Ferry, near where the Fairy yacht left her moorings, to as far as New Brighton. On the river were innumerable vessels, of all sizes and description: merchant ships, steamers, flats and pilot boats, gaily decorated with flags, and having on board thousands of people, anxious to fill every possible space in order to get a view of the royal visitor. The "Prince", a Dublin steamer, was gaily decorated and had the foreyard and topsail-yard fully manned with mariners dressed in blue jackets and white trousers, which presented a striking effect, and gained the warmest commendations from those who were present. The river boats, which had advertised to convey parties to the royal yachts, were in great demand and numbers took advantage of the opportunity this gave. Several people even planted themselves precariously in the rigging of the vessels, they were so anxious to get good viewing positions.

Robert and Sarah were soon down by the docks. "Right," said Robert, "keep looking out for granny and grandda' – we dinnae want tae miss them!" Agnes walked with Mary and John. It was hard for Robert and Sarah to keep up with them. They kept them in view, though. William carried the hamper for his father part of the way and Robert watched him with pride.

On the other side of the river, however, much more was happening, and those on the Birkenhead side could only imagine how the events were unfolding. The railway station at Lime Street was the great focus of attraction. Thousands of people had congregated in Lime Street, and the large area opposite the station was filled – everybody anxiously waiting to catch a glimpse of his Royal Highness, and to give him a hearty reception. Many had been there since early in the morning, dressed in their best clothes. They passed the time talking about whether the Prince would be early or late, and many other things.

The people waited patiently. Everybody seemed happy, forgetting all about work – for this day, at least. After all, Prince Albert had come to honour the town with his presence, and open the dock, named after him.

Entrance to the station itself was by ticket, only, which limited the number of people who were present on his arrival to the authorities of the town and the principal officers of the Railway Company. The gentlemen connected with the press were afforded every facility by direction of Henry Booth, the Secretary to the Railway Company.

Shortly after 10 o'clock that morning, the main dignitaries had assembled at Lime Street station, and they were anxiously awaiting the Prince's arrival. Amongst them were the Mayor and Town Clerk, Thomas Sands, Earl Talbot, Henry Booth, secretary to the Railway Company, Benjamin Poole, Manager of the Government Department, Captain Evans, Conservator of the River, Charles Lawrence, Chairman of the Board of Directors, Samuel Mosley, James Longton, George Hall Lawrence, William Rotherham, James Ilbery, Engineer to the Company, who was particularly active in making the necessary arrangements for the Prince's arrival. About half past 10 o'clock Lord Sandon had arrived in his carriage and took up a position in the railway yard; also there were Generals Sir William Ward and Sir William Arbuthnot, the Dean of Chester and Lady and Lord Adolphus Fitzclarence.

A company of the 36th regiment, under the command of Captain Ridge, with their band, and a portion of the 4th dragoon guards, under command of Captain Fune, were there. The latter were to be a guard of honour to receive the Prince.

A large body of the police force were present under the direction of Commissioner Dowling. The Prince's private carriage and attendants were in waiting to receive him on his arrival. The windows of the offices and other buildings connected with the railway station were filled with well-dressed ladies, who had been admitted to view the arrival of the Royal guest and every available position that would afford even the slightest view of the proceedings was occupied.

A temporary stage or platform had been set up on which his Royal Highness was to alight and pass to his own private carriage. It was covered with a red carpet. Considerable interest was aroused when it was known that the train, in which the Prince was to arrive, had reached Edgehill station and everybody at Lime Street station were full of expectation. At 25 minutes to 12 o'clock the royal train arrived, and everybody was ready to receive him.

On alighting from the railway carriage, in company of Lord Morpeth and Colonel Anson, he was received by the Mayor and Directors and principal officers of the Railway Company. The Prince returned the congratulations of the Mayor with great courtesy and freedom of manner. The band of the 36th regiment of hussars struck up God save the Queen, at the conclusion of which there was considerable cheering from all present. The Prince was in plain clothes, wearing a light waistcoat, grey pantaloons, and light neckerchief. Across his breast he wore the band of the Order of the Garter.

After the necessary courtesies were over, his Royal Highness entered his private carriage in the company of Lord Morpeth and the Mayor, in order to proceed to the Judge's lodgings in St. Anne Street.

As soon as those present outside the station realised that the Prince had arrived, the crowd gave several hearty cheers and the excitement was kept up until he made his appearance in Lime Street, upon which there arose such a burst of popular enthusiasm as literally rent the air.

The Prince then proceeded to the Judge's lodgings in St. Anne Street. He was escorted by the chief Commissioner of Police, Matthew M Dowling, with a body of the police force on horseback. There then followed a guard of honour, consisting of the officers and troop of the 4th Dragoon Guards, and immediately after, the Prince, in his private carriage. His staff followed in another carriage and the rear was brought up by a body of police to keep the people off and prevent any interruption.

The cavalcade moved on through Lime Street, Commutation Row, Islington, to St. Anne Street to the Judge's lodgings, where the Prince arrived about a quarter to 12 o'clock. He was received by a guard of honour of the 36th Infantry, with a military band. Soon after, the Mayor left the Judge's lodgings in his carriage and proceeded to the Town Hall.

The Prince had some refreshment and a short rest, then again left the Judge's lodgings at about half past 12 o'clock and proceeded to the Town Hall, under the same escort as before. The royal carriage, drawn by six horses, passed on through St. Anne Street amidst the shouts and cheers of the assembled crowds. The Prince and his staff continued on their way, through Islington, where they were again greeted with load cheers and roars, not only from those who followed the train, but also from a large company of ladies and gentlemen, assembled at the various windows on the route, several of which were handsomely decorated with flags, banners, and other demonstrations of respect for the Royal visitor.

On passing through Lime Street, Church Street, Lord Street and Castle Street, to the Town Hall, the cheering continued just as strong. During these outpourings of loyalty, the Prince waved to everybody and he smiled in appreciation.

Huge arrangements had been put in place in Castle Street to keep order. Round the entrance to the Town Hall a strong barricade had been erected. A body of the police force were stationed inside and the outside was guarded by a body of the 65th Regiment of Foot.

In the centre drawing-room, awaiting the arrival of the Prince, a large number of ladies and gentlemen had been admitted with the Mayor's orders. The ladies were richly and elegantly attired. Amongst them were Lord Sandon, Lord Talbot, Lady Sarah Ingestrie, Mrs. and the Misses Wright, Mr. and Mrs. Cardwell, one of the late Trustees of Mrs. Bowman, Pudsey Dawson, Mr., Mrs. and Miss Greenwood, Guildford Hartley, Edward Parry and his daughter, Mr. Roscoe, Mrs. Mann and her daughter, Mrs. Swainson, Mrs. Allen, Mrs. W and Mrs. J Burkett, George Grant and his wife, Mrs. G Lawrence, the Reverend Hugh McNeile and his daughter, Sir Haward Douglas, the Misses Hodgson, sisters to the Mayor, the Reverend Mr. Barker and his wife, of Edgehill, the Misses Bushby, Mrs. J H Linnor, Mrs. Phillips, Colonel Tempest, John Wybergh, the Misses Brancker and Lady Brancker, the Misses Molyneux and Stapley, Mr. J Langton and the Misses Langton, the Reverend C Lawrence, Mrs. Rector Campbell, Mrs. Aspinall and Mrs. Clay, Rector Brookes, Miss Brookes, Mrs. and the Misses Shuttleworth, Miss Myers, Mr. W J Myers, Miss Crook, Mrs. Brampton Sands and the Misses Sands, the Misses Cropper and Mr. Edward Cropper, Mr., Mrs. and Miss B Hill, Mr. H Hornby and his wife, Mr. Robert Neilson and his accompanying lady.

In the vestibule, the members of the Town Council took their places on each side of the path leading to the grand staircase. The crowd round the Town Hall was, of course, immense. Shortly after 12 o'clock, the Mayor's carriage, preceded by several gentlemen and officials, drove up to the Town Hall. Some people thought it was the Prince in the carriage and they began to shout. At the same time, the band of the 68th regiment, from Chester, who were stationed outside, started playing "God Save the Queen".

Disappointingly, however, the Mayor and the Town Clerk were the only people who stepped from the carriage. They brought the news that the Prince had arrived and he would be arriving shortly. During the wait, the line which had been formed by Councillors became broken, as they moved from their places. Taking the opportunity, some members of the press, who had stood behind the members of the Council, now pushed forward.

Councillor Thornhill immediately sent one of the Mayor's footmen to force them back. This was an officious act, as unwarranted under the circumstances, as it was ungentlemanly. Shortly afterwards the Mayor stepped in and requested that gentlemen of the Council would follow the Mayor and the Prince, four abreast, and that gentlemen not of the Council should follow in the rear.

The grand staircase, which had been redecorated by Mr. Tyram, of Birmingham, was thrown open for the first time. It presented a magnificent appearance and the effect was greatly heightened by a large supply from the Botanic Gardens of richly tinted plants, fuschias, evergreens, and more, in full flower.

The Mayor, in his official gown and with his wand of authority in his hand, awaited the arrival of the Prince. The Town Clerk was also in attendance in his robes. Gilbert Henderson was the recorder, in a full-bodied wig and gown, and Peter Wright, the Clerk of the Peace, in his official robes, were also there.

Meanwhile, back by the river, shortly before 1 o'clock, the Foulkes family were spotted by the McWilliam children. Robert and his family had finally arrived down by the Priory. "I've found them!" Agnes called to her parents, then she and the little ones ran on ahead to them. Thomas was the first to see them coming.

"Well done," he said. "You found us, then."

Sarah, pushing the baby carriage, came level with them. "Da'," she said, "you've done us proud! This is a perfect viewpoint. What time did you get here?"

"Your ma' and I came first," Thomas said. "We got here about 9 o'clock and secured this spot. Hannah and John got here about

10 o'clock. She arranged with John to meet her at home, so she had to wait for him to arrive from New Brighton before she could leave. Robert, Jane and the children came about 11 o'clock so the children wouldn't get too bored. The Fairy is due to leave Liverpool pierhead about half past 1 o'clock, so it should be coming through just here about 2 o'clock. So, we've about an hour to wait."

"You must be famished, then," Sarah said. "Just as well we brought a hamper of food with us. We can have something to eat while we wait." William had just put the hamper down on the grass beside them, so Sarah got down and opened it up. There were barm cakes, pork pies, cheese, tomatoes, simnel cake, apples, pears and much more besides.

"What a wonderful spread!" Mary said to her daughter. Over the next half hour the food was eaten with relish by the whole family.

By this time, the younger children had all gathered together in a group and were talking excitedly to each other about the assembled spectacle.

Robert McWilliam looked about him and took in the panorama. "I've no' seen so many people all in one place," he said. "I never imagined there'd be scenes like this... Look at all those boats in the water... It's so colourful!"

"Oh... It's beautiful," added Mary, senior. "There's so many boats out there on the water – look how pretty they are!"

Jane moved nearer to her father-in-law. "There's so many different sizes," she said. "What do all those flags mean?"

"They spell out words or sentences," he replied. "They're all spelling their congratulations to the Prince. Then there are the Union flags and all the bunting. Some of them are taking passengers up and down the river, for a fee."

Sarah asked, "Where is the Fairy setting off from?"

Thomas, pleased to be asked all these questions, replied, "She's leaving from the Egremont Pier. Look up there," he pointed to his left, "where the headland on this side disappears round to the left?"

Sarah looked in the direction he had indicated and nodded. "Well," he continued, "on the opposite side of the river, just above that point, is where the pier is."

Back on the Liverpool side of the Mersey, the outriders and Guard of Honour appeared at the Town Hall, followed closely by the Prince in his private carriage, and at 10 minutes to 1 o'clock precisely, his Royal Highness alighted at the Town Hall. All the assembled crowds cheered and the regimental band began playing God Save the Queen. The Prince was received by the Mayor, who conducted him into the vestibule and up the grand staircase.

As he passed the members of Council he graciously bowed in acknowledgment of the manner in which he was received by them. In ascending the staircase, the attention of his Royal Highness was directed by the Mayor to the statue of Canning, by Chantrey, and the Prince expressed satisfaction at seeing it.

On reaching the centre drawing room, the Address of the Corporation was presented to his Royal Highness. It was read in a clear, distinct, and energetic manner by the Recorder and after being deposited in the box, was handed to the Prince by the Mayor.

The box was about 8 inches in height, 6½ in breadth, and 2 in depth. The inside was lined with white satin and the exterior was covered with purple velvet. A gold border surrounded the lid and four elaborately worked gold ornaments decorated the corners, and the Albert arms in gold occupied the centre. Attached to the large box by a ribbon was a small silver box, richly chased, the lid having the Liverpool arms executed in relief. In this was placed the Corporation seal.

The Prince was very pleased and, turning to the Mayor, he read, "I experience the greatest satisfaction from the cordial welcome which the address you have just presented to me, gives me upon my arrival in this town.

"I am glad to perceive that my coming amongst you, in order to take part in two ceremonies connected with your mercantile industry and enterprise, should have been gratifying to you, and on my part, I have only followed the bent of my own inclination in at once responding to your kind invitation.

"Your expressions of loyalty and attachment to the Queen, cannot fail to be most satisfactory to me and, I am sure, will be felt as much by her Majesty."

The Prince spoke with a rich, sweet voice, slightly touched with a foreign accent. The ceremony of presentation being over, the Mayor conducted his Royal Highness through the principal apartments in the Town Hall, showing him around.

The cornice over the centre window, which had been fitted up by Messrs. Hand and Sons, of Bold Street, particularly attracted the attention of the Prince and he said how well the rooms were dressed. The windows fronting Castle Street were then thrown open and his Royal Highness presented himself to the assembled crowd, who greeted him with the most enthusiastic cheers.

The Prince did not remain long at the Town Hall. He shortly afterwards entered his carriage and drove to the Pier Head. On leaving the Town Hall, the royal carriage and staff proceeded down Water Street, along George's Dock, passing the Old Church, (the bells of which on his arrival there gave several loud peals) and crossed the south gate of the Prince's dock to the Egremont slip, where the Royal Yacht Fairy was stationed.

Along the whole line of road he was enthusiastically cheered and in those parts of the route which allowed large masses of persons to congregate, the applause was almost deafening. The masts and the yards of the various vessels which lay on those sides of the George's and Prince's docks adjacent to the route, were studded with "tars", who were ready and willing to honour the royal visitor and no sooner did they catch a glimpse of him, than one vast cheer suddenly arose.

The ship Georgina, lying in the Prince's Dock gut, was prettily dressed. Every mast and spar were crammed with the "protectors of our commerce", all neatly attired. On his Royal Highness embarking on board the Fairy, he was presented by the Mayor with a beautifully embossed red morocco bound Guide to Liverpool and a Plan of the Docks.

Back down by the Priory, the cheers of the people grew louder. "Did you hear those bells ringing? They must be on their way at last!" Mary said to her family.

Oh, Look!" Hannah shouted. "They've sent some balloons up!"

Sure enough, several balloons had been set off from the baths at George's Pier, which caused considerable amusement to the assembled spectators. They remained in sight for a good while and eventually went off in the direction of Egremont.

About half past 1 o'clock, the Prince and his staff, with several of the authorities, embarked at the Egremont Pier on board the royal yacht, amidst the cheers of the people and several salutes of cannon. The royal yacht set its course down the river, towards New Brighton, followed by an immense number of steamboats, but they all trailed in its wake, the Fairy was so fast. As the boats passed the Prince's Basin a most novel sight presented itself, a vessel called the William Fisher was placed with her head towards the river, manned with about 200 seamen, dressed in the naval uniform of blue jackets and white trousers, covering the whole of the yards and rigging. One of the seamen was actually on the mast head, and he waved his hat several times, as the Royal yacht and the other vessels in the train passed along. Great crowds were assembled on the numerous heights in Bootle Bay and also on the opposite shore, to be witnesses of the event that presented itself on the river.

With the sound from the guns, Robert Foulkes was the first to notice. "Look! There's movement over there!"

"It's so far away," sighed Hannah. "Is it a big boat?"

Thomas answered her. "She's getting on for nearly 150 feet long, 21 feet wide and weighs over 300 tons."

"Is it new?" Mary asked.

"She was launched last year," he replied.

Jane interjected, "Why do you keep calling it a "she"?"

Proudly, Thomas answered her. "A ship is called 'She' because there is always a great deal of bustle around her; there is usually a gang of men about, she has a waist and stays; it takes a lot of paint to keep her good looking; it is not the initial expense that breaks you, it's the upkeep; she can be all decked out; it takes an experienced man to handle her correctly, and, without a man at the helm, she is absolutely uncontrollable. She shows her topsides, hides her bottom and, when coming into port, always heads for the buoys."

Everybody laughed and Robert Foulkes said, "Oh, that's really clever, da'. Makes sense when you say all of that!"

As they watched, and after receiving a salute at the Battery, the Fairy steamed up the river towards Birkenhead, close in shore, the crowds on the shore exhibiting the same ardent demonstrations of loyalty which had greeted the Prince throughout the previous part of his progress.

"Look!" Hannah called out once again. "She's coming! I would love to have a ride on a boat."

John looked at her, smiling at the child in her, rising to the surface. "I'll have to see what we can do," he said.

"She's moving fast," Robert McWilliam added.

"The screw helps her go fast," answered Thomas.

"What's a screw?" Mary asked.

"It's a type of propeller," explained Thomas. "She's a steamship, so she has an engine that works the screw. This one is a new design and it makes her go faster. See how she's leaving all the other ships behind?"

Everybody all looked in the direction of the ships and watched as the Fairy pulled away.

Agnes had been watching the children, to make sure they remained safe. She began to talk with them.

"Look!" Agnes told them. "Watch for the yacht to go by. See who's the first to see the Prince."

The children strained to see if they could spot him. The adults were just as excited and looked as well.

Sarah McWilliam and her niece, Sarah, called out at exactly the same moment. "There he is!" Little Sarah pointed in the direction of the Fairy.

"Well done, Sarah," said Agnes to her cousin. "Doesn't he look fine?"

"Doesn't he look handsome!" Hannah added.

"What's that band across him?" Mary asked her sister Agnes. Agnes looked at her father.

"It's a sort of badge that his wife gave him. It's called The Order of the Garter"

Mary Foulkes, who had been watching and listening to everything said, "He isn't in a uniform – I wondered if he might be."

"It's just a grey suit. Very smart, though," added Sarah McWilliam.

"What's the Order of the Garter?" William Foulkes asked.

His father answered, "It means he's one of the Queen's knights. Do you know what a knight is?"

Little Mary was the first to answer her uncle. "Is that like George and the dragon?"

"That's right," he replied.

"That yacht looks so different from what we normally see on this river," mused Thomas, almost oblivious to the other conversations going on around him.

She continued her course as far as Rock Ferry, where she turned round and crossed over to the opposite shore at the Herculaneum Dock.

"Look, Hannah," said John. "He's coming back again."

Everybody turned to look in the direction of Tranmere and watched as the yacht passed back on the other side.

"She's further away, now, but she still looks wonderful!" Hannah remarked.

"It's all happened so quickly," said Mary, disappointedly.

Her daughter-in-law tried to cheer her up. "But there's still the fireworks, later. They're to be on the river, so we can watch them. It'll be a wonderful end to a beautiful day."

"What time are they?" Sarah asked her husband.

"It willnae be before sunset," Robert replied.

Mary looked down at her daughter's empty hamper. Had they really managed to eat everything? She was still hungry. "We'll soon be going back to our house for food," she said. "We can stay there until it's time for the fireworks. We'll be close enough at our house – better than you," she spoke to Robert and Sarah, "going back to your place and then coming out again." Sarah nodded in agreement.

"If it's all right, ma'," said Hannah, "I'll be going to John's cousins' house with him. They've also laid on a spread."

"I expected as much," answered Mary, chuckling to herself as she spoke.

Once again, the Prince was received with fresh manifestations of popular feeling by those assembled on the pierheads, which he acknowledged at intervals. His Royal Highness and staff were on the quarter deck of the yacht during the whole time of their cruise on the river, and appeared to be engaged in inspecting the various objects which presented themselves. Opposite the King's Dock, the William Fisher, manned as previously described, made her appearance, having been towed up by a steamer. The Victoria and Albert royal yacht was also on the river, but she did not accompany the Fairy on her route.

The Fairy then passed along the Albert Quay and entered the dock, about half-past 2 o'clock, amidst the most enthusiastic cheering and the firing of guns. The various steamers, having parties on board, remained there a while longer but then returned to land their passengers at the different pier heads. During the afternoon one or two collisions took place amongst the fleet of steamers following the Prince's yacht, but, happily, nobody was injured and there was just a small amount of damage to one of the vessels entering the dock.

The loud pealing of the cannon and the opening of the bridge at the Albert Dock, announced that the Prince was approaching. All eyes were now directed to the entrance. First came one of the Liverpool lifeboats, fully manned; next followed the Queen's state barge, belonging to the Victoria and Albert and then two gigs belonging to the Fairy. The Prince stood on the quarter-deck, gracefully bowing in acknowledgement of all the cheers and thunderous applause that greeted his appearance.

The families on the Cheshire shore tried desperately to see more of the spectacle, but the people were too far away to be seen clearly.

Also on the quarter deck stood John Bramley Moore, the Chairman of the Dock Committee, the Mayor, Lord Sandon, Lord Morpeth, Colonel Sir Thomas Arbuthnot, Captain Bevis, Major-General Warre, Lord Adolphus Fitzclarence and the royal staff. Captain Crispin, the commander of the Fairy, conducted her into dock, Captain Arthur of the Steam Tug Company acting as pilot at this time. The appearance of the Fairy as she entered the dock was truly imposing. The rich uniform of the naval and military officers on the deck, the neat and clean appearance of the sailors and the superb outfittings of the vessel, commanded general attention. From her stern hung a union jack, whilst high over the dock hung a rich gold standard.

As soon as the small boats had entered they saluted the Royal yacht by pointing their oars, the regimental band on the quays at the same time struck up "Rule Britannia". The Fairy steamed into the centre of the dock and approached the south end. She turned round by the sole aid of the screw, passed along the west and north sides and came alongside the quay at the east side. As the vessel passed the crowds assembled in every corner of the quay, the Prince was again and again greeted most enthusiastically.

A few minutes elapsed before the temporary gangway was lowered upon the deck of the Fairy, during which time the Prince seemed to take much interest in viewing the magnificent warehouses at the Albert Dock. As soon as it was in place, Lord Adolphus Fitzclarence and Captain Crispin helped the Prince to ascend. On the quay the Chairman of the Dock Committee and other members, along with the Mayor, were waiting to receive him. The cheering was at fever pitch. Jesse Hartley, Dock Surveyor, from whose plans nearly the whole of the docks and all the warehouses had been built, was introduced to the Prince, who complimented him on the wonderful construction of the stupendous docks and warehouses.

After a few moments' pause, during which the Prince was again cordially greeted, his Highness was conducted by the chairman of the dock committee up the private staircase. He was closely followed by the principal guests and the whole of his staff.

Returning to the dock, after the Royal yacht had entered the dock, two of the yachts belonging to the Royal Mersey Yacht Club followed. These were followed by the Redwing steamer, the Government tender of this port and several other yachts belonging to the Royal Mersey Club. The Redwing and the whole of the yachts were literally covered with flags. A number of small river boats, crowded with passengers, followed in the wake of the yachts. The bridge of the dock was then closed, in order to accommodate the people who were congregated on each side, and some time elapsed before the William Fisher, the merchant vessel appointed to go into the dock first, entered. More than 500 people, exclusive of 250 sailors, who manned the yards, were on board. The masts, yards and spars were crowded with "jolly tars" and one of them had actually taken his place at the topmast head. He returned the cheers of the crowd by waving his hat in good style.

"Well, that's it," began Thomas. "She's gone into the new dock now."

"Well, I must say," said Robert McWilliam, "it's been a wonderful day. It's getting hotter by the minute, too."

John Corless was getting restless. "Shall we go and find my cousins, sweetness?" He asked Hannah.

Hannah looked at her mother. "Do you mind, ma'?"

"Of course I don't mind," Mary replied. "Off you go... Have a good time."

It was precisely 3 o'clock when the Prince ascended the staircase to the refreshment room. His Royal Highness and his immediate attendants having entered, the door was closed and he was taken to that portion of the building intended to be submitted to his inspection.

Hannah and John said their goodbyes to everybody and took their leave. All around, people were starting to move off since there was nothing more to watch. Thomas and Mary led the group as they walked back to Albert Terrace. After tea they waited for it to get dark, then everybody went out to see the fireworks. It had been a wonderful day.

The next few days things carried on as normal. William became a full-time apprentice at the foundry so he left home to live in with his new master. Sarah missed him greatly, especially since Agnes worked such long shifts. He had been a great help with the children.

A couple of weeks later, on Saturday, 15 August 1846, Mary came to visit Sarah. On her way in she saw her grandchildren playing with the neighbours' children. They all got on very well. Anne Beech was down there with them, to make sure they were safe. Mary knocked at the door and Sarah answered it.

"Hello, ma'," Sarah said, "come in."

Mary came in. "Did I see your little ones playing downstairs?" Mary asked, as she sat down.

"Yes, ma'," Sarah replied. "They're playing with the Mill-ward and Beech children. They go to the same school, so they're good friends." Sarah looked at her mother. "There's something on your mind, ma', I can tell."

"That's for sure," answered Mary. Little Jane, who was by now crawling, came over to her grandma and begged to be picked up. Mary did so, and Jane sat on her lap.

"What is it? Tell me, ma'," said Sarah.

"It's Hannah," Mary continued, with a smile.

"What about Hannah?" Sarah asked.

"I think there might be something in the off-ing," Mary said.

"You mean with John?" Sarah replied. Mary nodded.

"They seem to be spending so much time together," said Mary. "I wouldn't be at all surprised if John doesn't come to see us soon."

"Oh, that would be wonderful!" Sarah brought her hands together, almost in prayer, as she spoke. "It's about time she had somebody in her life."

"Yes," agreed Mary. "And John knows that she needs a lot of looking after, so I think they make a wonderful couple."

"Oh, ma'," said Sarah, "I never gave it a thought those few months ago that all this would happen from just a visit to a concert hall. It came along just at the right time."

At the beginning of September John did, indeed, come to ask Thomas for Hannah's hand in marriage. Everybody was over-joyed. At last Hannah would be able to live a life that most people think of as routine, but for Hannah it was something that, six months earlier, she would never have dreamed possible.

On Sunday, 20 September Sarah came, alone, to visit her parents. Agnes had come to visit, so she urged Sarah to go out for some air while she and Robert looked after the children. Sarah took her up on her offer and she decided to visit her parents, unannounced. Thomas and Mary were alone, downstairs, in the house. Sarah sat talking to them.

"Where are Robert, Jane and the children?" Sarah asked. The house was so quiet it seemed strange.

"They've gone to stay with Jane's parents," Mary answered. "They've moved back to Wales and there's a need for masons where they live, so Robert took the opportunity to go there for a while."

"Hannah is poorly," said Thomas.

"So Hannah is in bed?" Sarah asked.

"Yes," Mary replied. "She's got a bit of a fever, and she isn't sleeping very well, so we all told her to stay in bed and get some rest."

Sarah looked worried. "That doesn't sound very good," she said. "What do you think's causing it?"

"I'm not sure," Mary replied. "I'm hoping it is only a chill, but you never know."

Sarah knew that Hannah wasn't one for being ill, but she said, "She'll be fine. Just keep her warm and in bed – she'll soon be back to normal."

"Well, I expect you're right," said Mary, nodding. "She'll be back to her normal self soon enough!"

As an afterthought, Sarah asked, "Does John know she's ill?"

"He was here yesterday," answered Thomas. "He was the one told her to stay in bed today and that he'd call round tomorrow to see how she's feeling."

"Shall I go up and see her?" Sarah asked. Mary nodded so Sarah went up to Hannah's room. She stayed there for a while, talking with her, but Hannah wasn't really up for talking. So, Sarah left her alone and went back to see her parents. She told them to let her know how Hannah was over the next couple of days, then she returned home to her own family.

But Hannah did not recover, in fact she grew worse. Mary and Thomas tried to look after her, but nothing seemed to be working. Robert had called in on the next Sunday and insisted they call in the doctor. Mary promised she would and then would let them know how things were.

Next evening, Monday 28 September, Thomas called to see Robert and Sarah. Robert answered the door, and he could see immediately that things were not good.

"Your ma' sent me. She says for you not to go..." Thomas began, but Sarah interrupted him.

"Did you fetch the doctor?" Sarah asked.

"We did, lass... We did," Thomas replied.

"What did he say?" Sarah demanded.

Robert was also anxious, but he could see that Sarah was not making things easier for her father. "Sarah," he said, "will you let your father speak!"

Thomas nodded and continued. "He says Hannah has dysentery – badly. She caught a bit of a chill as well, and that's why the dysentery caught hold so much."

Sarah was in shock. She sat down and shook her head in dismay. "No! This cannot be happening... Not now!"

Robert could see the pain that Thomas was in. "Sit down, man," he said, ushering Thomas to a chair. "What's tae be done?"

Thomas sat down and continued, "The doctor is to arrange for a nurse to come in every day to help look after her as soon as he can. John came while he was there...

He's devastated, what with having lost his wife a year past."

Sarah sat there saying nothing. Robert looked at her, seeing how distressed she was. He urged Thomas to continue. "Will she get better? This dysentery is bad."

Thomas shook his head. "He didn't say. He was very worried, though... In any event," Thomas turned to Sarah, "Sarah, your ma' has told me that you mustn't go round. She doesn't want you catching anything – because of the children. Either she or I will come round and let you know what happens."

Finally, Sarah managed to speak again. "How is ma'? I just said Hannah would be fine when she first told me… Was the fever the start of it?"

"It was," replied Thomas. "That was the chill, which she couldn't shift. Then the dysentery started, about a week later. That was it."

Robert sat down in front of Sarah and held her hand. "Sarah, once this has got hold there's no telling… Dinnae blame yourself… You could never have known this was coming."

Thomas could see that Sarah was blaming herself. She had told them not to worry. He said, "Robert's right, Sarah… This isn't your fault… I'd best be going… I need to get back to your ma'… She needs me just now."

"For sure she does," said Robert. "Go home, man… I'll look after Sarah, you look after Mary and Hannah."

Thomas stood up and went over to Sarah. He stroked her hair. "We'll get through this," he said, turning to leave. Robert opened the door and let him out. He walked slowly away and Robert shut the door. He turned to look at Sarah. There were tears streaming down her face. She began to sob.

For 2 weeks Hannah was gravely ill. Every other day Thomas came and told them there was no change. Finally, on 12 October, both Thomas and Mary came to call. Robert opened the door and let them in. Mary looked devastated and sat down in the first chair she could reach. She began to sob uncontrollably. Thomas went over to Sarah and held her as she realised what had happened. "No!!!" She screamed. "Please don't tell me… No! It can't be…"

"I'm so sorry, lass," said Thomas. "When it was clear the treatments weren't working we knew it was always going to end like this… The doctor's been with us for the last 2 hours. By the end she was fitting most of the time and she was in so much pain… This is what the doctor said she died of – he gave us the death certificate." He held the certificate out to her so she took it and read what the doctor had written. "Dysentery and remittent fever."

Sarah began to cry, silently, but the tears were rolling down her cheeks. "It's just not fair! She was just beginning to enjoy her life… She'd found a man who loved her as she was… Why did this have to happen?"

The tears affected Thomas, and his eyes began to water, too. "At least she did have John for a few months… At least she did get to know love… She was going to get married – for her a fairytale come true. John made her life so rich, so full of joy… Don't think this was all wrong… Remember her as she was… A happy, innocent young woman, in love for the very first time."

Struggling to stay composed, Sarah replied, "Oh, da', I know… But why did this happen to her? Of all people."

"Oh, ma'," Sarah went over to her mother, knelt down and hugged her. Sarah tried to remain strong, as she continued talking to Mary. "She's over it now… We have to be strong – for the others – the children… They all loved her… She was almost one of them… They're going to miss her."

Mary began to calm down and she started to regain her composure. "It was seeing her lying there," she said. "So still, so quiet… She was always so full of excitement… It seemed so strange… It wasn't my Hannah."

Robert walked over to Sarah and held her. "I feel for you, I really do," he began. "I understand sae well what it feels like tae lose one you love. I felt like my heart had been ripped out when Agnes died. I thought I couldnae go on. I just wanted tae be with her. It's so empty after their life is gone. You still expect tae see them walk through the door as if they'd just gone for a walk…

"But it does get better. It's bad enough losing a parent; it's much worse losing your first love; I felt inconsolable when the bairn died, and she was only 4 weeks old… Dear, sweet Hannah was 35. The love she's given has been overwhelming… She will be badly missed… I've only known her for nine years but she's been more of a sister tae me than my own sisters. I've no idea where they are… I suddenly feel I ought tae have taken more interest in my own kin."

Sarah listened, enthralled. She had never heard her husband talk with such emotion. "Oh, Robert," she said, "that's beautiful."

Hannah was buried two days later, 14 October. The service was held in St. Mary's Church and then Hannah's body was taken to the municipal cemetery next to Bidston Hill. The Curate, Reverend William Handcock performed the service in the church and went with the family to perform the rites in the cemetery. The family chose 'Amazing Grace' and 'The Day Thou Gavest' for the hymns. It was a cold day, with heavy rain. It seemed as though the weather was trying to hide everybody's tears. The whole family was there. Robert and Jane had come back from Wales with their children. Even Agnes, William, Mary and Jane had been given a dispensation by their employers to attend. Most upset, though, was the man who Hannah had been due to marry in a few weeks' time. He was heartbroken. The service was performed and the family returned to the Foulkes home for the wake. Agnes and William stayed for a toast to Hannah and then they both had to leave to go back to their positions.

There was ale for the menfolk, tea for the women and lemonade for the children. The men were sitting at one end of the room (Thomas and Robert Foulkes, Robert McWilliam and John Corless); the women were sitting at the other (Mary Foulkes, her daughters Mary, Jane and Sarah, with her baby, Jane, and her daughter-in-law Jane Foulkes). The children (Mary and John McWilliam, William, Sarah and Mariah Foulkes) sat in the centre of the room, talking for a while before they disappeared out of the room to go to play elsewhere in the house.

The men were gathered together at the window; Thomas was sitting while the younger men were standing.

Thomas tried to make conversation. "So how's it going, down at the docks?" He asked his son-in-law Robert.

"It's hard graft," Robert McWilliam replied, but the work's coming on fine."

"Are you involved in the new bridge to Seacombe?" Thomas asked him.

"Aye – well, our part in it's mostly finished. We were sinking the bases for the bridge tae stand on. It's tae be like a drawbridge, when it's done."

John was interested in this construction. "When do you think it'll be finished?" He asked.

"There's at least another couple of months yet afore the south side is finished. The north side – Seacombe end – is barely started," replied Robert.

"It'll make travelling from New Brighton easier when it's done. The journey time will be almost halved, I should imagine. John stopped, realising the futility of what he was saying. "Not that I'll have reason to come, now," he added, dejectedly.

Thomas looked at John. "Now, John... Enough of that... Hannah wouldn't want to hear you talking like that. She loved you so much... You gave her so much – even if it was only a few months... You'll always be welcome here."

"But it's the memories," John continued.

"I understand how hard it must be for you, being here," said Robert Foulkes, "but I've never known her so alive as she was these last few months... Doesn't seem possible..." He broke off, almost unable to contain his grief.

Meanwhile, at the other end of the room, the women were sitting and talking. Mrs. Jane Foulkes was the centre of attention. Mary, senior, asked the question that everybody was thinking.

"So when's the baby due, Jane? I wasn't expecting to see you looking like that when you came back!"

"I'm only about three months," Jane replied, coyly. "It should be due about May time by my reckoning."

"You're going to need more room, now," said Sarah. "You'll be needing a place of your own very soon!"

"When we've sorted out Hannah's room you can spread out," added Mary, a tear running down the side of her face. "You and Robert have her room with the baby, then the other children can have their own room."

"I wasn't saying it so you'd suggest that," Jane replied, embarrassed.

"I never thought you were!" Mary replied. "But it makes sense…"

Sarah tried to change the subject, and she turned to her sisters. "So how's life below-stairs? Any gossip?"

Young Mary was the first to answer. "We get on well enough. There's only two of us working for the family. He works at the bank as a book-keeper, so, no – there's no gossip!"

"There's three of us, where I am," answered Jane. "Mind, it's a well-to-do family… There's talk of them moving abroad soon."

"Abroad where?" Mary asked.

"Well," Jane began, "the husband spends quite a lot of time in America, so they were thinking of going over there."

"Will you go with them if they do?" Sarah asked her.

"If they ask me, I'd say yes in a moment!" Jane replied.

Finally, the wake was over and everybody returned to their homes. Mary and Jane to their employers and Robert and Sarah to Back Beckwith Street. They were all very subdued. The children had finally gone to bed, after such an emotional day, and Robert and Sarah are having a discussion before going to bed themselves.

"Well, Sarah," Robert began, "she had a good funeral. Still doesn't seem possible, though."

"She's not in pain any more," Sarah added.

"Aye… But life must go on," Robert said. "It's Agnes' birthday tomorrow."

Sarah nodded. "Not the best of birthday presents. Do you know when she moves in at the Bull?"

"Aye," he said. "She told me today at the funeral… She moves in at the weekend. The place will seem almost empty without her."

Sarah sighed. "I shall miss her evening reports of the daily goings on at the Bull."

"I know, hinny, but life goes on."

CHAPTER 5

A Day out

"Ma'," said Nathaniel, bringing Sarah back to the present day, "I never knew you were such a good story-teller... This is the best birthday present, ever!"

Sarah sat there, smiling, watching the children. "So I'm guessing you want tae hear what else happened tae us and the rest of the family."

"Yes, ma'... Please do," pleaded Nathaniel.

"Well," said Sarah, "you'll have tae wait. I need to make myself a cup of tea tae wet my whistle. It's hard work, story-telling!"

"We can wait, can't we, boys?" Nathaniel said to his nephews.

"Aye! That we can!" Both Walter and Alexander replied. Finally, Alexander had started to listen to his granny's story. He had stopped playing and was just sitting there, propped up against his uncle.

Sarah stood up and stretched. She had been sitting in the chair a good while, now, and she was feeling a little stiff. She walked over to the stove and put some water on to boil. As she waited she looked out of the window. It was a beautiful day outside, too good for the boys to be inside, but they wanted to hear the story. Sarah sat back down to wait for the water to boil. She continued.

"The next couple o' years were very ordinary. Well, they opened the big new park in Birkenhead, near where we lived, in 1847 – that was a mighty fine place, though...

"Robert and Jane had another daughter in May 1847. They called her Jane. Funny things, names," Sarah stopped and chuckled to herself. "I never realised until now how confusing it can be wi' names – especially when you name children after family members! By now we had 3 Marys, 4 Janes, 2 Sarahs, 2 Williams and 2 Roberts. There'd have been 2 Johns if my big brother hadn't been away in the merchant navy!

"Any way, Jane's baby, Jane, was a bonny wee thing, too. They finally found a place o' their own tae live – 2 Morpeth Buildings – one o' the new tenements built for the dock workers. They were a lot like our flat, but they weren't well liked because o' their style – two flats on each floor, four floors in total – still, a home's a home…

"By 1849 there were lots of Irish in Birkenhead. That's when the potato famine was at its worst. It was a terrible time for the Irish. Where we lived half the families were Irish – and Back Beckwith Street was only half full!"

Sarah heard the water beginning to boil. "Right," she said, "water's boiling, so I'm making my tea. She got up again and went over to the stove, took the pot off the top, got herself a clean cup, and made her tea. She then went back to the boys and sat down. She looked at little Alexander. He was falling asleep.

"Nat, lay Alex down afore he falls down," Sarah said. Nathaniel did so and Sarah continued her story.

The afternoon of Sunday, 4 February 1849 was cold, the temperature not rising much above 47° Fahrenheit and the afternoon was rainy. Robert, Sarah and the children were visiting Sarah's brother Robert and sister-in-law Jane. Their flat was laid out in a similar fashion to Robert and Sarah's home, with the same amenities except that whereas there was only one flat on each floor where Robert and Sarah lived, here there were two, which mirrored each other. Robert and Jane had the smaller of the two bedrooms so that their children could all fit into one. Their furniture was sparse – they were just starting out at buying things for their first home, although both Thomas and Mary and the Salisbury family had helped them out.

By now, Sarah was about 5 months pregnant, as was Jane. All the younger children were there, the Foulkes children: William 12, Sarah 8, Mariah 5 and Jane 18 months; and the McWilliam children: Mary 10, John 8 and Jane 3. The two mothers were sitting drinking tea whilst the children were playing together, albeit the boys were in one group and the girls in another. Both husbands had gone out to the local public house for a drink.

Jane was so pleased to see Sarah. As soon as the children were out of earshot she began to talk excitedly. "There was such a commotion last night," she started.

"Do tell," said Sarah.

"Well," said Jane, "we'd been in bed some time, but what with this being on the ground floor, we hear every noise outside... It must have been about midnight when there was this terrible commotion... So loud, it woke us up. Well, I looked out the window and such a sight there was out there." She paused.

Sarah urged her to continue. "What did you see?"

"It was one of our neighbours," Jane continued. "She's been acting a bit strange for some time now... Well, last night she was out again – and completely in a state of undress!"

"What? Nothing?" Sarah asked in amazement.

"Not a stitch!" Jane replied. "And the local police were out – they had to arrest her!"

"Oh, my!" Sarah said, putting her hand to her mouth. "So where is she now?"

"Well, I have heard tell," continued Jane, "that she tried to burn herself while at the police station, so she was taken to hospital, where she currently is... Apparently all she was heard to say was that she wished to 'be regenerated by being baptised in the waters of Birkenhead'."

The two women laughed at the thought.

"Well," said Sarah, "you'll have to keep me informed if you hear any more! I expect it will appear in the newspaper."

At that moment the door to the flat opened and in walked the two Roberts. The two women almost blushed. Robert looked at Jane and he could tell from her appearance they had been discussing the events from the night before.

"I imagine Jane has been telling you about the occurrence last night," he said to Sarah.

"Indeed she has," Sarah replied. "I expect the whole block is talking about it!"

"It was certainly on everybody's lips at the inn!" Robert McWilliam replied.

"That poor woman," Jane added.

Robert McWilliam looked at the sky. It was clear there was more rain on the way. He turned to his wife. "Well, Sarah, we should be going home now. Get the children ready – it's going to start raining again soon. If we're lucky, we can get home before it starts."

"Yes Robert," Sarah replied. She went off in search of the children. They weren't far away, and it wasn't long before they all had their raincoats on, ready to go. The McWilliams said their goodbyes and walked the short distance back to their own home. Not a moment too soon, either, for they had not long got in through the downstairs door than the heavens opened again.

"Just in time," said Sarah, relieved.

The story did make the headlines. It was in the Liverpool Mercury that Tuesday. Robert was reading it after his evening meal. Sarah had cleared away and was sitting opposite him.

"That woman died," said Robert. "It says here in the newspaper…"

"What woman?" Sarah interrupted.

"You know – The one Robert and Jane were telling us about… The whole tale's here."

Sarah began to nod. "Oh, yes. Read it to me."

Robert began to read. "It says here: Death under singular circumstances. A woman named Ellen Griffiths, died on Thursday last, at Morpeth-buildings, in consequence of willfully burning her arm on the 3rd of February last. The deceased, who was the subject of religious melancholy, and had become much reduced in circumstances, got up at midnight and ran into the street almost in a state of nudity. She was taken tae the police station, where she accounted for her presence in the street at so unreasonable an hour by saying that she wished tae be regenerated by being baptized in the waters of Birkenhead. She subsequently thrust her hand into the fire, saying that she was desirous tae suffer, seeing that our Saviour had suffered. In consequence of the injury she sustained tae her arm, the limb was amputated on Sunday week, but the deceased only survived the operation a few days."

"That pour soul," said Sarah. "Whatever must have come over her, to take off so?" She shook her head. "I am so thankful we are happy here… We have enough to live on, a roof over our heads, and each other for company."

"Aye, that we do," replied Robert.

Sarah and Robert continued happily for the next few months. Work was good, Sarah's pregnancy progressed normally, and the rest of the family were all well.

On Tuesday 15 May 1849, during the afternoon, Sarah went into labour. This was her fourth child, and Sarah knew that her labour would be quick. She had arranged for a midwife to come round, so as soon as contractions started she went to see Sarah Beech, with her children. Sarah had said she would look after them for her in the event something should happen while Robert was at work. Immediately, Sarah Beech sent her daughter Anne to fetch the midwife. There was one who lived not far away, so she came very promptly, and immediately sent Sarah to bed. Robert had come home after work to the sound of his wife giving birth.

In a very short while after he got home the baby was born. The midwife opened the bedroom door and let Robert enter. "You've a healthy girl, Mr. McWilliam," she said. Your wife's doing just fine. I'll be taking my leave of you both, now."

"Thank you." Sarah called out to her.

The midwife picked up her bag and went out of the room. Robert followed her, briefly, to let her out of the flat. He then returned to be with Sarah and the baby. He walked up to Sarah, lying in their bed and looked down at both of them. "So, it's another girl, then," he said, smiling.

"We seem to be building up a family of girls, that's for sure!" Sarah replied. "John must be feeling outnumbered!"

"Dinnae worry, hinny," said Robert. "I love every last one o' them." He picked up the baby. "It was quick, this time."

"It always seems to get quicker, the more you have," replied Sarah, "but never easier!" Suddenly Sarah remembered the children. "Robert, you should go up to the Beech's and get the children. Sarah will want to know what I've had, any way!"

"Right," said Robert. "You take the bairn, then, and I'll be off upstairs." He passed the baby back to Sarah and went to get the children.

When he came back with the children Mary and John both wanted to see their new sister. Little Jane had fallen asleep and Robert had laid her in her cot.

"What's her name?" Mary asked.

Sarah looked at Robert. "We're goin' tae call her after your mother," he said. "Sarah."

The children clamoured round their mother and the new baby.

Two weeks later, Jane Foulkes went into labour. This, too, was her fourth child, and the same midwife attended her. Jane's sister Margaret was visiting at the time, so she looked after the children while the midwife was there. Her baby, Mary, was born on 31 May 1849.

Next month, Thomas and Mary decided to invite their children to Sunday tea. 24 June 1849 was a fine and sunny day. It was passably warm. The house seemed really big for Thomas and Mary, now it was just the two of them. Thomas and Mary had taken back the upstairs front room and made it their bedroom, so downstairs their old bedroom became their living room and they turned the front room into a parlour.

The women were sitting in the parlour, talking. The children were playing on the floor, whilst the men were getting ready to go to the inn. They were waiting for Thomas, who was upstairs.

"The house seems so big, now," said Sarah.

Mary replied, "Well, we decided to move our bedroom back upstairs, so it made sense to put the dining tables in the other room. But this house is too big for us."

"Meaning what?" Jane asked.

"Well," began Mary, slowly, "we're thinking of moving back to Tranmere... To somewhere smaller."

Thomas came downstairs, finally ready, so they headed for the front door. "We're just off, ladies," said Thomas. "See you in a while." He looked at his daughters' faces and knew Mary had spoken.

"You've told them, haven't you?" he asked. Mary looked over and nodded.

Sarah continued, "But we're all so close here... Don't move!" She looked at her father. "Whose idea was this?"

"It was your ma' decided," replied Thomas. "But she's right. This place is far too big."

"Well," replied Mary, "it won't be for a while, anyway... Now let me see these babies."

Thomas and the others left the house, and the women talking about babies. Sarah passed her baby to her mother. Mary looked down at her tiny face.

"Sarah is a bonny baby, that's for sure," she said. "And big."

"That she is," replied Sarah. "She's 5 weeks old now and doing well."

Jane countered, in an effort not to be outdone, "My Mary is 3 weeks now. Strange how we had our babies so close together."

"Well," said Mary, after a pause, "these two make eleven grandchildren, including Agnes and your two Williams."

As Mary cradled Sarah in her arms, she spoke to her daughter. "So, is your Robert still alright for work?"

"Well, the work at the docks are getting less and less," Sarah replied, "so he's having to look further afield, now. It's dangerous, but they're building a new railway tunnel under Liverpool. They need some more masons for putting the stonework up when the blasting's been done, and he's working there."

Mary looked concerned. "Are you not worried in case it collapses?" She asked.

"Of course, ma'," said Sarah, "but it's work... And it's not like they don't know what they're doing – it's the third tunnel under Liverpool."

Sarah turned to her sister-in-law. "How's your Robert doing with work?"

"He's managing," Jane replied. "He works for a firm of stonemasons, now, so he goes where they send him. It means he has more chance of regular work."

"Who's he working for?" Sarah asked, with interest.

"Alexander Heron," answered Jane. "They're in Brook Street."

"Do they have any more places?" Sarah asked.

"I don't know," replied Jane. "You should ask Robert when they get back."

Mary stood up. "Here you are, Sarah," she said, handing baby Sarah back to her. She turned to Jane. "Let me see my new namesake."

Jane passed her baby to Mary so she could hold her. Mary looked lovingly down at her, too.

"Oh, they're both so beautiful," she cooed.

A while later the men returned and the family all sat down to tea. Sarah asked her brother about work at the stonemasons, but he told her there were no more vacancies. He also said that he would have spoken with Robert if there had been any.

After tea the families went back home. The two families walked together to Morpeth Buildings where they said their goodbyes. Robert, Jane and their family went indoors, and Robert and Sarah, with their brood, continued on the way to Back Beckwith Street.

The summer came and went, and life in Birkenhead carried on much the same. The work in Liverpool, on the tunnel, carried on apace and both masons were busy with work. Autumn was fast approaching, and this particular Sunday afternoon, 16 September 1849, Robert and Sarah were relaxing at home. The rain had just stopped. Robert had been watching out the window to see if the weather would let up, when there was a knock at the door. Robert turned and went to answer it.

He opened the door and was pleasantly surprised to see his sister-in-law there.

"Why, Mary! How wonderful to see you. Come in," he said.

Sarah stood up. 'What was Mary doing here?' she wondered. She went to the door to greet Mary as she entered. She stopped still when she saw her come in with a young man.

"What a lovely surprise!" Sarah remarked. "And who is this?" She looked at the handsome young man beside Mary. He was much taller than Mary – by about six inches. You could tell he worked outdoors – he had a tanned skin. His hair was dark brown and he had a moustache. They made a lovely couple. Mary and her young man took their coats off and Robert hung them up on the hooks just inside the door.

"Sarah, Robert," said Mary, "this is Henry Wilson. We're walking out together."

"Pleased to meet you," Sarah replied. She looked at Mary. "How long has this been going on, then?" she asked, grinning. Robert shook Henry's hand.

Mary gave Sarah a coy smile, and then she turned Henry around and introduced him to her nieces and nephew. They took one look at their aunt and came over to her together, and Mary hugged each one in turn.

"Calm down," Sarah called out. "you've plenty of time to talk to Auntie Mary. Mary, Henry, sit down. I must hear all your news!"

Robert pulled up two more chairs and everybody sat down.

"You missed the rain, then," Robert began.

"We came on the Horse Bus," Mary replied, "so we didn't get wet. Have you travelled on them?"

Sarah looked interested. "No," she said, "we walk everywhere. There are too many of us to take it!" Sarah looked at Henry. "So, Henry, tell us about yourself."

"Well, there's not much to tell," Henry replied. "I'm local and 25 years old."

Mary looked at Henry, annoyed. "Oh, Henry, you don't do yourself justice!" She turned to Robert and Sarah. "He's got a 4-year old son – his wife died having him."

Robert looked sad. "I've been there," he said. He shook his head, as he remembered his Agnes.

159

Sarah noticed his pain and brushed her hand against his knee. She turned to Henry.

"Oh, that must have been hard for you," she said, "having to bring him up on your own... You can't have been married long."

"We'd been married a year when John was born," replied Henry. "He's living with my parents now."

"So what do you do for a living?" Robert asked.

"I'm a carter," said Henry. "I work for Robert Hogan, the auctioneers. It's not a bad job – pretty steady work."

"I imagine you must be kept pretty busy," added Robert. Henry nodded.

Sarah turned to Mary, eagerly. "How did you meet?"

"Well," Mary began, slowly.

"I was making a delivery to the house," interjected Henry. "The family had bought some furniture at auction – and I met Mary when she let me in."

Mary gathered herself and continued. "We got on well that day, and he came back after work to see if I'd like to walk out that evening, and I had the evening off, so I did. We've been together two weeks."

"Oh Mary," said Sarah, smiling. "I'm so pleased for you... Have you been to see ma' and da'?"

Mary shook her head. "We're going from here to see them," she said, "then Henry's taking me back home."

"Would you like to have some tea?" Sarah asked. "I'm sure the children want to talk to you. You can have some time with them, while I make it."

Mary nodded. "I'd like that," she said.

Sarah got up and went out to the kitchen. Henry and Robert began talking together and Mary sat on the floor with her nieces and nephew. They tried to talk to her at the same time, but Mary made them slow down. Sarah stood in the doorway, watching as she waited for the kettle to boil. She smiled. Life certainly carried on. They may have lost Hannah just before she was due to marry, but Mary was taking on a new man. Hopefully, a wedding would soon follow. The family certainly needed something to look forward to after all the heartache they had recently suffered.

Sarah went back to the kettle as it began to steam. She turned it off and made tea for everybody. She took it into the living room and they all drank and chatted. Finally, Mary said it was time they should be going. They were going to call on Robert and Jane first, and then go to see Thomas and Mary afterwards. Robert fetched them their coats, which they put on. Sarah gave Mary a hug and told them both to come again soon. Robert then opened the door and they walked out. Robert closed the door and went back to Sarah.

"Well," he said, "that was a pleasant surprise. They looked very happy together."

"Do you think they'll get married?" Sarah asked.

"Gie them a chance!" He exclaimed, "they've only been together a couple o' weeks!"

The rain had stopped for the duration of Mary and Henry's walk to her brother Robert's home. When they arrived there Robert and Jane were overjoyed to see them. Their children also wanted to play with Mary. Mary, once again, introduced everybody to Henry. Jane asked if they wanted a cup of tea but they declined. Once they had finished their short chat with Robert and Jane, they left to walk to Thomas and Mary's home. They made it just in time, too. As they knocked at the door the heavens opened.

Here, again, they were met with a smile. Thomas and Mary were just preparing their tea, so Mary asked her daughter and Henry if they wanted to join them. They said they would love to eat with them, so two extra places were set at the table. Over the meal they talked about many things. Mary was eager to know more about her daughter's suitor, and Thomas talked with Henry about work. Eventually, Mary announced that they would have to leave for home. They said their goodbyes and set off.

The next few weeks all talk was about Mary and her new beau. All the women wanted her to be happy and wondered when Henry would ask for her hand. The husbands were getting used to not being the topic of conversation for a few weeks, at least.

Back at the McWilliam home, Monday, 15 October, all was quiet. It was the early hours of the morning when little Sarah woke up with a start. Her screams pierced the quiet night. Her mother got out of bed to comfort her, and she looked out of the window as she walked round the room, trying to quieten the screams.

What a beautiful sight met Sarah as she peered out through the window. Way off in the distant sky she could see the Northern Lights. She had seen them before, of course, but she loved watching the lights dance across the night sky. She would ask, in the morning, if her neighbours had seen them.

Next morning she got the children up ready for school as usual. It hadn't taken long to get Sarah back to sleep, so nobody else had been disturbed. Robert had already left for work by the time Sarah and the children were up. It wasn't long before everybody was ready for school, so the family left to meet their neighbours.

Both Mary Millward and Sarah Beech were just leaving for school, with their families. All the families were much larger now. John Millward was in his last term at school, before he was to be apprenticed, but for now, he was a great help to his mother as she had three under 9 plus an infant (Ann, aged 8, Mary, aged 6, Charles, aged 2 and infant, James, aged 9 months). Ann Beech was working as a domestic servant now, but she didn't live in with the family as Agnes did. She worked in one of the big houses on the way to school, so she often helped her mother with her brood. There were three under 8 plus a toddler and an infant (Sarah, aged 7, Joseph, aged 5, Emma, aged 2½, John, aged 21 months and a new baby, Arne, aged 2 months).

The families were dressed for the colder weather for this time of year. It was a dry morning, but there were plenty of clouds in the sky. Mary Millward was the first to speak.

"Morning, Sarah… Everything alright?" she asked.

The children organised themselves into groups, as they did every morning. They had all built up great friendships amongst them. It was a pleasure to see.

"We're fine," replied Sarah. "Did you see the sky before dawn?"

"Now, why would I be up before dawn?" Mary answered, with a smile. "Did Sarah wake you?"

"She did, and I'm glad she did," replied Sarah. "The Northern Lights were in the sky! They were beautiful."

"I saw them!" Sarah Beech added. "Little Arne would not go to sleep last night!"

"Have you not seen them before?" Mary asked them both.

"I have," replied Sarah McWilliam, "but they never fail to delight me. It's the way they dance across the sky."

"It was the first time I'd ever seen them!" Sarah Beech said. She was taking in all the new faces as they walked along Back Beckwith Street. "I can't believe how many Irish are living here now... They're bringing all their harsh ways with them. Do you think they'll ever go back?"

Mary Millward shook her head. "Would you go back? They're living the life of Reilly over here... There's enough labouring jobs to go round. I don't blame them for coming over. "

"It's been three years, now, the potatoes have failed," Sarah McWilliam commented. "Surely, they must get a crop next year?"

"Who knows," answered Mary Millward. They turned the corner into Victoria Street and continued the journey to school. Ann Beech arrived at her place of work, so she said her good-byes to everybody and went indoors. The conversation continued about trivial things all the way to school.

By November Thomas and Mary Foulkes had found a little cottage back in Tranmere. Sunday, 11 November they invited all the family round to tea. The house had hardly been so full for months!

Robert and Sarah McWIlliam were there with their children, Mary, John, Jane and baby Sarah. Robert and Jane Foulkes were there with their children, William, Sarah, Mariah and baby Jane. Mary was there with Henry Wilson. Jane and John were missing from the group. Jane had gone abroad with her family, but John hadn't been heard of for years. The adults were laughing and talking, while the children found space to play.

Thomas began to speak. "Your ma' and me have finalised our decision. We've had enough of the big town now, and this house is far too big for us to keep on. So we're having this little get-together to tell you all about it."

Sarah turned to her husband. "I knew this was coming," she whispered.

Mary continued. "Well, it's not so hard to get to Tranmere now. There's the railway and there's the Horse Buses. So we can still keep in touch. There's a lovely little cottage, near where we used to live, up for rent after Christmas, so we asked for first refusal on it. We've just had word that it's ours."

"So are you going back on the Tranmere Ferry?" Robert McWilliam asked.

"I'm not going back on any ferry, Robert," Thomas replied. "I've had enough of all the to-in and fro-ing. All the idiots who try to jump on and off the ferry when it's set sail... I just want a peaceful life!"

"Has something else happened on the ferry, da'?" Sarah asked her father.

"Did you not see it in the Mercury in the week?" Thomas asked. The families all shook their heads.

"I was on the late ferry last Sunday," began Thomas, "and this chap arrived just as we were setting sail. We'd cleared the mooring – just. Well, he does no more, but he tries to jump the gap! I mean, nobody in their right mind would do that! Well, them on shore grabbed him out of the water and took him to the doctor, but he didn't make it. Crushed between the steamer and slip, he was!"

Young Mary whispered to Henry as Thomas was talking. Henry looked at Mary and she gave him a nudge. Henry walked over to Thomas. "Beg pardon, Mr. Foulkes, but could I have a word?"

Everybody turned to look at Henry as he spoke. Thomas answered, "Yes, Henry?"

"Well," continued Henry, nervously, "I was wondering if you'd oblige me... by giving your permission... to marry Mary."

Thomas stood quietly for a moment, looking at everybody. He knew what he was going to say, and had been waiting for Henry to ask. Finally, he spoke.

"Henry, my lad... of course you can marry her – if it's what she wants!" He looked at Mary. "Well?"

"Oh, yes, da'... I do so want to marry Henry!" Mary shouted, with joy.

"Then I think congratulations are in order!" Thomas concluded. Everybody cheered and, one by one, they went over to Mary and Henry. The men shook his hand and the women gave Mary a hug.

"If you'll excuse me," said Henry, finally, "there's something I need to do. He reached his hand into his coat inside pocket and fetched out a box. He got down on one knee in front of Mary and opened the box.

"Mary," he began, "will you do me the honour of becoming my wife?"

"Yes, Henry," Mary replied, with a tear in her eye, "I will."

Henry put the ring on her finger. Then he stood up and he kissed her.

Henry and Mary were in no rush to get married. Henry was adamant that they should have somewhere to live first, and Mary wanted her wedding to be perfect. So a date was set for mid-April.

Meanwhile, Thomas and Mary were organising their removal back to Tranmere. They wanted to be back in the village for the New Year, so they had a lot of things to sort out, and furniture to downsize. They had hoped that Mary and Henry would marry sooner, so they could have given their furniture directly to the couple, but as that wasn't going to happen, Mary had asked that they hold onto the things for just a while.

Thomas and Mary moved mid-January, as it turned out. By New Year had been rather more difficult to achieve than they had hoped. They had to avoid the snow that had fallen. The ground was hard, but not snowed over on the day they moved. They took everything with them and managed to store the surplus furniture around the cottage, until such time that Henry and Mary could get a place of their own to live.

By late March Henry had found a property to rent. He moved in and all the furniture was brought over so that everything was in place ready for the day that Mary would move in.

Mary stayed with the family she worked for until two days before her wedding and then she said her good byes. She had saved hard over the last few weeks, and had managed to make herself a lovely dress. For the last two days she stayed with her brother, Robert.

Finally, the day of the wedding arrived. Sunday, 21 April 1850. Thomas and Mary came to Morpeth Buildings on the morning of the wedding. Thomas was to give Mary away and she had two bridesmaids, Mary McWilliam and Sarah Foulkes. Robert and Sarah arrived with Mary and their other children late morning. They didn't want to overcrowd the flat, but there was really no easy way to avoid it.

The two bridesmaids were ready and very excited. They wore dresses in pink, full length satin. The bodice had a "V" neckline, also edged with a layer of lace. The sleeves were elbow length, and they were very full and gathered at the bottom. Mary and Sarah were soon dressed and it was all that Sarah McWilliam could do to keep them still. Sarah and her mother put pink flowers in the girls' hair. They looked a picture.

Jane helped Mary get dressed. Her dress was beautiful. It was in white satin, since Queen Victoria had started the fashion. It had a waist set at the front a couple of inches below, coming down to a slight "V" shape at the front. The skirt had two layers, the top one scolloped with bows and about 8 inches shorter than the skirt underneath (at the scollop's lowest point). Each layer had a lace frill, as did the join at the waist. The bodice was covered in a layer of lace and had a "V" neckline, also edged with a layer of lace. At the centre front, at the bottom of the "V" was a matching bow. The sleeves were elbow length, and they were very full, gathered at the bottom with another edging of lace and a bow at the side. Mary wore a simple veil with a ring of flowers holding it in place.

When she came into the living room Thomas and Mary were speechless.

After a moment Thomas said, "Well, my girl, you look amazing!"

Mary couldn't believe her daughter had made this dress herself. "I see now, why you wanted to wait to get married," she said. "And you made this all by yourself?"

"Well," replied Mary, coyly, "I did have some help from the mistress."

"Your Henry will be as stunned as I am," said Thomas.

Jane said, "I will leave you and da' with my Robert. I shall go with Robert and Sarah to the church. Come along, children." She took her remaining children and disappeared with Robert, Sarah and their remaining children.

Henry had hired a horse and carriage to take Mary, her father and the bridesmaids to church. Mary's mother was the children's chaperone, so she went with them in the carriage.

Robert Foulkes waited with Mary and her entourage until it was time for them to leave so he could lock up, and then he jumped up with the carriage driver and they set off for church.

It was a fine and sunny day but there was still a chill in the air. All the families had gathered at St. Mary's church for the service. The Foulkes families were gathered in force, still growing, but also, this time there was a large party of Wilsons. Besides Thomas Foulkes and his family, his two brothers came with their growing families.

William Foulkes, now 58 years old, and his wife Ann, now 49 years old, brought their son John, now 19 years old and his girlfriend Mary Maginnis, aged 20 years old, who had moved over from Dublin, Ireland. They also brought their daughters, Annie, now 15 years old, Mary, aged 10 years and Sarah, aged 8 years.

Robert Foulkes and his wife Mary, both now 55 years old, came with their son John, who was 27 years old and his wife Katherine, aged 22 years, moved over from Carlow, near Dublin, along with their son John aged 1 year. They also brought their other sons Edward, now 25 years old, Robert, now 19 years old, William, now 14 years old and Samuel aged 10 years.

Robert and Sarah McWilliam came with their whole family. Both Agnes and William were able to get away for the day.

Robert and Jane Foulkes also came with their whole family. Jane and John Foulkes were the only two of Thomas' children who didn't attend due to them being elsewhere.

William Wilson, aged 56 years and his wife Mary, aged 49 years brought their son William, aged 25 years and his wife Ann, aged 24 years, who was expecting, and daughter Elizabeth aged 1 year. They also brought their other sons John, aged 23 years, Thomas, aged 21 years, Joseph, aged 20 years, George, aged 19 years, James, aged 8 years, and their daughters Mary, aged 17 years, and Ann, aged 11 years.

Thomas Wilson, Henry's uncle, aged 54 years and his wife Elizabeth, aged 51 years were also there. They brought their daughter Jane, aged 17 years and son Thomas, aged 15 years.

All the families were waiting in the church for the bride to arrive. Henry was nervously waiting at the front with his brother John. The organ announced the arrival of the bride so everybody stood up. Henry turned to see Mary enter the church.

Thomas and Mary walked in, followed by the two brides-maids. Mary's mother had crept in as quietly as she could just before Mary made her entrance. The guests were all enthralled by the scene that met them. Thomas couldn't have been prouder.

Mary joined Henry waiting, with his best-man, at the altar and the curate, the Reverend William Handcock conducted the service. Everything went off beautifully. Mary's mother cried and the bridesmaids behaved themselves with decorum.

After the service everybody talked about how beautiful the dresses were. Then Robert Foulkes spoke to Henry.

"So, I understand you're moving in to Morpeth Buildings – at the other end from us."

"Yes," Henry replied. "We've got number 48. They're very well built and will do us well enough for the time being."

"When do you move in?" Robert asked.

"I've already spent the last few days there," said Henry, "getting everything sorted."

He took hold of Mary's hand. "Mary will be moving in with me today."

"I'm so excited!" Mary said. She was joined by her sister Sarah.

"I'm so glad you will be living close by," said Sarah.

"Yes," replied Mary, "we'll all be near each other."

Finally, it was time to leave the church grounds. All the families said their goodbyes and each went off to their own homes. The wedding was the talk of the family for weeks.

The next couple of months flew by. Mary and Henry were now settled. Mary had found it easy to adjust to married life. Henry had brought his son, John, to live with him and he was getting to know his step-mother. She was often at her sister's, but not so often as she was at her brother's.

But on this occasion, Saturday, 22 June 1850, she hatched a plan with her sister Sarah.

"Henry came home last evening and told me about this new garden that has been opened to the public," Mary began. "It's called Alton Towers. I think it would be a great place to visit."

"How did he find out about it?" Sarah asked.

"Somebody he was delivering to had been there and was saying what a lovely place it was," Mary explained.

"Sounds interesting. I suppose it's a bit like Birkenhead Park," added Sarah.

"So what do you think, Sarah?" Mary asked. "Would you and the children like to come out with us for the day?"

"Where is this place – Alton Towers?" Sarah replied.

"It's in the village of Alton, on the way to Uttoxeter," replied Mary. "The home of the Earl of Shrewsbury. He's made these ornamental gardens for people to go round."

"And how will we get there?" Sarah asked.

"By train," said Mary. "It will be great for us all to go out together. I shall invite Jane and her children if you come. It will be a sisters' day out. We'll all be taking children – I shall be bringing John, and it will be good for him to get to know everybody."

"Well," Sarah began, "It would be a good way for everybody to spend some time together. I must say, I've never travelled anywhere without Robert, so I'm not sure."

Mary looked disappointed and Sarah could tell she felt let down. Sarah thought about it some more. Finally, she said, "Alright, if Jane says she will come, then so shall I."

Mary's face transformed instantly and her eyes lit up. She stood up. "I shall go and ask her directly!" She said. "Don't worry about letting me out," she said. As the weather was warm she had no need of a coat, so she put her bonnet on and left to go and see Jane.

Jane was as unconvinced as her sister-in-law, but when she realised that Sarah had agreed to go she changed her mind. Mary was so happy. She rushed off home and began to plan the day out.

Robert, Sarah and their children took it in turn to visit Robert, Jane and their children on Sundays. 30 June was the turn of Robert and Sarah to go to Morpeth Buildings. As usual, they arrived straight after lunch. The two Roberts went out to the public house – Robert Foulkes had been eagerly awaiting Robert McWilliam's arrival. The children set straight to play. Young John was feeling left out, however. He was the only boy amongst the four girls, since William was out. He decided he would sit and read while the girls played.

Meanwhile, Jane and Sarah began to talk about their impending day out.

Jane started the conversation as soon as Sarah sat down. "I am so glad you said you would go to Alton Towers," she began. "If you had not said you would go then I'm certain I would never have agreed. But after thinking about it, I'm sure it will be lovely for the children. We never take them anywhere. They can spend time with each other and we can enjoy the beautiful gardens."

Sarah nodded. "Has Mary said anything more to you?" Sarah asked.

"She said she would come round this afternoon," Jane replied, "as she knows you come to visit this Sunday."

Almost on cue, there was a knock at the door and Jane got up to answer it. Sure enough, Mary and young John were standing there. Jane invited them in, "Hello, Mary," she said, "I was just telling Sarah you were going to call in today." Mary came and sat down. John sat beside his step-mother, rather shy. Jane looked at John. "Why not go and play with your cousins?" She asked. John just sat there, clinging to Mary.

John McWilliam realised he was no longer alone, but he could see how timid his namesake was. He came over and sat beside him. "What's your name?" he asked.

John Wilson sat there, shyly, trying to hide behind his step-mother.

"My name's John," continued John McWilliam. "What's your name?"

John Wilson looked surprised. "I'm John, too," he said, quietly.

"We both have the same name, then," John McWilliam continued, smiling. He realised he had broken the ice, but could see that the young boy was shy, so John left it at that.

Meanwhile, the women continued to chat about the day out Mary had suggested. "Yes," said Sarah, "we were just talking about this trip you want us to go on."

"You haven't changed your minds, have you?" Mary asked, uncomfortably.

"No," replied both Jane and Sarah together.

Mary showed her relief. She continued. "I was just coming to let you know the details. We will be going on Wednesday, 3rd July, from Lime Street on the quarter to 9 o'clock train to Uttoxeter. It stops at Alton Towers and the fare is 2 shillings 6 pence each for the adults, half price for the children."

"That's quite a lot of money," said Sarah. Jane nodded.

"But how often will we be going there?" Mary asked. "It it's not as if we shall be doing it every week."

"Well" said Jane, "put like that, I think we could manage it."

Sarah nodded, having thought about it.

By Wednesday morning everybody was excited about the trip. They all met at Jane's home, bright and early. They needed to leave for Liverpool by half past 7 o'clock. It was a glorious day, just the sort you need for a day out. With everybody gathered together, they set off.

The walk to the ferry didn't take as long as Sarah had expected it would, and they arrived at Lime Street station in good time.

They all stood outside the station and looked on in awe. This was the first time that any of them had seen it. The station was a vast construction, of stone, metal and glass.

"Come on," said Mary, "let's find the ticket office." She strode off, holding John's hand and the others followed on behind her. Mary went under the first main arch and looked around her.

Inside was just as big and daunting as the outside had been. There were people and carriages everywhere, but it was very smoky. There was one train in on a platform at one side, and empty platforms on the other. Mary located where the ticket office was and led everybody over to it.

She stood outside, waiting for everybody to catch her up. As they did so there was a horrendous noise coming from outside the station, and Sarah looked over in the direction the noise was coming from, near the empty platform next to them. As she did so there was a whistle and a squeal of brakes as a train came hurtling down the track. The train strained under the pressure of the brakesmen, trying to stop it. Finally, still travelling at speed, the lead carriage careered into the wall at the end of the platform. The carriages following on behind continued on into the back of the one in front. It was only the good construction of the carriages that stopped them from concertina-ing up entirely.

Horrified, Sarah asked, "Is that the train we are to travel on?"

Mary was almost in tears. "I don't know," she began. "I was going to ask at the window which platform we needed."

The smaller children had begun to cry and were clinging on to their mothers for dear life. John Wilson, Jane McWilliam, Mariah and Jane Foulkes would not let go of their mothers. It was all that the mothers could do to keep their older children in check. Mary McWilliam and Sarah Foulkes were fussing round the little ones attached to their mothers' skirts. John McWilliam and William Foulkes were desperate to get closer to see the scene of chaos unfolding before them.

Sarah McWilliam and Jane Foulkes stood there, each holding their toddlers and trying to stop the boys running off to get closer to the wreckage.

As they stood there, people staggered off the train, some injured slightly, others not at all. There were station staff rushing about helping with the injured.

"Please, ma'!" John McWilliam called out to his mother, "Please let me get closer to see what it is!"

Sarah struggled to hold him. "You can't go off there, John" Sarah replied. There's too many people milling about. You would only get in the way!"

"But ma'!" John continued.

William Foulkes was also straining to get closer. Jane's response was the same as Sarah's. Mary Wilson was the only one of the group who was able to stay calm.

"I'm not sure I want to travel on a train, now," said Jane Foulkes, upset at seeing so many people in distress.

"I don't think we'll be able to for a while," replied Mary Wilson. "Look how the carriages are bent."

"Those poor people," added Sarah McWilliam, "look, they are covered in blood!"

"They're having to carry some of them – look!" Jane screamed. "I don't want to stay here. Can we go home?"

Mary agreed. "I think it's best we do... We won't be travelling anywhere until they clear up and help all these poor people."

By now her step-son John had overcome his fear of the day and was trying to get closer like his cousins. Mary tried to pull him away. "Come on, John," she said.

"I want to see!" He shouted. Now all three boys were trying as hard as they might to propel their mothers towards the disaster.

Mary finally took control of the situation. "Come on, John," she called as she tried to pull him in the direction she wanted to go. "We have to leave... We have to let them save those people!"

Slowly, all three mothers managed to leave the station. It was such a relief when they got outside. Apart from the noise and distress that had occurred inside the building, once outside there was no smoke from the engines.

Once outside all the children began to regain their composure and the walk back to the ferry was uneventful. Once on the ferry they were soon across the river and back home again. They all trooped into Mary's home where the ladies had some tea. The children all played happily amongst themselves. The boys played train crashes, much to their mothers' annoyance, and the girls played with their dolls. At least one thing had been achieved that day – all the children were playing happily together.

Finally, it was time for the families to go their own respective ways. Sarah and her children to Back Beckwith Street and Jane and her children to the other end of Morpeth Buildings. They all said their goodbyes and left. Oh, what tales the women would tell their husbands, that evening!

So it was with much gusto that evening Sarah related the sad chain of events that curtailed their day out. The evening meal was over and Robert and Sarah were sitting in their favourite chairs.

"It was horrible, Robert," she said. "The train came in so fast... It was such a big bang – we wondered what on earth was happening!"

"Were there many injured?" Robert asked.

Sarah pondered for a few moments. "Considering how big the train was," she said, "I don't think so. We didn't stay to watch – the little ones were crying, so we left quickly. There were so many carriages – I counted more than twenty. That's not usual, is it?"

Robert looked surprised. "More than twenty?" He said in amazement. "That's about twice as many carriages as normal. There must have been hundreds on that train, then... No wonder it didnae stop at the buffers!"

Sarah reflected. "I don't think I ever want to travel on a train, now," she said.

Robert chuckled. "You'll be fine," he said. "They'll not lay on a train so big, again, I'm thinking!"

"Well, maybe. We shall see – only time will tell." She sighed. "I was actually looking forward to going out today. Oh well, never mind. Maybe we'll get to go on another day out – but I think it will have to be much closer to home. It was a good idea of Mary's, just a shame it didn't work out the way she planned. Mind, the children were all talking together about it for ages afterwards!"

That Friday, 5 July 1850, Robert came home with the newspaper. As he had expected, the train crash had made page six of the Liverpool Mercury. He waved the newspaper at Sarah. "It's all here in the paper!" He said. "Do you want me tae read it to you?"

Sarah nodded, so he began.

"On Wednesday an accident, by which upwards of thirty individuals were more or less injured, occurred at the station of the London and North-Western Company, Lime-street. It appears that at 6 o'clock in the morning an excursion train belonging tae the North Staffordshire Railway started from Uttoxeter, calling at Alton Towers, Leek, etcetera.

"This train consisted of 26 carriages, containing about 500 passengers. On reaching the Edge-hill station the engine was detached, and the train entered the tunnel incline in charge of two breaksmen. When about half way through the tunnel it became evident from its velocity, that those in charge had lost their control over it. The line was clear at the moment, and, without encountering any obstruction in its course, the train dashed with fearful violence against the station-wall.

"The concussion was terrific. The passengers were thrown against each other and the sides and roofs of the carriages: many of them were rendered insensible by the shock; but, on examination, it was found that although upwards of 30 or 40 persons were cut about the head and face, and severely contused in various parts of the body, no life was lost.

"One man, named Daniel Pride, about 30 years of age, sustained a concussion of the brain, and is suffering from congestion. The sufferers were removed tae the Queen's Arms Hotel, where medical assistance was obtained, and everything done which the nature of the circumstances demanded. Mr. and

Mrs. Curchod, the proprietors of the hotel, were unremitting in their attention.

"Pride, who received the most serious injury that occurred, was conveyed to the house of Mr. Callan, surgeon, Islington, almost immediately after the accident, where he received the most prompt attention. Yesterday he was so far recovered that he returned to the Queen's Arms, where he now remains.

"The accident evidently occurred from the non-acting of the breaks, the cause of which is said tae have been want of sufficient power tae regulate a train with so large a number of passengers."

Robert paused for a moment. "See, that's why the train didnae stop – it was too long!"

"Ahh," replied Sarah, now understanding. Robert continued.

"Mr. Henry Booth, one of the secretaries of the company, was at the station when the accident occurred, and rendered every assistance in his power; and the same observation will apply tae every servant of the company.

"In the evening the train returned tae Uttoxeter, carrying back most of the injured passengers. A large proportion of the sufferers were ladies, and several respectable women appeared with swollen and discoloured eyes. One woman, a Mrs. Armitt, of Leek, suffered so severely from the shock that she lost the use of her limbs, and had tae be lifted into the carriage."

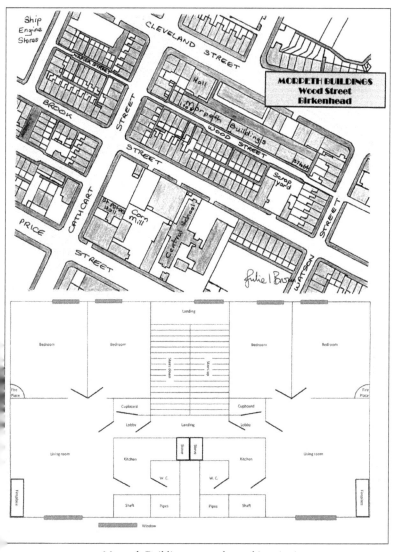

Morpeth Buildings street plan and interior inset

CHAPTER 6

A new start

Six months flew by and Robert McWilliam grew restless. The work wasn't so easy to come by locally, but he had heard there was a lot of work in Glasgow. After work on Wednesday, 22 January 1851 he was found arguing with Sarah. They were standing in the living room after the children had gone to bed. Sarah was trying to be quiet, but the more they spoke, the louder they got.

"I want tae go home to Scotland," he said. "There's plenty o' work in Glasgow, and there's less people in Scotland."

"But I thought you were happy?" Sarah asked.

"Dinnae get me wrong," he continued, "I love being here. If we'd no' come I'd never have met you, and you're the best thing that could have happened tae me next tae Agnes."

"Then why?" Sarah asked.

He gave her a wry smile. "I remember the days when you said you'd like tae visit my home."

"Yes," she replied, "visit. Not live there!"

"Scotland's a beautiful place tae live," he continued. The air's cleaner there. It's more open."

"What? Glasgow?" Sarah retorted. "It's a big town!"

"Aye, you're right, there," he conceded. "Well… What if I found somewhere not in Glasgow, but in easy reach of all the work?"

"Well," Sarah began, "that's a better idea – something I could probably come around to." She looked at him and could see he was visibly distressed. "I can see you've made your mind up."

He nodded. "Aye, I have."

"But does it have to be now?" Sarah asked. "Can't we wait for a while longer?"

"Why? What now?" Robert replied.

"I think I'm pregnant again," Sarah answered. "I don't want to go just yet, if I am. If you've made your mind up I know I'll not change it. But can we wait a few months?"

"Another bairn?" Robert couldn't believe it. He paused to look at her and smiled. "Well, I know you suffer in your first few months."

"I do." Sarah replied. "It'll also give me time to get used to the idea of moving away. It's a big thing, you know... All my family's here... I'll be in a strange country with nobody outside of these four walls that I know."

Robert smiled and nodded. "I know I'm asking a lot o' you. I realise that, now. I forget what a close family tie is. Mine never was." He moved next to Sarah and brushed his hand down her cheek. "I love you so much." Robert stood and looked at Sarah. She had been the perfect wife, done everything the way he'd wanted. Perhaps just this once, he could give in to her. He continued, "Fine. I'll wait till about March and then I'll make a start in earnest wi' sorting out a move back home. How does that sound?"

Sarah breathed a sigh of relief and nodded in agreement. "That'll do just grand." Sarah paused and looked at Robert. "It's not that I don't want to move – it's just that I wasn't expecting this." She looked down at her hand and caressed her wedding band. Then she looked back at Robert and continued, "I know you miss your home. But I love you... I will come round to the idea – now you've planted the seed."

She began to calm down. This was all she needed now she was expecting again. But she did understand. Robert was full of contrition. "Sit yoursel' down and I'll go make you some tea. She sat down in the rocking chair. She felt drained. A cup of tea would be most welcome. Robert went out into the kitchen and soon returned with a brew for her. He handed the cup to her and pulled up a chair to sit beside her.

As Sarah drank her tea she thought about how she would tell her family about moving away. What would the children say? Next day she began to think it wasn't such a bad idea, after all. Mary got up before her siblings, and before Robert had left for work. She was the first to mention the conversation. "Ma', what were you both shouting about last night?"

Sarah looked at her, concerned. "What did you hear? Did we wake you?"

"Not really," Mary replied, "I hadn't quite gone off to sleep. I did hear Scotland mentioned, and moving. Are we going somewhere?"

"Well," said Sarah, "your da' thinks there's not so much work hereabouts now, and he's read they're doing a lot of stone building up in Glasgow."

"That means everybody we know will be miles away from us!"

"We shall make new friends," said Robert.

"I don't want new friends. I'm happy with the ones I've got!" Mary retorted.

Sarah looked at Mary. She understood how her daughter felt. Until she had thought it through, that was exactly the way she had felt. "Just think about it, Mary. It won't be anytime soon, and besides, we won't go anywhere unless we've somewhere to live."

"When were you going to tell us?" Mary asked, indignantly.

Sarah looked at her and smiled. "Today, of course, but not one at a time. I was waiting until you were all up. Besides, there's other news." Sarah patted her tummy. "I'm having another baby."

Mary stormed off into the bedroom. John came out almost immediately afterwards. "What's up with Mary?" He asked.

"We're moving away, son," Robert said. "Tae Scotland – in a few months."

John stood there, open-mouthed. "And that's why Mary's upset?" He asked. Sarah nodded.

"But I like it here. I don't want to go!" John shouted at his father.

"It's no' up tae you, boy," Robert began, "if we move you move. You ma' didnae want tae go at first, but she's got used tae the idea. So will you."

Just then, first Mary and then Jane appeared from the bedroom. When they were all up and having breakfast Sarah began to tell them the news. Mary looked almost despondent, but John was considering the idea. After the shock he realised he could do nothing to change anybody's minds, and besides, it would be an adventure.

Robert was ready for work, so he left Sarah telling the children about the move. He was happier now that Sarah had accepted his idea.

Sunday afternoon, 2 February 1851 Robert and Sarah were visiting Mary and Henry. Robert, Jane and their children were there as well. They now alternated as a threesome with them and Robert and Jane. Their home was the same style as Robert and Jane's home but the Wilsons lived on the top floor whilst the Foulkes lived on the ground floor. The only difference here was that both Henry and Mary had been working up until the wedding, so they had managed to fit the place out with new furniture.

Mary was also pregnant, just a month more than Sarah. Sarah was telling her sister about their plans.

"You mustn't go! I don't want you to go!" Mary shouted. Jane looked just as concerned.

"Why do you have to go all the way to Scotland?" Jane asked.

"Robert wants to go home," Sarah said defiantly. "I must admit when he first told me I felt the same, but the idea is growing on me, now."

"It's a big thing," added Henry. "Moving everything up north... Do you have work?"

"There's a great deal of building going on in Glasgow just now," Robert McWilliam replied, "so I know I shall find work when I get there."

"Maybe we could go," suggested Robert Foulkes, jokingly.

"Don't even think of it!" Jane replied, angrily.

Mary was crying. "So, what, are you all going up there together?" She asked, through the tears.

"No, Mary," replied Robert McWilliam. "I shall go up there first and get work. I'll stay in lodgings tae begin wi'. Once I have work I shall find us a home. When everything's in place I shall be back tae sort out down here."

"Dry your eyes, sister," said Sarah. "There are trains, you know. We're not moving overseas – you can come and visit. In fact," she added, "I insist you do!"

Mary seemed to approve of that, and the tears slowly dried up. "You must think me silly," she added.

"No," replied Sarah. "That I do not. To be fair, I didn't think it was a good idea on the day that Robert said he wanted to go, but on reflection, it will be an adventure. He has promised to take us somewhere quiet, and who knows, we may even move near to where he is from!"

"How are you going to get all your furniture up there?" Henry asked. "You'll be taking it with you?"

"Aye, for sure – I'll no' leave it behind!" Robert replied. "I was wondering if –"

Henry interrupted. "You'll be needing a cart... I have a cart... Just how far is it?"

"About 200 miles, gie or take." Robert McWilliam said.

"That far?" Robert Foulkes interjected. "Well, I suppose it must be. Good job you're not going to the highlands!"

Sarah looked shocked. "200 miles? I had no idea!"

Mary looked as if she was going to cry again. Sarah turned to her. "No more tears," she said. "You will come to visit." Jane comforted her sister-in-law.

"I thought it would be something similar," replied Henry. "It'd take us two to three days to get up there. Less to get back – the horses wouldn't be pulling so much."

"Could you spare the time, man?" Robert McWilliam asked.

Henry smiled. "You're family, now! Of course I can spare the time!"

Robert McWilliam was relieved. "I was hoping you'd ask," he said. "Now we can start making our plans."

Mary cheered up under protest. She was still convinced she would never see her sister again. The families had tea and then Robert, Sarah and the children went home, leaving Robert and Jane still there.

The news travelled fast and Sarah's mother, Mary, discussed the proposed plans with her husband, Thomas, first, before asking Sarah anything. On Saturday, 15 February Mary went to visit her daughter. It was the first thing she spoke about upon her arrival at Back Beckwith Street.

"I've been talking with your da'. Do you think it's a good idea to be going all that way?" Mary asked her daughter.

"Yes I do." Sarah said convincingly. "Robert's going up first – on his own – to get work," said Sarah. Once he's got a job he'll get us a place to live."

"But it's so far," added Mary. "I'll not see you again!"

"No it is not 'so far'," said Sarah. "You can catch a train. I had all this with Mary the other week. Besides," she added, "you can always write! It'll be great to get letters from you all."

"But it won't be the same. I shan't get to see my grandchildren," added Mary. "Will you be alright? And who's going to deliver that baby of yours?"

Sarah smiled. "Ma', it's not the middle of nowhere. Besides, it'll be a brand new start for us all."

"What about Agnes and William?" Mary asked. "Will they be going with you?"

"It depends on what they want," Sarah replied. "Agnes is a fine, independent woman now. I daresay William still wants to be in the army. His apprenticeship is up soon and he'll be his own man."

Mary sighed. "It's sad to think the family is breaking up."

Sarah smiled. "Oh, ma'," she began. "We all move on. Look at John – we've no idea whether he's living or dead. And then there's Jane – she's living overseas as nanny with her family. There's poor Hannah, plus your other little ones that didn't survive, in the ground, and us three married. Everything changes."

Mary nodded. Sarah thought for a moment and then gave a chuckle. "Can you imagine what your life would have been like if we all lived in the same house with our families? There'd be no room to move!"

Mary wiped a tear from her eye as she thought about the scenario. "I know you're right... Doesn't mean I have to like it though!"

"I know ma'. But try to be happy for us," added Sarah. "You'll still have Robert and Mary with their families."

"So, when does Robert leave?" Mary asked.

"In seven weeks," Sarah replied. "I shall miss him, but it won't be for long."

Seven weeks passed by very quickly, and the closer it got the more uncertain Sarah became. Were they doing the right thing? Robert certainly thought so, and Sarah knew that her place was by her husband's side. Finally, Saturday, 5 April 1851 arrived.

Sarah had packed a bag for Robert and was fussing round him. She wanted to be sure that he had everything he needed. Outside, the morning was very hazy and the temperature a few degrees above freezing. Robert was getting exasperated. "Will you gie over, woman!"

"I'm just making sure that you have everything," Sarah replied.

"I have everything I need – for now," he said. "Dinnae worry, hinny – we'll be fine. I'll be back afore you know it!"

"I shall miss you," she said, trying hard to hold back the tears.

"Dinnae cry, hinny. I want tae see you wi' a smile on your face afore I go," said Robert.

At that moment the older children opened their bedroom door and came into the room.

Robert looked anguished. "I didnae want tae wake you," he said, apologetically.

Sarah was cross. "You couldn't go without saying goodbye to them, surely?"

"I didnae want tae see their sad faces," he admitted.

Mary, John and Jane huddled round him. They all told him how much they loved him, and his heart melted. He began to cry.

Sarah went into the bedroom to get their remaining daughter. She brought Sarah out and Robert gave all his children hugs and kisses. He then walked over to Sarah.

"Come here, woman," he said. "I shall so miss you. It will-nae be long – you wait and see!"

Sarah looked at him and smiled. "I know," she said, "it's just that we've never really been apart."

Robert nodded. "I know, but I'll be back soon enough – you'll see."

Robert gave Sarah a hug and a kiss on her forehead. He picked up his bag, opened the door and went out, closing it behind him. Sarah just stood there, transfixed.

Young Mary was the first to speak. "It'll be alright, ma'. You'll see."

She took her mother by the hand and sat her down in her rocking chair. Little Sarah climbed up on her lap and Sarah cuddled her. Mary, John and Jane went into the kitchen to organise breakfast. They could see that their mother was upset and wanted to help her.

Sarah sat in the chair and her daughter looked lovingly up at her. She didn't really understand why everybody was so sad. Sarah sat there, bouncing her daughter.

"Oh, Sarah," said her mother, "what are we to do? We're going away and I'll never see this place again... I wonder what life holds in store for us?" She could hold back the tears no longer, and began to sob uncontrollably.

Mary came in from the kitchen. She took Sarah from her mother's arms and put her on the floor. She knelt down in front of her mother and made her look at her. "Shush, ma'," she said, "shush. Everything is going to be alright, you'll see." Mary stood up and held her hand out to Sarah. "Come to table, ma', we'll make you breakfast. There's a cup of tea on the table for you."

Sarah stumbled through the next week in a daze. She went through the motions of a normal life but her heart wasn't in it. All she wanted was her husband back. Mary was worried about her mother, and despite also being sad to be without her father she kept everybody going. Agnes came round to see them during the week and Sarah asked her what she wanted to do.

"Ma', I'm settled here," Agnes told her mother. I've a good job at the Park and I'm not going with you. I thought about it long and hard when you first told me." Sarah was upset at first, but she had almost been expecting that answer. Agnes would be 18 next birthday. She was just beginning her life. She had a good job and would undoubtedly find a young man, soon.

Finally, news arrived on the following Saturday. There was a knock at the door so Sarah answered it. The postman stood there, with letters. "Morning, missus," he said, "here's your letters." He was a jovial man, medium height and well filled out. Sarah looked through them – there were quite a few. Finally, she saw one that she needed to read. The postman could see she was anxious so he tried to make conversation. "I understand they'll be putting slots in the doors here soon – it'll make my life easier."

Sarah looked up at him, realising what he was trying to do, but it didn't make it any better. She smiled at him as she spoke. "Thank you," she answered. "but I don't suppose we'll be here to see the slots. We're moving away."

"Anywhere interesting?" The postman asked.

"I'm not sure," Sarah replied. "We're going to Scotland. It's where my husband's from. He's up there just now, trying to get things ready for us."

The postman nodded, understanding. "You've a letter from Scotland there. Goodbye till next post."

Sarah closed the door and went to her rocking chair. As she sat down she began to open the letter. Little Sarah saw her mother sit down and decided she wanted to sit with her, so her mother put her on her lap and held on to her as she read.

Robert had written the letter on the Wednesday. She read it aloud to her daughter.

> *Wednesday, 9th April*
>
> My darling Sarah,
> I arrived safe on Saturday evening. It was cold, but dry.
> I found myself lodgings on Sauchyhall Street – number
> 183. The owner is a widow, Elizabeth McAllister. She had
> just one room left. Her other tenants were two young men
> and a young woman. On Sunday I acquainted myself with
> what building works were going on so I'd know where
> to look on Monday. They're building a bridge across the
> Clyde, so I tried there first thing. They did have a need for
> stone masons as they've only just started the work, so the
> first part of my business is done. I shall look for a place to
> live come Saturday.
> I miss you so much, and I can't wait until I see you again,
> your ever loving husband,
> Robert.

A tear rolled down the side of her face and she kissed the letter.
She looked at it for a few minutes then put the letter back in its
envelope, picked up Sarah in her spare arm, stood up and laid the
letter down on the mantlepiece above the fire.

Mary and Jane came into the room, shortly followed by their
brother John. Mary could see that her mother had been crying.
"Are you alright, ma'?" Mary asked.

"We've had a letter from your father," Sarah replied. "He's
doing grand. He's got work and he'll be looking for somewhere
for us to live, now."

Sarah pulled herself together for the sake of her children. "Can
I read it?" Mary asked.

Sit yourselves down, and I shall read it to you," Sarah replied.
They did so and Sarah put her toddler down on the floor beside
them. She took the letter off the mantlepiece, out of its envelope, and read it to them.

"Will he be home soon?" John asked.

187

"I certainly hope so," Sarah replied. "I miss him… Anyway, enough of that… I've jobs to do."

Sarah put the letter back in its envelope and replaced it back on the mantlepiece, then she went into the kitchen to prepare breakfast.

The children could see how much their mother missed their father, and during those few days that Robert was away they almost took over looking after her. Sarah was also suffering from the effects of her pregnancy, so life was doubly hard for her just now.

When she had a quiet moment, Sarah sat down and wrote a reply to Robert. She told him that both Jane and Mary were bringing their families round on Sunday, and how she couldn't wait until he returned home.

While Robert was away in Scotland Henry, Mary and John and Robert, Jane and children all came to visit Sarah. It made a welcome change, therefore, the next day, when her visitors came to call.

Mary was busying herself by mending a dress that she had outgrown. She was a capable young girl and she was making it smaller so that her sister Jane could fit into it. Sarah had been shopping and had already prepared tea for everybody.

As soon as the younger children got together they all disappeared into a corner to play.

When everybody had arrived, and all the adults had sat down, the first thing that Sarah did was to show the letter she had received from Robert to her brother-in-law, Henry.

Mary looked at Sarah and was worried. She voiced the concerns that the rest of the family had. "Are you coping without Robert?"

"It's hard," Sarah replied, "especially expecting and with children already – but then again, you know that."

"But I have only John," replied Mary, "and Henry's home every evening."

"Well," said sister-in-law, Jane, "I don't know how you are managing! I know I couldn't be without Robert every day."

"John and the girls are good children," answered Sarah. "Mary helps me a lot around the house – look at her now," Sarah smiled, "she's taking one of her old dresses in for Jane to wear. Besides," she added, "it's only a few weeks now, and we'll be back together again."

At that moment, Mary McWIlliam stood up. She put her sewing things away and held the dress up. "That's done it," she said, "it's sure to last a bit longer now." She folded the dress up and turned to the adults.

"Would you all like a cup of tea?" She asked.

"Why, thank you, Mary," said her mother. "That would be lovely."

"What a treasure you are," added her aunt Mary. I'd love a cup. What about you, Henry?"

Henry looked up from reading the letter. "That'd be grand, sweetheart."

Robert and Jane also accepted the offer of a cup of tea so Mary went out to the kitchen.

Henry turned to Sarah. "She's a credit to you, Sarah."

Robert asked, "Are the children happy to be moving away?"

Sarah thought about the argument she had with Mary and John when she and Robert had broken the news to them. It didn't last long, though, and by the time Robert went away they were looking forward to the adventure as much as their younger sister Jane was.

"John and Mary didn't want to go at first," Sarah replied, "but Jane thought it was an exciting adventure, so after a few days they all changed their minds. I worry about Agnes and William, though."

"Are they not going with you?" Mary asked.

"No," Sarah replied. "Agnes is happy where she is. She's moved on from the Bull, now. She works at the Park. She's not lived here for the last five years. Nor has William, come to that."

"Five years?" Jane asked, incredulously.

"It can't be!" Mary agreed. "Five years? Where did they go?"

"I know," replied Sarah. "When I told Agnes she said she didn't want to move away. Said she was old enough to know her own mind and that she'd do fine."

189

"Well," interjected Jane, "you've no need to worry. We shall look after her!"

Sarah continued. "As for William – his apprenticeship is finished in a few weeks, and he's told me he wants to volunteer."

"Volunteer?" Mary asked, incredulously. "Why would he do that? He has a trade, now – he should be set for life!"

"He's wanted to be in the army since before he was apprenticed," Sarah explained. "I know him well enough. Once his mind's made up there's no talking to him."

"Hah!" Mary exclaimed, "A bit like his father, then!"

"Shush, Mary," said Henry, angrily. "There's no need for that!"

Mary made her appearance carrying a tray of teacups, pot, milk jug and sugar bowl. She proceeded to put the tray down on the table and poured out all the teas, asking the guests, one by one, if they wanted sugar and milk. She then handed the teas round.

"So, Mary," began her aunt Jane, "What do you think of moving to Scotland?"

"It's not for me to decide," she said. "Ma' and da' have made their minds up, so we shall be going. It will be quite an adventure."

They drank their tea and then presently, Sarah began to bring the food out for everybody to eat. As she carried the food in from the kitchen Mary was getting more and more upset.

In between coming and going between the kitchen and living room Sarah tried to persuade her that everything would work out. Jane was as annoyed as Sarah was about the way that Mary was reacting. It was Jane that spoke out.

"Why do you not want Sarah to move away, Mary?" She asked.

"It's alright for you," she said, upset. "Your family is not that far away in Wales. My brother John is away at sea. I don't even know if he is still alive. Then there's Jane. She's living in America with her family. Probably having a right old time."

"But you still have your brother here," Jane replied, struggling to understand Mary's angst.

"But I won't have a sister!" Mary said, angrily.

Henry and Robert could see that there was no way to reason with Mary, so they stopped trying. Jane accepted defeat.

Sarah, now understanding what was really Mary's problem, comforted her sister.

"Mary, I know we're all moving away, but surely you don't begrudge me doing what my husband wants of me?"

Mary wouldn't answer.

"We will only be a train journey away from each other, you know," Sarah continued. "It's not like a seven or eight week sea voyage to see me, is it?"

Mary began to relent. She turned to look at Sarah, directly. "Well," she said, "if you put it like that, it doesn't sound so bad."

"Of course not!" Sarah added.

"But I shall so miss our chats," Mary added, "and I shan't see that new baby of yours when it's born!"

Sarah smiled. "You'll be busy enough on your own with the new baby that you're expecting. Or had you forgotten that?"

"No, of course I hadn't!" Mary retorted.

"So come and eat this food I spent so long preparing," added Sarah. Mary dried her eyes and stopped complaining, and everybody went to the table to get some food. There were more people than there were places to sit at table, so they picked the food they wanted and went to sit back down to eat it.

After they had eaten the guests went back to their homes and Sarah waited anxiously for the next letter from Robert. She didn't have to wait too long. The next Thursday, 17 April, the postman knocked at the door again. "You've another letter from Scotland!" He called out, jovially. She took it from him, anxiously, and quickly opened it. There was only little Sarah there to act as audience, so Sarah decided to read it to her. Not that Sarah took any notice; she was playing with her farm animals.

Monday, 14th April

My darling Sarah,

Thank you for your wonderful letter. It came on Friday. I'm glad you are all well and that Mary, Henry, Jane and Robert will be coming round every Sunday. The company will do you good. Good news! I have found some lovely little cottages about 25 miles south of Glasgow, in a village called Lesmahagow. I was told about them by a workmate. He comes in from Lanark, which is about 7 miles from the village and about the same distance from Glasgow, give or take. During the week he stays in lodgings and goes home at weekends. I shall find out who owns them this week and see if we can rent one. The weather is still good here. The air is so beautiful in Lesmahagow – so clean, so fresh – I'm certain you'll love it.

I do so miss you, and I long to see you and the children again,

Your ever loving husband,

Robert

Sarah returned the letter to its envelope, stood up and put it on the mantlepiece with the other one. She looked down at little Sarah, playing happily on the floor.

"Oh, Sarah," her mother said, "How is your father going to take the news that William's gone and volunteered?"

Sarah sat upright on the floor and looked at her mother. She held out her arms, so Sarah bent down, picked her up and walked out to the kitchen. She had the evening meal to prepare and it helped her take her mind off what she had to tell her husband. The weekend came and went. As the week before, the families came round to see Sarah, to save her from having to go out. It made Sarah feel special when they were there. Mary was getting more used to the idea, which helped ease the pressure on Sarah. Henry had been busy trying to persuade Mary that it wasn't such a terrible idea for her sister to move.

Sarah was beginning to get more used to being apart from Robert. She looked forward to the letters that Robert was sending her. She so enjoyed reading them to her children, who also wanted to hear everything that Robert wrote about. The children were now, excitedly, telling all their friends about how they were moving away. Their friends were positively jealous, which made the McWilliam children even more certain they were doing the right thing.

Another letter arrived on the Wednesday, 23 April and after Sarah had read it she and baby Sarah went round to see her sister-in-law, Jane. All the other children were at school but Jane was there with baby Mary. Sarah showed her sister-in-law the letter.

"This is the third letter he's sent me in just over two weeks," said Sarah. "If I needed any proof that Robert missed me, this is it!"

Sarah handed the letter to Jane, who read it. As Jane read the letter, Sarah continued to talk to her.

Sunday, 20th April

My darling Sarah,

Don't worry yourself about William. We always knew he wanted to be a soldier, even before he was apprenticed. He will do his family proud. You'll see. I have spoken to the owner of the cottages in Lesmahagow. As I thought, one is empty and we should be able to move in by the end of the month. They are big rooms, a bit like the cottages in Tranmere, but there are only two in each cottage. It is raining a little today – the first rain since I arrived, but it is still warm. I shall let you know when I intend to return home to collect the furniture. You will need to give the landlord notice of intention to leave at the end of the month.

Not long, now. We'll soon be together again, keep your spirits up.

Your ever loving husband,

Robert

"I've told Robert about William volunteering," continued Sarah. "He wasn't surprised. We always knew William would leave the foundry as soon as he could. Robert's found some cottages in a place called Lesma...hah...goe – I don't know how you say it – a bit like the cottages in Tranmere."

"I can't believe how calm you are," said Jane, once she had read the letter. "You'll be leaving us all behind."

Sarah was adamant. "I'm looking forward to it, and besides, I'll be with my husband and my children. We do fine." Almost as an afterthought, she added, "I hope."

Jane looked at her, long and hard. "You don't sound very sure," she said.

"I am," replied Sarah, "but every now and then I wonder about the unknown part." After a momentary pause, she added, "We will be alright. I know it!"

Sarah received another letter from Robert on the Friday, 25 April. They were coming thick and fast, now. This one, however was more urgent than the last, so Sarah went to her sister Mary's as soon as she was able. She first had to go to the landlord's and give him their leaving date. She had already told him they would be going in May but didn't have a fixed date. Moving day was now set in stone.

It was a cold day, but at least it wasn't raining. It was lovely to be out walking with little Sarah in her baby carriage, but she would have to look after it. It would be needed again when the new baby came along. Sarah went, with this latest letter from Robert, to see her sister.

Mary answered the door and let Sarah in. She was there alone as Henry was at work and John was at school.

"Why, hello," Mary said as she opened the door. "Come in."

Sarah looked at her sister as she went inside. "It's final, now," she said. "Robert has paid the rent on the cottage and we move next month. I've brought you the letter to read." Mary took Sarah's coat and they both sat down. Sarah took the letter out of her bag and gave it to Mary to read. Mary read it, slowly. She looked up at Sarah and then back at the letter, comparing the date.

My darling Sarah,

Arrangements have been made for us to take over the cottage on 1st May. I have spoken to the building site foreman and he has given me a week off so that I can come down and bring up the furniture. You will need to tell Henry that I will be arriving back home on Saturday evening so you and the children will have to move in with them after we start out on the journey north.

So looking forward to seeing you all again, keep your spirits up.

Your ever loving husband,

Robert.

"My," said Mary, "he arrives tomorrow!"

"I know," added Sarah, "I can't believe how quickly everything is happening. Will Henry still be able to help?"

Mary nodded. "He has already told his foreman about the trip. Everything will be fine. I shall tell Henry to come to see you as soon as he gets in from work tonight. Have you given notice?"

"Yes," replied Sarah, "I told the landlord we will be leaving at the end of April. He said to take the key back when we've cleared everything out. Mary –"

Mary looked at her sister. "What, Sarah?"

"I'm scared, now," Sarah replied. "What if it doesn't work out?"

Mary chuckled. She knew her sister was stronger than this. This was just last minute nerves. She spoke. "You? Scared? No! I know you too well, Sarah McWIlliam – you'll do just fine!"

"I suppose you're right," replied Sarah. "Anyway, I will expect Henry later. I shall go now – I need to be back for when the children come home."

"I shall make sure he knows," said Mary. "Now off you go."

Mary opened the door and Sarah left for home.

Mary looked at the time. It was not often that she did something on the spur of the moment. But, if Henry was to be able to take the next few days off he needed to know immediately. She set off to go to Robert Hogan's auction rooms in Grange Lane. It wasn't far. Right into Adelphi Street; left into Dacre Street; right into Argyle Street and Grange Lane was the third turning off on the right. The auction house was down there on the left hand side. She hoped Henry would be there.

That evening Henry arrived at Sarah's straight from work. He had brought with him some crates so that Robert and Sarah could start packing. She let him in and showed him the letter as he sat down.

"Mary came round and told me about your letter," he said.

"She went to the auctioneers?" Sarah asked, surprised.

"I'm glad she did. I wondered what she was doing for a bit, but afterwards I could tell the foreman I needed this week off."

"Did he say you could?" Sarah asked, nervously.

"Of course he did," Henry jovially replied.

"So," asked Sarah, "everything is alright then?"

"Yes," Henry replied. "We are all set. Now, let me read this letter."

Henry read the letter. "It's all happening very quickly," he said. "Are you sure you're ready for this?"

"I did have my doubts earlier, but now the time is finally here, I can't wait," replied Sarah.

"That's good. Well, I should think he won't be home before evening, so I shall go home now and be back tomorrow at about 4 o'clock."

"I shall have dinner ready. I was going to cook, anyway. Robert is sure to be hungry," said Sarah.

"Grand!" Henry stood up. "I shall be going now," he said. Sarah opened the door and let him out. She closed the door and leant on it. She held the letter in her hand and put her hands together in prayer.

"Oh, Lord, let him come home soon!" Sarah prayed.

Next day, it was still dark in Glasgow when Robert got up. It was to be a long journey. He packed his things and said goodbye to his landlady. He told her he would be back in just over one week. His work was in Glasgow, so he would stay there week-nights and go home only at the weekend.

He turned right out of his lodgings on the south side of Sauchy-hall Street and headed down to where it turned into Cathcart Street. He turned right into Renfield Street, on into Union Place and walked on to Jamaica Street, where he crossed the bridge over the Clyde into Bridge Street. He walked down Bridge Street as far as the junction with Bedford Street, where he turned left into it. He walked the length of Bedford Street and turned right at the end into Surrey Street. He could see Southside Station at the end of the road.

He bought his ticket in the booking hall and waited for his train to arrive. It would be a long journey. The first leg was to Carlisle and from there he would have to travel to Liverpool. He wondered what Sarah would be doing, and if Henry was still able to help out.

Meanwhile, Sarah and the children had begun to pack things into the crates. They kept a minimum of things out that they would need to last them before they left. The kitchen would be the last room to pack.

Henry arrived mid-afternoon, as Sarah was about to start cook-ing the evening meal. She had no idea as to what time Robert would arrive, but she knew he would be hungry. Henry contin-ued with the packing, instructing Mary and John as to the best way to fill the crates. The family had only been in the property for about two years, but they had collected a lot of things dur-ing that time.

Sarah was glad to have something to do. It took her mind off watching the clock and stopped her worrying about Robert.

The children stayed up a little later than normal. Mary and John went to bed later than Jane, but after all the strenuous exercise filling the crates the children were all more tired than normal. It began to get dark and the children were beginning to fall asleep. The family had all eaten, leaving enough for Robert when he arrived. Most of the belongings had been packed into the crates.

Finally, at about 6 o'clock, there was the sound of movement outside. The front door opened and Sarah jumped up out of her seat in anticipation.

"Robert!" Sarah shouted, with joy.

"Aye," said Robert, as he walked in through the door. "Well who else did you expect tae see?"

Sarah rushed over to him and gave him a hug. Robert returned the embrace with gusto.

"I've been waiting too long for that," he added. "How I've missed you, woman." He looked at Henry. "Glad tae see you here, Henry," Robert said.

Mary and John roused from their reverie and rushed over to greet their father. He hugged them both, then he sat down and gave tired Jane a hug. The children sat at his feet, listening to his every word. As they sat there, though, sleep began to overtake Jane, despite how hard she tried to stay awake. Soon, she was sound asleep at her father's feet.

"Look at her," said Sarah. "They were determined to wait up for you…" She smiled down at Jane, happily asleep on the floor. "I've made you dinner," said Sarah, "you must be famished."

"Well, now, I could certainly eat some o' your cooking." Robert replied.

Sarah went out to the kitchen to get him his meal while Robert and Henry were moving Jane to her bed. When they sat back down, Robert began to talk with Henry.

"You've had no problem getting the time off?" Robert asked.

"No, that was easy. I'm due some time off," replied Henry. "After Sarah told Mary she came down to the auctioneers to tell me. So, all I had to do was to confirm the dates with the foreman. I had said provisionally this next week coming, so there was no problem. So, what's the plan for the removals?"

Sarah brought in the food and Robert ate as he spoke.

"The journey tae Lesmahagow" – Robert began.

Sarah interrupted. "Say that again – Lesmah – hag-goe?"

"No' quite," replied Robert. "It's said LESMA-HAY-GO."

Sarah repeated it until she got it right.

"That's right, you've got it!" Robert finally told her. He continued to talk to Henry. "The journey should take no longer than three days, and we can get in the cottage from Thursday. We've tae leave here by Tuesday at the very latest so you can be back by the weekend."

"That's a lot to do in just over two days," replied Henry, worried.

"There's not a huge amount o' furniture tae take," said Robert, "so it shouldnae take long tae get everything done."

"We've started packing already," added Sarah.

"Yes, da'," added John, "we all helped!"

"Aye, I can see that. And I'm right glad you're helping your ma'." He turned to Sarah. "Once we leave, you and the children will have tae go straight to Mary's, where you'll stay until Friday."

"Why do we have to stay until Friday?" Sarah asked.

"Because I need tae be sure I've got there, and all the furniture put where it needs tae be," answered Robert. "Besides, I need tae be at the station when you arrive or you'll not know where tae go!"

"Why can't we stay here until Friday?" Mary asked.

"There'll be no furniture here, silly!" John retorted.

Sarah smiled, "Oh, of course!" She said. "So how do we travel?"

"Well," began Robert, "you get the train tae Carlisle from Liverpool first. At Carlisle you'll need the train to Glasgow through Lanark, and when you get tae Lanark I'll be waiting."

"The train?" Sarah said, in horror. "I have to take the train?"

"Well, how else did you think tae get there, woman?" Robert chided.

"I've not been on the train before," said Sarah, nervously.

"You'll be fine," added Henry. "The children will help you."

"Yes, ma'," said John, proudly, "I shall look after you!"

Sarah looked upset. "It's just, I – I – I keep thinking about the train accident we saw. It will be alright, won't it?"

"The train's the safest way to travel," said Henry. "That accident was a one-off occurrence."

Robert smiled. "Anyway, as I was saying," continued Robert, "Make sure you dinnae get the train that goes tae Dumfries, for that'll no' take you tae Lanark. There's no railway any closer than Lanark tae Lesmahagow, so I will meet you at Lanark station and we can get the coach tae Lesmahagow."

Sarah knew Henry was right, and that she shouldn't be worried about going on the train, but she remembered the last time she went to Lime Street and shuddered. She shook herself back to reality and asked, "What time will we have to leave?"

"You must get the 8 o'clock train tae Carlisle from Lime Street," said Robert.

Sarah was just about to protest at the earliness of the hour, but Robert spoke first.

"I know it's early, but you've a long journey tae make, and we still have travelling tae do when you get tae Lanark – so you cannae be late."

Sarah submitted to everything that Robert had told her. She knew he was right. Henry was smiling at her. "You'll do fine, Sarah," he said, "mark my words." He stood up and turned to Robert. "Right," he said, "I'll be going now – you need your sleep. I'll be back early in the morning and we can get on with packing everything up."

"Aye, you're right," said Robert. "Well, we'll see you tomorrow."

"Say goodnight to your uncle Henry," Sarah said to both Mary and John. "Night, Uncle Henry," they both said together. "Now, away to your beds," added Sarah.

The sleepy children gave their father another hug and then went to their room.

Robert stood up and walked over to the door. He opened it and Henry left. Robert shut the door and turned to face Sarah.

"Come here, woman," he said, playfully. Sarah walked over to him and Robert kissed her. "Oh, how I've missed you!" Robert whispered to her.

"I've been counting the days," added Sarah. "Let's go to bed."

Over the next few days the McWilliam family continued to pack their belongings. Henry brought his cart and horses round on the Monday so they could load everything. It made it easier, as the flat was emptied, to see what else needed packing. The weather didn't help, though, and it was lucky that Henry had brought a tarpaulin with him.

"You will need to secure the things that have been packed on the cart overnight," he told them, "and it will also protect against the weather."

Finally, the morning of Tuesday 29 April 1851 arrived, and the last of the possessions that Robert was taking by road were loaded. It was sleeting, so everybody was dressed almost for winter, despite being well into spring. Henry, who had taken the horses back home with him the night before, harnessed the horses to the cart. Robert made sure the tarpaulin was secure and Sarah stood under cover, as much as it was possible, with the children as they watched Robert prepare to leave. Robert took the valise that Sarah had packed and loaded it on to the front of the cart. He and Henry would go past Morpeth Buildings on the way out, so Henry was to take the valise up to his home ready for when Sarah got there. Finally, everything was ready and Henry climbed up on to the cart. Robert walked over to Sarah. Mary took Sarah from her mother's arms.

"Now, you have all the details for travelling?" Robert asked.

"Yes, Robert," Sarah replied. "It's all written down on paper – and it's in my bag."

"Good," he replied, nodding. "You should arrive at Lanark station about 4 o'clock. I'll be waiting until you arrive – however long it takes. We'll soon be together again."

Robert kissed Sarah on the forehead and held her.

Then, one by one he said goodbye to his children. Sarah took her toddler from Mary and Robert finally climbed up on to the cart. Henry drove off. Sarah waved until they were out of sight.

But it was a normal Tuesday morning for everybody else, and Sarah realised that the normal, daily things were still going on around her. For those few minutes it was if she and her family had been held in a bubble where time stood still.

A few moments later, Mary Millward and Sarah Beech, with their respective families (Ann, Mary, Charles and James Millward plus Sarah, Emma, Joseph, John and Arne Beech), emerged to see Sarah standing outside.

"Why, Sarah – is it today?" Mary Millward asked as they walked to school.

"Yes, Mary," Sarah replied. "Robert's just left with everything. He and my brother-in-law are off to Scotland as we speak."

"So when do you go?" Sarah Beech asked.

"We leave on Friday," answered Sarah. "Tomorrow will be the children's last day in school."

Sarah began to get a little emotional as she thought about it.

"Have you given up your place here?" Mary asked.

Sarah nodded. "We have. I shall drop the little ones off at school, take the key back to the landlord, and then go to my sister Mary's place in Morpeth Buildings. I'll not be back here again."

Sarah struggled to hold back the tears as she thought about not seeing her neighbours again.

Both Mary and Sarah looked concerned. Sarah Beech spoke. "Will you write? We must know how you get on."

Sarah tried to regain her composure. "I shall write," she began, "I can't lose touch with everybody… I'll be isolated enough – to begin with. I have to know how you're all doing."

They continued their daily walk to school with not much more being spoken. Her friends could clearly see that Sarah was upset, and they did not want to make it worse for her. Finally, they arrived at the school and Mary and John went inside. Sarah turned to go to return the key to the landlord. "I shall say goodbye now because I shall not see you both tomorrow," she said.

She left her two neighbours and set off with Jane and little Sarah. It didn't take long to return the keys and then Sarah set off for her sister's. When she got there Mary was waiting for her with open arms. "Oh, it is so lovely to have you staying here with us – even if it is only for a couple of days," she said.

Mary and John made their own way back to their Auntie Mary's. They had done the journey enough times to know the way without thinking. Next morning they went to school by themselves as well.

Friday morning soon arrived. It was cold but at least the weather was fine. Sarah and her children were ready to go. She stood outside Morpeth Buildings with her sister and brother. All the children were there, laughing amongst themselves. There was a small valise beside her on the ground that Sarah was to take with her. Both sister Mary and sister-in-law Jane were crying, which was making Sarah feel upset.

Mary finally managed to speak. "Do you have everything?"

"We do," replied Sarah. "There isn't much to take, most of it is already gone, and probably inside the cottage by now." She sighed. "I shall miss you."

Robert looked at her. "Not for long," he said. "You'll do fine. You always do, sis." He held her hands. "You better write when you get there!"

"I shall," she replied, "and you must keep me updated with your news."

"You should go, Sarah," said Jane, "or you'll not get that train. I'll keep my eye on Agnes for you, but we both know she'll be fine."

"Come on," said Robert, picking up the valise, "I said I'd take you to the station – it's not that far from where we're working today. I shall make sure you get there on time."

Everybody hugged and kissed each other. Robert and Sarah gathered together the four children and left for the station.

Robert got Sarah and the children to Lime Street Station for half past 7 o'clock.

They bought the tickets and went in search of the train. Sarah looked nervously around for anything that might remind her of the awful events the last time she was here, but there was nothing to suggest anything had ever happened. Robert led her over to a train and on to the platform. They walked along until Robert found an empty carriage.

"This is the train, Sarah," Robert said. "These are the second class carriages. This one's empty, so up you go. It's going to be a long journey, so make yourselves comfortable."

Sarah climbed up the steps into the carriage. The train consisted of carriages with compartments accessed only from a door to the platform on either side. There were seats facing each other that went all the way across from side to side.

Once Sarah was inside the carriage, Robert passed the valise up to Sarah and began to help the children climb up. First, Robert picked up Sarah, now well into her second year, but still too small to manage the steps. Robert passed her to her mother's waiting arms.

Next was Mary. "Up you go, Mary," said Robert as he helped her get on the first step. Once she had her footing she made light work of the remaining few steps up and was quickly sitting opposite her mother, looking out of the window.

Robert went to help John, but he was feeling far too independent. "I can do it myself, uncle!" John told him.

Jane, on the other hand, was grateful of her uncle's helping hand. As she stood at the top of the steps she turned to her uncle and blew him a kiss. "Stand back," said Robert, "I need to shut the door." Jane did as she had been asked, and Robert shut the door.

Sarah leant out of the window and stretched out her hand to him. Robert held it as he said, "I have to go now, Sarah... You'll be fine. You have your instructions, so if you get confused just speak to somebody. They'll put you right."

Sarah nodded, "Thank you, Robert." They let go of hands and Robert walked back down the platform and out of the station. Sarah watched him as he went and began to cry. Will I ever see you again? Sarah was woken out of her reverie by little Sarah, who wanted to sit on her mother's lap. Sarah turned to look at her children. They were all brimming with excitement. Mary had the window seat opposite her and John and Jane sat by the other windows.

The train left Lime Street at 8 o'clock, right on time. They left the dark station and built up streets of Liverpool and were soon out in the countryside. The sun shone but it was still cold. Sarah took the blanket out from the valise. Robert had told her it would be cold on the train before he left with Henry, so Sarah made sure she had one. She wrapped herself and Sarah up in the blanket. The other children were too excited and running about in the carriage to feel cold. Just like Sarah, this was their first ever train journey and they were enjoying the space.

The seats were hard and uncomfortable, though, and Sarah soon stood up. Robert always thought of everything! She put the Sarah down and walked about a bit. They had also packed a cushion. Sarah smiled as she took it out of the valise and on to her seat. After a while, the train stopped at Maghull station, just a few miles north of Liverpool. It was still early and not many people were on the platform. For those who were boarding the train there were still a lot of empty carriages, so, for a time at least, Sarah and her children were alone.

The train moved off again and was soon back in the country-side. Sarah sat down again. Little Sarah wanted her mother, and there was no way Sarah could stand for long holding her 'almost' 2-year old. The train stopped at Ormskirk and Burscough stations and still nobody else needed to share the carriage. At each station they stopped at Sarah looked eagerly out of the windows. The stations all looked so different.

Finally, at Rufford station a couple got in to their carriage. They looked at Sarah and the woman said, "Good morning." Sarah replied, "Morning," in response. John and Mary stood up, wondering where the couple would choose to sit. They finally sat down by the opposite windows, facing each other. Mary and John came and sat down opposite their mother, and Jane moved to sit beside Sarah.

Sarah looked over at the people opposite. They were well dressed and didn't have any luggage. She wondered where they might be going at this time of day.

There were so many stations, that, after a while, Sarah stopped looking at them, and she concentrated on her children – particularly the little ones – to make sure they were alright on the journey.

The train ambled along, stopping at all the stations on the way. Three stations later, the train pulled into Preston, where the couple alighted and more got on. The train began to fill up as they continued on. There were seven stations until the train reached Lancaster. The countryside was beginning to get more undulating.

Ten stations later the terrain was much more uneven. There were a lot of hills around. The station at Shap was high on one such hill. When the train got to Tebay a second engine was attached to the train, in order for it to make the climb to the next station. The children were enthralled at the changing landscape by now, and they could see the steep hill ahead of them. They encouraged Sarah to look out of the window on her side, and finally, reluctantly, she did. She could not believe the hill ahead of the train.

But with two engines, the train made it to the top and into Shap station, where they waited for a while, until the train caught up with the timetable.

The closer they got to Carlisle the fuller the train became. Finally, shortly after noon, the train pulled into Carlisle station. It was an impressive building. Sarah and the children got off the train. They were all very hungry, so they found somewhere to sit down and eat the packed lunch that Mary had provided. There was plenty of time before the family had to catch their next train, so after they had finished eating they ventured outside the station.

Inside the station it had been dark, but when they got outside it was a gloriously bright day, but still very cold. Sarah turned back and looked at the exterior of the station. It was beautiful. The children ran around her. There was a small park with a fountain over to her left, so Sarah propelled the children in that direction.

They remained here for a short while before returning to the station to get the train to Glasgow. By now it was nearly 2 o'clock and everybody was beginning to get tired. The train was due to leave at half past 2 o'clock and there were a great many people waiting for it. The train had just arrived at the platform, so not only were there people waiting to get on, but there were also many others getting off the train.

Sarah walked up to one of the station staff to make sure this was the correct train. The attendant on the platform told her it was the one she needed. He could see that she was alone with her children so he offered to assist her getting on the train. Sarah gladly accepted his offer and they walked down the platform together.

This time there were no empty carriages, but the attendant found one that had only two people in and he assisted Sarah and her family to climb up into it. They sat and waited for the train to leave. The couple who sat in the carriage with them were deep in conversation, and Sarah realised that Robert's Scottish accent had been softened over the time he had been in Cheshire. Sarah could barely understand some of the things she heard.

Finally, the train set off and they were, once again, deep in the countryside. The further north they went the more hills they encountered. The viaducts they crossed over continued to be impressive. One by one, they stopped at the stations on the way, until, finally, they arrived at Lanark. It was, by now 5 o'clock and in just under two hours it would be sunset. This was a tiny little station, by comparison to the other ones the family had alighted at. There were barely any buildings to speak of. The station staff had to put steps up to the carriages so that people could get off.

The beauty of this being such a small station was that Sarah could see Robert waiting for them before he even had an inkling where they were. Sarah and the children got off the train. John helped the two little ones down while Sarah began to call out to Robert.

Robert had arrived at the station early and had managed to find a coach to take the whole family across to Lesmahagow. When the train came in he couldn't wait for it to come to a halt, so he began rushing down the platform, peering in all the windows of the carriages. By the time he saw them they had found him.

Robert ran up to them and he called out, "Sarah!" As he got close to her he held her in his arms.

"Oh, Robert!" Sarah exclaimed, relieved that she had found him. "Thank the Lord! We made it!"

"Was the journey alright?" Robert asked, as he picked up his youngest daughter and twirled her around.

"It was an adventure – that's for sure!" Sarah replied. "Not something I'd like to do again, mind!"

"I thought it was brilliant!" John exclaimed. "I looked after everybody," he said, beaming proudly.

"Good man," replied Robert. He turned to his wife. "You'll no' have tae go anywhere on your own again," he said.

His two other daughters demanded to be held so he handed little Sarah to her mother and gave his other daughters a hug each. Robert picked up the valise and the reunited family then turned and began to walk away from the train and out to the road. Sarah thought about all the stations she had seen on their journey. She decided that the one at Carlisle was the prettiest. But, nothing more mattered. She had her husband by her side again.

They walked on to where the coach was waiting for them and Robert helped them all inside. The coach driver set off and Sarah watched as they went up and down hill along tree lined roads on the way to Lesmahagow.

This, too, was a long journey, but the seats were more comfortable, and Sarah was no longer on her own. She snuggled up against her husband and watched the children as they excitedly looked out the windows.

Robert told her about his journey up with Henry. The weather had been kind to them and they arrived in good time.

He had put all the things in the cottage as best he could but it would be up to Sarah to make sure everything was where she wanted.

Sarah told Robert of their journey up from Liverpool, and how much the children had enjoyed the train journey.

By now, Jane had fallen asleep, as too, had little Sarah. John and Mary were quieter now. The journey to Lesmahagow was more sedate than the train. It had been smoky, and things had gone past so fast. The coach, though took much longer as it travelled at about eight miles an hour, which meant the journey took about two hours.

Finally, the coach pulled up outside a row of tiny cottages. It was almost dark, now and only Robert and Sarah were awake. "Welcome to Auchtykirnal," he said.

Robert got out of the coach and Sarah passed little Sarah to his waiting arms. Sarah gently woke the other three children and they climbed out, sleepily. Sarah was the last to get out, bringing the valise with her. She put the valise down on the ground. They stood there, in the half-light, peering at the cottages.

"So, which is ours?" Sarah asked.

"It's the second one from the right," he replied. "Come on, let's go in!" Out from his pocket Robert produced a key. He gave it to Sarah. She picked up the valise and they walked towards the cottage. She put the key in the lock and turned it. John pushed the door open and they all went inside.

There was an oil lamp just inside the door. "Put the bag down", said Robert to Sarah. "There are some matches on the table by the lamp. You'll need tae light it."

Sarah did as she was asked, and the lamp started to glow. As the light brightened Sarah and the children could see the room more clearly. From the outside, the cottage didn't look very big, but once inside there was a roomy feel to the place.

The first room was the living area, with a fireplace in the centre of the wall adjoining the next cottage. There was a range in the centre of the fireplace and Robert had put the cupboard from the kitchen in Birkenhead against the wall to the right of the fireplace, furthest away from the window.

The table and chairs were up against the same middle wall, and the rocking chair was over by the window. Sarah could see beds built into the wall on the opposite side of the front room, by the front door. Even with the fixed beds and the furniture that Robert brought with him there was a lot of room.

Robert watched Sarah as she looked around the room. Even the children were silent – most probably because they were tired.

"Well," he asked, "what do you think?"

Sarah thought for a moment more before answering. "When I saw it from the outside I thought it was going to be so small, but inside there's more room than I could have imagined." She turned to face the closed door to the other room. "That must be the bedroom."

"Aye," said Robert. "Open the door, and we can put this little one tae bed." Sarah walked forward and opened the door, carrying the oil lamp as she went. They went into the room and Robert walked over to one of the set-in beds, in the furthest corner, and laid little Sarah down with her head on the pillow. He covered her over and then proceeded to go and pick up another oil lamp, which he lit, making the room brighter.

Here there were two more beds sunk into the wall, as before, one of which was now occupied. Also, however, the beds that Robert and Sarah brought with them had fitted easily into the room, each one facing into the centre of the room, one from the window wall and one from the centre wall.

Sarah looked around the room and smiled. "Well," she said "it's bigger than I expected. You did well, Robert. Just one thing. Where do I do my washing?"

Robert looked sheepish. "There's no running water tae the cottage, but there's a well a ways up the road tae the main village. We fetch the water back and do our washing outside."

Sarah glared at Robert. "That's all well and good in the fine weather, Robert... What am I to do in the wet weather and the winter?"

"Same as everybody else here!" he retorted. "You'll get used tae it."

"Hmph! One step back!" Sarah angrily replied. "Well, that's the way we had to do it in Tranmere, so I suppose I will get used to it. Or maybe I'll use a corner of the kitchen, out of the way." Sarah knew there was no getting away from it. She began to calm down. She continued, "Anyway, let's sort out these beds. Jane, you can share with Sarah. Mary, you can have the other set-in bed, and we'll have one of the ones we brought – looks like this is ours. Is this the one you've been using?"

"Aye, Sarah." He realised he hadn't gotten everything right. "I'm sorry I didnae get the place you were looking for."

Sarah ignored him for the moment. "John, you can have the other bed we brought. Let's get some sleep. Everything will look better in the morning."

Sarah was still holding one of the oil lamps. She turned and walked out of the bedroom and Robert, sheepishly, followed her. The children began to get ready for bed. Sharing a room with each other was nothing new. It had been quite a while since they had shared with their parents.

Back in the other room, Sarah sat down in the rocking chair. Robert knelt down in front of her. "I've missed you," he said.

"I'm sorry I got angry with you," Sarah replied. "I expect I was spoiled in Birkenhead. We had everything under one roof, and now we've gone back to this."

"Do you want anything? Tea, perhaps?" Robert asked.

"A cup of tea would be lovely," Sarah replied.

Robert made them a cup of tea each and they sat for a while talking. It had been an early day for Sarah and she was soon tired, so they had an early night.

Next morning came quickly. Sarah had gone straight to sleep the night before, she was so tired. Robert was already up when Sarah woke. She got out of bed and looked out of the window. The day dawned bright and sunny. It was warm, but there were clouds in the sky.

Sarah got dressed and went in the living room. Robert had bought in some food so he was getting the stove lit, ready for breakfast. He had heard her get up and had made a cup of tea for Sarah. She took it from him gratefully and sat down to drink it. "I must have needed that sleep," she said.

"Aye," said Robert, "you didnae even wake in the night when Sarah cried."

"Was she alright?" Sarah asked.

"Nae bother. I saw tae her and she went straight off again," replied Robert.

The children soon woke up. Sarah was the first. She cried. Sarah put her tea down and went to get her. She gave Sarah a hug and got her get changed and dressed. The other children were soon all dressed and ready to explore. Sarah stepped outside to get acquainted with her new surroundings and Robert started cooking. As she did so, the front door of the cottage at the end of the block, next door, opened. A woman walked outside with a bucket.

Sarah was the first to speak. "Good morning," she said.

"Morning," said Sarah's new neighbour, with a thick Scottish accent. "So you'll be my new neighbour. I met your husband the other day. My name's Sarah. Sarah Crossan."

Sarah smiled. "I'm a Sarah, too! Sarah McWilliam. We got here last night – it was just getting dark."

Sarah's neighbour smiled. "I see you're expecting, then. When's it due?"

Sarah replied, "September. It'll be our fifth. We've three girls and a boy."

"Five!" exclaimed her neighbour. "We've just the three girls – all in their teens."

Robert came outside. "Sarah," he began, but then he saw Sarah was talking. "Sarah – Oh, morning Mrs. Crossan. How're you doing today?"

"Fine, Robert," she replied. "Call me Sarah, let's no' stand on ceremony here."

"Aye, I could do that," he replied, "but it might get a wee bit confusing when you're both stood together!" He chuckled. "Sarah," he said, turning to his wife, "breakfast's ready."

"Oh, Robert," replied Sarah, "I wasn't expecting you to do breakfast for me!"

"And nor should you," he answered. "This is just for today, as I'm so glad tae see yous all here wi' me now!"

Sarah Crossan looked on, smiling. She turned and walked off round the back of the cottages. Sarah McWilliam walked inside her cottage with her husband and shut the door.

The food was on the table and the children were all eating. There was a plate of food at an empty chair and Robert sat Sarah down at it. She looked for his plate. "Are you not eating?" She asked.

"Aye," Robert replied, "but there isnae room for us all tae sit at table, so I shall sit over here."

"You'll do no such thing, da'," said John, standing up. "I've just finished my breakfast, thank you, so you can come and sit in my place." John moved away and Robert brought his breakfast over and sat down, opposite his wife.

"So where will you be working?" Sarah asked Robert.

"Glasgow – on the same job when I first got here," he replied. "I shall go from here early Monday morning and will be back Saturday."

Sarah looked shocked. "So I shall not see you until the end of the week?" Sarah asked, incredulously.

"Aye. Well, you saw how far it was and how long it took tae get here. I cannae do that every day!"

"And just exactly how will you get there?" Sarah asked.

"Well," replied Robert. "I shall make my way tae Lanark station wi' the other workers, early in the morning. There's a carriage that goes tae the station first thing in the morning. The same thing happens on a Saturday when we come back."

"So, what am I to do while you're away in the week?" Sarah demanded.

"You'll find something tae do. Meet the women in the village."

"Hmph!" Sarah said. She had finished her breakfast, so she got up and took the plates off the table.

Over the next two days Robert and Sarah explored their new surroundings. They took their children down into the village and found where everything was that they would need over the coming months. Sarah didn't want to be out walking for too long, however. She was, by now, into her fourth month of pregnancy. She had come to terms with the fact that she would only see her husband at weekends. It had come as a big shock. She had gone from a modern home and seeing her husband every day, to a weekend wife in a village cottage. It wasn't what she had expected but she would do what was wanted of her, just the same.

Monday, 5 May, came, soon enough. Robert was up at just after 4 o'clock. He had a bag packed to take with him for the week.

He could see that Sarah was unhappy but she told him she would be alright. John had promised he would be the 'man of the house' while his father was away, and Sarah was proud of him. Robert kissed Sarah on the cheek before he crept out of the house. Sarah curled up in bed and tried to go back to sleep, but she found it difficult. She lay there in bed for a while but then decided to get up. She got breakfast ready and the children got up a while later.

They left for school at 8 o'clock. It was about three-quarters of a mile to get to the school, so Sarah knew they would have to set off in good time. They walked up to the village, Sarah pushing her youngest in the baby carriage they had brought with them. It was a cool day but it wasn't raining. To begin with Sarah found it easy to walk the children up into the village, but by the time the school came into view Sarah was struggling. They walked up to the junction and finally the school was on the other side of the road.

Mary was as relieved as her mother was to see the school. "I can see it ma'!" She said. "It's just round the corner."

"At last!" Sarah answered, struggling to get her breath. "I can't walk all this way again. You'll have to come on your own tomorrow."

"'Course we can," replied Mary. They walked into the school and found the schoolmaster. "Good morning," he said, "I've not seen you before – are you new here?"

Sarah answered. "Yes, we just moved in on Saturday. I'm Mrs. McWilliam, and these are my children. I'd like them to start school."

"Well, I'm Duncan Campbell, the schoolmaster," he replied. "How old are they?"

Sarah pointed out each child in turn. "Mary, here, is 12, John is 10, Jane is 5 and the little one is almost 2."

The schoolmaster eyed each one up in turn as their names were called out. "I take it they've attended school before?" Mary and John both nodded.

"Well," the schoolmaster began, "Mary's about leaving age, so there's little point her starting now, but we can take John and Jane. Jane's not attended school before, I take it?"

"No," replied Sarah. "She would have been due to start after Christmas, but as we knew we'd be moving we thought it sensible to wait, rather than get her started back home and then started again here."

"Very sensible," Duncan replied, nodding. "You're from England, I notice. Whereabouts?"

"Birkenhead," Sarah replied.

"Oh," Duncan answered with a smile. "Well, if you leave John and Jane here now they can start their first day in their respective classes. School finishes at 4 o'clock. Is John sensible enough to bring his sister home?"

"Yes, sir," answered John, boldly. "I know the way. It's out of the school, take the road opposite – not the one going left and right – and then go left at the fork. It's a straight road after that."

"Well done, boy," replied Duncan. "He be fine, Mrs. McWilliam. You get yourself back home and rest. I can see you have a bairn on the way."

"Thank you," said Sarah. She turned to her two children. "Bye John. Bye Jane. See you both later."

"Bye, ma'!" John and Jane both answered, almost together. Almost before Sarah had turned the baby carriage round to leave the two children had been sent to the playground to find the other children. Sarah smiled. "Right Mary, we shall go back down into the village and get acquainted with the shops."

"Yes, ma'," Mary replied. Sarah, pushing the carriage, and Mary left the school and headed back.

Finally, mother and daughter arrived home. They had been into the local shops to see what they sell and to meet their new neighbours. Sarah had written some letters back home and she wanted them posting. They bought some more provisions with them. Mary put the shopping away and Sarah sat down to rest. Mary brought her mother a cup of tea. She could see she was exhausted.

Finally, home time came and Sarah eagerly awaited John and Jane home from school. It was shortly before 5 o'clock when an out-of-breath John opened the door, closely followed by an out-of-breath Jane.

They both sat down on the floor and told their mother about their first day at school. They had enjoyed it but it had been a little difficult to keep up with the different way of speaking. Having been used to the gentle accent from their father they had expected the accent to be the same, here. But it was much harsher. They both agreed they would pick it up, though.

Sarah had made them their evening meal so they all sat down to eat. Afterwards the children played for a while and then they went off to bed. Sarah stayed up afterwards, tidying up, but she wasn't late to bed either. The long walk of the day had tired her out.

This was Sarah's new routine, and she was beginning to get used to it. She packed John and Jane off to school then took a leisurely stroll up to the village a while later on, with Mary and little Sarah. By Saturday she was eagerly awaiting Robert's return from work. It was lovely being with Mary, but she was still only a girl, and Sarah desperately needed some adult stimulation.

Throughout the Saturday the children played with their neighbours at Auchtykirnal. There were so many new faces to get to know. Mary spent her time with Jane Crossan (aged 13) and Helen Carruthers (aged 10). John made friends with Alexander Day (aged 13), his brother, Robert Day (aged 10) and Thomas Carruthers (aged 8). There were some children Jane's age, too. There were Mary Day (aged 7) and Jane Carruthers (aged 5) and they were thrilled to have somebody new to play with. There was another youngster, who was just the right age for little Sarah, but both of them were too young to be left alone to play. But, during the week, when Sarah and her neighbour, Jane Carruthers, had a spare five minutes, they would let little Sarah and Andrew Carruthers play with each other. It was these quiet times when Sarah Crossan would join them and the women would talk about their families. They all got on well together.

It was early Saturday evening when Robert returned home, and Sarah was ready for a hug from her husband. They spent a wonderful weekend together, making the most of the time they could share. Sarah knew that the children needed him as well, and it was only right that they should. Finally, too soon, it was Monday morning, and Robert departed for work again.

By Friday, 23 May Sarah and her children were all becoming used to their new routines but Sarah needed news from home and she was feeling homesick. It was raining, so Mary offered to go to the shops for her mother. Sarah thought it was a good idea. It would make Mary feel more useful. While Mary was out she collected the post. She walked in the door and handed the letters to her. Mary took her wet coat off and hung it up. When she turned round she could see her mother was upset.

Sarah stood there, holding the letters, with tears running down her face. "Oh, ma'," said Mary, "what's the matter?"

"I don't know," Sarah replied. "I thought things would be better up here. Robert always said they would. But I never expected Robert to be away so much. And now there's these letters – they just remind me of what I've left behind."

"Are you going to open them?" Mary asked.

"I started to open this first one," Sarah replied, "but that's as far as I've got."

"Give 'em here, ma'," said Mary, authoritatively. "I'll read them for you."

Mary took the letters out of her mother's hands. "Go on," she said, "sit yourself down." Sarah did as she was told, all the energy, suddenly gone from her body.

Mary continued to open the first letter. She read who had sent it. "This one's from Uncle Robert and Auntie Jane."

She read through it first, so that she could understand what had been written. She smiled as she read it to herself, then she began to read it aloud to her mother.

Dear Sarah and Robert,

Hope you arrived safe and sound and are settling in alright. Robert said he got you safely on the train, so that put my mind at rest. I miss our little weekly chats but it was lovely to get your letter. The cottage sounds different. I wonder if it's anything like the ones in Tranmere. Agnes is doing fine. She calls in to see me from time to time and says you have written to her. The Mercury has announced that a man called the Manx Giant will be coming to Liverpool. He is so very tall – about 7 feet 6 inches and he's only 22 years old. I can't believe how somebody could be so big. Robert has said we shall all go to see him on Saturday. I am so excited. I shall tell you all about him in my next letter.

All for now,

Your sister-in-law Jane

After Mary had read the letter to Sarah she looked up at her. Sarah had stopped crying. "Oh, ma'," Mary began, smiling and giggling as she spoke, "can you imagine that! I can't even picture a man so big as all that."

"That's nearly two feet taller than your father!" Sarah replied, looking up, as if she was looking at him. "Oh Mary, it must be very difficult for the man. That's almost as tall as a ceiling – he'd have to bend down to get into a room!" Sarah paused as she realised she no longer felt unhappy. She continued, "I'm enjoying this, now we're reading them together. Pass me one, and I shall read it to you."

Sarah and Mary continued to read all the letters in this manner and by the end Mary was pleased to see that her mother was returning to her sparkly self.

Next morning, Robert came home with a very excited air about him. He had barely shut the door before he began to talk to Sarah.

"Sarah! Sarah!" Robert called out.

"Why, Robert, whatever is it?" Sarah asked, very curious. She gave him a hug and Robert made her sit down in her chair. He pulled up another one and sat beside her.

"Such a surprise," Robert continued. "A man on the same gang as me today… Michael Donachie… We were talking, and he asked what part o' Scotland I was from originally as he couldn't place the accent. Well, I told him I'd been living in England for a few years but that I was born in Port Logan, and he said that he knew somebody who was also from those parts." Robert paused for breath.

"Go on," said Sarah, intrigued.

"Well, Michael is from Greenock," said Robert, "that's away tae the west of Glasgow – and he lives just up the road from the bakery there, in Market Street. He's lived there some time and knows the baker's well. The owner's name is Matthew Anderson, but his assistant is a good friend of his – and the assistant's name is John McWilliam. Well, my brother John was a baker last I heard."

Sarah sat there open-mouthed. Finally she spoke. "So, is this man YOUR brother?"

"Well," continued Robert, "it might be, but McWilliam is a common name where I come from. Anyway, Michael's given me the man's address, so I shall write him and find out."

Sarah was so pleased for Robert. She knew he thought he didn't have any family left alive. "Oh, Robert, wouldn't it be grand if he was your brother? You thought you'd lost touch with all of them."

"Aye, hinny, I thought I had. I'll write him tomorrow and take it wi' me when I go on Monday."

After they had all eaten and Robert was more relaxed, Sarah showed him the letters they had received from home. He, too, tried to picture a man so tall as the Manx Giant. There was one more letter that had arrived that day, from her sister Mary, so Sarah read this to Robert as they sat and relaxed.

Monday, 19th May

Dear Sarah and Robert,

I am so glad the move went well. Henry had so much to tell me when he got home. The cottage sounds so big. He says we should move away from Birkenhead to somewhere more open. I do believe you have given him ideas. He keeps talking with his brother Joseph about it. I don't know if it was Henry filled Joseph's mind with the idea or the other way round. In any event, he and Joseph are going to Shropshire on Saturday – to a town called Oswestry. I hope we don't move anywhere until after the baby is born. I am getting bigger by the day. There are only about three months left before it is born. Just think – I shall soon be a mother.

I will tell you all about Henry's trip in my next letter.

All for now,

Your sister Mary

When Sarah finished reading the letter Robert thought for a moment, then began, "Now I come tae think of it, Henry couldnae stop talking about the countryside hereabouts. Well, it's no bad thing tae get out of the big towns."

Sarah nodded. "Even ma' and da' did it this year," she added. "They're doing fine. My da's working on the local farms and growing his own vegetables. We can do that, now, can't we?"

"Aye, hinny," Robert replied, "that we can. We have a part o' that field behind us. I shall check wi' the neighbours tomorrow tae find out which is our plot." So next morning, Robert went to see Thomas Carruthers, who lived next door, and found out which was their garden plot. Sarah and Mary started to plant vegetables and tend it over the next few months. John and Jane also wanted a small plot but they often got bored with gardening, so Sarah and Mary looked after their plots for them when they didn't care to do the gardening themselves.

The weekend came so fast, and before Sarah knew it, it was time for Robert to leave again. The family made the most of the Sunday they spent together. The rest of the week the children played with their neighbours, but nobody wanted to be anywhere but home on a Sunday.

The next two weeks passed by as normal, with one exception. One of the letters that arrived on the latter Friday came from Scotland and not England. Sarah had put it safely propped up at the back of the table, so it rested against the wall. Every time she walked past she looked at it, wishing she dared open it.

Finally, on the Saturday, Robert returned home. He had no more chance than to open the door, but Sarah jumped up. She grabbed the letter. "At last!" She said, excitedly. "You've had a letter come – yesterday."

Robert looked shocked. Nobody ever wrote to him. "What? A letter tae me?" Robert put his bag down on the floor beside him.

"Yes, Robert," said Sarah, nodding, impatiently. "Maybe it's from Greenock." She handed the letter to Robert, who stood there looking at it. Sarah watched him, willing him to open it. Finally, he turned it over and tore the envelope open. He took the letter out of the envelope and slowly read it to himself. As he read he began to smile. Still he kept the contents to himself. Sarah was becoming more and more curious.

Eventually, she could bear it no longer. "Well? Is it from him? Is he your brother?"

Robert began to smirk. "Will you gie me a moment, woman… Let me read it tae you!" He began to read the letter aloud.

Friday, 30ᵗʰ May

Dear Robert,

Well, what a surprise – hearing from you after all this time. I thought for sure you were dead! I am well and have been living in Greenock about 5 years now. I became a master baker after you left home all those years ago. I married in 1839, to Ann Pettigrew, in Dundonald. We've no children, and have lived happily without the worry they bring. We shall have to come and visit you – it will be easier for us to travel than you. I am so glad you are happy, and much saddened to hear that your Agnes died so long ago. I look forward to meeting your new wife and children.

We can come to see you on a Sunday as our shop is closed. We shall get the coach from Lanark to come to Lesmahagow. If you would like, we can come on 22ⁿᵈ June. Please write and let me know how to get to you.

Your brother,

John

Robert finished reading and looked up at Sarah. He was positively beaming. Sarah spoke first. "Oh Robert! That's wonderful! Please write and tell him he can come."

"Aye," Robert replied, "I shall. It will be grand tae see him again after all these years. But, first," he added, I must take my boots and coat off!"

The children had all seen their father return home and were now piling in through the front door. Robert handed the letter to Sarah, to save it from being crushed and Robert greeted his children.

There was such excitement in the McWilliam household. Everybody was looking forward to meeting Robert's family. Robert had replied the same day and Mary had posted the letter first thing on the Monday morning. John and his wife were coming early on the Sunday morning, 22 June 1851. They were going to catch the train from Greenock to Glasgow, change there for the Lanark train, and once at Lanark would get a coach to Lesmahagow. The train journey would take two hours, what with changing at Glasgow, and then there was the two hour coach ride to Lesmahagow. They would arrive in the village just about noon.

They had directions to the cottage, so they would walk down to meet them. The weather was warm but there were unsettling clouds in the sky. Robert and his children were outside, the children playing and Robert watching up towards the village. Finally, in the distance, he saw a couple walking towards them. "Sarah! They're coming!" Robert called out. The children emerged from the different parts of the cottage and its surroundings, and Sarah came outside with little Sarah. Robert walked off towards them, almost running, in his excitement.

Finally Robert reached the couple and they stood for a short moment, then the two men hugged each other.

"My God, Robert!" John exclaimed, "You look sae much like our father, I cannae believe it!"

"Oh, John!" said Robert, "It's a miracle we found each other after all this time!"

John nodded. "This is my wife, Ann," said John, introducing her to Robert. "Pleased tae meet you," she said.

By this time they had walked within sight of the cottage and Sarah and the children walked up to meet them. Robert introduced them all. "This is my wife, Sarah, and these are our children – Mary, John, Jane and Sarah."

"Pleased to meet yous all," said John. "I'd like yous tae meet my wife Ann."

They walked down to the cottage and Robert looked up at the sky. They had arrived in good time. "Shall we all go inside? I think it may just be starting tae rain."

Everybody went inside and Sarah closed the door behind them. John and Ann sat down with Robert and Sarah and they talked for hours. Sarah brought out the food she had prepared and they had a wonderful day together. John and Robert reminisced about their parents and brothers and sisters, and living with their aunt and uncle after their parents died, while Ann talked with Sarah about Liverpool and Birkenhead. She was so interested to learn about where they had come from.

Meanwhile, the children sat and listened to the stories of Robert and John. They were far too much in awe of their uncle to dare to speak. They spoke of their sisters, Susan and Elizabeth, and the tricks they used to get up to with them when they were children, then they spoke lovingly of their grandparents, Nathaniel and Elizabeth Mean, and visiting them in their cottage on the seafront at Portnessock.

But, all too soon it was time for the visitors to leave. John had to be back in good time. Being a baker he had to be up before the dawn. So, Robert walked with them to the village, where they caught the coach to Lanark in time for the train home.

The day had brought back many happy memories for the brothers, and they promised to keep visiting now they had found each other again. After Robert had seen them off he returned to the cottage and sat with Sarah for a while before bed.

"Well," said Sarah, "if nothing else good should come of it, at least by moving back to Scotland you're been reunited."

"Aye, hinny, that we have."

But next morning life was back to normal, and Robert left early in the morning for work. Sarah did not have to rush up this Monday morning, as school was finished for the summer harvest. Mary took the children up to the village to do some shopping and get any post that may have been delivered. Sarah was getting bigger, so she was pleased not to have to make the walk to the village. She stood outside, talking to her neighbours. Little Sarah was far more adventurous now, and Sarah needed to keep a sharp eye on her. Mary Day chuckled when Sarah pointed out how fast little Sarah was. She agreed that this was the age they were most fearless, and she, too, was having the same problem with her toddler, Andrew.

Mary and the children were soon back with the provisions, but no post, not this day, anyway. The days were getting warmer, but not so warm as they had been in Birkenhead. The week flew by and finally, Saturday, 28 June 1851, Robert was home again. More post had arrived during the week, this time from Henry and Mary. Sarah put out the evening meal and the whole family ate it with gusto. After Robert had started to relax in what was barely a weekend, Sarah read the letters to Robert.

The first one was from Agnes, and Robert delighted in hearing what Agnes got up to. Then there was one from William. He was out in India now, with the East India Company. All was well and Robert was pleased how his two eldest children were getting on.

Then Sarah moved on to her sister's letter. This one had concerned her most of all.

Tuesday, 24 June 1851

Dear Sarah and Robert,

We hope this letter finds you all well. For myself, I am well, although I blame you for instilling the wanderlust into my dear Henry. To explain, when Henry returned he was so excited about you travelling, as I previously mentioned, and then his brother Joseph moved in with us. Those two things alone I could cope with, but Henry infected Joseph with the same wanderlust, and one day, when Henry came back from making a delivery to a town in Shropshire, he could not contain his enthusiasm for the place.

Well, to cut a long story short, we have moved. We are now living much closer to the Welsh than I had ever dreamt of. Our address is 5 Drenewydd Place, Whittington, Shropshire. The menfolk both have found work, but I have only John for company when they are at work. It is so lonely. I do wish I had your stamina, sister.

All for now, your loving sister

Mary and Henry

She began to talk about the contents. "I can't believe that everybody is moving away. But Mary did say that Henry and Joseph were of a mind to go there. Whatever next? And Mary so close to having her baby, as well! Henry and Joseph both have work there. Joseph is lodging with Henry and Mary. They have a two storey house in Whittington, on the outskirts of the town. She's put the address – **Drene...**

(Spells it out loud: D R E N E W Y D D) – Oh I can't say that!"

Robert had no idea what Sarah was talking about. The words were spilling out so fast he couldn't understand one from the other.

"In the name o' the wee man! Slow down, will you, woman!" Robert shouted. "Where did you say they'd moved tae?"

Sarah stopped, realising that she was the only one who could understand what she was saying. She was getting used to the new Scottish sayings she was hearing when she was out and about, because there were some that Robert used from time to time.

She started to talk again, but this time much slower. "Whittington. It's on the north side of Oswestry. Look, there's the address. I thought Scottish words were bad enough – how do you say that?"

She showed the letter to Robert and he looked at it. He puzzled over it for a few minutes and then replied, almost exasperated, "I have no idea, hinny!"

The next month flew by, each week much the same as the last, until, finally, unexpectedly, Sarah went into labour a month early. Thankfully, labour had started while Robert was home, so he was able to stay with his wife. Sarah chose to use one of the set-in beds in the living room rather than disturb the other children. Mary was despatched to get the midwife, who had arrived just in time for the baby to start to crown, much to Robert's relief. The baby arrived shortly after midnight, in the early hours of Monday 4 August 1851 and it was a boy. The midwife cleaned Sarah up and left the McWilliams with their new arrival. Sarah can't believe her luck. "A boy! I was beginning to think I'd not have another. What shall we call him?"

"You choose," Robert replied. Sarah lay there, for a moment, holding the baby. "What about David? I like David."

Robert looked puzzled. "Is that a family name? I've no' heard it afore."

"Does it have to be a family name?" Sarah asked.

"It's traditional," Robert began, but he saw disappointment in Sarah's eyes. "But, if that's what you want."

Sarah nodded. "Yes, it is," she said. "David."

"David McWilliam it is then," agreed Robert. He kissed Sarah on her forehead. "Do you want tae go to your own bed, or shall you stay here?"

Sarah thought for a moment. "I'll just stay here for now. You go to bed – you should get some sleep before you go to Glasgow."

Robert smiled at her. He didn't want to leave her there on her own. "I'll be fine," he said. "I'll just lay awhile with you here." He got ready for bed, put baby David in the cradle beside her and climbed in on the other side. They snuggled together for the few hours left before Robert had to leave.

Next morning, Mary was first up. She walked out into the living room and found Sarah asleep. She saw the cradle out and went round to look in it. She smiled when she saw the little baby lying there asleep. She looked over at her mother. She, too, was fast asleep. As quietly as she could, Mary tiptoed back into the bedroom.

She told the other children about the baby. They all wanted to see it but Mary made them stay quietly in the room. "I will make us breakfast," she told them, "and I shall bring it in here. Be quiet when I leave the room." Mary opened the door, left the bedroom and closed the door behind her.

The children promised they would, but eventually, curiosity got the better of them. John tried his best to make them do what Mary had told them, but even he wanted to see the baby. More and more noise came from the bedroom, and eventually, Sarah woke up. She looked over at the baby and smiled. He was fast asleep. She then saw movement down by the fireplace and lifted her head to see what it was. By now, she could hear the murmurs coming from the bedroom.

Mary saw that Sarah was awake. She went over to her. "Ma', I'm sorry," she said, "I tried to get them to stay quiet so you could sleep."

"It's alright," Sarah replied. "Let them in. They only want to see their new brother."

"It's a boy?" Mary said, pleased. "I know you and da' wanted it to be a boy." She went over to the bedroom door and opened it. The other three children almost fell through the door, they weren't expecting it.

Sarah sat up in bed and straightened herself up. The children all gathered round their mother and Sarah pulled the covers back on the cradle and lifted the baby out. He was tiny. He was early, like his brother had been. "Say hello to your brother David," she said. All the children looked on in awe. Finally, John spoke. "I'm not the only boy any more!"

Mary was a godsend that week. She did all the running around for her mother and was amazing. Sarah told Robert that weekend how proud she was of Mary, which in turn made Robert pleased. They had letters again, during the week, from Agnes, telling them how well she was getting on and how pleased she was for them that she had another brother. They had letters from Thomas and Mary, and Robert and Jane.

Mary and Henry had news of their own. Mary had also had her baby, but, unlike Sarah, Thomas Wilson was born late, so he was born a week after David McWilliam. Thomas Wilson came into the world on 14 August 1851 (Mary had been a month earlier than Sarah in getting pregnant).

The next couple of months were hectic with the new baby. He had a good pair of lungs on him, that was for sure. John had been a noisy baby in his first few months, but he had been nothing like wee David. The children were back at school now, and autumn was setting in fast. It was a Saturday morning at the start of October, and Sarah, John and Jane were all tending the garden. It was drizzling with rain but Sarah was determined to get in the crops that were ready for picking. They had potatoes, turnips, swedes and curly kale in their garden. Mary was indoors with little Sarah and baby David.

Now that Sarah had given birth she was more able to do the gardening. "It's grand that we can grow our own food, even if we only have a small space."

"It's hard work, though, ma'," said John.

Sarah pointed to a patch of Kale that was growing. "That Kale is ready to be picked; and those parsnips," she said. They all moved over to the spot that Sarah had pointed to and started to collect the crops. While they were doing this the light drizzle they had been working through turned into much heavier rain, and Jane ran indoors. Sarah and John picked as much as they could of the produce.

"Ma'," John called out, "can we go in – the rain's coming down now."

Sarah decided he was right, but she wasn't going to be beaten. "Let's just finish up with these few parsnips. I've got what kale is ready."

Between them they gathered up the crops they had picked and ran inside. They made it just as the heavens opened fully, and the heavy rain clattered against the windows. Not long after they got in, Robert appeared, soaked to the skin.

"It couldnae wait for me tae get home, could it?" Robert said, as he ran in through the door. He stood there, with the rain dripping from his clothes. As quickly as he could, he took the wet clothes off and Sarah got a towel to dry him. He went straight to the bedroom and changed, then came back to say his hellos to his family.

The weekend had no sooner arrived than it was time for Robert to go again. The village was starting to make plans for the Hogmanay celebrations, and Robert had asked his brother to come to the village to spend it with him and his family. John and Ann had sent a letter saying they would love to come, and how much they were looking forward to the festival already.

Very soon, it was Hogmanay. John and Ann arrived early afternoon for the celebration. The village school was decorated for the evening dance and everybody had contributed something, be it food or drink or decoration. The evening party started late in the evening, so the children all had an afternoon nap in readiness. Finally, everybody was assembled at the school and the ceilidh band began to play. The band was made up from some of the locals and they played well together.

There was much food provided, including steak pie and stew, and drinking to be had. Robert and Sarah came with all of their children. John and Ann McWilliam came to spend the celebrations with their new-found family. All the other villagers and children were there too. The family was beginning to integrate in the village and Sarah was becoming more settled. Mary was talking with children of about the same age while the other children were all playing together. Robert was talking with some of their male neighbours in one part of the room, while Sarah was talking with her female counterparts, while still watching the children.

The men were gathered together. They all had glasses in their hands. Some had ale, some had whisky and some had both, but they were talking and laughing, and generally having a good time.

Thomas Carruthers was talking. "Is it grand tae be back in Scotland, Robert?"

"Aye, that it is," Robert replied. My family's settling in, well, too, and what's more, I've found my long lost brother!"

"Where is it you're from originally?" William Crossan asked.

"Kirkmaiden parish – Port Logan – Wigtownshire," replied Robert. "It's warmer here, for sure, but then again, we're further inland." Robert took a swig of the whisky he was holding. "So, Thomas, how much land do you farm?"

"112 acres," Thomas replied. "I grow wheat amongst other crops. It's hard work, but I've hands tae work wi' me. You're a mason, I understand?"

"Aye," answered Robert. "I go tae Glasgow on a Monday, back on a Saturday. It makes it a long week, but it pays the bills."

George Day asked Robert, "What are you working on?"

"The new Victoria Bridge across the Clyde," replied Robert. "Work had just started when I came up and they were looking for masons. It was perfect timing. And by amazing co-incidence, it allowed me to find my brother here, through a fellow workmate." Robert slapped John on the back as he spoke, making poor John nearly choke on his ale.

"That must have been real emotional for you both," said George.

Having got his breath back, John answered, "For sure it was – I thought I was the only one left, as, it turns out, so did Robert!"

"So, what's your trade, John?" William Crossan asked.

"I'm a baker – I work in a shop in Greenock," replied John.

"Is it a thriving business?" William asked John.

"It does well enough," John replied.

Thomas turned to Robert. "So, how does Sarah cope weekdays wi' you in Glasgow?"

"It was hard for her in the beginning," said Robert, "but she's beginning tae settle now."

Meanwhile, in another corner of the school, the older children were also all gathered together, talking in groups. The girls from Auchtykirnal were standing together in one group and the boys were hovering round them. Alexander Day had his eyes on Mary, being the new girl in the village, but she was happy to be talking with Jane Crossan. That notwithstanding, Mary was perfectly aware of Alexander's interest.

"Do you plan on being a weaver forever?" Mary asked Jane Crossan. "Or have you ever considered doing anything else?"

"It's a trade," she answered. She, too, was watching Alexander. "Alex, will you stop bothering me!"

"What makes you think it's you I'm interested in?" Alexander replied, curtly. "Do you want tae dance, Mary?"

Mary looked at the dance floor. "I've never seen this sort of dancing before. I don't think I can do it!"

Jane was becoming angry at Alex's attention. Or perhaps she was just jealous that she wasn't the object of Alex's affection, tonight. After a moment she said, "Will you leave the girl alone, Alex!"

Mary hesitated. "Have a go, Mary – you'll do fine," Alex urged her.

The band struck up another reel. Alexander grabbed Mary's hand and pulled her onto the dance floor. She held back for a moment or two, and then gave in and went with him. "What are they playing?" Mary asked.

"It's the Virginia Reel," Alex replied.

"But I'll make a mess of it!" Mary wailed.

"You'll do fine," he said. "Even the best dancers end up looking glaikit!" Mary looked puzzled and Alexander explained that it meant foolish.

The dance floor began to fill with couples and Mary and Alex soon found themselves part of a set. There was no backing out, now. Mary looked around her and shrugged her shoulders. The other women could see she was panicking. "Just do your best!" They yelled.

The music began and the women in Mary's set kept telling her what to do. To begin with she didn't have a clue what was going on, but she soon picked up the dance, and by the end of it she realised she didn't want to stop.

Over in a corner of the room, the mothers and younger children were sitting in a group, too. All the neighbours from Auchtykirnal were there with the exception of Jane Weaver, the elderly woman. They were chatting together, but being mindful of the children. The boys were aged between 8 and 10 years – Thomas Carruthers, Robert Day and John McWilliam – and they were running round as boys do, teasing the girls, Helen and Jane Carruthers, Mary Day and Jane McWilliam. Sarah McWilliam and Jane Carruthers were the only mothers with toddlers and baby.

"How is baby David doing?" Jane Carruthers asked Sarah. "He must be getting on for 5 months now?"

"He's doing grand," replied Sarah. "He'll be 5 months next week. When's your Andrew's birthday?"

"He turned 2 last month," Jane replied. "He's into everything now!"

"I'm so glad mine are all past that stage, now," added Mary Day.

"How old's your eldest, now, Mary?" Sarah Crossan asked.

"James is 25, and finally married!" Mary replied almost with relief. "He and Euphemia have moved to Lanark." Then she shook her head. "Agnes is 23," she continued, "and still not settling down any time soon. There she is over there," she said, pointing to a young woman dancing, "but she's not walking out with anyone."

Mary looked at Sarah McWilliam and then back to the dance floor, then back to Sarah again. "Where's your Mary?" she asked.

Sarah looked up, nonchalantly. She had been watching Mary's every move, not that Mary had any idea. Sarah pointed as she spoke. "She's over there, dancing."

Mary Day looked over to where Sarah was pointing and realised who Mary was dancing with. "Oh, aye – wi' my lad!" Then, changing the subject, Mary turned to Ann McWilliam. "So, Ann, what's it like to have relations you never knew existed?"

"Well," Ann began, "it was a bit of a shock when we got Robert's letter, but it's thrilling, now we all know each other. It's grand to know the family will go on – we had no bairns of our own, you see."

"Did yous no' want any?" Mary asked.

"It wasnae that," began Ann, "But I couldnae have any. No' that it matters now – I just treat my nieces and nephews as my own!"

Sarah McWilliam added, "You should have seen the look of joy on Robert's face when he realised John was still alive – so was I. I come from a big family, you see, so I've always been used to seeing them all the while. This is the best celebration for the end of the year I could have imagined! "

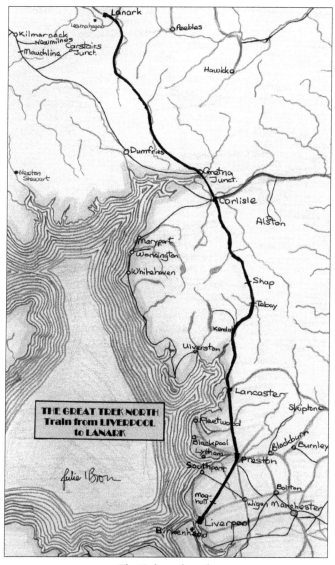

The Trek northwards

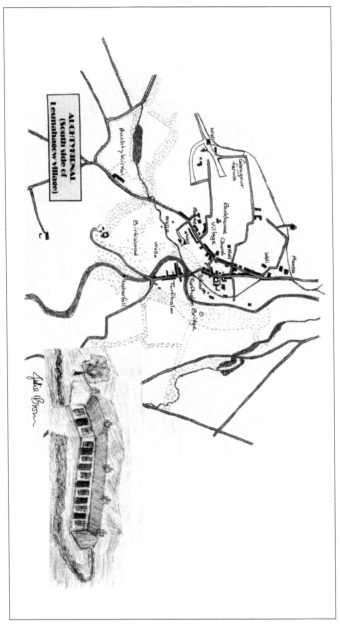

Map of Lesmahagow with inset of cottages

CHAPTER 7

Life and Loss

Walter interrupted his grandmother. "That must have been really hard for you, Granny, not living wi' Grandad."

Sarah looked at him and smiled. "I got used tae it after a while. Just seemed normal. But he didn't always work away – he followed the work. So, when one job finished he moved on. That's the way the trade works. But, as it happened, by the end of 1852 the work was beginning tae come tae us. They passed a bill allowing a railway tae be built that went from Glasgow through Lesmahagow tae Cotcastle, so your Grandad was going tae be able to stop working in Glasgow and live at home 7 days a week.

Sarah and Robert were sitting at home one weekend and Robert was reading the newspaper. He jumped up from his seat and began to wave the newspaper in front of Sarah's face. "Look, Sarah! Look!" Robert shouted.

Sarah was trying to keep calm but she was afraid Robert would hit her with the newspaper. "How am I supposed to look at anything with you waving that under my nose! Whatever is it?" she replied, annoyed.

By now Robert was dancing, something Sarah had rarely seen him do. He continued. "It's the railway! They're putting in tenders for the railway sleepers, rails, and other stuff!"

Sarah still did not understand what Robert was talking about. "And that means?" she asked.

Robert was beginning to get exasperated with Sarah. He explained. "Oh, woman! Tenders for the railway – the one that's coming down here!"

Sarah began to understand. She repeated, "The railway that's coming down here," She looked at Robert. "So, does that mean you'll be finishing in Glasgow?"

"YES!!" he said, excitedly. "It means I can go tae work every day from here!!"

Sarah now could barely hide her joy. "Oh, Robert! That's wonderful news! So, when do they start the work?"

"The tenders have tae be in by 21st June, so it'll be quite a few months yet afore the work starts proper. I'll just keep my eyes peeled for when they're after labour," Robert explained.

Robert kept looking at the newspaper but there was nothing more about the proposed railway line. He dare not say anything to Sarah because of the way he got so animated. He just continued to watch the papers.

Meanwhile, there were other things to take Sarah's mind off Robert's suspect news. By June, the family had arranged to go and visit John and Ann in Greenock. They decided to go by train, even though there were a lot of them. Thomas Carruthers had offered to take them to the station in Lanark that morning and would collect them from the station when they came back in the evening.

Sunday 19 June 1853 dawned clear and sunny. A perfect day to travel. Mary and Jane helped little Sarah and David get ready to go. Thomas Carruthers brought his cart round and the family started to climb up. John, now 12, climbed into the back of the cart. Robert hurried the others up. He was eager to go. Finally, everybody was outside and waiting to get on board. "Right," called Robert, "are we ready?"

"Yes," replied Sarah, "all waiting to get on."

"Good," said Robert, "well, John's in the back, so let's get everybody else on."

Robert passed the younger children up to John, while Mary got herself up in the cart. Finally, Sarah and David were the only two waiting. She and the baby were to travel up front with Thomas Carruthers.

"Right, Sarah, you climb up," said Robert, "and I'll pass David up tae you."

Sarah handed David to Robert and she climbed up into the front. Robert passed the baby up to Sarah and he then jumped up in the back to sit with his other children. They headed off to Lanark for the train. Thomas told them he would wait for them on the 9 o'clock train the same evening.

They left Auchtykirnal early in the morning, to catch the 8 o'clock train to Southside Station, Glasgow. The journey from Lanark to Glasgow by train took them over an hour and then they had to go to Bridge Street Station.

At Bridge Street Station they waited about 20 minutes for the connection to Greenock. This journey was by far the longest, taking just under 2 hours, but finally they arrived at Central Station, Greenock.

The train pulled into the station and the family alighted the train.

They came out from the station and found themselves in Cathcart Street. Once out into the bright sunshine they saw John and Ann waiting for them in the street.

"Have yous been here long?" Robert asked his brother, shaking him by the hand.

"No, we'd not long been waiting." John answered. "It's grand tae see yous here at last."

John and Ann gave a warm hug to Sarah and the rest of the family.

"Aye," said Ann, "yous must be hungry. Let's be away tae the house. Dinner's waiting. It'll be ready in a wee bit."

John and Ann took the family on the short journey to their home at 8 Market Street. It wasn't far to their house. They continued west along Cathcart Street, coming into Cathcart Square, left into Church Place and then right into Market Street.

They all walked down to the McWilliam's house and John unlocked and opened the front door. This was one of the few houses in between two parades of shops. Everybody went inside. John and Ann had a neat and tidy home. There were only the two of them, so it was well furnished. The two women and Mary sat down to talk at one end of the room, while the two men and John sat at the other. The younger children (David and Sarah) sat playing on the floor while Jane kept an eye on them.

Robert looked around the room they were in. "It's a good size place you have here. You must be doing well." Robert said to his brother.

"Aye," John replied, "Aye, Matthew Anderson pays well. It's quiet with no children, mind."

"But, it does mean you have no distractions during the day," added Robert.

"Well, aye, but I'd no' have minded the distractions," added John, "but it wasnae tae be."

"Uncle John, began young John, "why did you live here?"

"Well," John (senior) began, "wi' al our family gone from Port Logan there was nae point me staying there. I moved to Dundonald eventually, where I met and married your aunt Ann, here. I stayed there a while and then we decided tae move closer to Glasgow, so here we are."

Young John nodded. His father continued. "So what's life like here in Greenock. I have tae say it's a bigger town that I was expecting."

John chuckled. He thought of Robert working in Liverpool, and how that must have been far bigger than Greenock could ever be. He replied, "It's a seaport just like any other. After the shop shuts we're baking again, so there's no' much time in the week tae do anything, particularly. So I'm truly pleased we've managed tae meet up again – especially since you have your own family. We can spend time together. It'll surely be wonderful."

Meanwhile, at the other end of the room, the women were also talking. Ann asked about the journey. "How was the journey? It surely is a beautiful day. Yous couldnae have picked a better day for the trip."

"Well," began Sarah, "Our neighbour, Thomas Carruthers has a big cart, and he offered to take us to Lanark Station to get the train. He'll be there at nine o'clock to pick us up tonight." Sarah sat back and relaxed. "It's been so lovely to get away from the house – and the village – even if it is only for a few hours. It's the furthest I've been since we moved up here."

"I read somewhere they're talking about putting a line in tae Lesmahagow," said Ann. "Do you know when that'll be?"

Sarah nodded. "Robert was telling me they're putting out the tenders for the equipment for the line, so it won't be for a while yet."

Mary interjected, "Does that mean that da' won't have to go to Glasgow every day?"

"Indeed it does!" Sarah replied, smiling.

Mary was truly pleased. "Oh, ma'! That's wonderful news."

Ann stood up. "If you'll just excuse me, I've tae see tae the dinner."

"Can I help you, Auntie Ann?" Mary asked.

"Why, that'd be grand, Mary," Ann replied, "and while we're out there you can tell me all about your family back in England."

Ann had prepared sweet mutton hotpot with dumplings. The last thing she needed to do was the potatoes to go with the meal. There weren't many because they were expensive, but Ann intended to prepare a meal the family would not forget in a hurry.

Everybody thoroughly enjoyed their dinner. Ann stood up to collect the plates. "I hope you've left some room," she said.

They all looked at her. "What else have you prepared?" John asked his wife. "Cranachan."

Sarah looked at Robert. Mutton she understood. "What's Cranachan?" She whispered to him.

Robert smiled. "It's made wi' raspberries, hinny. You'll love it."

"Do you need any help, Auntie?" Mary asked.

"Aye, a spare pair o' hands will come in useful," Ann replied.

Mary stood up and picked up some more plates. She followed her aunt out to the kitchen and reappeared a few minutes later with two desserts. She put them down in front of her parents and then went back for some more. Ann carried in some more on a tray, and Mary brought the spoons. Sarah had never tasted anything so wonderful before.

After they had eaten and Ann, Sarah and Mary had cleared away they all sat talking some more. Finally, it was time to leave. John needed to have an early night, being a baker. John and Ann walked the family back to the station and they waited for their train. The journey home was uneventful, just the way Sarah liked it.

As they travelled home they talked about their wonderful day. It had been gloriously hot and everybody had enjoyed it so much. They finally arrived back at Lanark just before nine o'clock, and, true to his word, Thomas Carruthers was there waiting for them.

At the start of July Mary went up to the village to do some shopping for her mother and came back home singing. "Ma'!" she called out.

Sarah stopped doing her washing and looked up. "What is it?" she answered.

"I went in the Post Office on Abbey Green and Mary Scott asked me if I wanted tae work there, as she'd just had tae let Euphemia Campbell go on account she was having a baby."

"So, what did you say?" Sarah asked, hopeful.

"I said I'd be happy tae work there." Mary looked at her mother. "Are you pleased, ma'?"

"Oh, Mary, I couldn't be happier," answered Sarah. "You needed something tae keep you busy during the day, well done, lass."

Sarah gave her daughter a hug. Sarah realised her daughter was, at last, showing some welcome initiative.

That weekend Robert came home from work with a skip in his step. He opened the door to their cottage and called out to Sarah, "Sarah! I start work on the new Lanark railway station next week!"

Sarah, who was in the bedroom, came out in a rush. "You didn't tell me!" she said, annoyed but happy at the same time.

"I wanted tae surprise you, hinny," said Robert. "I made the mistake of telling you about the Lesmahagow line, and nothing's happened yet. Well, I didnae want tae jinx the Lanark work, so I said nothing. And it worked out for the best!"

Sarah was overjoyed. "Oh, Robert," she said, "that is wonderful news... How long will it take tae build?"

"Should be a couple o' years' worth o' work, for sure," replied Robert. "It's going tae be a big build – plenty tae keep me busy! And by that time – hopefully – the Lesmahagow line will have started, so I can just move over the way a bit!"

"And that's not the only bit of good news... Mary has got herself a job in the village – at the Post Office on Abbey Green," added Sarah.

"Well, it's about time she got herself working," replied Robert. "She's been left school long enough! Agnes had been working a full year before she was Mary's age!"

As they spoke, Mary came in from the village. Robert turned to look at her. "I hear you've been busy while I was away," he said to her.

"Did ma' tell you I got a job?" she asked.

"Aye, lass, he replied. "It's braw news! Come here and gie me a hug."

Mary ran over to her father and he hugged her. "I've some news o' my own," he said to her. "I shall be living at home every day for a good while now."

"Oh, da', that's grand," Mary replied. "Does ma' know?"

Robert nodded. He was pleased. For the first time in a few years he felt sure that everything was finally going alright.

The next week was so different for Sarah and her family. For the first time since they had moved to Scotland she was happy. She prayed that he would never have to work away again. The children, too, were overjoyed at Robert being at home all week.

Mary enjoyed her new job. She was happy to be doing something during the day, and earning money was a bonus. John now wanted to work. He had finished with school now, but for the time being he found something to do that he enjoyed. The village had a quoits team. They were very competitive and John joined them. He did very well for a beginner, and had high hopes of joining their main team.

Summer turned into Autumn, and there was love in the air. Agnes Day had met and fallen in love with William Prentice, also from the village. William asked for her hand in marriage and George Day told him how pleased he was that William wanted to marry his daughter. Agnes was overjoyed and a date for the wedding was set.

Sunday 18 December 1853 dawned very cold, but fine. The wedding was due to start at the kirk at 2 o'clock, so the bridal party were going to leave the cottage half an hour earlier. Thomas Carruthers had brought his cart out for the bride to travel to the kirk. All the neighbours were watching for the door to open. Finally, the door opened and Mary Day came outside, followed by the bride and the rest of the family.

Sarah Crossan was the first to speak. "Oh, look – here they come."

"Aye, ma'," replied her daughter Agnes, "Aye, ma', oh what a pretty dress."

"It's a bit like my sister Mary's dress was," added Sarah McWilliam, "when she got married a few years back, only hers was more summery. It's funny how everybody gets married in white these days."

Mary McWilliam added, "I dinnae want tae get married when it's cold. I want to be able tae wear a summer dress!"

They watched Thomas help Agnes into the cart, followed by her father. They set off, walking slowly. Their neighbours fell in behind the cart, following them to the kirk. Jane Carruthers gave the signal. "Right, let's fall in behind the family." Everybody walked behind the cart to the kirk for the wedding.

It almost felt like one of the McWilliam family was getting married, the families lived together so closely. Mary McWilliam became determined she wanted to get married as soon as possible. She sat with Alexander Day at the kirk. He was quite happy to be seen with her.

The days passed and Winter became Spring. It was another year passed by and Russia had annexed the Crimea. By 31 March

1854 the newspapers were full of the details of Britain's declaration of war, and the various campaigns. Robert was discussing the situation with Sarah as she cooked the evening meal.

"What about William?" Sarah asked. "Will his regiment go to the Crimea?"

Robert shook his head. "William's wi' the East India Company, hinny. He'll continue tae be in India for the time being. Mind, there's more than enough trouble in India tae keep them busy!"

"It seems so long since we last saw him – or heard from him," Sarah added. "He hasn't written for ages."

"He's a young lad," said Robert. "His mind's on other things."

"Hmph!" retorted Sarah, "I suppose so… Still, it wouldn't hurt for him tae put pen to paper once in a while!"

A few days passed and the declaration of war was all around the village. Young men were volunteering, simply to get away from the dull village life. On 1 May 1854 Sarah was preparing the evening meal and Robert had just returned from work.

Suddenly, the front door opened and in ran Mary. She had a thick coat on, reflecting how cold it was outside. She was clearly upset. Sarah looked at her, concerned. "Why, Mary, whatever's the matter?"

"Alex Day has only gone and volunteered!" Mary exclaimed. "He's just come in and told his ma' and da'!"

Sarah was very surprised. "Alex? Volunteered? Where were you, then? I thought you were supposed to be at the Carruthers' – with Helen?"

"I was," Mary replied, "but there was such a commotion outside we had tae go look and find out what it was all about. His ma' was real upset. His da' was shouting an' everything."

"Oh, my," said Sarah, not knowing what to say, but thinking about William.

Robert sighed. "There'll be a lot o' young men doing the same – I'll warrant! Just you see."

Mary was more than upset at Alex enlisting. Sarah realised that Mary must have grown up feelings for him. It came almost as a shock to Sarah to realise that her daughter was becoming a woman.

But life carried on. Mary calmed down as she realised there was nothing she could do about Alex. That Friday, however, she came home with a skip in her step. She had just left the Post Office after work and was walking through the village when she saw a soldier coming towards her. She thought nothing of it, as by now there were many soldiers in the village. This one, however, was making a beeline towards her.

As he got closer she saw who it was. Her heart began to beat faster and she ran towards him.

"Alex!" she called out. He, too began to run towards her and he grabbed her and lifted her up in his arms.

"Oh, Mary!"

He put her down and they stood there for a moment, holding each other. Then Mary stepped back and looked at him.

She smiled. "Just look at you," she said. "All smart in your new uniform."

Mary stood there, taking it all in. He had on his head a black pill-box style hat with a red and white chequered band. There was a red bobble on the top and two black ribbons down the back.

His tunic was red, with a white stand-up collar, white horizontal leather straps, buckled together, looking like stripes across the front, red epaulettes with white horizontal stripes and white border, a white bandolier across from left to right and his cuffs were yellow.

He wore a kilt in the traditional regimental colours, black green and blue, which was fastened with a white belt and gold buckle. Around the front of the kilt was placed a large sporran with white tassels. He had on long white socks with spats, and the top of the socks were edged in red and white with a red ribbon hung on the outside of the leg.

"Aye, it's good tae see you, Mary," he replied. "I was hoping I'd get the chance tae speak wi' you."

"Why?" Mary asked, now feeling shy.

"We're away come Monday, so we've been allowed home tae see our loved ones afore we go."

"Go where?" Mary asked, naively.

"Crimea," was his reply.

Mary stood still. Her jaw dropped in horror. "Crimea?" she said.

"Aye, Mary," he replied. "It's what I enlisted for."

"I know," she said, regaining her composure, "I just wasn't expecting it so soon."

They began to walk on to Auchtykirnal. Mary had recovered from the shock, now. "Come see ma' and pa' first," she said.

"Aye, Mary," he said, "I'd intended tae do as much."

They continued to walk, talking as if nothing had happened, now. Finally, they reached Mary's cottage.

Inside the cottage, Sarah was cooking the evening meal. John was reading the previous day's newspaper and the other children were playing on the floor. The front door opened. Sarah was expecting her daughter home from work, so when she came in it was no surprise.

Sarah continued with her cooking without looking up, until Mary spoke.

"Look who I met on the way home!"

Sarah looked and couldn't believe her eyes. "Why, Alex… Look at you, in your smart red uniform. I would hardly have recognised you!"

"Thank you Mrs. McWilliam," Alex replied. I'm off to the Crimea on Monday, so we've been given leave tae return home for the weekend tae say our goodbyes tae our families."

Sarah was shocked. "Oh, no! So soon? But you've not been enlisted very long."

Alex nodded, "Aye, but they need the troops. Tae be honest, I'm glad Mary brought me in tae see you. I was wondering if you'd be sae kind as tae keep your eye on my ma' while I'm away – since my da's no' sae well at the moment."

"Come, sit down," said Sarah, sitting down, herself. Alex did as she asked.

"So, what regiment are you in?" Sarah asked him.

"The 93rd Highlanders," he replied.

It meant nothing to her, but she continued, "and how long will you be away?"

247

"I dinnae ken. How long can a war go on for?" he replied.

"Well, don't you worry yourself, Alex," said Sarah. "I'll see your ma's well looked after – I know she's having problems with your da' – I hear it sometimes. Now, you must be away and go see your family."

Alex looked relieved. They both stood up and Alex turned to go. "Aye, I will. Thank you, Mrs. McWilliam."

Alex went outside, with Mary following him. She gave him another hug. Sarah watched him do this and then returned to her cooking.

Alex could hold back no longer. He held Mary's head and kissed her. Mary struggled for a second and then relaxed. She realised this was wonderful. Her first ever grown up kiss. Finally, Alex let go. "I'll no doubt see you later," he said, as he disappeared into his cottage. Mary stood there, watching him go. She smiled to herself, then she turned and walked back inside her cottage.

"Doesn't he look smart, ma' – in his uniform," Mary said, as she closed the door.

Sarah turned to look at Mary. "Well, yes, he does." She stopped to think for a moment. "I'm glad my John's not old enough to volunteer!"

Next day, straight after the evening meal Mary went out. Sarah knew where she was going. She knew that Mary was in love with Alex and she hoped it wouldn't end in tears – especially now he had enlisted.

Robert didn't notice Mary go out, but he saw John reading his old newspaper. He felt proud of his children. The younger children went to bed, so Sarah and Robert were at last able to talk.

"Where's our Mary gone?" Robert asked.

"She's round at the Day's," Sarah replied. "Alex is about tae go tae the Crimea and he came home yesterday for a last couple of days with his family. She gets on really well with him."

Robert shook his head. "This war's a bad thing. There'll be lots o' young men die – you'll see."

Sarah looked horrified. "I don't understand why we have to go all the way tae Russia. What's so important we fight against the Russians?"

Robert tried to explain. "It all started wi' talk of religion and partitioning Turkey, which didnae go down well wi' the Turks. Then, last year Russia invaded parts o' Turkey tae see what would happen. They didnae expect us tae declare war on them."

"So, the Crimea's in Turkey?" Sarah asked.

"No, it's part of Russia," Robert continued," but it's where there troops are. The main place that's disputed is the Black Sea, which is why Crimea is so important – it's right in the middle. The other side o' the Black Sea is Turkey."

John looked up from his newspaper. "I think it's exciting, being a soldier," he began.

Sarah was horrified. "Don't' you go talking like that my boy!"

"Why," John asked. "What's wrong with being in the army? It's better than working on a farm!"

"Well, you're too young, for one thing!" Sarah retorted, afraid he wanted to enlist. "William was allowed to enlist. Why can't I?"

"Oh, Sarah," said Robert, trying to calm Sarah down, "it's only natural... He's a boy – granted he's no' old enough yet for the army, but who are we tae talk. Look at William."

"Well, yes," Sarah began, "but he was nearly sixteen when he volunteered. And we weren't at war!"

Robert could see he would not win against Sarah. "Hmm," he said, changing the subject. "What time did you say Mary would be back?"

"I didn't," said Sarah, curtly. "Let the girl enjoy herself. She likes Alex, and he'll be gone tomorrow."

Mary wasn't late in. Alex had left that evening, so once he'd gone she had no reason to stay out. She was very quiet when she came in, but kept reading through the newspapers every day to scan for news of the 93rds.

Meanwhile, life carried on in the village as normal. John continued to play for the Lesmahagow Quoits Club in their junior side. They had been revived 2 years earlier and their results were impressive. They took on all the teams in the district, and it was rare they were beaten. John was learning the game, but he was a quick learner.

Bad news came by way of a telegram during the early afternoon of Friday 26 May. It said, "MA DIED SUDDENLY OF HEART FAILURE 25 MAY. FUNERAL MONDAY. ROBERT." Sarah read the message over and over again. She would never again see her mother. It was so final. She wanted to go to the funeral but she knew it was impossible. How could she go and leave Robert and the children? She sat down and cried. Mary was in the bedroom and she heard her mother crying. She came out. "What's the matter, ma'?" she asked.

"It's your granny," she said, holding the piece of paper out. Mary took it and read it.

"No!" cried out Mary, in dismay. "We're so far away! It's not fair!"

"We have our happy memories of my ma'," said Sarah, calming down. "It'd be grand tae go to the funeral, but it's not going tae happen, and we both know it."

"But it's not fair!" added Mary.

Robert was deeply upset when he came home from work that evening. Not only because his mother-in-law had died but also because he knew that Sarah would have liked to go to the funeral. They both knew it was just not possible. She would have to have taken all the children with her on her own. It was bad enough coming up to Scotland the first time, but there were more of them now.

The best they could do was to spend a few hours on the day of the funeral in deep respect for the woman they owed so much. Sarah didn't have time to stay maudlin, though. There was far too much going on in her household. As the days passed she reflected less and less. Her mother had lived to be in her sixties, so she had done well.

May turned into June and the McWilliam brothers saw more of each other. It was easier for John and Ann to come and visit Robert and his family, and this particular sunny, summer day,

Sunday, 25 June 1854, Sarah saw fit to pack a hamper and take everybody out for a picnic to Birkwood, near the waterfall. The younger children, Jane, Sarah and David, were running around, enjoying themselves and the adults were sitting talking.

"This is lovely," began Sarah. "It's a beautiful day, my family is all here…"

"The sun's shining," continued Mary. "This is so pretty."

Robert nodded. "It's days like this when I'm glad we made the move back tae Scotland."

"For sure," replied Sarah. "I cannae imagine anywhere so beautiful back in Birkenhead!"

John turned to his brother. "I expect Birkenhead is a wee bit like Greenock, is it not?"

"Well," Robert began, "it is a port on a big river, but it is much more built up than Greenock. I was so glad when Sarah agreed tae moved back up here."

John turned to his nephew. "So, John, have you left school now?"

"Aye, uncle, just this term," he replied.

"Have you decided what you'll do wi' yourself?" his uncle asked.

"No, uncle – no' yet," replied John. "I expect I'll work on the land for a bit for now. I've just taken up playing quoits wi' the local team."

"Quoits?" John's uncle repeated. "Well, it's something tae keep you occupied, I suppose. Mind, being in a village, there's no' a great deal otherwise tae do."

Ann was listening to all the conversations. "Strange how things turn out, isn't it? If you'd stayed in England we'd never have been able to get tae know you!"

"True," Sarah replied. "I'm so pleased for Robert – and for me, too. It's lovely tae have family close by. We were such a close bond at home – I was afraid I was going tae be lonely."

Young Jane walked over to her aunt. "Auntie Ann, will you come with us to the waterfall?"

"Aye," replied Ann, standing up as she spoke, "and that's another thing – we'd never have had little ones around us. They make life so rich, so much fun! Come on!"

Ann ran off with the three children, and out of sight, on their way to see the waterfall.

Sarah and Mary chuckled as they watched them go. Sarah said, "It's almost like we've injected new life into John and Ann!"

Finally, the lovely day had to come to an end. It was time for John and Ann to return home. Sarah packed up the remains of the picnic back into the hamper and the family went back to the cottage. John and Ann said their goodbyes and they set off for home.

The seasons moved on and summer turned into autumn. It was Monday 13 November 1854 and it was a dismal day outside. Sarah was at home doing her washing while John played with his siblings. He had been trying to teach Sarah to read but she didn't want to learn, so he had given up. Jane was at school and Mary was at work.

There was a knock at the front door so Sarah went and opened it. Mary Day stood there with a crumpled piece of paper in her hand, tears streaming down her face.

Sarah took one look at her and then the piece of paper, and said, "Why, Mary, whatever is it?"

"I'm sae sorry tae bother you," Mary began.

"It's nae bother, Mary – come on in!" urged Sarah.

Mary slowly made her way inside, despair etched on her face. "This came today," she said, handing the piece of paper to Sarah. Through her tears she managed to say, "It's Alex!"

Mary collapsed into Sarah's arms and she propelled her to a chair. Sarah looked at the piece of paper and saw that it was a telegram. As she read it she understood.

"Oh, no!" said Sarah. "How can this be? Balaklava? I know the troops were going there – Robert's been telling me all about it from the paper. Does George and the children know?"

"George is out," Mary began, somewhat regaining her composure, "and I've no' told the bairns – the young ones are at school, and the older ones are working. I dread tae think how George will take it. He was so angry when Alex joined up."

"My Mary will be so upset, too," added Sarah, "she had a real soft spot for your Alex."

"That she did!" replied Mary.

"Do you want a cup o' tea, Mary?" asked Sarah.

"Aye, that'd be grand," Mary answered.

Sarah got them both a cup of tea and the two women then sat talking. Mary felt a lot better having spoken with Sarah and was soon able to go home.

After she had left, John stopped playing with the little ones. "Ma'," he said, "Do a lot of people die when they go to war?"

"Too many!" she said, angrily. "Now do you understand why I dinnae want you to join up?"

"A bit," he said. "What's Mary going tae say?"

"I don't know, lad, I don't know," Sarah replied.

Later that afternoon, John went to collect Jane from school. It wasn't too long before they were home again. Sarah began to cook the evening meal. She was trying to work out the best way to tell Mary about Alex. Soon, Mary arrived home and took her coat off.

"Evening, ma'," she said, jovially. Sarah looked up. "Why so sad, ma'?"

Sarah let out a big sigh. "Sit down, Mary," she said. Mary sat down.

"What is it, ma'?" Mary asked.

Sarah came over and knelt in front of Mary. "It's Alex," she began. "Mary came round to see me today, with a telegram." Sarah stopped and looked at Mary, hoping that she wouldn't have to say any more. Mary just looked quizzical.

"There's been a big battle, Mary," Sarah took hold of Mary's hand. "There were a lot of casualties."

"NO!!!" Mary shouted. "NO! Please don't tell me he's dead!"

"I'm so sorry," Sarah said. "His mother was devastated, as I know you must be."

"NO! NO!" Mary jumped up. "You can't know how I feel. You can't!" She started to walk around the room. "It has to be a mistake. He's not dead. Maybe he's just been hurt."

Mary grabbed her coat and walked out of the door. Sarah thought she had gone to see Mary Day, so she let her be. She'll be back soon.

But Robert was home first.

Robert walked in the door. There was no joy in the air, tonight, and no Mary.

"What's the matter?" Robert asked.

Sarah looked up from dishing up the food. "It's Alex... Alex from next door... Mary's had a telegram," she said.

Robert looked shocked. "He's dead?"

"Aye," replied Sarah. "Balaklava."

Robert sat down in surprise. He put his newspaper down. "I've just been reading about it," he said. "It was a bad decision that caused a lot of unnecessary suffering. The cavalry rode tae their deaths – and the 93rd's were badly outnumbered. They formed a thin line – they're calling it "The Thin Red Line". That poor boy – he didnae stand a chance! Where's our Mary?"

"She's out," Sarah replied. "Don't ask where. I don't know."

Robert was confused. "What d'you mean "you don't know?"

"Well," said Sarah, "she came in from work and I told her about Alex. You know she had a soft spot for him."

"Aye, she did like him," mused Robert. "How's Alex's family doing?"

Sarah continued, "well, no sooner had I said about him, she put her coat back on and went out – without a word. She's upset. I thought she'd gone round tae see Mary, but she's not there."

"So how's Mary Day, now?" Robert asked.

"Mary was devastated this morning," said Sarah. "She was on her own when the telegram came. She came straight round here, and stayed with me for most of the day. She didn't know how she was going to tell George."

"Does he know now?" Robert asked.

"Aye, he does," answered Sarah. "He came home about an hour since. I'm guessing she told him, for there were some raised voices and then he stormed out."

"I suspect you'll find him down the ale house," Robert replied. "He spends a lot o' time down there."

"I thought as much." Sarah paused. "Oh, and I'm expecting again."

There was silence. Robert did a quick double-take. "That was a quick change o' subject!" he said in surprise. "What is it wi' you women? Every woman in this village is forever having babies! And when is it expected?"

Sheepishly, now, Sarah replied, "In the summer."

"Right."

"It's not all my fault, you know," Sarah said defensively. "You had a part in it!"

The family ate their dinner. Sarah kept a plateful back for Mary, for when she did return home. The evening wore on and the children went to bed. Finally, the door opened and Mary walked in.

"So where've you been all this while?" Robert demanded.

"I was up in the village – wi' Jean Gibb, from Turfholm," Mary replied, subdued. "I know her from working at the post office."

"Oh, aye," said Sarah. "And how old's she?"

"She's just a bit more than a year older than me," answered Mary. "She works at James Scott's grocer's shop. I needed someone tae talk to about Alex".

"And you didn't think it important enough tae tell me where you were going?" Sarah snapped.

"I didnae think you'd understand," answered Mary.

"Oh, Mary," Sarah began. "Has this family not seen enough tragedy? Of course I understand, but it'd just help if you tell me what you're doing. Do you not think I care about you?"

"I'm sorry, ma'," said Mary, now beginning to cry. "I just wanted tae be out of the house."

Sarah went over to Mary and helped her take her coat off. She gave her a hug.

"Right, at least we know now," said Robert, calmer now, "and you'll tell us in future?" Mary nodded.

"Away tae your bed, lass."

"Aye, da'," said Mary. Slowly, she went to bed, drying her eyes.

"She's growing up," said Sarah. "She'll be fine."

Robert looked at the closed bedroom door and then at Sarah. He tutted. "She's nothing like Agnes. She's going tae be trouble."

Mary did recover from her loss. Sarah saw her get over Alex as the days passed. Hogmanay passed and the spring came around again. Sarah got bigger and was looking forward to having this baby. She would have no more. Six was enough!

Sunday 1 April 1855 was a day for John and Ann McWilliam to visit. They knocked at the door and Sarah opened it.

"Come in!" said Robert, jumping up. "It's grand tae see you again. How're things?"

"We're fine. And yourselves?" said John.

"Aye," said Sarah, "everything's fine. Sit yourselves down."

John and Ann sat down, each in different parts of the room. Ann sat with Sarah in the kitchen end while Robert and John sat over the other side of the room.

"Would you like a cup o' tea?" Sarah asked. "I've put the water on."

"That'd be lovely," answered Ann. "You've grown quite a bit since we were here last."

"Aye," replied Sarah. "I'll be glad when it's been born."

Jane, Sarah and David were out back, playing, when they heard their aunt and uncle arrive. They came crashing in through the front door to greet them.

"Hello!" they all shouted in greeting. They clamoured to be first with their uncle and then their aunt.

"John and Mary not here?" Ann asked.

"No," Sarah replied, "they're in the village wi' the other youngsters – it being Palm Sunday – and they're doing a walk round the local district. We've gone before, but wi' me expecting I just cannae do it."

Sarah went over to the stove and made the tea. Little Sarah held out some papers to her aunt. "Auntie Ann, would you like tae see some o' my drawings?"

"Aye, Sarah," replied Ann, taking them from her. "I'd love tae – are these them?"

Meanwhile, at the other end of the room, the men were talking.

"John," said Robert, "would you like some beer?"

"Aye, Robert… I would," replied John.

Robert got a glass of beer for himself and John and then sat down with him. John took a drink from his glass. "Ahh... That's grand... So, how's work going?"

"It's almost done now. We're working on the railway station at Lanark. That should be finished soon."

The two men stopped to take a drink. John started to speak. "What'll you do –" John's question was interrupted as John had a huge coughing fit. He managed to control it and then continued his question. "– when the Lanark work's finished?"

"Are you alright, man?" said Robert, concerned.

Almost at the same moment in time Ann asked, "Is that you coughing again, John?"

"Aye," replied John, "it was my ale – just went down the wrong way."

Ann returned to Sarah's pictures. "Why, Sarah, these pictures are wonderful!" she exclaimed.

"John helps Sarah wi' lots o' stuff," Sarah told her sister-in-law. Drawing, writing and reading. He's a real help wi' the little ones."

"That's grand," said Ann. She turned to Jane, who was waiting patiently for her turn. "And what have you been up tae lately, Jane?"

Beaming, Jane relied, "When I'm no' at school I help at the Day's house wi' the weaving."

Looking up at Sarah, Ann asked, "Do they have a hand-loom, then?"

"Aye, they do, and they have bobbin-winders, to get the thread ready for weaving." Sarah replied. "Jane's useful, for their children are growing now, so there's not so many tae help."

"I start school soon," announced David. Ann looked at David. "How old are you now then, Davy?"

"I'm 3 years and 8 months now," said David, proudly.

Ann smiled at him. "You're getting tae be a big boy, now, aren't you?"

"Aye, Auntie," he said, going all shy.

Returning to the men, Robert comforted John after his coughing fit. "Oh, Ann seems tae think it's a wee bit more than something going down the wrong way, man."

"That woman's a born worrier!" John retorted.

"Aye, they all are that." Robert remembered the question that John had asked before he had begun to choke. "When the station's finished? They've started on the Lesmahagow line already, so I'll probably work for them afterwards. There's a few big viaducts and tunnels there for sure!"

"I bet your Sarah's glad tae have you at home all the while," said John with a smile.

"Aye, she is that!" answered Robert. "And that's half the trouble," he chuckled, pointing at Sarah's belly. "Mind, I'm glad tae be here, as well!"

With that, Sarah stood up and went over to the stove. She checked the stew pot. "Right, folks, food's ready."

Sarah dished up the food and the family ate a hearty meal. Eventually, it was time for the visitors to return home. John and Ann said their goodbyes and left for the train.

The next week passed by uneventfully. An unexpected letter arrived that Friday. Sarah opened it and read it.

> *Tuesday, 3rd April 1855*
>
> Dear Robert and Sarah,
>
> You will recall the coughing fit my dear John suffered on Sunday. This was not the first time he struggled to breathe, and he suffered another one yesterday. He is driving me mad by denying there might be a problem, so I took it upon myself and I went to the apothecary yesterday and told him about it. He thought it might be an irritation in his throat and suggested I buy some peppermint drops.
>
> I did this and gave them to him in the hope that it will bring him some comfort. I discussed our visits with him, and much as we enjoy coming to see you all, we have decided for a while, at least, to stay home in case travelling was making the irritation worse.
>
> We shall continue to write while we cannot come to see you, and look forward to the time we can visit again.
>
> All our love
>
> Ann and John

"Oh dear," she said, sitting down.

"What is it, ma'?" John asked. "Who's the letter from?"

"It's from your Auntie Ann. Uncle John's not too well," Sarah answered him.

"Da's no' going tae like that," John replied.

"Dinnae say a word till I've told your da'," Sarah told him.

"Fine, ma'," John replied.

Sarah waited until everybody was home. The younger children had all been fed and dinner was almost ready for the others. Robert had come in and taken his coat and boots off.

"Sit yourself down, Robert," said Sarah. "We've a letter from Ann."

"A letter?" said Robert, as he sat down. "But we only saw them at the weekend."

"Aye," answered Sarah, "but remember John had a coughing fit?"

"Well, he said something had gone down the wrong way," Robert replied.

"Aye, but Ann seemed tae think there was more to it than that," added Sarah. "I could tell by the tone of her voice."

"I'm guessing by the way you're talking that she was right," said Robert, less nonchalantly.

"Aye," said Sarah, nodding. "Come Monday the cough started to get more noticeable. She's bought him some peppermint tablets to take to see if they'll help. She says she'd rather they don't come for a while – till it's cleared up."

"Well, that's sensible," said Robert, relieved. "I thought it was something troubling – when you told me tae sit down!"

"Well, I'm troubled!" said Sarah, angrily. "I don't like tae hear of anyone ill – not after Hannah!"

Robert looked at John and Mary, then heavenward. "Women!!" Almost as an afterthought, Robert turned to Sarah and asked, "How's the dinner coming on?"

"Almost ready!" Sarah replied, now in a temper. Robert put it down to her being pregnant.

At dinner John made an announcement. "I've got on tae the main quoits team now," he said.

"Well done, lad," replied Robert. "When's your first game?"

"We play away to Motherwell in two weeks, but there's a home game against Mauchline on 5 May. Will yous come?" he asked.

Sarah looked at him. "Will it be up in the village?" she asked.

"Aye, ma', down by the kirk," John replied.

"That'll be a grand day out. O' course we'll come," she said.

So Saturday 5 May arrived and the villagers all descended on the playing field down by the United Presbyterian Kirk. There were ten members on each team, and Mauchline was the opposing side. Young John McWilliam was one of the 10 for Lesmahagow. All the family came to watch the game on a warm, sunny day. Lesmahagow was a force to be reckoned with, and Mauchline was their toughest adversary.

The family arrived in good time to get a spot to view the match. Mary helped watch the two youngest children, who got bored easily. Jane was as interested as her parents. John was the sixth team member to play.

"Oh, Robert, look!" said Sarah, "it's John's turn tae play, now."

"Aye, he's sure tae do well," answered Robert, "he's been practising enough!"

"I've never seen this game before," said Sarah. "How exactly is it played?"

Robert smiled, and began to explain. "Those are the quoits over there – see those big flat metal discs?"

Sarah looked in the direction Robert was pointing and saw them. Robert continued, "Well, they weigh about 11 pounds and you have tae throw them about 18 feet tae the pin that's in the clay. See the clay over there?"

Sarah peered as hard as she could. She could see the clay area but that was all. "Aye, I see the clay, but I cannae see the pin!"

Robert smiled. "That's because it's flat to ground."

"Well how the hell am I supposed tae see it then?" retorted Sarah.

Robert tried to stay calm. He continued. "That man stood over there, by the clay will put a marker on where the pin is, so the thrower knows where tae aim."

"Well, I cannae see any marker!" replied Sarah in disgust.

"Will you just watch, woman, and you'll understand," said Robert, in exasperation. "Watch – here goes John now."

They both watched the play. John threw his first quoit and it landed close to the mark, but about a foot out. Sarah peered as hard as she could. "Did it land where it should have?"

"Almost," answered Robert. "Now his opponent has tae make his play, tae see if he can get closer. Then they'll each go again."

The opponent made his attempt. John and he then alternately took their remaining two turns each, getting closer each time. His opponent's all landed on the opposite side of the pin, but a fraction further off than each of John's did. The distances were measured and the result went to John. The result was put up on the board for all to see.

"See," said Robert, "John's quoit was closer tae the pin – he won the point."

"That's grand!" Sarah replied, excitedly, thinking to herself that she didn't see at all. "So how many goes are there?"

"Each man has three goes," said Robert. "It depends on how many play. There can be as few as ten on each team, but there can also be more. Today there's ten men on both teams."

Sarah began to understand the game a little, anyway. Robert continued, "So at the end of the game they tally up which men won their game, and the team with the most wins are declared the victors. Does that make sense?"

"After a fashion," replied Sarah.

The game continued. Mauchline was a hard team to beat, but so was Lesmahagow, and all the other villages knew it.

"Is it over?" asked Sarah, as she saw the men patting each other on their backs and shaking hands.

"Aye, hinny," Robert replied. "They're just working out the score. Look – there's five from either side won their games."

"So who won?" asked Sarah.

"It was a draw, hinny," said Robert. "They both scored the same number of wins per person."

"Oh, that's a shame," said Sarah, disappointedly. "I wanted the village to win."

All the players started to pack up the game and they then walked over to their families.

"Here comes John, now," said Robert, standing up.

"Did you see me win?" John asked.

"Aye," said Sarah, as Robert helped her stand up. "That we did. You did well."

"Shame the team didn't all win their matches, mind," added Robert.

John nodded. "Mauchline are a hard team tae beat, so we did well tae get a draw. Are you coming tae the inn for a celebration drink, da'?"

Robert wanted to go with him, but he looked at Sarah and could see she was tired.

"You go, John," Robert said. "Your ma's tired, and it's a way tae walk home. We've the little ones, as well. We'll see you later, lad."

"Fine, da'," said John, fully understanding. "Glad you enjoyed watching the game. See yous later." With that, John walked off to where his team mates were standing and when all of them were together they walked off.

Mary came over with David and Sarah. "Do you mind if I stay in the village with the other girls?"

Sarah looked at her. "Will you be long before you get home?" she asked.

"Let the lass be out wi' her friends for a while," added Robert, feeling generous.

"Alright, then, lass," said Sarah, unconvinced. "We'll see you later, too."

Mary went over to her friends and they, too, walked off. Robert, Sarah and the three other children slowly strolled home.

Sarah was relieved when she got home. She was getting much bigger, now. There were only two months left to go before the baby was due, and going out anywhere was more and more difficult for her.

Mary wasn't late home, which pleased both Robert and Sarah. John continued to play quoits, and did better in the games he played throughout the summer months.

Finally, Saturday 21 July at about 7 o'clock in the evening, Sarah went into labour. Both Robert and Sarah knew the signs by now, so Robert had asked Mary to go up to the village to get hold of the midwife, who had come directly, knowing that this baby was Sarah's sixth. The baby came naturally at a quarter to midnight with no problems. In fact, Sarah's labour was so quick, she hardly had any time to be in pain.

"You do realise," said the midwife before she left that Sunday morning, "you need to get the baby's birth registered."

"Registered where?" asked Robert.

"At the Bankhouse," the midwife replied. "Duncan Campbell is the new Registrar."

"What, the schoolmaster?" Sarah asked.

"Aye, well he was – until he took this job," answered the midwife. "They're getting a new schoolmaster for the new term."

"We'll be sure tae get the bairn registered," said Robert, as he showed the midwife out.

"What shall we call him," Sarah asked Robert. "I know you wasnae keen on my last choice."

"My grandfather's name was Nathaniel – on my mother's side," he answered. How does that suit?"

"That's a grand name," Sarah answered. "Will you put Nathaniel in his cradle and then come tae bed?"

"Aye," said Robert. He went over to Sarah and took the newborn from her. He gently laid him in the cradle, then got ready for bed and blew the light out. It was well after midnight when Robert finally got into bed with Sarah. They were both tired, but happy. Robert lay there beside Sarah, pleased that everything had worked out in the end.

Robert woke early that morning. Sarah was asleep. Baby Nathaniel had woken in the night and Sarah had fed him. Robert got out of bed quietly and began to see to breakfast. The aroma of the cooking woke the children, who got up, one by one, and came out to the living room.

Jane was the first to emerge. She looked around the room and saw the cradle out again. She looked at her father. "Did we have another sister or brother, da'?" she asked. David and Sarah joined her to look at the new arrival.

Robert turned to Jane and nodded. "It's a boy. Go say hello tae your brother Nathaniel – but quietly, mind."

Mary was up now, hearing all the commotion. She rubbed her eyes as she walked in the room. "What time did it happen, da'?" she asked.

"Fifteen minutes afore midnight, lass," Robert replied. "Your ma' was hardly in labour this time, it seemed!"

"Well, at least now there's three of us," remarked John, first pointing to the baby, then David and finally himself, "and three of them!"

Baby Nathaniel woke up, crying, which woke Sarah up. She sat up and picked the baby up, She put him to her breast to feed. Robert looked over at her. "Morning, Sarah. How're you feeling now?"

Sarah yawned as baby Nathaniel fed. She looked at Robert. "I'm exhausted. This is definitely the last one!"

Robert sniggered. "Where've I heard that afore? Do you want a cup o' tea?""

"Aye," she replied, "that would be grand."

The next three weeks went by in a blur. Sarah was busy with the baby, Mary helped with the other children – when she wasn't at work, and John helped out when Mary was at work. The station at Lanark was now finished, and Robert was now working on the line to Lesmahagow, along with the railway station.

By Saturday, 11 August 1855 things had settled down a bit. Sarah had gotten into a routine with her new baby. Sarah decided as it was such a beautiful day she would sit outside with the new baby to do some chores. Agnes Crossan was walking back from the village. She saw Sarah, sitting outside on a blanket, and decided to come over and see the baby. It was a lovely warm day, but there were clouds building. Sarah Crossan was already outside, on her knees, tending to her garden, as she saw her daughter walking up the road to see her.

Agnes sat down with Sarah McWilliam to see the baby. "Oh, Mrs. McWilliam, he's beautiful."

"How much longer do you have to go wi' your pregnancy?" Sarah McWilliam asked.

"I've another couple o' months tae go yet," she replied. "It's been hard."

Sarah Crossan came over to talk with Sarah McWilliam. Sarah looked up at her neighbour. "Morning Sarah, how're you today?" she said to Sarah Crossan.

"Fine thanks," Sarah Crossan replied. "I see you've brought your latest addition outside. Let me have a look."

Both Sarah McWilliam and Agnes Crossan stood up. Agnes struggled for a bit, but she finally managed to stand erect. Sarah took baby Nathaniel over to show him to her neighbour.

"I didnae know your Agnes was walking out wi' anybody," Sarah McWilliam said.

"She's not," Sarah Crossan retorted, angrily, looking across at her daughter. "William Matheson didnae want tae have anything tae do wi' her – after he's caused all this grief. He said it was a mad moment o' passion and he didnae have any feelings for Agnes. Tae make matters worse he's enlisted and gone tae the Crimea!"

"Oh, you poor girl," Sarah McWilliam replied. "So you'll have your grand-daughter and daughter living with you, then."

"Aye," answered Sarah Crossan. "Not what I'd anticipated at my time o' life!"

"I'm sorry, ma'!" said Agnes, guiltily.

"Aye," replied her mother, "well, you should have been more careful! But what's done is done." Sarah Crossan went back to tending her garden. She knelt down on the ground and went back to clearing away the weeds.

Trying to change the subject, Sarah McWilliam remarked, "You're garden looks pretty."

"Well," Sarah Crossan replied, "I'm getting it ready for the judging – at the Floral and Horticultural Show – at the start of September."

"The show?" Sarah McWilliam answered in surprise. "Oh! I'd clean forgot about that!"

"Well, you did have something else on your mind this year!" Sarah Crossan replied, chuckling away.

"So, I did!" answered Sarah McWilliam, smiling. "What's the date this year?"

"6th September," Sarah Crossan replied. "I hope the weather holds."

"Well," added Sarah McWilliam, "the last couple of weeks have been glorious. Let's hope for more of the same."

"Aye, lass," said Sarah Crossan. "Right, that's me done for now." She stood up. "I'll be seeing you later, Sarah, I'm sure. Come on Agnes, let's be getting inside."

Sarah McWilliam said goodbye to her neighbour and went back to her blanket. She sat there for a short while longer, but felt it was necessary to go inside. There were jobs to be done, and lovely though it was, to be outside in the fresh air, the mid-day meal needed to be cooked. Sarah packed away her sewing when her other neighbour came outside. He looked over at Sarah.

"Morning, Sarah," said Thomas Carruthers, walking towards her. "Glad I spotted you. Is your John working yet?"

"Why, no, Thomas," Sarah replied. "Why, do you know of anybody as wants tae hire him?"

"Aye, I do," answered Thomas. "That would be me. I'm need-ing another farm hand, 'specially now it's coming up tae harvest time. Would he be willing tae work on the land?"

I shall just take my baby inside," said Sarah, "and I'll bring John out so you can speak with him yourself."

"That'd be grand," Thomas replied.

Sarah stood up, picked up baby Nathaniel, and went inside. She soon returned with John, picked up the blanket, and went back indoors.

"What was that all about?" Robert asked Sarah when she went back inside.

"Thomas said he needed another farm hand and wondered if John was working. I told him that he wasnae doing anything yet, so he asked tae see him. That's why I fetched him outside."

A while later John came back indoors with a grin on his face.

"So, do you have a job?" Robert asked.

"Aye, da'," John replied. "I start on his farm on Monday."

"You don't sound very enthusiastic about it," said Sarah.

"I am," John replied, "it's just that I hadnae thought about working on a farm."

"Well, what sort of' a job did you want, then?" asked Robert.

"That's just it – I don't know!" replied John.

"Well, see how you go on the farm," said Sarah. "Gie your-self a chance to find out if you like it. If it doesnae suit, then try for something else."

"Ay, ma', I will," answered John. "I shall gie it my best."

So, on Monday, John was up bright and early, ready to work for Thomas Carruthers. As it turned out, he did enjoy the work.

Maybe it was being out doing something instead of being at home helping with the children. In any event, Jane was now Sarah's main assistant.

Sarah went up to the village, as usual, to get her shopping in and to collect her post. She walked up the road with a skip in her step. Everything seemed to be working out well. Perhaps moving to Scotland had been a good idea, after all. She went to the Post Office to collect her mail, which she put in her bag. She saw Mary there, working behind the counter.

She said hello to the postmistress and the other villagers who were also in there. After the Post Office she went to the grocer's shop to get food for the next few days. She had noticed that there was a letter there from her sister-in-law Jane, so with all her shopping done, she eagerly rushed home to read it.

Once indoors, Sarah put her shopping away and opened the letter from Jane. She stood, reading it, silently, but almost as soon as she started she gasped and had to sit down.

"No! It cannae be!" gasped Sarah.

Jane, who had just sat down with Sarah and David, looked up at her mother. "What is it, ma'?"

"It's a letter from your Auntie Jane in Birkenhead," Sarah replied. "Your sister Agnes is very ill and Uncle Henry's been killed."

"Read it to me, ma'," Jane asked. Sarah, slowly, read to her daughter.

Tuesday, 7th August

My Dear Sarah and Robert,

I apologise for my delay in writing to you, but there has been a tragedy in Oswestry. Our darling brother-in-law Henry Wilson was killed on 26 June. He was out at work when his horses were startled and they bolted. The result of which was that the cart overturned, with him now underneath it.

The harnesses broke and the horses fled. While somebody rescued the horses the cart, which was full to heaving, was lifted off dear Henry. He was still alive, but his injuries were so severe that shortly after his arrival at hospital in Oswestry they were told he was dead.

Our dear sister Mary is heartbroken. She was taken ill after hearing the news, but, thankfully, her brother-in-law Joseph, who was still staying with her, was able to help look after her. Elizabeth Price, who was Mary's neighbour's daughter, helped him look after the children. Mary was ill for almost a month, but the doctor finally said she was fit to travel, as Mary was desperate to return home to us, and she arrived back here last week. Both the boys are currently staying with Henry's parents until Mary has decided what she wants to do.

Joseph remains in Oswestry to finalise Henry's affairs and then he, too, will return. The shock of what happened has upset Joseph, too, we understand.

A further piece of bad news, I'm afraid, is that your Agnes has been taken ill with Smallpox. We will let you know as soon as we hear any more news.

On a brighter note, Robert and I are both doing well, as are all our children. Sarah, Mariah and Jane are out working now, and Margaret and Hannah are growing fast. Margaret has just had her third birthday, and she is a real charmer. Hannah, too, has just had her first birthday – how funny that both girls should be born on the same day, two years apart! Hannah will be walking soon, I am sure. I can't believe it is almost three years since our Mary died.

Wonderful news that your new baby has arrived. Nathaniel is an unusual name – I am sure you have a reason for calling him that.

I am so sorry to be the bearer of such bad news.

Waiting to hear from you, Love,

Robert and Jane

"Oh, ma'," Jane began, "poor Auntie Mary, poor Agnes. What are we tae do?"

"What can we do?" Sarah began, almost in tears. "We're stuck up here in Scotland when we should be home wi' my family!"

Sarah managed to compose herself enough to carry on with her jobs for the day. Finally, Robert came home from work. Dinner was waiting on the table but he could see that all was not well. Sarah showed him the letter. "It's bad news," she added.

Robert sat down and read it. He, too, was shocked. "I cannae believe it," he began. "Why do you no' invite Mary to stay for a while? I know we cannae get tae see our Agnes, but Mary could come here. The change might be beneficial. It's been so long since you saw any of your family."

Robert looked at Sarah as she thought about the idea. "Do you think she'd come?" She replied. "It would be lovely tae see her again, after all this time."

Robert smiled. "Write and ask," he replied. "You'll never know otherwise!"

"Aye," replied Sarah, now enthused with the idea. "I'll do it while yous eat your dinner!" She got out her writing set and began a letter straight away.

When the letter was written Robert coaxed Sarah to eat. She had not wanted to eat anything after the news that had come with the post, but the thought of her sister coming to visit made her realise that she was, indeed, hungry.

The letter was posted next morning, and a reply received a week later. It had taken some persuasion from her brother, Robert, but Mary finally agreed to come. She planned to arrive on Saturday 25 August.

There was so much joy in the cottage. Despite it being autumn, the place had a good spring clean. Not that it was dirty, but Sarah was so overjoyed at having visitors she insisted on the place being spotless. It also gave her something to do with her pent up energy. Finally, the day arrived and Robert took Thomas Carruthers' cart to Lanark station to meet her.

It had been a long journey for Mary. She had travelled the same route that Sarah took, but Mary had travelled alone, so she was overjoyed to see Robert waiting for her at the station when she arrived. He ran up to her and helped her down off the train. He picked up her luggage and they started to walk back to the cart.

"It's wonderful tae see you, Mary," he said, "your bad news, notwithstanding."

"It's grand to be here," she replied. "It was a lovely idea for me to come here. I feel better already."

"Well," replied Robert, "I daresay your sister is desperate tae see you as well."

They got to the cart and Robert loaded Mary's luggage in the back. He then helped Mary climb up and they began the 2 hour long journey back to Auchtykirnal. Back at the cottage, Sarah was full of anticipation. It was a beautiful day, almost as if heaven sent. Sarah kept looking out of the window. The children were playing outside, also watching for their father to arrive with their aunt. Finally, the cart and horses came into view. Jane was the first to see.

"Ma', ma'," Jane called out. "They're coming!"

Sarah rushed outside to see them coming. Finally, Robert pulled up outside the cottage and helped Mary down. Sarah rushed up to her and they hugged each other. Robert fetched the luggage down and returned the cart to Thomas Carruthers.

"Oh, Mary, Mary!" Sarah cried out, with relief.

"Oh, Sarah!" gasped her sister. "Oh, it's so wonderful to see you again. It feels like an eternity since I last saw you"

Robert walked back from the Carruthers' barn. "You must be tired," he said to Mary. "Come on, let's get you inside."

Jane picked up some of her aunt's luggage and carried it inside. "Oh, what a helpful girl you are, Jane," said Mary. "You've grown up so much since I saw you last!"

The whole family then walked inside the cottage and Mary sat down with Sarah.

"I've missed you so much," began Sarah, almost losing the Scottish accent she had begun to acquire. "I can't believe what has happened in so short a time. You must tell me all about it."

"I will, I will," Mary replied.

"Shall I get you a cup of tea?" Sarah asked her sister.

"That would be most welcome," Mary replied.

While Sarah made the refreshment, the children clamoured around their aunt.

David stood in front of his aunt, whilst his sisters sat on the floor in front of her. Mary looked at David. "So, you must be David?" she said.

David nodded in reply. His aunt continued. "I'm your ma's younger sister, Mary. I've a little boy back home who's almost the same age as you."

David's face brightened up. "Where is he?" he asked.

"He's staying with his grandparents just now," answered Mary.

David looked disappointed. "Why didn't you bring him?"

"I've been poorly," Mary replied, "and I needed some time to get better."

The cup of tea was ready. Sarah had already boiled the water, so she was prepared. Sarah brought a cup over for Mary and one for herself. She sat down again.

"I am so glad you decided to come to stay for a while," said Sarah. "Everybody has been so looking forward to seeing you again."

"Where are Mary and John?" Mary asked, "and where's this new baby?"

Sarah stood up and fetched Nathaniel out from his cradle. "Here's Nathaniel," she said, handing him to her sister's waiting arms. "Mary and John are both at work, but they'll be here soon."

Mary looked lovingly down at the baby. "So, why did you call him Nathaniel?" she asked. Sarah explained the reasoning behind the name.

"So, what do you think of the place?" Robert asked.

"I think this place is beautiful," Mary replied, looking around the room. "It sort of reminds me of Tranmere, but it's got a kind of uniqueness about it. The cottage is bigger inside than I imagined."

At that moment the front door opened and John ran in, straight from the field. He rushed up to his aunt. "Auntie Mary!" John cried out. "Oh, it's grand you could come! Mr. Carruthers told me you were here so he let me off early tonight, but said I have tae start early tomorrow."

Mary looked at him. "How you've grown!" she said. "You'll be taller than me, soon!"

"I'll be back in a minute," John said, "I just want tae get out o' my work clothes."

John disappeared into the other room to get changed. Mary took a drink from her cup of tea while John was out of the room. Sarah then stood up and went over to check on the food that was cooking.

"Oh, that's just what I needed," said Mary, putting her cup of tea down for a moment. "I've missed everybody so much. I never really liked Oswestry. I only went because Henry –" Mary began to stifle a sob, but managed to compose herself again – "and Joseph wanted to go. Maybe if he hadn't gone he'd still be here." Mary began to sob, but through the tears she managed to say, "We were so happy!"

Sarah came back and sat down with her sister. "I know you must miss him, Mary," she began. "I don't know what I'd be like if anything happened to Robert, especially up here."

The front door once again opened, and in came Mary, excited to see her aunt again. She rushed up to her aunt, who is desperately trying not to cry.

"Auntie Mary!" said Mary, "I've been desperate tae get home all afternoon."

Mary looked at her. "Just look at you," she said. "This Scottish air has given you a wonderful complexion!"

Sarah smiled and stood up. She went back to her cooking while Mary was occupied. Being with the children was stopping her from crying, at least.

Mary sat next to her sisters on the floor. Mary finished her cup of tea. She stood up and put baby Nathaniel back in his cradle. "Oh, you sweet thing," she said to him. She went and sat back down with her nieces and nephew and they talked.

By now, John had returned, dressed in other clothes. He, too, sat down with his siblings and he joined in with their conversations. Meanwhile, at the other end of the room, Sarah was dishing up the dinner.

CHAPTER 8

Growing pains

The two weeks were blissful. The two sisters, reunited, spent a lot of time reminiscing. Mary loved being with her nieces and nephews.

The day after Mary's arrival, they visited Craignethan Castle, a few miles south west of Crossford. They borrowed Thomas Carruthers cart and horses again. He was more than happy to let the McWilliams use it. It was about a two hour's journey from Auchtykirnal. They left their cottage mid-morning so they could make a day out of it.

The castle was glorious, even though in ruins. They found a place to stop and they had a picnic on the grass, with the castle as a backdrop in the distance.

"This is so beautiful," said Mary.

"Tae think," added Sarah, "we've lived here all these years and this is the first time we've ever come here!"

After lunch they ventured up to the castle ruins and looked round. It was very peaceful there. There were a few other people there looking at the ruins, but the McWilliams were left to wander without interruption. They saw the Keep and the Inner and Outer Courtyards, and marvelled at their beauty.

Finally, they headed back home. They enjoyed the day out so much Mary was beginning to look more like her usual self. Sarah was so pleased that Robert had taken the time to ask people about places they could go to visit.

The younger children were back at school now. Jane was the eldest, now almost 10 years old. She was in charge of the journey through the village with her sister Sarah and brother David, who was 4 years old and ready for school. While the children were at school Sarah involved Mary in visiting the village. Sarah was proud to be showing her sister off to her neighbours.

The following Sunday they visited the Falls of Clyde, just south of Lanark. Once again they borrowed Thomas Carruthers' cart and horses for the two hour journey to New Lanark. It was another glorious day and the family again took a picnic with them. They stopped near Dundaff Linn, the first of the three waterfalls, where they had lunch. It was such a beautiful view of the river Clyde.

"The waterfall is so small," said Jane. "The one near us is much bigger!"

"Aye," said Robert, "but this is the first o' three waterfalls along the river."

"Can we go see them?" Jane asked.

"We can certainly get tae see the next one," Robert answered. "That'll be Corra Linn. It's a way down the river." He pointed away from New Lanark, to where the river curved out of sight.

After they had eaten their picnic they packed up and headed down along the river path to the Corra Linn. When they got down to the bend in the river they could see the Corra Linn, leading down to where the castle sat on the next bend. This was much more spectacular than the Dundaff Linn had been. Robert turned to his sceptical daughter.

"Well, Jane," he said. "What do you think o' this one then?"

"Now, that is much bigger!" she replied. Robert smiled. They stayed there for a while, taking in all the views, but finally, the day out was over, as the family needed to get back home before it began to get dark. Mary was truly happy to have come to Scotland, and now Sarah could also see what her husband liked about it so much.

All too soon, the two weeks were over and Mary had to go home. Saturday 8 September dawned another beautiful and warm day. The family were all outside the cottage with Mary whilst Robert fetched the cart and horses. He drew up outside and loaded Mary's luggage. She had collected some trinkets from the places they had visited – some leaves and flowers. She had also done some drawings of the places. Sarah was impressed with her sister's capabilities. "You are so clever!" Sarah had remarked that first day out, when Mary sketched the castle.

"It's been really wonderful here," began Mary, "these last two weeks. I've loved every minute of it." She had been hiding something behind her back, but she now brought out one of her drawings. "I want you to keep this to remember how happy these two weeks have been for me," she said, handing the sketch to Sarah.

"Oh, Mary!" said Sarah, "It's beautiful! We shall put this up after you've gone. It will remind us of such a happy time."

"I'm so glad you like it," added Mary. "I shall miss you."

Sarah took the picture inside the cottage. When she came out Mary could see she had been crying.

"Don't you dare cry," Mary scolded, "I want to remember your happy face for my journey home."

"It's been so long since I saw anybody from home," replied Sarah. "I'm going to miss you."

"You'll be fine, Sarah McWilliam," said her sister. "You've six healthy children around you, a wonderful husband who idolises you, lots of friendly neighbours. I expect you'll be a bit sad after I've gone – but you'll do alright!"

"Just listen to you," said Sarah, now smiling. "That's the Mary I know and love. Aye, I know I'll be alright, but the place will feel a wee bit empty for a while."

"Now where are my girls and boys?" Mary turned her affection towards her nieces and nephews. The two younger ones clamoured round her but John, Mary and Jane stood back, watching.

Mary bent down to them. "Now promise me you'll both be good," she said. Both Sarah and David, almost together, replied, "We will!" Mary gave them a kiss each, then she stood back upright.

She walked over to the older children. "I still can't get over how much you've grown," she began, "and not only in size! You are all so grown up now." She turned to Mary. "You, especially, Mary. Who'd have thought, sixteen years ago, when I was looking after you as a tiny baby, that we'd have gone through all this, all these ups and downs."

"You take care, Auntie," replied Mary. She gave her aunt a big hug. Mary then turned to John. "And you, John!" she said, "what a strapping young man you are! You'll make some young woman proud."

"Oh, don't!" John replied, embarrassed. He, too, gave his aunt a hug. Then Mary turned to Jane. "Come here, Jane," she said. "Quiet, studious, Jane. You're growing up to be another beauty."

"Will we see you again, soon?" Jane asked.

"Not soon," Mary replied, "but I would love to come again." Jane then hugged her aunt. Finally, Mary walked over to Sarah and gave her a hug that it seemed would never end. They parted and Mary took hold of her sister's hands. "Always, you were my conscience," Mary began. "Even now." Mary smiled at Sarah. "When I came here I was dead on the inside – you've brought me back to life. You are such a treasure to have as a sister. Never forget that!"

"I won't forget," replied Sarah. "I shall miss you, but go back to those boys of yours – both of them – and give them the love I know you have inside you. You won't let everything that's happened get in the way of your happiness. Remember Henry with pride. You both loved each other so much – he'd hate to see you hide away from everyone and everything... Let Henry live through your children!"

Robert was beginning to get impatient. Mary had a train to catch – had everybody forgotten? "I hate tae put a damper on the proceedings," he began, "but we've a train tae catch, and if you're no' careful you'll miss it – and your connection. I dinnae want tae see you stuck at Carlisle overnight!"

With that, the family was brought back to reality. "I'm coming!" said Mary. She hurried over to where Robert stood and he lifted her into the cart. He jumped up beside her and they set off. The others all stood there, waving for all they were worth till they could see the cart no longer. The holiday was over and everything had to go back to normal.

Mary caught her train and got back to Liverpool before it was too late. Robert and Jane were overjoyed to see her and they couldn't conceal their envy at all the places she went to. Sarah received a letter on the Thursday from her sister. She eagerly read it as soon as she got home from the Post Office with it.

Monday, 10th September

Dear Sarah, Robert and children,

Thank you so much for having me these last two weeks. I truly enjoyed every minute of it. It did what nothing else had been able to do. I feel totally restored to health. I shall treasure every minute I spent in Scotland.

You were right, of course, but then you always were, dear sister. I have a hole in my heart where Henry's memory will, forever, live on, but I cannot abandon his dear children. I have spoken with Henry's parents and I intend to move in with them, temporarily, until I can find somewhere else to live. At least being there I will be with the boys. Robert and Jane could barely accommodate me in their small home with all their children, so I know moving on is the right thing to do.

I will write again soon when I know what is happening. All my love, your ever loving sister,

Mary

When the rest of the family came in during the evening Sarah showed them the letter.

"It was such a good idea of yours, Robert," she said, after he had read the letter.

"Aye, hinny," he replied, chuckling to himself, "I do know a wee bit about women!"

The next Saturday morning, 15 September, a telegram arrived from Birkenhead. Sarah handed it to Robert to open because she dare not do it. She sat down before it was opened. There were no babies expected to be born in the family, so it must, therefore, have been bad news.

Robert cautiously opened it. "Well?" asked Sarah, "What does it say?"

Robert stood there reading it for a moment and then he took a sharp intake of breath. Sarah could bear it no longer. "Will you tell me what it says!" she demanded.

"It's Agnes. My dear, sweet, Agnes." He shook his head and his eyes began to water. "She's gone!"

Robert almost fell into the chair that stood beside him. He could no more speak than control his tears. Sarah stood up and walked over to him. She gently knelt down beside him and prised the missive out of his hands. She quietly read it to herself, so that Robert would not hear her as she stumbled over the words. It was a simple telegram, but it said it all.

"AGNES FIGHT WITH SMALLPOX OVER. SUCCUMBED 13 SEPTEMBER IN HOSPITAL. FUNERAL TUESDAY 18TH. WE WILL GIVE HER GOOD SEND OFF IF YOU CANT MAKE IT. ROBERT"

Mary came home from work early that day. She had been there when the message arrived and knew before her parents. She had struggled at work after learning the news, so had been sent home. When she walked in through the door tears were streaming down her face. Sarah watched as she came in from her position at Robert's feet.

"Oh, ma'," Mary cried, "why did He have to take our Agnes?"

"Come here, Mary," said Sarah, standing up but still crying. "Life isn't fair. I don't know why she had to be taken from us. I will never understand." Sarah held Mary and Mary collapsed, sobbing into her mother's arms.

Jane had been playing with Sarah and David in the bedroom, but she came rushing out at the sound of such crying. "What is it, ma'?" she asked. "What's happened?"

Robert managed to regain some of his composure. "It's your sister, Agnes," he managed to say. "We've had a telegram from your uncle. She's passed away."

"Our Agnes? Gone? Why, da'? Why?" Jane couldn't say any more. She, too, began to cry for her sister. Robert held out his arms for her and Jane rushed over to him.

When John came in from the fields the crying had abated somewhat, but he could see immediately that there had been bad news. The telegram had, by now, been put on the table, so he picked it up and read it for himself.

"No! No! It can't be! It can't be!" John cried out in anguish. He looked at his father. "Can we get to the funeral?"

"One of us can," he replied. "It's too expensive for us all tae go."

"It should be you, Robert," said Sarah, standing up from her rocking chair. "She's your child."

"Aye, but you were her mother." Robert said, looking at Sarah.

"Not her proper mother," added Sarah. "It's your duty tae go."

So, arrangements were put in place, and Robert did, indeed, go to his daughter's funeral. A telegram was sent back to Sarah's brother in Birkenhead to let them know that Robert was going. He left for Liverpool on the Monday evening immediately after work. He caught the night mail train from Carlisle to Liverpool and got there first thing in the morning. He made his way over to Birkenhead and got to Morpeth Buildings before there was hardly a soul on the roads. He knocked on the Foulkes' door and Robert opened it.

"Come in man," said Robert Foulkes to his brother-in-law. "Jane," he called, "he's here!"

Robert went inside and sat down with his in-laws as they explained how Agnes had first become ill, and her struggle for life. They were with her at the end and it was a happy release from her pain and suffering. The service was held in the morning at St. Mary's and she was buried in the cemetery, near Hannah. Robert spent a short while with the Foulkes at the wake before returning home to Scotland.

Life, slowly, went back to normal at Auchtykirnal. There were many periods of sorrow and crying, but as life and work continued, the moments of sadness grew less and less. They knew there would, forever, be a hole in their hearts for their dear Agnes, but they also knew that she had been in great pain and was now out of her misery.

The next week, Sarah asked Robert if he could get Mary's sketch put in a frame for her and he said he would. It took him a few days, but finally, the sketch of Craignethan Castle was framed and Robert hung it in the living room on the wall facing the window.

Saturday, 29 September 1855, was a warm, sunny day. Sarah was out in her garden, working on her plants. Baby Nathaniel was outside with her in his carriage. Sarah was taking advantage of the last of the warm weather. Sarah Crossan came out to join her. As the two women were gardening they chatted.

"Morning Sarah," said Sarah Crossan, "another sunny day."

"Aye, that it is," replied Sarah McWilliam. "Has that baby arrived yet?"

"Aye," answered Sarah Crossan, "she gave birth on Sunday. A boy – she's called him William. He's a bonny wee thing. How's your Nathaniel doing?"

"Fine," Sarah McWilliam replied, "he's doing just fine."

They continued gardening for a few minutes and then Sarah Crossan resumed conversation.

"Your sister got home alright after her stay?"

"Aye," replied Sarah McWilliam, "we had a letter from her last week. She's feeling much brighter now. We've heard, though, that our oldest daughter, Agnes, who stayed in England, after we left, has died of the smallpox. It's very sad. She was such a good girl – so loving – I couldn't have done without her." Sarah began to cry again.

"Oh, Sarah, I'm so sorry about that news," replied Sarah Crossan. She didnae come wi' yous, did she?"

"No," answered Sarah, regaining her composure, "she was 18 and decided she wanted to stay. My brother and sister-in-law lived nearby, so they watched over her. But none of them could beat the Smallpox. I so wish we all could have got tae her funeral, but it's so far to go – and there's all the children tae think of up here. Robert did go, but just for the funeral and wake." Sarah felt like she would cry again, so she tried to change the subject. "Your family doing well?"

"Our Bill's not been so good lately," said Sarah Crossan, "but we'll do."

Agnes, had come outside. She heard her mother talking and wanted to show off her new baby. "Oh, it's you, Mrs. McWilliam," she said, feigning surprise. "Come and see my baby."

Sarah McWilliam followed Agnes into their cottage and looked at her baby William. "He is a bonny thing," said Sarah. "Is he feeding well?"

"I'm finding it hard," answered Agnes, "but it's getting easier."

"That's grand," said Sarah. "Well, I must be away. Nathaniel's out in the sunshine and I was almost ready tae take him back inside. You take care, now."

With that, Sarah turned and said her goodbyes to the Crossan family, and went back to her own.

The next month went by quietly enough. Finally, on Saturday, 27 October 1855, a long awaited letter arrived from Greenock. John came down from the village with it and the other mail. He handed all the letters to his father, before going out to work with Thomas Carruthers. Robert looked through them and picked out just the letter from Greenock. The rest he put on the table for later. Sarah was busy doing the housework, Sarah and David were sitting on the floor playing and Jane was reading.

"We've a letter from Ann and John," said Robert. "Shall I read it to you?"

"Aye, I can listen to it as I'm working," replied Sarah.

Robert read out the letter to her, struggling as the letter continued. Halfway through, Robert had to sit down and stopped reading aloud. Sarah stopped what she was doing and went to him.

Wednesday, 24th October

Dear Robert and Sarah

I hope you're all well at your end, sadly the same cannot be said here. As you know, John developed a wee bit of cough when we visited last April. It did seem to get better during the warm summer months, but now that there is a chill in the air, the cough has returned. John went to see a doctor this week, and we now know that he has consumption.

We don't quite know how bad it is, or how long he might suffer with it. We are trying the various remedies offered for sale at the pharmacy, but nothing seems to have much effect. As long as John takes it easy he seems to have good days. He is currently taking Cod Liver Oil, which seems to be helping a little, but I suspect he will not get much better. I seem to be free of the disease myself, so I am taking as many precautions as I am able. We have separate bedrooms now – it was John's insistence – but I wish we did not. I know John would like to see Robert again, if he would like to come, but please, only Robert should come. Now you have that new baby I would not wish any of you to get this horrible disease.

If you cannot come we do understand.

All our love

Ann and John

Sarah took the letter from Robert and finished reading it. "Oh, no! Not more bad news!" she exclaimed. "We've just got used tae being wi'out Agnes and Henry, and now it looks like we're going tae lose your brother. It's no' fair!"

"They want me tae go visit," Robert began. "What do you think? Is it wise?"

"He is your brother," said Sarah. "He may linger for a while. I've heard of people suffering for years wi' it. What did Ann say was helping? Let me read the letter again." Sarah sat down in her chair and read through the letter. "Ah, here it is… Ann says that Cod Liver Oil is helping. Perhaps you should take some before you go. You never know – it might stop you getting it." She looked at him, tenderly. "I think you should go."

"Aye, I will," said Robert, somewhat recovered. "But first, I'll take some of this Cod Liver Oil!"

So, over the next few weeks, Robert prepared himself for the visit. Sarah bought some cod liver oil and Robert took it, disgusting though it was. It was agreed that Robert should visit the first weekend of December.

Saturday, 1 December 1855 Robert caught the 10 o'clock train from Lanark and was in Greenock in just over 3 hours. He arrived at his brother's house and Ann let him in. He put his small bag down.

"Oh, Robert," said Ann, "I am so glad tae see you. John will be pleased you've come." She took Roberts coat and hung it up.

"How is he?" Robert asked.

"No' well," replied Ann, "but come in and warm yoursel' up. Do you want anything tae drink or eat?"

"Aye, now you come tae mention it," Robert replied, "I could do wi' a bite tae eat and a beer or something."

Ann made Robert sit down and she fetched him a sandwich. While he was waiting, John shuffled into the room. This once tall, fit man was now reduced to a shadow of his former self. He made his way over to a chair and turned to Robert. "Oh, man," he said, quietly, "it's sae grand tae see you again. Wish I felt better."

"I cannae believe it," said Robert. "We've just got back together again after all these years and now this happens!"

"Aye," said John, catching his breath, "but at least we did meet up." John leaned back into the chair and sat quietly for a few minutes.

Ann soon returned with the sandwich. She sat down on another chair in the room with them.

"How is everybody back home?" she asked.

"Fine," replied Robert, "fine." He sat eating his food. "Agnes died a couple o' months ago," he added.

"Oh no!" said Ann. "The poor girl. We didnae meet her, did we?"

"No," said Robert, shaking his head. "She stayed on in England after we left. She decided she was old enough and had a good job, living in at Birkenhead Park. The wife's brother and sister-in-law were making sure she was doing alright."

"What did she die of?" Ann asked.

"She had the smallpox," answered Robert. "I made it tae the funeral. She was only 22." He sat thinking of the last time he had seen her alive. "It's just one thing after another."

They looked over at John. He had fallen asleep in the chair. "He does a lot o' that," said Ann, looking at him fondly.

John slept for a lot of the weekend, and Robert found himself getting to know Ann a lot better. He could see she was devoted to John and was glad he had somebody to care for him. Ann had a spare mattress that she put down on the floor for Robert in the living room, which is where he spent the night. Next morning he got up early, had breakfast and spent some more time with his brother, who was still in bed. By lunchtime Robert was ready to go home. He knew it was only a matter of time before he would be the sole survivor of his family. He said his goodbyes and left for the station. In just under four hours he was back home again. He put his bag down and took his coat off.

John was relaxing in the living room with a book. "Evening, da'," he said. Jane and the other children came up and gave Robert a hug. He patted Jane on the shoulder and picked Sarah and David up in turn, saying hello to each of them.

"How was it?" Sarah asked.

"He's no' good," replied Robert. "Since we met up again he's become a different man… This disease has just drained him."

"How's Ann holding up?" said Sarah.

Robert sighed. "She's just existing." He paused. "Oh, Sarah, why? We'd just started tae get tae know each other again after all these years. We're the last two o' my family left."

"Why does anything happen?" Sarah replied. "Why did we lose Agnes tae smallpox? Or Hannah in the best year of her life? Who knows? We just have tae come to terms wi' it."

The front door opened and Mary walked in after an evening spent in the village with her friends. She could see her parents were upset. "What's the matter, ma'?" she asked.

"It's your uncle John," Sarah replied, "he's very ill."

"Is that why da' was away this weekend?" Mary asked.

"Aye, lass," Robert replied. "Your Auntie Ann asked me tae go. She disnae know how long your uncle will last." Robert tried to brighten up for his daughter. "So, what have you been up tae today?"

"I've just been talking wi' my friends after church," Mary replied.

"Church?" said Sarah, shocked. "It must have finished late today, then?"

Sheepishly, Mary added, "Well, I went round one o' my friends' house afterwards."

Sarah and Robert looked at each other, puzzled. Robert turned to Mary. "Ohh," he said, not sure whether to believe her or not. "Fine, well, away to bed wi' you, lass."

Mary carried on into the bedroom. Sarah stood there, as if watching her through the bedroom door. She turned to Robert. "She'll be fine. She's young. There's no' much she can do here in the village."

"Aye," replied Robert, "I suppose you're right."

The Hogmanay celebrations would not be so happy this year. As Sarah thought about it, she decided it was a year best forgotten. Two deaths and another one on the way. The only good thing about it, she mused, was the fact that new life had arrived. The sooner the next year arrived, the better!

With the New Year came the snow. The village always seemed so beautiful when the snow lay around, but it was so hard to go anywhere. Life carried on as normal as possible. Finally, the end of the Crimean War was announced. On Wednesday 6 February 1856 Robert was sat at home reading the newspaper. "I see Russia has finally given in over the Crimea," he said.

"Does that mean all our boys will be coming back home now?" asked Sarah, stopping from putting away the dishes.

"Eventually," answered Robert, nodding his head. "There'll be a lot tae do before they'll leave the Crimea, but at least there should be no more loss o' life."

Sarah sighed with relief. "It's a start, I suppose." Sarah came over and sat down with Robert. "Our Mary turns 17 in just over two weeks. It disnae seem possible," she added.

"Aye," added Robert. "I reckon there'll be a lot of boys after our Mary, when the soldier boys get back here, in the next few months."

"She'll be fine," said Sarah. "She's a good girl."

"Hmmm," said Robert, not so sure. "The work on the railway is getting less and less now. I'll soon need tae be thinking o' where the next job will be."

Sarah looked shocked. "What, is it all finished now, then?" she asked.

"No," Robert began, slowly, knowing that Sarah was not going to like what he had to say, "but the work that needs tae be done is for the younger, less experienced men, and the navvies."

"Navvies? What do they do, then?" Sarah asked.

"Most of them are Irish," Robert replied. "The navvies do all the menial, but important, jobs o' track laying and such."

Almost afraid to ask, Sarah said, "So where will you go?"

"At this moment I've no idea," answered Robert. "It's something I shall be looking into over the next few months."

"So there's a while yet, then?" asked a relieved Sarah.

"Oh, aye," Robert added. "I shall take my time and get the best work I can. But if I have tae go after the work, it has tae be done." He looked at Sarah, almost asking for her understanding. "It's no' that I want tae do it, any more than you do."

Sarah sighed. "Let's go tae bed," she said. Robert nodded and stood up. They both went into the bedroom.

The next few weeks flew by. Mary had her birthday but everyday seemed the same as any other. By Wednesday, 5 March 1856 the weather began to get warmer and Sarah made the most of the good weather by walking up to the village with Nathaniel in his baby carriage. He was nearly 8 months old now, and forward for his age.

As Sarah walked up the road she saw one of her friends, coming out of the Grocer's shop. Janet Wilson also saw Sarah and they met up in the street. Janet was 37 years old, of average build and very pretty. "How's your Robert doing for work?" Janet asked Sarah. "My Walter says he'll have tae soon start looking further afield for decent work."

"Aye," replied Sarah, "Robert says that too. Does Walter have any ideas where?"

"There's work tae be found south o' the border and over tae Dumfries," Janet answered. "He's seeing what looks tae be the best."

Sarah thought for a moment. "Perhaps you could let me know what he finds out."

"Aye, I'll do that!" answered Janet. "Good day for now." Janet continued on her way down the street while Sarah went into the Grocer's for supplies.

"Good afternoon, Mrs. McWilliam," said James Scott, the Grocer. "What can I get you, this fine day?"

Sarah returned the reply, nodding. "I need some flour, tea, sugar, salt, please, Mr. Scott."

James Scott got the items ready for Sarah and she put them in her shopping bag. "Thank you kindly," she said to him. She turned to leave the store. "I'll be by again tomorrow."

"Aye," he said, "till tomorrow!"

Sarah opened the door and left the shop. Just outside, Sarah bumped into Mary Stewart. "Afternoon tae you, Sarah. Your little one's doing well."

Sarah returned the greeting. "Afternoon, Mary, thanks. Your family well?"

"Aye, thanks, answered Mary Stewart. "I see your Mary up the village a lot these days."

"Aye," answered Sarah, a little confused, "well you would, since she works at the Post Office."

"Other times as well!" Mary Stewart added.

"Well, she does have friends of her own age in the village," Sarah replied.

"True," began Mary Stewart, realising Sarah's ignorance, and almost gloating, "but, Ellen, my youngest, says she's seen her about wi' John Blaney – an' he's two years older than your Mary – she's about 17, isn't she?"

"Oh, right," said Sarah, feeling small. "I didn't know that. I'll have a word with her later. Thanks."

"Nae bother," said Mary Stewart, feeling conceited, "I'll be away, now." Mary went into the Grocer's and Sarah went back home. Such thoughts were going through Sarah's head on that journey home. When she arrived home she had made her mind up to confront Mary and she worked out what she would say to her while cooking the dinner.

Finally, Mary arrived home from work, on time. "Evening, ma'," she said.

Sarah straightened up and looked at her daughter. "I was talking with Mrs. Stewart in the village today."

"Aye," replied Mary, "and what did she have tae say?"

Sarah came over from the kitchen end and sat in her rocking chair. "She says you've been seen wi' John Blaney. Is there any truth in that?"

"And what if I have?" retorted Mary. "I've done nothing wrong!"

"But you've not mentioned him afore!" continued Sarah. "When we've asked you where you were you only told us you were wi' your girl-friends. You didnae mention any boys!"

"We're just good friends!" replied Mary, curtly. "I don't only go around wi' him. There's a group of us stay together. It's no' like there's lots tae do in the village, ma'!"

"Well, mind you take care!" answered Sarah. "I don't want you ending up like Agnes Crossan, next door but one!"

"Hah!" retorted Mary, "I'm no' going tae do anything stupid, ma'! Anyway, I'm in tonight."

With that, Mary stormed off into the bedroom. As Mary went in, Jane and the others came out. "What's up wi' Mary, ma'?" asked Jane.

Sarah sighed. "I said something she didnae want to hear, that's all. Go and sit down there on the floor. Food will be ready soon."

Sarah went back to her cooking and Jane and the children sat down on the floor. John came in and tried to talk to Mary after Sarah told him why she was upset. Nothing would coax her out of her room. A while later Robert came in and Sarah explained what had happened. He went to talk with Mary.

"Hey, lassie," Robert said to Mary, quietly, "your ma' was a wee bit upset that you didnae confide in her."

"Oh, da'," said Mary, turning to look at him, "I know that, it was just I lost my temper."

"Right," answered Robert, "but your ma' worries after you. She wants the best for you. Go say you're sorry, lass. It'll all be fine."

"It's just," Mary paused for a moment, trying to find the right words, "I feel like ma' doesnae want me tae grow up."

"Oh, Mary," Robert said, "You're her eldest. Wi' Agnes dead and William in the army, she doesnae want anything bad tae happen tae you. Gie her a wee bit o' time. She'll come round."

Mary looked at her father and nodded. She got off the bed and went and hugged her father. She then went out of the bedroom and over to Sarah, who was putting the dinner on the table.

"I'm sorry, ma'," Mary said, contritely.

Sarah looked at her. She could see her daughter had been crying. "Oh, Mary," she said, "I didnae mean tae be so angry wi' you. I just want you tae be able tae confide in me. If you dinnae tell me what you're doing, how am I tae trust you?"

"I understand that now," Mary replied.

Sarah gave Mary a hug. "Come sit at table, now," she said. Robert stood watching in the doorway, smiling. He, too, came over with the others for their dinner.

Over the next few days Mary tried hard to talk to Sarah and tell her everything she was getting up to. Both Robert and Sarah were pleased, and Mary saw this and began to cheer up.

Friday 4 April, Sarah was reading the newspaper during the day after Robert had finished with it the evening before and she read about a new craze that had started. People were beginning to give birthday cards. When Jane got back from school Sarah explained what she had read.

"It's Uncle John's birthday on 18th April, and I thought it'd be a lovely idea tae make him a card. What do you think?" Sarah asked Jane.

"Oh, ma'!" exclaimed Jane, "I know he'd love it!"

Sarah smiled. "I thought you'd say that," she continued, "so I've looked out some bits and pieces tae decorate this piece of card I bought from the grocer's this morning."

"I'll start now!" said Jane, excited.

"Remember, though," added Sarah, "this is tae be from all of us!"

Jane began to design a birthday card for her uncle. Sarah mixed some flour and water together to make some glue to stick the things on with. The little ones helped her stick bits of cloth and twine on to make a pretty design. Jane tried her hand at writing poetry for the inside message. Mary and John also thought it was a wonderful idea when they came in and they made their own contribution. They took their time to make it special.

When the card was finished, halfway through the next week, all the children signed it and Sarah then showed it to Robert. She explained how she had read about it in the newspaper and Robert thoroughly approved of the idea. He signed the card alongside Sarah's name and the next day, Thursday, Sarah took it, now placed inside an envelope, to the Post Office to send it to Greenock. The card was going to arrive a few days before John's birthday, but it was decided better for it to be there early rather than arrive too late.

Almost two weeks had passed when a letter from Robert's brother arrived. Sarah handed it to Robert when he got home that Wednesday, 23 April 1856. He sat down, afraid it contained bad news, and then opened it.

He read the first line to himself, then, confident that there was no bad news, he read it aloud to Sarah.

Dear Robert and Sarah,

We hope this letter finds you all doing well. John seems to be doing a little better now the weather's warming up, but he is still poorly. Thank you so much for your lovely birthday card – it meant so much to John to get it. Another new fad, but a wonderful idea. Whoever thought it up, I wonder?

We have to share our little house now – we cannot afford to pay the full rent, so we have the downstairs rooms while a new family live upstairs.

We really miss seeing you all, but dare not invite you to visit. All for now,

Your loving brother and sister,

John and Ann

Sarah sat there, smiling, as Robert read the letter to her. "Oh, Robert, I do miss them," she said. "It was lovely when they were able to visit us."

"Aye," replied Robert. "He's doing well, though – it's a year on since he found out what he had, and he's still here!"

"The weather helps, though," added Sarah. "The warmer air seems to ease the congestion."

Robert looked around him. "What's our Mary up to tonight?" he asked.

"She's in at the moment," replied Sarah, "she's in the other room wi' the others. She's helping them wi' their reading." Sarah stopped and smiled to herself. "That talk we had with her seemed to do wonders," she added. "Any news on where you'll next be working?"

Robert shook his head. "No," he began, "we're moving a wee bit further afield wi' the work now – but still local. They'll be doing another section of line next, so the work will still be there. Walter Wilson and I were discussing this, only today. Apparently, there are some new workers coming down from Glasgow in a couple o' months – the local lodge has asked if the railway will take on some trainee masons for a while." Robert seemed a bit rattled with this idea and scowled, as he continued, "well, o' course the railway will take 'em – they're cheap labour! I shall wait until the youngsters arrive and then look for work elsewhere. I know it's been wonderful living with you all week, every week, but we always knew it wasn't going to last, didn't we?"

"I know," sighed Sarah, "we'll just have to make the most of our weekends."

For the next few weeks, though, life continued on as normal. Sarah hoped nothing would change and if she didn't speak to Robert about him changing his job she thought it might go away. There was still a lot of track to be put in place – the work could go on for years – couldn't it?

Monday 16 June 1856 Robert came home from work with some news that would affect him and many other experienced masons.

"They've sent us the first lot of trainee masons. They're no' bad." He told Sarah.

Sarah looked upset. "So what does that mean tae us?" she asked.

"Well, I've taken a couple of 'em under my wing," he replied. "We'll have tae see."

The next couple of weeks passed well enough and Robert felt he was working with a good team. He had been assigned two young masons, Walter Brown and Alexander McMillan, both 21 years old. In the evenings Robert talked about them and how well they were doing at work.

"Invite them tae dinner one evening," Sarah remarked. "It'll be grand tae see some new faces."

So, Monday 30 June 1856 Robert took her up on her offer. He invited his trainees to dinner. Normally they ate in the public house, so it made a lovely change to be able to eat elsewhere. That evening, at the end of a lovely warm day it was just beginning to rain. Robert and his trainees were walking back to Auchtykirnal. They were working just outside Lesmahagow station, so they didn't have far to walk.

Mary was just coming home from work after a long day and she saw her father walking home in the distance with two men. She had no idea who they were but decided to run home to let her mother know they were coming.

"Ma'!" Mary shouted, running indoors, fair out of breath, "Da's coming wi' two men!"

"I thought your father might do that today," said Sarah. "Just as well I put more food on!"

Meanwhile, the men continued on their way. It was only light drizzle, so they didn't quicken their pace. In fact it made a welcome change from the heat they had experienced during the day. As they walked along they chatted.

"You must find it very strange," said Robert to Walter, "what with being apart from the wife and the bairn so soon after he's been born."

"Aye," replied Walter. "She's still in Edinburgh at the moment, living wi' friends, while I'm here tae find a place tae live. Are you sure your wife won't mind us calling in?"

Robert smiled. "She'll be fine. In fact it was her who suggested you come. Mind, I didn't say it'd be today," Robert chuckled as he thought of the look on Sarah's face when they walked through the door. "We're just coming up tae the place now."

The children were waiting outside to see these strangers that Mary had been talking about. Mary was helping Sarah finish the dinner.

"Ma'!" called Jane, "they're coming!" With that, the children ran indoors.

Sarah came outside, leaving Mary watching the food. She met them at the door to the cottage. "Oh, Robert," she began. "Mary said she saw you coming with some men. I just wondered who they might be."

"It's the new masons," Robert began. "I thought they might like a bit o' company after your suggestion. This is Walter Brown and this is Alexander McMillan."

"Pleased tae meet yous," said Sarah. "Well, there's plenty of food to go round – come in!"

They all went inside the cottage and Robert introduced his family to the men. Sarah dished up the meal and the whole family and guests sat down to eat. It was clear the younger men missed home cooking because they ate their meal with gusto. They didn't leave anything on their plates and afterwards Mary and Jane did the washing up for their mother.

Finally, all the chores done, John went out to Quoits practice, shortly followed by Mary, who was going out with some friends. The masons sat with Robert and Sarah. Sarah wanted to know more about these young men, so she began to talk to them.

"So, where are you staying, Walter?" Sarah asked.

"I'm lodging wi' Alexander, here," replied Walter. "We're with an old gent in Turfholm – Mr. Stodhart. He's a widower."

"Aye, I know him," said Sarah, nodding. "His wife died last year. You'll do fine there."

Walter looked at Alexander and he motioned the door to him. Alexander responded in similar manner by nodding. Alexander spoke. "Well, we'll no' take up any more o' your time, so we'll head for home now."

The two men both stood up. "Thank you for your hospitality," said Walter. "Goodnight Ma'am, Robert."

"Aye, thanks indeed," said Alexander. "The food fair reminded me of home. Goodnight."

Robert stood up to let them out. "I'll see yous tomorrow, then," he said. Robert opened the door and the two young men went outside. They began to walk up to the village as Robert watched them go. When they had gone a fair distance Robert shut the door.

He walked back into the room and sat down. "They're a couple o' fine lads, there," he said, nodding to himself. Sarah looked disappointed. "Does this mean you'll be changing job soon?"

Robert smiled and shook his head. "The bosses want me tae work with the new lads for a few months until they've settled in properly. They're paying me extra tae do the work, so I'll happily do it."

Sarah let out a sigh of relief and looked heavenward. She had been praying for a while longer with Robert at home. It seemed her prayers had been answered – for a while at least.

For the next six weeks life continued on as normal. Once a week, Robert brought Walter and Alexander over for dinner. He could see how Sarah enjoyed having them over, and he was beginning to think of the men as sons, almost. But always, at the back of Robert's mind was the thought of working elsewhere. When the railway reached Douglas that would be the end of the work for a while. With all the men they had working up and down the line that time wouldn't be too long in coming.

Tuesday 12 August, though, Robert brought a different visitor. He came home late from work after stopping off in the village. They arrived back at Auchtykirnal and Robert opened the door. He walked in with his visitor. This was Walter Wilson, Janet's husband. He was three years older than Janet and was well built.

"Sarah, you know Walter Wilson, don't you?" began Robert. "We've decided to find out where else we can work, so he's come over wi' some details of places looking for masons."

Sarah's jaw dropped. She sighed. "So soon?" she said, almost in tears. "Have you eaten, Walter?" she asked, regaining her composure.

"Aye," Walter replied, "thanks anyway, for the offer."

Sarah turned to Robert and glared. "I wondered why you were so late. We've all eaten but I'll get your dinner."

Robert and Walter sat at the empty table while Sarah fetched Robert his dinner. Walter got out the various pieces of paper he had been collecting and laid them out on the table. They looked at them as Robert ate his dinner.

Walter spoke as he showed various things to Robert. "I've done a fair bit o' work looking tae find out who's building what, and this is the best bet.

Robert looked at the document as he ate. "Are you sure there's no alternative?" he asked.

Walter shook his head. "Grange-over-Sands is at the centre of a new railway line," he continued. "They're building around there all the while. There's to be a huge viaduct at Arnside, and they'll be putting up new buildings all over the place. That's where we should go!"

Robert sighed and shook his head. Sarah watched out of the corner of her eye, pretending not to notice, but her insides were churning.

"The wife won't be happy," said Robert.

"Neither will mine!" added Walter.

"Shall you write to them and find out what they're needing?" asked Robert.

"I shall, indeed," answered Walter. "And I'll be off now. See you tomorrow, Robert. Thanks, Sarah."

Both men stood up and Robert opened the door for Walter. He went out and Robert shut the door after him. Robert went back to his dinner, trying to pretend nothing had happened. But Sarah knew. She just wanted to know how much longer she would have her husband by her side. She stood up and went over to Robert.

"So when do you finish with the railway here?" she asked, almost dreading the answer.

Robert took his last mouthful of food and looked at Sarah. He held her hand. "Not for a while, yet, Sarah," he said. Sarah was so very sad. Despite Robert's protestations, she knew she could not change the future. She must make the most of the short time she could spend every night with her husband.

The next week, however, 18 August, Robert came home with his two trainees and another, older, man in tow. By now the two young men have gotten comfortable around the family and they chatted happily with everybody. Robert introduced the new man to Sarah.

"Sarah, this is James Purdie. He's just come down from Glasgow. He didnae know anybody, so I didnae think you'd mind another mouth tae feed."

"That's fine," Sarah replied. "There's plenty tae go round."

They ate a hearty dinner and afterwards sat around, talking. Robert and Sarah were getting to know their new visitor whilst Mary was talking with Walter and Alexander.

"So where are you from, James?" asked Robert. "I recognise the accent."

"Well," replied James, "I've come down from Glasgow – Barony, but that's no' where I was born. I was born in a wee village in the far west o' Scotland."

"Oh, aye," replied Robert, "and where was that? My accent's changed some having spent almost fifteen years in England, but I came from that side o' Scotland originally."

James looked a little surprised, and Sarah got more interested. She'd not seen Robert like this for a while.

"Maybe you do know, then," he said. He paused. "Kirkmaiden."

Sarah grew wide eyed when she heard the name, and Robert almost choked on his mouthful of beer. James was concerned. "Are you alright, Robert?" he asked.

After the coughing fit subsided, Robert was able to answer. "I'm from Port Logan!" he spluttered. "Hang on – Purdie – are you my Aunt Martha's boy?"

James was in shock now. He nodded, then he realised who he was talking to. "Martha Main and James Purdie were my parents. Were your parents Jean Main and John McWilliam, then?"

Robert had, by now, fully recovered from the choking fit. "Indeed they were!" he exclaimed. "What a chance meeting this was!" Robert turned to Sarah. "Jimmy here is my cousin on my ma's side. He's about 14 years younger than me, and one of a larger brood." Robert turned back to speak with his cousin. "So, do you keep in touch wi' the others?"

"Aye," replied James, "now and then. Your aunt Susan Palmer still lives in the village." James smiled and then a thought occurred to him. "There's tae be a wedding soon," he added. "Grace – their daughter – she's marrying John Galloway in November."

Sarah was so pleased. Her eyes lit up and she gasped. "A wedding!" she said, "and more family! Oh, Robert – you promised me you'd take me… Can we go?"

"What do you reckon, James?" said Robert. "Would we be welcome?"

James chuckled. "For sure, man! In any case, I'll write and tell them."

Meanwhile, Mary was talking with the other journeymen. This was the first evening that they hadn't sat talking with Robert, and since Robert and Sarah were obviously getting on well with the newcomer, Mary decided she'd get to know a bit about the other two.

They were standing near the stove when Mary started talking. "So where are you from, Alexander?"

"Call me Xander – it's easier," Alexander replied. "I'm from Cupar, in Fife."

"Is that far?" asked Mary, naively.

Alexander chuckled. "Aye, lass, it is – it's on the east side o' Scotland."

"Ohhh," said Mary, almost in awe. "What about family?"

"It's just me and my parents," Alexander replied. "I'm their youngest. My father's a mason, too."

"What about you?" Mary asked Walter.

"I'm from over that way," Walter replied. "But I've a wife and son back home."

Mary almost ignored Walter. He was married. Xander was not. 'I can go out wi' Xander', she thought.

Eyes firmly fixed on Alexander, Mary continued to question them. "So, why did you come all this way?"

"Well," began Alexander, "I wanted tae see what the other side o' Scotland was like. There were quite a few of us came from the east side."

Mary began to flirt with Alexander and he quite liked it, but he knew better than to show Mary what he thought while still in her parents' home.

Walter was watching Robert and Sarah talking to James. He felt a little left out. "I didnae think Jimmy knew anybody hereabouts," he said to anyone who might be listening.

"What?" asked Alexander, suddenly realising what Walter had said.

"Over there," continued Walter. "They seem tae know each other." He pointed to Robert and Sarah, talking with James.

Alexander stopped listening to Mary as he realised the conversation at the other end of the room was gaining momentum.

As Robert started to choke, Mary began to understand what they were talking about.

"Kirkmaiden," she said, suddenly realising what that meant. "Kirkmaiden!" she repeated. She turned to Alexander and Walter. "My da's from Kirkmaiden!" she announced. "Jimmy must be someone he knows from home!"

Finally, the two younger masons decided to make their way back to their lodgings. They bade the family a good night and left. Jimmy stayed a while longer, then he, too, left for the evening.

Over the next three weeks Robert and Sarah saw a good deal more of James Purdie than they did of the other two masons. They all continued to visit, but James was a more frequent visitor.

On Saturday 6 September Walter Wilson came to call. It was a warm, sunny morning, so Sarah was out in her garden. She saw him walking along the road. "Robert!" she called, "Walter Wilson is here!"

Robert came outside to greet Walter. "Do you have news from Grange-over-Sands?" he asked.

Walter walked up to Robert. He nodded as he replied. "Aye, Robert. They've not a great deal of the line tae work on just now, but there'll be building work in Grange-over-Sands in a few months, so we've tae get in touch in about three months."

Robert sighed. "Then we'll just have tae keep on wi' this work for now," he said. "Well, it's no' too bad at the moment – especially since I'm training the young 'uns. Three months – ready for the start of next year. I'll leave that wi' you, then, Walter."

Sarah looked disappointed. She knew it was coming, but even so, the thought of being days on end without her husband was daunting. "Three months?" she said, sadly. "I know you have tae do it, but I'd got so used tae you being here all the time."

Robert took her in his arms. "I'll miss being wi' you all the time, hinny, but I have tae go where they'll pay me enough tae live on, you know." He put his hand on her chin and raised her face up so he could look into her eyes. "We'll just have tae make the most o' the next few months."

Sarah looked at Robert and she knew he was right. She couldn't help but shed a tear, though. Robert gently wiped it off her cheek.

Walter felt a little insignificant watching the tender moment. He interrupted their reverie. "Shall we pop tae the inn for a wee dram, Robert?" he said.

"Aye, Walter," replied Robert. "That's sounds like a good idea." Sarah stood back and dried her eyes.

"Off yous go then," she said, "but mind you're not too long. Food'll be ready soon."

"Right-o," replied Robert. He and Walter strolled off up the road to the village, leaving Sarah to get on with her gardening and preparation of the lunchtime meal.

Sarah spent another half hour in the garden and then returned indoors to concentrate on the dinner. Jane was helping David with his reading and Sarah practising her sums. Little Nathaniel was now into everything. He had started walking about a month earlier, so Jane was keeping an eye on him, too.

Robert was home about 1 o'clock, just as the family had sat down to eat. His timing was impeccable. After they had eaten he sat down with Sarah and began to explain to her where they were thinking of going for work.

"So where is this place?" Sarah asked.

"It's called Grange-over-Sands," answered Robert. "It's in England, just down from Kendal."

"Kendal?" said Sarah, staring at him. "Did we not come through Kendal on the way up here?"

"Well, yes, you would have done," answered Robert, surprised she had remembered.

"And if my memory serves me right," added Sarah, "we weren't too far long out of Liverpool when we passed it."

Robert realised that Sarah was now angry, and he was beginning to understand this was going to be a difficult explanation for him.

"Well, tae be fair, it'd be about half-way between Liverpool and Carlisle, but they weren't working on the part o' the line they're doing now," he tried to explain.

"So," retorted Sarah, "you moved us all the way up here tae Scotland. Away from my family, so you could get work."

Robert knew this was going to be hard to explain to Sarah, but he tried.

"Well, aye, but the work was in Glasgow then," he floundered.

"And now, you're going tae be working nearer tae my family than me while I'm stuck up here in the back o' beyond alone wi' our children."

"It wasnae how I expected it tae end up, hinny," Robert answered, sadly. "Are you telling me you want tae move back home?"

"I'm no' moving again," said Sarah. "when you've finished there you'll move on again, no doubt."

"Well, that's how it is. How it's always been for stonemasons," Robert explained.

"And how often will you be home?" she asked. "It's no' like working in Glasgow, is it? It's tae be at least two train journeys each way."

Robert sighed. He hadn't expected Sarah to like the idea, but neither had he expected to hear so much anger and resentment. "We dinnae expect tae be home every weekend," he continued. "Probably every two weeks, but we'd have a wee bit longer at home when we do come."

"And there's no other option?" asked Sarah, reluctantly accepting what Robert said as inevitable.

"No' one that'll pay sae well," answered Robert. He paused and looked at her. "I'm sorry, hinny," he pleaded. "I dinnae want tae work sae far away, either!"

Sarah stood up and walked outside. Robert knew not to antagonise her any more. He'd had this reaction when they moved to Scotland, and he had left her to come round to the idea by herself and it had all worked out for the best. The rest of the weekend passed by with little being said between husband and wife. Sarah wasn't talking and Robert knew better than to try to talk to her.

Sarah's mood mollified over the next few days and she began to get back to her normal self. The younger masons visited again, and she spent a lot of the time talking with James about his family. By the Friday Robert had news that would lift Sarah out of the doldrums.

That Friday evening Robert opened the door and came in with a big grin on his face. Sarah looked up at him from the cooking end of the room. She looked puzzled.

"Well, lass," Robert began, "Jimmy's had a reply from Port Logan. Would you like tae go tae the wedding?"

Sarah smiled. "Aye, Robert, I would," she said, "but how far is it to go?"

Robert sat down on a chair and Sarah came over to sit next to him. Robert looked at her, and smiled. "'Tis a fair way, for sure," he began, "but not so inaccessible as it once was. We can get a train from Lanark tae Glasgow, a train from there tae Dumfries, and then get a coach tae Stranraer. From there it's a short distance. It'd take about half a day tae get there. We should go Tuesday, stay at the Inn in Port Logan and come back Saturday. I've a bit o' money saved, so if you want tae go, we can."

Sarah looked at Robert. It meant he would lose some days at work, and money. But the more she thought about it, the more she realised she wanted to go. After all, Robert had promised her to show where he came from…

"Oh, Robert!" she began, excitedly, "it would be so lovely tae see somewhere else – even if it is only for a day or two. Now that we cannae go tae see your brother I feel so trapped here. And a wedding, as well –" her words trailed off as she thought about the excitement.

Robert nodded. "Then we'll do it! The wedding is Thursday 13 November. We'll take the little ones, but it'll be up tae the older children as tae whether they want tae come wi' us."

Sarah stood up and almost began to dance. "Aye," she said, "I'll ask them when they come in. Mary and John should be home soon. I'll go tell the others what we're doing." Sarah went into the bedroom to tell the children about the wedding.

Robert sat there, thinking. This was going to be quite an adventure for Sarah. If she thought this was the back of beyond, what would she think of his home?

John and Mary both had their jobs to think of, so they told their parents that they wouldn't be going to the wedding, which didn't surprise either parent. Meanwhile, Sarah was now filled with enthusiasm in preparation of the trip. She went down to the village and bought some cloth to make new clothes for everybody. She had become quite adept over the years at dressmaking.

The days soon passed and life was happy again in the McWilliam household. Preparations for the trip were going ahead, and new clothes were being made, one by one, for all those who were going. But, Sarah came down to earth with a bump on Monday 27 October as a telegram arrived. It was lunchtime, and John had come in from the farm for a sandwich. Sarah gingerly opened the telegram, afraid for what it might contain.

"Who's that from, ma'?" John asked.

Sarah sighed. "It's from your Auntie Ann, in Greenock," she answered. She sat down.

"Is it about Uncle John?" John asked, almost knowing what the news was, now.

Sarah nodded. "Aye," she said, "The news we were hoping never tae arrive. He died on Saturday morning. His funeral's tomorrow afternoon."

"Poor da'," said John with real emotion. "How do you think he'll take the news?"

Sarah sighed again. "Well, we were expecting it, really. He lasted well, all things considered." Sarah shook her head. "Your da' is the last now. He'll come tae terms wi' it."

"I'd like tae go, ma'," said John, standing up. "Send her a telegram back saying we'll be there. Then if da' is too busy tae go at least one of us'll be there."

Sarah stared at John. "Are you sure you want to go?" she asked.

"Aye, ma'," John replied. "It's my uncle – it's my decision. I want tae go."

Sarah smiled. "Oh, you are a good boy," she said. "I'll go tae the post office and send a telegram now." She got herself and little Nathaniel ready to go to the village. It was a warm day for the time of the year, so they didn't need to put too many layers on. The sky was clear and the day dry. John put his coat on, too.

"I'll be off tae the farm, to let Mr. Carruthers know about tomorrow. See you, ma'!"

"Aye, son," she said, as she opened the door. "See you later." They both went outside. Sarah closed the door behind her and they both went their separate ways.

That evening Robert came home from work with Jimmy. He sat down to relax, and Sarah came over with the telegram. "We had a telegram this morning from Greenock," she said.

"John?" asked Robert. Sarah nodded and handed the telegram to him.

"When did he die?" he asked, not even looking at the telegram.

"Early Saturday morning," Sarah replied. "The funeral's tomorrow. John said he wants tae go. Will you be going?"

"Aye, of course I'll go!" Robert replied, with some irritation. "He's my brother. It'll be grand John coming wi' me." He paused for a moment. "I'd best go up tae the village and tell Walter so he can pass on the message tae my team of journeymen. What time is the funeral?"

"3 o'clock," answered Sarah. Robert finally looked down at the telegram in his hand. He hadn't wanted to look at it because it made everything so final, but it made little difference now.

He shook his head, sadly. "That'll gie us plenty o' time tae get there."

Sarah put the dinner on the table and they ate silently, thinking of Robert's sister-in-law. Afterwards Robert walked up to the village to tell Walter he would not be at work the next day. Walter wished Robert well and said he would make sure the lads would be fine.

Next morning, bright and early, Robert and John set off for the station. They didn't have so far to travel now the line was in place at Lesmahagow station. They caught the train to Glasgow and from there on to Greenock and to Ann's house. She was so pleased to see them.

"I am so glad yous could both make it," she said. "Come in, come in!"

They went indoors and met some of Ann's relations, and some friends of John's and hers. They were all in sombre mood. After the funeral Robert and John went back for the wake, but they couldn't stay long. They needed to get back to Lesmahagow in good time. By 6 o'clock they had said their goodbyes and were off to the station for the return journey. They were back home by 9 o'clock.

Two weeks passed and it was time to leave for the wedding. New clothes had been made for everybody. Sarah had quite a talent – well, as they say, necessity is the mother of invention, and Sarah could turn her hand to anything! John and Mary were not going to the wedding. They both had their jobs to go to, which meant they would keep house while Sarah and Robert were away.

Sarah didn't like the idea of leaving them behind, but as Robert pointed out, they were both older than Agnes had been when she left home.

It was 11 November and this Tuesday morning the travellers had got up very early and they were all ready to leave. David was very excited. He had never been on a train, and his siblings were telling him what they remembered of their journeys.

Sarah had left Jane in charge of getting the younger children ready while Sarah fussed over her two older children. "Are you sure you'll be alright on your own?" she asked them both.

"Aye, ma', we'll be fine," replied Mary, distractedly, in her head wishing them on their way so she could get on with her life.

"Stop your blathering, will you, ma'!" said John. "Go and enjoy yourselves!"

"You will be careful on your own, won't yous?" Sarah asked.

"You dinnae need tae worry, ma'," added Mary. "Just go! Have a good time."

Robert had been standing there, quietly waiting, but even his patience was wearing thin. "Will you come along, woman," he called, "or we'll miss the train!"

306

John opened the front door and Robert, carrying two cases, led the children outside. Sarah hesitated one more time. John pushed her outside, saying, "Mother will you go. You've no need tae worry. We'll be fine."

Finally, Sarah was outside and John shut the door. She picked up her one case, turned and followed after Robert and the children as they walked up to the station.

It didn't take long to reach the station. The family was full of anticipation, but Sarah was concerned. "Are you sure we can afford this trip?" she asked, as they stood waiting on the platform for the train to pull in.

"How many more times do I have tae say?" replied Robert. "There's a lull at the moment, so work is light. I've been canny wi' my money. We'll do just fine."

As they stood there a train pulled in going the opposite way. David looked at it closely. "Are we going on a train like that da'?" he asked.

Robert smiled. "Aye, son," he replied, nodding. "That's like our train. It's big, isn't it?"

David stood there, just nodding. "This is so exciting!"

Little Sarah puffed herself out. "I've been on one before," she said, proudly. Nathaniel had just had enough of standing and called out to his mother. Sarah picked him up and he watched the trains from her arms.

Sarah smiled. "Aye," she said to her daughter, "but you were only little then – just about two – do you still remember?"

"Aye ma'," Sarah answered, defiantly.

"Oh, look!" Jane called out, "the train's coming."

The train pulled into the station and drew to a halt.

The other people on the platform began to get on the train. Robert found the third class carriages and helped the family on board with their luggage. Once on board they waited for the train to leave. David was so excited he could barely sit still. Finally, the train blew its whistle and they were off.

For a Wednesday morning, the train was busy, stopping at all the stations on the way in to Glasgow, but finally they arrived at Southside Station. Here they waited for their connection to take them to Gretna Station. Sarah felt as if she was going back to England, remembering her journey north from Carlisle. The train arrived at the station and the family boarded. As this was a much longer journey Robert bought second class tickets so they had a pleasant journey. By the time they got to Gretna it was nearly 12 o'clock and everybody was beginning to get hungry.

As they waited for their connection at Gretna Sarah brought out some sandwiches she had prepared before leaving home. The food lasted as long as it took them to wait for their connection, they were so hungry. Not a scrap of food was left as they got on their final train. There were only five stations on this part of the journey, and they were soon at Dumfries.

They got off the train and Robert led the family to find a coach for the remainder of the journey, as the railway had not got that far west. It was 72 miles to Stranraer, so they were going to stop overnight in Newton Stewart, just east of Stranraer.

Once on board the coach they settled back into their seats and Robert explained to the children where they were. "This is going tae be the longest part o' the journey. There are no trains in this part o' Scotland yet."

"Why not?" asked David. "I liked being on the train."

His mother, Sarah, smiled at his innocence. Robert continued. "Coaches don't travel as fast as the train, so we'll not get all the way to Kirkmaiden today."

"The time taken to travel disnae matter a bit to me," Sarah said to her husband. "I'm enjoying every minute of this. Are you enjoying yourselves, children?"

All the children joined in with their reply. "Aye, ma'! It's wonderful!"

The coach set off on its long journey. Halfway between Dumfries and Newton Stewart the coach had a change of horses. David was intrigued. "Why can we no' keep the same horses, da'?" he asked.

"Because they get tired, son, just like we do," Robert answered. Finally, the family arrived at Newton Stewart and they headed for the Galloway Arms Hotel. The owner led the tired travellers to a bedroom for the night. They ate dinner in the hotel then retired to their room. It wasn't long before they were asleep. They'd had a busy day.

Next morning Robert and Sarah woke early and got the children up and dressed. They went downstairs and ate breakfast before starting on the last leg of their journey. They took another coach to Stranraer, which took almost as long as the journey from Dumfries. From Stranraer they found another coach to go down to Portnessock.

Finally, they were there. It was late afternoon but they had enjoyed good weather all the way. After the coach had left them by the roadside Robert looked around him and smiled. It didn't look any different than it had on the day he had left.

"Well, Sarah, what do you think?" he asked.

Sarah had been looking at everything around her and understood why Robert spoke of it so lovingly. "Robert, I think it's the most beautiful place I've ever seen! How could you ever want to have left it for so long? Why did we not move here instead of Lesmahagow?" she said.

Robert laughed. "I think it pretty obvious why we didnae come here tae live. Look how long it took us tae get here. Do you see any new building happening here?"

"Well, if you put it like that," Sarah replied, "aye, it is very basic here, to say the least – but I love it!"

Robert picked up his two cases. "Let's go tae the Inn and get our room," he said. Sarah picked up her case and they walked down the road to the Inn.

Robert, Sarah and family entered the Port Logan Inn and they saw the landlady, Margaret Millvie, and her barmaid, Elizabeth Thomson, standing behind the bar. There were also a few people inside with drinks. Robert put his bags down and walked up to the bar.

"Good afternoon," he said to the older woman. "We've a room booked for two days."

"Aye, McWilliam?" Margaret Millvie asked. "We don't often get travellers here, mind."

Robert smiled as he remembered the last time he was in this bar. "That's right," he said. "We wrote tae you. I was born here, and I'm bringing the family back for my cousin's wedding and tae show them where I lived."

"Oh, you mean Grace Palmer's wedding?" Margaret stopped and studied Robert's face. "You're from here, you say? Whereabouts?"

"Up the road towards Byer Croft. There's only me left now."

Margaret thought for a moment. "Hmm... Aye, I do remember you now," she said. "Your father was John and your mother was Jean, were they not?"

"Aye," replied Robert, astonished. "That's right. I didnae expect to be remembered!"

"Well, we have so few visitors," said Margaret. She came out from behind the bar. "Come upstairs," she said, "I'll show you tae the room."

Margaret led them upstairs and through dark corridors until they got to the room she had allotted to them. She opened the door and they were greeted with bright daylight, after the dark corridor. It was a large room, with two double beds in it.

Margaret walked into the room and the family followed. "Well, here you are," she said. "It's a big room wi' two beds in, so you'll all fit. Have you travelled far?"

"We've come from Lesmahagow," Robert answered. "The wife's never been to this part o' the world, and I'd promised her we'd come before we moved from England a few years back. So, here we are."

"Well, I hope it lives up tae your expectations," Margaret said to Sarah. She turned back to Robert. "Well, I'll leave you tae get settled in," she said to him. "I can cook for you tonight, if you're wanting."

Robert was famished, and he knew everybody else must be. "That'd be grand," he said, "we've not eaten for a while."

Margaret smiled. "That's fine, then – come down about 7 o'clock." She turned and left the family to settle in. Robert closed the door behind her and went to look out the window.

He stared for a while at the view. It was good to be back, even if it was only for a few days. He thought about his last day in the village. It was a week after his mother had died. That was November, too. 33 years past.

There had been little reason to stay after that. John and Susan had moved in with the Palmers – they were the youngest, him 9 years old and her 7 years old. James and Elizabeth, his siblings nearest in age to him, had both died as children, so there was nobody else left to take them in.

Sarah came over to him at the window and nudged him. "A penny for them," she said. Robert turned and looked at her. "Oh, Sarah, it takes me back," he said, sadly. He sighed. "The last time I was here my mother had just died."

"What did you do after that?" she asked.

"I moved on. I was nigh on 20 by then, and the rural life wasnae for me. I wanted a craft that'd pay good money. Aunt Susan took John and Susan in so I'd no need tae stay. Off I went tae Stranraer tae make a living."

Robert turned to look at Sarah. She smiled at him. "Do you wish things had been different?" she asked. "God, no!" he said, defiantly. "If I'd stayed here I'd have gone mad, besides, we'd never have met, and you're the best thing that could have happened tae me."

Robert was interrupted by young Nathaniel, tugging at his trousers. "Dada," he called, his arms held aloft, waiting to be picked up so he could look out the window. Robert picked him up and Nathaniel put his hands up to the glass.

Robert then turned to look at the other children, who were sitting patiently on the bed they had decided was to be theirs for the duration. "So, what do yous think o' the place?" he asked them.

"Different," said Jane, "in a good way."

"I want tae explore!" said David

"Can we meet our cousins?" asked Sarah.

"There'll be plenty of time for that tomorrow," said Sarah. "Right now it'll soon be time for dinner, so we'd best unpack and put our clothes away." She set the example by putting one of the cases on the bed and opening it. The clothes were neatly laid on the bed in piles as to who owned them. There was a tall chest of drawers in between the beds, with four large drawers and two smaller ones at the top. David and Nathaniel were to have one of the smaller ones each for their clothes, then the other drawers, which got larger in size the further down they went, were allocated in turn to Sarah, then Jane, then Robert, and finally Sarah had the largest.

"Why do you have to have the largest, ma'?" little Sarah asked.

Sarah smiled. "Because I have the biggest clothes!" she said. Besides, I've also got some extra baby things in my drawer – for Nat."

By the time the clothes had been put away it was time for dinner, so everybody went downstairs to eat. As they were eating it became apparent that all the children were more tired than they had thought, so as soon as they were done the children went to bed. Robert and Sarah sat downstairs together, in the bar. Something Sarah had not done for years, but they were with the children, so they could relax.

They had a couple of drinks – Robert had a beer and a whisky chaser and Sarah had a gin. They felt almost guilty at sitting there without the children, but it was lovely, all the same. Soon, too, they began to feel drowsy – or was it the effects of the drink? In any event, it wasn't long before they, too, went to bed.

Next morning, Thursday, 13 November, they were awake early. Robert got out of bed and looked out of the window. "It's no' bad out there, hinny," he said. "Well, it's dry, anyway."

They all got up and dressed and went downstairs for breakfast. Finally, they were going to see the village. After breakfast they put their coats on and went outside. Directly in front of them was the bay. There were a few boats in the bay, but most of them were out. There was a lighthouse-type beacon on the far left as they looked at the bay. It was so peaceful. The children were running from one vantage point to another to compare what they could see.

Robert pointed over to the far right where there was a building out on its own. "Right hinny, over there is the fish pond. Can you see?" he asked.

Sarah looked as hard as she could. "Fish Pond?"

Robert chuckled. "See that house? It's over by there. It's big – no' just a pond, but that's what we call it."

Sarah looked at him with disdain. "Robert, just take me wherever you think I'd like to go," she said. "I want tae see everything. This is the first time I've ever had a holiday."

Robert smiled. "Right, then," he said. "We'll go tae the Fish Pond tomorrow. Right now we should head tae Aunt Susan's. It's just up the way here – 5 cottages up from the Inn."

They walked the short distance along the road until they came to the Palmer's house. Robert walked up to the door and knocked. They waited a couple of minutes and then the door opened. Adam Palmer was there to greet them. He looked for just a moment. "It's Robert, isn't it?" Robert nodded. Adam continued, "I recognise you – you look so much like your father!"

Robert smiled, "Aye, it is," he replied. "This is my wife, Sarah, and these are my four youngest – Jane, Sarah, David and Nathaniel."

Adam chuckled. "Nathaniel, eh? I know where you got that name from! Come in! We're just getting ready tae go tae the church."

Adam led the family through to the living room. Sarah was in awe. The room was so much smaller than her main room, but there were so many more rooms than she had. A rotund woman came over to meet them. "Robert!" she said, "Welcome."

Robert introduced his family to her, and in turn, she introduced her family to him. There was Grace, the bride, aged 19 years, and their younger children, Ann, aged 17 years, and Adam, aged 14 years.

"It's grand you were able to come," Susan began. "It's been sae long." She stood back and looked at him and smiled. "You just look like your father." She stopped and chuckled. "I daresay you've been told that afore!"

Robert nodded. Susan turned to Sarah and they began to talk. They sat down together. Young Adam went over to the children and asked them who they were. Jane was their spokesperson. She got on well with Adam, him being only four years older.

It wasn't long before the families were ready to leave for the kirk. They had a cart ready and waiting, and it would be large enough for everybody. They set off down the lanes. They were soon at the kirk and they got off and went inside.

There were more people inside. Friends of both sides, and the groom's family. Robert didn't have a clue who Grace was marrying, he realised. Oh well, he thought, he'd soon ind out.

Sarah thought how beautiful the kirk looked that day. It was such a tiny one and the interior lighting made it look homely. The ceremony began and Robert found out who Grace was marrying. John Galloway. The wedding went off without a hitch and afterwards everybody stood outside talking for a while.

Susan came over to Robert again. "Sorry I didnae get much time tae talk wi' you earlier, but we were in a wee bit of a tissy."

"That's nae bother, aunt," Robert replied.

"It's sae wonderful that you could be here, Robert," Susan continued. "It's been quite a while since we last saw you."

"Aye," Robert nodded, "Aye – your Grace wasn't even born when I left!"

"Was it that long ago?" said Susan, much surprised. "Time flies, that's for sure! We're really pleased tae see you again, and your family. Do you know where your John is?"

Robert's mood changed. "He's dead," he said. "He died from consumption last month."

"Oh, no!" exclaimed Susan. "The poor wee lad." She suddenly laughed, a sad laugh. "Listen tae me," she said, "calling him a 'lad'! He must have been in his forties!"

"Aye," replied Robert. "He was 42,"

"That's no age!" she shook her head. "Still, life must go on." She brightened up. "Anyways, it was quite a surprise when James wrote and told us he'd seen you."

"How do you think I felt?" answered Robert. "Mind, I did recognise the accent."

Sarah had come to stand with Robert as they spoke. She knew nobody else and felt isolated. The children were happily mingling with the others. She joined in the conversation. "Robert nearly choked on his beer when James said!"

As they spoke James Purdie came over to say hello. "Yous made it, then!" he said.

"Aye, said Robert, "but it was quite a journey, what wi' the bairns."

Robert seemed to be the centre of attention, despite it being Grace's wedding. Next to introduce herself was Elizabeth Galloway. "So you're the son of Susan's eldest sister, then?"

"Aye," he said, "the last – we buried my brother John last month."

"Oh, I'm sorry tae hear that," she said.

"Aye," he said, "still, it comes tae us all in the end. I understand you look after the Fish Pond?"

"That's right," said Elizabeth. "My husband passed away eight years ago, now. It's been looked after by the Galloway family for the last fifteen years, you know."

Sarah joined in. "Robert was telling me all about it. It sounds remarkable."

"Well, yous must come and see it tomorrow," replied Elizabeth.

"We'll do that," said Sarah.

Grace came over to talk with Robert. "Ma' says you've been left here for longer than I've been alive."

"Aye, lass," Robert replied. "I left when your aunt Jean died. After a while I went tae live in England afore moving back tae Scotland."

"It's grand you were able tae come tae the wedding," Grace added, "and wi' your lovely family!"

Finally, everybody started to go back to Port Logan and to have something to eat. The Palmers had put on quite a spread. Everybody had their fill of food, then all the menfolk disappeared to the Inn, leaving the women to clear away.

Next day, as promised, Robert took Sarah and the children to see the Fish Pond. Elizabeth greeted them and they went inside the small house. Elizabeth's son, James was there with his wife, Agnes, and their baby, Peter, just 2 months old. Elizabeth's daughter, Agnes, was helping her mother look after the Fish Pond.

Elizabeth took them through the house to another door that brought them poolside. The sight that greeted them was breathtaking. There was a huge, round pond, almost too big to be a pond, with a stone walkway all the way round, and a brick wall bordering it. On the far side was another doorway that led out to the rocky shore.

As Elizabeth took them round she told Sarah all about it. "The Fish Pond was built by Andrew McDouall in the 1780s, but nobody really knows why. It's a wonderful thing, though."

"Why would somebody do that?" asked Jane.

"It's certainly different," replied Sarah. The children were taking it all in.

"Look at all those fishes, ma'!" exclaimed David, not expecting to see anything.

"Aye, Davy – aren't they big!" Sarah replied.

"Oh, da', the walls are so high!" said little Sarah.

Robert smiled as he listened to his children. "This place never fails tae delight me."

Elizabeth nodded. "Aye, I know what you mean," she said. "I feel really privileged to be the caretaker."

The McWilliams continued to look around for a while, then they began to make their preparations for the return journey to Lesmahagow. They said their goodbyes to Robert's family and friends and caught the coach to Stranraer. From there they took another coach to Newton Stewart and stopped at The Galloway Arms for the night, as before.

Then, the next day they completed their journey. It was a very tired family that arrived back in Auchtykirnal that Saturday night. Mary and John were there to greet them. Mary had cooked a meal for the travellers to eat and they were very grateful. "See, ma'," said John, "there was nothing tae worry about!"

Over the next few days life began to return to normal. Robert went back to work with his journeymen and Sarah got on with running the home. Sarah's normal weekday shopping trips were interrupted on the Wednesday, 19 November, when she bumped into Jean Gibb, another mother of a similar age to Sarah.

"Sarah!" Jean Gibb called out. "Am I glad to have seen you! Did you have a good time at the wedding?"

Sarah walked up to Jean and stood still. She had Nathaniel with her in his baby carriage. It had lasted her well and she wouldn't need it soon. "We had a wonderful time at the wedding. It's such a beautiful place, Jean." Sarah paused. "Why, Jean, whatever is the matter – you look troubled."

Jean was flustered. "It's your Mary! Do you not keep her in check?"

Sarah looked shocked. "Whatever do you mean?" she asked.

"When she goes out," continued Jean, "do you not know where she is?"

Sarah was confused. "Well, she tells me she goes to her friends' houses." Sarah continued.

"Who in particular?" asked Jean.

Sarah thought for a moment. "Mostly Agnes Dyot, Anne Hastie, Helen Anderson and your Jean," she said.

"Well," said Jean, "she's not seen Jean for a wee while, but she does see the others, for sure. Do you not know where they go?"

Now it was Sarah's turn to get flustered. "I always thought she was at one or the others house. Is that not the case?"

Jean nodded. "Sometimes," she said. "Other times they hang around tae see what young men are about. You should ask her, Sarah. Get it out in the open!"

"Thanks, Jean, I will," replied Sarah, continuing on her way, feeling a little angry that she hadn't noticed anything going on. Jean disappeared home and Sarah headed for the Grocer's shop. She opened the door and James Scott called out "Good afternoon!" to her. She collected the items that she needed and paid for them. She turned to leave the shop and on her way out she saw Janet Wilson. "Hello, Janet," she called out.

Janet stopped and Sarah walked over to her. "Hello, Janet, how are you doing?"

"We're fine," answered Janet. "So, how was the wedding?"

"Oh, we had a wonderful time. I cannae understand why folk wouldnae want tae live there."

"Life's quiet round here," added Janet. "At least you have the children tae keep you busy."

"Aye," agreed Sarah, "Aye, but sometimes it's hard. Tell me, have you seen anything of our Mary while we were away?"

Janet thought for a moment. "No more than usual," she said. "Oh – I did see her wi' one o' the masons – Xander – the other evening."

"Thanks, Janet," said Sarah. "I'll ask her and see what she has tae say!" The two women said their goodbyes to each other and Janet continued shopping while Sarah made her way back home. All the way back home Sarah tried to work out what to say to Mary. She was still thinking as she prepared the evening meal. Mary came in but she was with John so Sarah decided to defer until later. Robert was the last to come home and he opened the door Sarah was dishing up. Sarah kept her thoughts to herself until she was clearing away, but it was Mary who made an announcement.

"I've fallen out wi' Jean Gibb," said Mary, unashamedly.

Sarah looked surprised. Had somebody told her daughter she'd been found out? "Whatever for?" Sarah asked, honestly.

With a shrug of her shoulders Mary continued. "She's jealous."

"Jealous?" repeated her father. "Whatever would she be jealous of?"

As if it was a normal occurrence, Mary continued. "How all the boys like me. I mean – I don't go after them – they all come tae me!"

"Do you do anything tae encourage them?" asked Sarah.

"No' really. I've no idea why!" answered Mary, nonchalantly.

"So where do you go that they all come after you?" Robert asked, intrigued.

"Just walking into the village," Mary retorted. "Anyway, they'll be out o' luck tonight – I'm staying in. I've had enough of 'em pestering me!"

Sarah had decided to come right out and ask, now. "What about Xander McMillan?" she asked. "I hear tell you went out wi' him while we were away?"

Mary looked embarrassed. "Who said that? And what if I did see him? I'm grown up now!"

"Aye, grown up, maybe," said Sarah, angrily, "but you've still a lot to learn!" Sarah sat down. She had to make her mind up now about who was telling the truth. Why would Mary come out with an answer to what Sarah was thinking? Had somebody prompted her? Or did Mary really just come out with that on the spur of the moment? She decided she would have to watch her.

Mary, having finished her chores went into her bedroom and sat with her siblings, helping them with their homework. Meanwhile, in the other room, Sarah was confiding to Robert what she had heard.

But, for a while at least, Mary stayed in more than she went out, so maybe it was bad feelings on the part of Mary's so-called friends. Sarah decided she would take more notice in the future, though.

A few more weeks passed. Hogmanay came and went and the year turned into 1857. Mary seemed to be showing everybody that her attitude was just a phase, after all. Robert and Walter got confirmation that they would be working at Grange-over-Sands for more money, and they would be working eleven days and home for three days, every two weeks. Their wives were not happy about them going, but what could they do?

Their first day of work was to be Monday, 2 February, so Robert and Walter had arranged to go down on the Sunday afternoon in readiness. Robert was packing his bag ready to take it with him. The journey would take the two men from Lesmahagow to Glasgow; then from Glasgow to Carlisle; and finally from Carlisle to Kendal, where the work was.

Everybody was home to see Robert off. They could see Sarah had been crying. "Do you have everything?" she asked.

"Aye, lass, I have," replied Robert. "Remember, I'm no stranger tae this working away lark." Robert put his hand on Sarah's chin and raised her face up so he could see it. "I shall be knocking at Walter's on the way up through the town. Will you be alright?"

"I got used to it once afore," Sarah replied, with a resigned look on her face. "I can do it again. It's just that you'll be away two weeks at a time, makes it hard."

"Aye," Robert replied, "but, it's much further this time."

Sarah sighed. "I know," she said, now smiling. "I'll be fine – you go."

Robert gave Sarah a big hug and he kissed her. He said goodbye to all his children in turn, kissing all the girls and the two young boys. He then turned to John. "You'll be man of the house while I'm away. Look after everybody."

"Aye, da'," replied John, proudly, "I will!"

With that, Robert turned, picked up his bag and opened the door. He looked at Sarah. "I'll be back afore you know it!" he said. Sarah mouthed "I know" to him and he was gone. Sarah and the children all went outside and watched him walk off up the road to the village. When he was finally out of sight the family all went indoors.

Sarah sat down in her rocking chair and sighed. John came over to her. "Dinnae worry yoursel', ma'," he said, "we'll do fine."

Sarah turned to look at him. "Aye, son," she said. She wiped a tear from her eye and then stood up, ready to clear away from the meal they had just finished.

The Port Logan Inn

**KIRKMAIDEN PARISH
(Port Logan and
Kirkmaiden)**

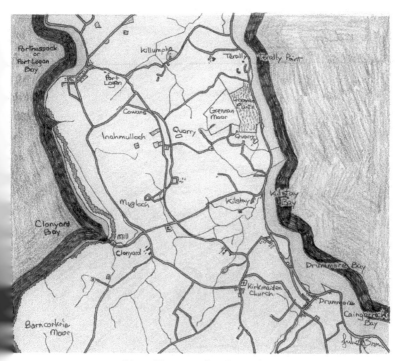

Map of Portnessock or Logan Bay

The Fish Pond

Kirkmaiden Kirk

CHAPTER 9

Bereft

"So, how long was Grandad working away for, this time?" Walter McWilliam asked his granny.

"Far longer than I expected, lad," Sarah replied.

"Are our cousins still living in Port Logan? Can we go there?" asked Nathaniel, excitedly.

"They may well be," answered Sarah, "but I've no' heard from them in such a long while."

"Carry on wi' the story, Granny, pleaseeeeeeeeeeee!" begged young Walter.

Sarah shook her head in defeat. "Alright! Well, it was hard wi'out Robert by my side most o' the winter, but the next few months went by wi'out much happening. By the end of 1857 we realised our Mary," she turned to Walter, "your ma', was beginning tae be a bit of a handful. It turned out all the stories I'd heard were more or less true. We were devastated. How could she do that tae us? Your father stuck up for her at work, but all the masons from this neck o' the woods knew her reputation, so it was a wee bit difficult. But she was mostly flirty – no real harm came of it. They finally finished the Lesmahagow part of the Caledonian Railway, but there was still much work tae be done on the rest of the line, so the masons were still out and about."

By the middle of 1858 Sarah had gotten used to the way Mary flirted with the men. She didn't approve, but no real harm came of it.

Friday, 27 August 1858 Sarah was just about to go to bed when she heard a noise outside. She turned the light out and was about to look out the window when the door opened. Mary came in, not seeing her mother by the window. "Bye, Walter!" she called.

Sarah moved away from the window and it made Mary jump. "Oh, ma', you're still up!" she said, startled.

"Aye, I am," replied Sarah, "and you're getting later and later!"

Mary turned her nose up at her mother. "Well, I'm no' working tomorrow," she retorted, "it's no' my day for working this Saturday."

"And who was that you were saying goodnight tae?" Sarah asked, indignantly.

"Walter Brown," Mary replied. "Him and Xander were in the village tonight."

Sarah was surprised. "Walter Brown?" she queried. "Has he no' gone home tae see his family yet?"

Feeling very cocky, now, knowing something her mother didn't, Mary answered, "His wife's taken the children tae visit friends in East Lothian for the week, so she's no' there. He decided tae stay here."

"You should be ashamed o' yourself," said Sarah, angrily, "going out wi' a married man!"

Mary squared up to her mother. "I wasnae on my own wi' him. Xander was wi' us wi' Annie Hastie!"

Sarah was almost at breaking point. "It's bad enough that I'm on my own most o' the time," she said, "without you disgracing the family!"

"I've done nothing wrong, ma'!" retorted Mary, indignantly.

"Let's hope so," sighed Sarah, resigned to the fact that she had no control over Mary whatsoever, "and let's hope it stays that way!"

Mary flounced off to bed, leaving a frustrated Sarah who sat down, and put her hands together on top of her head, looking skyward. "Oh, Lord, please look after us all!" she begged. Sarah sat there for a while trying to work out what she had done wrong in bringing Mary up. Finally, she gave up and went to bed.

Bright and early next morning, Robert arrived home. He had come home on the mail train overnight and would not be returning to England until the Monday. "Hinny, I'm home!" he called.

The younger children ran to greet their father, while Sarah looked up. She waited for the youngsters to finish saying hello to their father and then she stopped what she was doing and went over to Robert. "How I've missed you!" she said.

"Aye," replied Robert, "well, I'm here now, hinny. Is there something wrong?"

Mary, who had been sitting quietly, watched nervously in case her mother told Robert about the night before. She listed as her mother replied to Robert, "No, Robert. I just missed you! Do you want something tae eat or drink?"

Robert smiled. "Woman, I'm starved! Breakfast would be grand. Coming home on the overnight does wonders for your appetite!" Robert looked puzzled. Sarah didn't usually make such a fuss of him coming in these mornings.

"Sit yoursel' down, then, and you can tell me what you're up tae, now, where you're working while I cook." She turned to Mary, who was pretending to read. "Mary, will you go and get some more water."

Mary knew Sarah was picking her moment. She didn't want to leave the room, because she wanted to know what was going to be said, but neither could she refuse her mother's request. That would look even worse. She stood up. "Aye, ma'," she said. She went over to the kitchen and picked up the bucket. It would take a fair few minutes to fetch the water, so there was plenty of time for her mother to tell on her. She walked outside and out of view. Then she ran all the way to the well.

The younger children went back to their breakfasts and Sarah sat down next to Robert. "We're going tae have trouble wi' our Mary," began Sarah, "she's after all the men!"

Robert looked at Sarah. "She's no' that bad!" he said. Sarah shook her head.

"You weren't here last night," Sarah continued. "She was out wi' Walter Brown."

Robert looked surprised. "He didnae go home?" he asked.

"No," said Sarah. "He spun some tale about his wife being away for the weekend. Honest, everybody will be talking about her soon."

"You're worrying too much," replied Robert, hopefully.

"I hope that's the case," answered Sarah. Just then Sarah heard Mary walking back with the water. "Oh – here she comes." In an effort to hide the fact that she had been talking about Mary, Sarah got up and went over to prepare Robert's breakfast, in an effort to change the subject. "So, tell me, what are yous working on now?"

Mary entered the house as Robert was explaining his new job to Sarah. She smiled as she realised she wasn't the topic of conversation.

"We're working on a big new hotel now," Robert continued, "for all the visitors that'll now be coming by the new railway line."

Sarah sighed. "Oh, I wish you didnae have to go away again," she said. "I thought I'd get used tae this after last time, but it doesnae get any easier."

"I know, hinny," answered Robert, stroking her hair, "but you know I must. You have John you can rely on, you know."

"Aye, I know," replied Sarah, "but it's no' always easy." She stood up with a plateful of food that she had been preparing and walked over to the table with it. "Here, Robert," she said, "breakfast." She put the plate down and Robert came over to eat it. She sat down beside him at the table.

After breakfast Robert sat talking with John until he left for work then he went up the village. Sarah continued about her daily business, trying to keep one eye on Mary. Mary, in turn, kept a low profile for most of the day.

But that evening it was clear Mary was going out again. She put on one of her better dresses and tried to quietly leave the house. Robert was sitting in a chair, having read the newspaper. He appeared to be dozing, but the sound of Mary's movements were too much for him to sleep for long.

Mary thought her father was asleep as she tiptoed across the room, but the chair was facing away from the door, so she could not see his face. Robert sat there, stock still, waiting for her to go out of the door. Finally, she opened it and quietly closed it behind her.

As the door fell into its frame Robert was up out of the chair and peering out of the window. "Sarah!" he called. She came in from the other room.

"Well? What did she do?" she asked.

"I think you're right tae be worried," Robert replied. "She doesnae seem tae bother that he's married. I couldnae say before, but I've heard from others who've come from working here that she has a reputation. I just hope she doesnae do anything she'll regret. Mind, that Walter shouldnae be encouraging her. I'll go tae the village tomorrow and find out from people I know if there's anything tae be concerned about."

Sarah began to get upset. "Why, Robert?" she asked. "Why must she do this? What have I done wrong?"

"You've nothing tae reproach yoursel' for, hinny," Robert replied. "She's young and impressionable. That's why!"

So, next morning Robert went up to the village. He met up with Walter Wilson and they had a few bevvies at the inn before coming home. Amazing what you can learn while drinking. Anyway, Robert got home in time for lunch. He came into the cottage shaking his head. The children were outside playing and Mary and John were out. Sarah looked up, quizzically.

"It's worse than we feared, Sarah," began Robert. "Everybody knows about her comings and goings. She's a laughing stock o' the village. They're no' happy wi' her work in the post office. If she doesnae buck her ideas up they'll no' have working there anymore. She'll have tae get work elsewhere. And that Walter's as bad! It seems he's no' getting on too well wi' his wife. That's why he's staying here in the village just now."

Sarah was dismayed. "Oh, Robert! What are we to do wi' her?" she asked. "I cannae keep her in against her will."

"Is she here now?" Robert asked. Sarah shook her head.

"No, she's out," she answered. "She didnae say where she was going."

Robert thought for a moment. "Well," he began, "afore I go back tae work tomorrow I'll see what I can say tae her."

Sarah sat down, close to tears. "Oh, I don't know what tae do!" she said.

Robert sat down beside her. "There's nothing you can do, hinny," he said. "Just hold your head high. It's not you sullied our name."

Robert tried to speak with Mary but she managed to avoid him. She got up early to go to work and had left before Robert was even up. Robert made sure he had everything he needed to take with him and made his way to the station after breakfast. Sarah and the children walked with him as far as they could, but the children were going to school and Sarah and Nathaniel were going to the shops, not the station, so part way along the road they parted company. Robert promised Sarah that everything would work out. He gave them all a hug and then disappeared into the distance. Sarah continued on her way to the shops, with the children carrying on their way to school.

First place Sarah needed to go to was the Post Office as she had some letters to her family to post. She opened the door and she and the Nathaniel went inside.

"Good-day, Mrs. McWilliam," said Mary Scott, the postmistress. "How are you today?"

Sarah looked around to see where Mary was. "Fine, thank you, Mary," she replied. "And yoursel'?"

"Never better," replied Mary Scott. "I'm sorry we had tae let your Mary go – her mind wasnae on the work, and she was more interested in the young men's comings and goings."

Sarah was shocked. Robert hadn't told her that Mary had been let go, but she couldn't let Mary Scott know she was unaware of Mary's comings and goings. "I do understand," she improvised. "I don't know what's gotten into her these days." Sarah walked up to the counter. "I've a letter here for posting – tae England."

"That'll be two pence, please," said Mary, taking the letter from Sarah. Sarah took the money out from her purse and gave it to Mary Scott.

"Thanks," said Sarah. "I'll be off now." Sarah turned and walked out of the shop. She got outside and stood there, in the sunlight. She took a deep breath and looked around her. She felt that the eyes of the world were on her, but in reality, nobody was taking any notice of her. Then she spotted Janet Wilson, so she made a bee-line for her. "Hello, Janet. Are you well?" Sarah asked.

"Aye, Sarah," replied Janet. "And yourself?"

"No' bad," answered Sarah. "Have you seen our Mary today?"

Janet looked surprised. "No," she replied. "Is she no' working at the Post Office?"

Sarah shook her head. "I've just come from there," she said. "Mary was supposed tae be working there, but they've let her go. She left the house this morning saying she was off to work. I'm a bit perplexed, now!"

"Well," replied Janet, "you'll just have tae ask her when she gets home tonight."

Sarah nodded. "Aye, I will that!" she agreed. "How's your Walter keeping?"

"No' bad, no' bad," replied Janet. "He gets on well wi' your Robert – they're good workmates."

"Aye," replied Sarah, "Robert speaks highly of him. Well, I'll be off, Janet. Back home – tae wait for Mary!"

"Well," added Janet, "if I see Mary I'll no' say anything. Bye!"

The two women parted company. Sarah went off to the butchers and Janet continued on with her shopping before making her way back home.

Sarah bought what she needed from the butchers, went to the grocers and then made her way back home. She was very annoyed with Mary. It was bad enough that Mary Scott at the Post Office had let Mary go – it was a surprise, but not unexpected – but how could Mary lie like that? Sarah mused on this as she walked back home with her shopping.

Mary appeared to have vanished into thin air. Everybody who Sarah asked had no idea where she was. It seemed a lost cause, so Sarah gave up looking for Mary and went home. She did the chores and started to prepare the evening meal. Jane came home from school with the children.

Jane had left school now – she would be 13 in November – and she was far too old now, but she helped out in the school when she could. She enjoyed it. It passed the time while she looked for work elsewhere.

"Have you seen our Mary?" Sarah asked Jane as she walked in the door.

"Is she no' at work?" Jane asked, surprised.

"She doesnae work there now," replied Sarah. "Did you not know? I thought I was the only one who was ignorant of the fact."

The look of surprise on Jane's face convinced Sarah that her daughter did not know about Mary losing her job. "No, ma'," replied Jane, earnestly, "I did not know she wasnae there any more.

Sarah continued to prepare the evening meal and John came in. He didn't look at all happy. Sarah thought her mood must be rubbing off on everybody else. The dinner was ready and everybody present ate. There was a place still empty though. Mary had not yet returned from the village, and Sarah was not at all happy with her wayward daughter.

But, Sarah could see there was something pressing on John's mind. She waited until the younger children were in bed, then she turned to him. "Is there something the matter wi' you?" she asked.

John was sitting in a chair, reading the newspaper. He sighed and looked at his mother. "I'm going tae have tae finish with the Carruthers," John began, "he's giving up his farm, and just having a smallholding – so he'll no' be needing any farm servants. I'll have tae look elsewhere for work."

Sarah felt for him, but she tried to keep a brave face. "That's a shame," she said, "you're so close tae home working with him."

"Aye, but I didnae intend tae be working on the land all my life," he replied. "Is our Mary in yet? I've no' seen her tonight."

Sarah looked stern. She sighed and shook her head. "No, John, she is not," Sarah replied, angrily. "I've something I need to be saying tae her when she gets in, so I'd appreciate if you'd away tae your bed when the time's right."

"I've a notion I know what you're about tae say," John added, trying not to smirk.

Sarah glared at him. "Does the whole village know?" she asked.

John folded his newspaper up. "Well, she's no' discrete, ma'!" he said. "That Walter Brown is taking advantage of her, you know. It's no' all her doing."

"Maybe so," replied Sarah, "but she's of a responsible age now!"

Suddenly, they heard voices outside. "Quick," said Sarah, quietly, "I think she's coming! Away tae bed!"

John nodded and stood up. He hurriedly went into the bedroom and closed the door. Just at that same moment the front door opened and Mary tried to creep in. As she shut the door she realised there was a light on in the room still so she turned round to see her mother standing there, arms folded across her, in a defiant pose.

"Oh, ma'," Mary began, "you're still up."

Sarah looked at her. "And why wouldn't I be?" she asked.

Mary tried to think of something sensible to say. "Erm, I just thought it was a bit late," she floundered.

Sarah was now feeling confident. She could see that she had taken Mary by surprise. Mary certainly hadn't expected her mother to be waiting for her to come in. "I want a word wi' you, young lady," Sarah retorted, "although, I think lady is probably not the right word for you tonight!"

Mary tried to keep her composure, playing the innocent. "Why, whatever do you mean, ma'?" she asked, coyly.

"You know very well what I mean, madam!" said Sarah, huffing. "I was in the post office today."

"Oh, erm," Mary struggled to answer, "well, I expect you know then."

"You expect right, Mary," said Sarah, pointedly. "When did you finish at the post office?"

Mary had lost all her jauntiness now. "I finished on Friday," she answered, dejectedly.

"Hah!" said Sarah, "so that's why you weren't working on Saturday, and why you were out so late on Friday night."

It dawned on Mary that her mother knew more than she thought she did. Rather sheepishly, Mary replied, "Well, yes."

"And this Walter Brown business," continued Sarah, "I know all about that, too. His wife's not just gone away for a week. She's left him."

Mary's face turned bright red. She hadn't realised how easily she would be found out. "They're just going through a difficult time," she said. "He needed someone tae talk tae, that's all."

Sarah looked at Mary in amazement. Did her daughter really think she was stupid? Well, she thought, on Friday I must have been. "Someone tae talk tae?" Sarah said, pointedly. "Hah! And the rest. I wasnae born yesterday, you know! How dare you sully our name in this village!"

Mary didn't know which way to turn. She realised that her actions reverberated on other people as well as herself, and now she was hurting the ones she loved. Very contritely, she replied, "I'm sorry, ma'."

"Sorry? Sorry?" exclaimed Sarah, "you'd better be more than sorry, my girl! And what are you going tae do for work, now?" Sarah unfolded her arms and put her fists resting on each of her hips.

"I'll get another job," said Mary, beginning to feel a bit more confident again.

"You might find it a wee bit difficult round here," said Sarah, shaking her head, "everybody's talking about you."

"I'll be fine – you see!" said Mary.

Sarah stood there, still shaking her head, "Hmm… We shall see… Well, away tae your bed now!"

Mary turned to go to bed. "Night, ma'," she said, with little emotion in her voice.

Sarah watched her daughter go to bed and she stood there for a moment or two. She wanted to give Mary a chance to get into bed before she went in there. Finally, she followed her in to the bedroom.

Next morning, Sarah got up early. John was off to work with the sun, and Jane was helping Sarah get the little ones ready for school. Mary lay asleep in her bed. Jane turned to her mother. "Are you no' going tae get her up?" she whispered.

"What's the point?" asked Sarah, "it's no' like she's anywhere tae go, is it?"

Sarah opened the door and went into the kitchen to serve up the breakfast. Jane was just about to help the little ones with their coats when Mary appeared. Sarah was washing up the dishes. She turned to Mary. "So you've decided tae get up then," said Sarah, sarcastically.

"Aye, ma'," replied Mary, sleepily. She went over to the larder and got herself something to eat. A bit of bread and some cheese. "Any tea in the pot?" she asked.

"A bit – but it's well stewed," replied her mother. She watched Mary sit down with a mug of tea and her food. "And what are you going tae do today?"

Quietly, and confidently, Mary said, "I'm going tae get myself another job. That's what you wanted tae hear me say, isn't it?"

"And where are you going to go for one?" Sarah asked, bemused. "The hiring fair isn't until two weeks, so you'll no' get any work afore then." Sarah looked over at Jane who was shaking her head. "You'll have tae keep yourself busy helping me around the house." Sarah continued.

Mary looked confused. "Can I no' go into the village and see if there's anything tae be had there?" she asked.

"Hmph!" said Sarah, "You can go, but I doubt very much you'll get yourself any work. You'll be more help to me if you stay here and help wi' the washing!"

Mary looked annoyed. "So, am I no' tae go tae the village?" she asked.

Sarcastically, Sarah replied, "That depends on what you intend tae do when you get there!"

"Do you no' trust me, now?" Mary retorted.

"Tae be fair, Mary," her mother began, "I don't know what I think o' you just now! You do the washing that I had just put aside for doing and then you can go up the village this afternoon."

"Fine. I'll do that, then!" said Mary, pouting. She finished her breakfast and stood up. She could see the sheets that Sarah had brought out for washing, so she gathered them up and went outside. Jane and the others were, by now, ready to leave the house, but Jane couldn't go without seeing how Mary reacted. She was shocked at the way Mary had spoken to her mother. "Are you alright, ma'?" she asked. "What's up wi' Mary?"

"Never you mind," replied Sarah. "The less you know about, the better."

Jane walked over to her mother. She rubbed her hand on Sarah's arm. "Oh, ma', I know more than you think I know. If it's just about her losing her job at the post office."

"It's no' just that," replied Sarah, sadly. "I suppose you'll be telling me that you've heard what people are saying in the village, next."

"Well," began Jane, "I have heard things."

Sarah looked at Jane and smiled. Why, oh why couldn't Mary be more like her sister? "It's best left unsaid just now," replied her mother. "Off you go or the little ones will be late for school."

"Aye, ma'." Jane turned and ushered the younger children out of the door, leaving Sarah with Nathaniel, who was playing unconcernedly on the floor.

The next couple of weeks passed uneventfully enough. Mary did go down to the village, but she didn't stay long. Sarah was surprised at how helpful Mary had been. Sad, though, that it had taken this to make a change in her daughter. Evenings were when Mary saw no reason to stay in.

Early on Saturday, 11 September Robert came home again. Sarah prepared him a big breakfast. He enjoyed eating that when he came home. Mary was often out, despite her trying to be helpful, and Jane was helping the other children with their schoolwork.

Sarah sat down with Robert. She tried to spend as much time as she could in these few days she had with him. She had told him about what had happened in the village over the past few days while he was eating.

"So," he said, finishing the last bit of food off the plate, "do you think she'll get another job?"

"I've no idea," answered Sarah. "If she does, it'll be outside o' this area, for sure. We shall see on Tuesday. John has tae go, anyway, so he'll be my eyes and ears."

Robert looked surprised. "You've told him?" he asked.

"I've told nobody, but everybody knows," Sarah replied. "What else have you heard?"

"More than I care tae," replied Robert, with disgust. "Where is she, anyway?"

"Out – she went out early this morning – most probably tae avoid seeing you," said Sarah. "She's rarely in these days. She helps out a wee bit in the mornings and that's it. That Walter Brown's always hanging about, too."

As they finish speaking Mary flounced in. "So, you've decided tae show your face then!" Robert said, sharply.

Mary stood there, looking at him. "Can I no' come and go as I please?" she answered.

"You can come and go," Robert replied, "we cannae stop you, but do you know how you've hurt us? Do no' care about the shame?"

Mary put her hands on her hips. "I'm no' ashamed!" she retorted. "I keep telling you – I've done nothing wrong."

"Maybe so," said Robert, his tone softening, "but you're doing yourself no favours acting like this."

Mary, too, backed down, realising that she was not winning this argument. She knew they were right, despite not wanting to show it. "I'm sorry," she said. "I didnae mean for this tae happen. It just did."

Mary stayed in for the afternoon but went out again in the evening. Robert and Sarah realised whatever they might try to do they would not win. Had Robert been at home full time it might have been different, but he wasn't, and Sarah could not look after all their children and keep Mary in check as well.

The weekend went by far too fast and Monday came and Robert had to leave again. "Be strong, hinny," he said to Sarah. "I'll start tae look out for work round here. I'll no' put you through this any more than I have tae." He kissed Sarah. "I'll be back soon enough, in two weeks." He turned and left Sarah standing at the door.

Sarah stood at the door and watched him go. John came over to her. "Ma'," he said, "Everything will be just fine, you see."

Sarah looked at her son. He was such a loving lad. She was glad to have him around. "It's the hiring fair tomorrow, is it not?" she asked.

"Aye, ma'," he replied. He took her by the hand and led her back indoors. "Come on, ma', I'll get you some tea."

Early next morning both John and Mary left early to go to the hiring fair. Jane took the younger children to school and Sarah began the chores. She kept thinking of Robert back home every day and it seemed to lift her. The morning soon passed and John and Mary were back again. They walked in the door, bold as brass. "Hello, ma'," said John, "I've got myself another job!"

Sarah looked up, very pleased for him.

"So have I!" said Mary, looking very smug, in an 'I told you so' pose.

Sarah smiled. "Well done, both of you," she said. "So where are you working?"

"Well," John began, "erm – I have tae live in."

Sarah nodded in acceptance. She knew her children had to fly the nest at some point. "That's understandable," she asked. "But where?"

"Erm – Cambusnethan. William Pettigrew. He runs the Commercial Inn on the Edinburgh and Ayr Road and he has a small farm as well. I'm tae be his ploughman. He's a widower wi' two daughters."

"Well, that's no' bad," replied Sarah. "And what about you, Mary?"

"Well, I've been taken on at Birkwood Farm," she began. "The farm's owned by Jane Brown. She's a 78 year old widow.

337

It's her son, James, who runs the farm. It's 78 acres and they live there wi' her other sons. They've no house servants, so I'm tae help in the house."

"So, you'll both be going," added Sarah, stunned. "When do you leave?"

Mary was first to speak. "I start Saturday, 16th of October."

John jumped straight in after with, "And I start the Saturday after that!"

Sarah sat down. She smiled. It was clear she was glad that both her children had gotten themselves another job, but they would both be leaving. Jane would have to be her main support now. Sarah looked at Mary. "Mind you behave yourself," she said.

"I will, ma'," replied Mary. "I know I've been stupid. I lost my job at the post office being stupid – and it wasnae necessary. I could have stayed at home if I was at the post office. Now I have tae go and live in as a servant. I feel so foolish now."

"Well, what's done is done, and there's no turning back," said Sarah. "Just mind you keep yourself tae yourself."

"Aye, I will, ma'," replied Mary.

Sarah turned to John. "And you off, too," she said. "I shall miss you, my boy. Who'll be head o' the house when you've gone?"

"You'll do fine, ma'," John replied.

Soon Jane and the other children arrived home and Mary and John were telling them how they had done at the hiring fair. Jane was insanely jealous. "It'll be my turn, soon," she said.

The rest of the two weeks passed quietly enough. Mary had little time for the village now. It seemed she wanted to get herself ready for her new job, and she worked hard round the house, helping her mother. Soon, Robert was home and Sarah felt her world was complete. Robert was pleased to see everybody getting on well with each other. That was how a family was meant to be.

"Well, this looks a happier house than it was last week!" he said as he walked in through the door.

Sarah looked up and went over to him to say hello. "Things are no' so bad today," she added. "I think Mary's realised what she was doing."

"I should hope so," replied Robert. "I dinnae want another few days like these have been."

Mary came over to her father. "I'm sorry, da'," she said, "I didnae mean tae make you angry."

Sarah turned round, still hugging Robert's waist. She looked at Mary as she stood there. "Mary, look at me," she said.

"What is it, ma'?" Mary replied, looking at her mother, confused.

Sarah moved away from Robert and stared at Mary. "I think you have something tae tell us, Mary," she said.

Mary began to look concerned. "I've no idea what you're talking about, ma'!" she exclaimed.

Sarah looked at Robert. "Hmm, I take it all back," she said, "I think our troubles are far from over, Robert."

Both Robert and Mary now looked confused. They stood there looking first at each other and then both at Sarah. Robert could keep silent no longer. "But I thought you said things were getting back to normal?"

"Aye, so I did," answered Sarah. "But I've just noticed something. Something that's no' going away, no matter how hard Mary tries."

For a moment, still only Sarah knew what she was talking about, but, suddenly, Mary's confusion lifted and she realised there was nothing she could hide from her all-knowing mother. "How do you know, ma'?" Mary asked. "I wasnae sure."

Sarah gave a wry laugh. "I've no' been a midwife these years, tae not notice, missy!" she said.

Suddenly, the penny dropped for Robert and his happy demeanour was shattered by a look of dismay. "Oh, my God!" he yelled. "And who's the father? No – don't tell me – let me guess – Walter Brown. It is, isn't it? He's the only one you've been seeing."

Mary stood there, crestfallen. She knew now that everybody in the family knew. Both John and Jane stared at her, angry yet sad at the same time.

"I'm sorry, da', sorry, ma'?" said a very dejected Mary. "I didnae mean tae, ma', da'! I was trying tae be better!"

Sarah looked lovingly at her daughter. "Aye, lass, I know you were trying," she said. "But this didnae happen overnight. This must have been from a month or more ago."

Mary began to cry. Sarah immediately felt sorry for her. She went over to her and gave her a hug. Mary began to sob in her mother's arms, so Sarah took her into the bedroom to calm her down. Mary fell asleep on her bed and Sarah left her lying quietly there. She went back to her chores. A while later Mary woke up and got dressed to go out. She left the cottage without so much as a word. Sarah and Robert looked at each other.

"Well, what does it matter now?" said Sarah. "It's done. There's no going back now."

"Aye, you're right, as always," replied Robert.

Mary went up to the village and sought out Walter Brown. He was in the ale house. She made a beeline for him.

"Come outside, Walter," said Mary. "I need tae talk wi' you."

Walter didn't need telling twice. He had been drinking and thought Mary wanted some fun. "Well, lassie, here I am," he said. "What's it tae be tonight?"

"I'm no' in the mood for fun," said Mary. "I thought you should know I'm expecting."

"Expecting what?" Walter chuckled.

"A bairn!" Mary said, angrily.

Walter stood stock still. "You what?" he asked, no longer drunk. "You're expecting a bairn?"

"Aye," said Mary, "and it's yours."

"Oh, no! Oh, no!" replied Walter, backing off as he spoke. "I've two bairns o' my own. I dinnae want another. You were just a bit o' fun."

"Fun?" said Mary, shocked. "This isnae fun. This is me. This is my life. And it's your fault."

"Well, I'm away back home come Monday," said Walter. "Away back tae Jane. I've a mind tae stay there and make up wi' her. You're nothing tae me. Just a wee bit o' fun. You should have taken more care. Now, if there's nothing more on your mind I'll be away tae the bar again."

With that, Walter turned round and went back indoors. Mary stood there, speechless. She realised that Xander was standing there in the shadows, laughing. As the realisation that he had never really cared for her came to her she began to cry. She turned and ran back home.

She opened the door to the cottage and ran inside. She was still crying as she shut the door. Sarah stood up and went over to her. Hush, Mary," she said, soothingly, "everything will be fine." She led her daughter into the room and John pulled up a chair for his sister to sit on. He and his father were sat at the table, talking.

Mary turned to her mother. "What do I do, ma'? Walter's in the village but he says he doesnae want anything tae do wi' me now. He said he was going tae talk wi' his wife about their future."

"That was only a matter of time, Mary," said Sarah, softly. "I knew he'd go back tae her. You'll just have tae make do the best you can."

Robert stopped talking with John. "We'll get by, lass," he said, affectionately. "The bairn won't be born till the summer, so there's plenty o' time to work things out."

Mary began to calm her tears. "Do I still go and work at the farm?" she asked.

"Aye, lass," said Robert. "They'll see you changing, but you should tell them you'll be back wi' them as soon as the bairn's born. Does anybody else know yet?"

Mary thought for a moment and then remembered. "Xander was there. He heard Walter shouting about it being my fault, and my problem. I daresay it's all around the village now."

Robert shook his head. "That means it'll be following me around when I go back tae work after the weekend," he said. "But no matter."

"We'll get through this, Mary," said Sarah. "We'll all be fine."

Mary began to realise the full extent of what she had done. "I'm so sorry, ma', da'. I never even dreamed this'd happen."

Robert stood up. He could not bear to see his daughter upset like this. "Come here, lass," he said, holding his arms out. Mary went over to him and he held her. She sobbed, uncontrollably for a few minutes and then calmed down. She looked up at her father.

Through the tears she smiled. "I'll be fine, da'," she said. "I'll go tae bed now."

Mary disappeared into the bedroom and Robert turned to John. He had paper and pen out. "What are you doing over there, John?" he asked.

"I'm working out what I'll need tae take wi' me when I go," John replied. "I've never been away from home afore."

Sarah smiled. "You'll do fine, son," she said. "You've got your head screwed on right."

Sunday was quiet. Mary barely stirred from her room. Sarah was worried about her but Robert assured her Mary would be fine. He told Sarah that their daughter just needed a bit of time on her own. When she did come out, later that evening, she just sat reading.

Come the Monday, Robert was off again. He kissed his family goodbye and set off. With the younger children at school and Mary and John indoors she went up the village without Nathaniel. She was prepared for the stares and comments, but there were none. Amongst the womenfolk it was nothing new. Many of the mothers themselves had been in that situation, which was why they'd gotten married in the first place.

All her shopping done, Sarah returned home. Mary was prepared to hear what the villagers had said about her, but Sarah told her nothing had been said. She told Mary that she must venture out and show everybody she was fine. Mary said she would go the next day.

Mary went up to the village with Sarah the next day and realised that things weren't as bad as she had feared. But she stayed close to her mother's side. There would be no more misbehaving now.

They went back home and Mary did the cleaning while Sarah cooked the evening meal. Afterwards the little ones went to bed and Sarah sat with Mary and John, who was reading.

Suddenly, there was a knock at the door. "Who on earth could that be?" asked Sarah.

"Well, you'll never know until you answer it, ma'," said Mary.

Sarah got up and went over to the door. She opened it. It was the Wilsons. "Walter? Janet? What are you doing here? Are you no' working this week?"

"Can we come in, Sarah?" asked Janet.

"Aye, of course. Come in," said Sarah, confused. Walter and Janet came in. Janet looked around her.

"Oh, I'm glad tae see your children are here wi' you." said Janet, relieved.

"Whatever are yous doing here at this time o' day?" asked Sarah.

"Sit yourself down, Sarah," said Janet. Sarah sat down.

"Do you want us tae leave the room?" asked Mary.

Janet looked over at Mary and thought for a moment. "Perhaps it's best yous stay."

Walter and Janet pulled up a chair so they were sitting either side of Sarah. Sarah sat there, very confused. Walter began to talk. "They sent me home yesterday," he said. "It's bad, Sarah, it's bad."

He paused and looked at Janet. She indicated he should continue. He took a deep breath. "There was trouble yesterday. At Cartmel, where we're staying. After work. I dinnae ken how best tae tell you this, lass," he stumbled with his words, not quite knowing what to say.

"It's Robert, isn't it?" said Sarah, realising this was bad news. "Oh, for God's sake, Walter, just tell me!"

"Well," he said, "here goes."

As Walter began to explain Sarah visualised everything in her mind.

"It was after we got back yesterday. We took our bags tae the lodging house and went tae unwind at the Nag's Head. There were a dozen or so there already when we got there and they'd been drinking a while. There were a few of us arrived back the same time, some from the village and some from round about. Well, we sort o' kept ourselves tae ourselves for a bit, but some o' the others from the village were laughing wi' the others. Robert was drowning his sorrows. He'd told me about Mary – just as well he did – as it turns out. Anyway, he went for a leak and comes back wi' William Smith.

"Well, I was up at the bar getting in some more drinks, and I turned round to see it all unravelling. Afore Robert had the chance tae sit back down William was taunting him about Mary. Robert had just taken a swig from his tankard when William called her a slut…"

Robert slammed his tankard down on the table. "She didnae mean for anything tae happen," he yelled. "She's a young, innocent lass. If anyone's tae blame it's that fecking Walter Brown!"

"Hah!" laughed William Smith, "it takes two! If she'd no' egged him on none o' this would ever've happened!"

"He should've known better!" argued Robert. "He's a married man! No wonder he's having problems wi' his marriage – he cannae keep his parts in his trousers!"

"Well, everybody in your village knows what she's like!" retorted William. "She'll go wi' anybody. It was only a matter o' time before that hoor o' yours got in the family way!"

"Don't you dare talk about my daughter like that!" shouted Robert, getting very agitated, and red in the face. "Or – or –"

"Or what?" taunted William.

"Or – or – I'll beat the shite out o' you!" said an exasperated Robert.

"Dinnae take it like that!" said William, backing off, "I'm only talking wi' you."

"It's my daughter's name you're blackening!" replied Robert. "I willnae hear anything said about her."

Before Walter got back from the bar Robert took a punch at William. But William dodged out of the way. Walter tried to get back from the bar, but by now a crowd was gathering. Walter shouted over to Robert, "Robert, don't do it! He's no' worth it!"

But Robert was too worked up to hear. William, too, tried to diffuse the situation. "Gie over, Robert," said William. "She's no' worth it!"

"She's my daughter," yelled Robert. "She's every bit worth it. Put your fists up! We're having it out – now!"

Robert took a fighting stance but William tried to walk away, towards the orchard at the rear of the inn. "I'll no' take part in fisticuffs, man," William said.

"Hah!" said Robert, following him, putting his fists up and beginning to dart around as William tried to walk away. "So you're all mouth and no trousers, then!"

Another fellow mason, James Butler, realised that if William did get started there would be blood spilled, and despite it being entertaining, it wasn't a good idea. "Give over, you two!" James called out. "Calm down. Forget anything's been said."

"Aye, Robert – forget it," added William, sarcastically, now bitten with the fighting bug.

"I'll no' forget it," said Robert, taking some more swipes at William. Finally, Robert grabbed hold of William and William turned to face him. They both started to struggle with each other when, suddenly, Robert lost his footing and fell on top of William.

Walter finally managed to get through the gathered crowd. The scene in front of him shook him. Robert had hit his head on the ground when he fell and was now unconscious, laying on top of William Smith. William tried to push him off so he could stand up, but unconscious, Robert was a dead weight. Walter and James came over to try to wake Robert up.

"Robert! Robert! Wake up man!" yelled James, shaking Robert's head.

Slowly, Robert began to come round. James and Walter helped him stand, but he was unsteady on his feet.

"Are you alright, Robert?" asked James.

"My neck's a wee bit sore," answered Robert, rubbing his neck, "and my arm hurts a bit, otherwise I'm fine."

"Let's get you back home," said James.

"Aye," added Walter, "keep you out o' harm's way."

"And Billy!" added James.

Between them Walter and James staggered back with Robert to their lodging house, leaving William Smith to get up and walk away while the crowd dispersed.

They managed to get Robert back to Hodgson's Farm, where they were lodging. They struggled with him up the stairs and lay him down on his bed. Robert lay there, groaning. "Walter!" Robert called out, "you'll have tae get a doctor. My neck's killing me!"

Walter and James looked at each other. "Go, Jimmy, go get the doctor!" said Walter. "I'll wait here wi' Robert."

"Alright," said James, "I'll be as quick as I can." He rushed out of the room and down the stairs. Walter could hear voices downstairs. It was, most likely, Jimmy asking for directions to the doctor. Then Walter heard the sound of a door slamming and he knew that Jimmy was on his way.

Walter turned to Robert, who was beginning to look very pale. "Jimmy's gone for the doctor," he said to Robert. "Whatever got into you, man?"

"I'll have no-one speak o' my family like that," replied Robert. "Oh, man…" Robert's words trailed off as he lost consciousness once again.

"Robert!" Walter called, "Robert! Robert!" It was useless. Walter could not rouse Robert. At that moment there were noises coming from downstairs, getting louder. The door opened and in rushed Jimmy with the doctor.

"Where's the patient?" asked the doctor. He turned to look at Robert as Walter spoke.

"He's here, doctor," said Walter, directing the doctor's gaze towards unconscious Robert. "Help him, please!"

The doctor bent over Robert's lifeless body. He felt for Robert's pulse. "I'm afraid there's nothing I can do," he said. "This man is dead."

"He cannae be!" yelled Walter. "No! You've got tae do something!"

"I'm very sorry," replied the doctor, "but this man is past helping. Where's his next of kin? I shall have to tell them."

"What's your name, man?" asked Walter.

"Lomax, Dr. John Lomax," the doctor replied, "but there's still nothing I can do. Where's his next of kin?"

"You going tae tell them is going tae be difficult, even for you," replied Walter. "They live in Lesmahagow."

"Wherever's that?" the doctor asked.

"It's a few miles outside of Glasgow, man!" said Walter, annoyed.

"Oh, Scotland," the doctor mused. "Well, how did he get injured?"

"He got into a fight at the Nag's Head," replied Jimmy.

"A fight?" the doctor repeated. "With whom? I'll have to notify the constabulary." The doctor went to leave the room.

"Can we take his body back home?" asked Walter, putting his hand on the doctor's shoulder, stopping him from walking out the door.

"Take his body?" said Dr. Lomax, "why of course not! Under the circumstances there's got to be an inquest!" The doctor turned to Jimmy. "Young man, please go and fetch a constable, as you'll not let me out of the room. Tell him that I need an ambulance to take the body away so I can examine it. I'll wait here." The doctor sat down in the chair that was in the corner of the room.

"Feck's sake," said Walter, distressed. "You better go, Jimmy. Do as he says."

Jimmy looked uncertain. He looked at Walter again. "Go get the fecking constable!" repeated Walter.

So, without further word, Jimmy left the room, and was soon on his way.

The doctor looked at Walter. "What killed him?" Walter asked him.

"I do not know," replied the doctor, assertively. "That's why there's to be an inquest. That's why you cannot have the body."

They waited about five minutes, but the time passed far more slowly. Finally, James arrived with the police constable. They entered the room. "Ah, good!" said the doctor. "Did you organise the ambulance?"

"Yes, sir," replied the police constable. "They'll be bringing the meat – ambulance directly. Now, what happened here?"

"Well," replied the doctor, "this gentleman tells me that there was a fight at the Nag's Head and that is how this man was injured. That's when I sent for you."

"Very good, sir," replied the police constable. "Right thing to do."

At that moment the sound of a horse and cart pulling up outside could be heard. "That will be the ambulance," said the doctor. "I'll go and let them in." Dr. Lomax stood up and left the room. He went downstairs. With the doctor out of the room the police constable decided to take some notes. "Right, sirs, some information, if you please," he began. "Is there somewhere we can sit down?"

"We can go sit in my room if you want," said Walter, "although I'd rather wait here wi' Robert until he goes."

"I suppose we can wait here," answered the constable, reluctantly. "I'll sit over there in that chair." The police constable walked over to the chair that the doctor had just vacated and sat down. He took out his notebook and pencil and looked first at Walter and the James.

"Right," he said, "who'd like to start? What's this man's name?"

James stood there silently, looking at Walter. Walter looked at the policeman. "His name is Robert McWilliam," said Walter.

As Walter spoke the policeman began to write. As he finished writing he looked up again and asked another question. "Where does he live? Who's his next of kin?"

Walter continued to speak as he knew Robert better than anybody else on the team. "He lives in Lesmahagow. He's a wife and six children."

The policeman started to write but didn't know how. He looked up at Walter, questioningly. "Les – how do you spell that?"

Walter spelt out the name of the village letter by letter and the policeman wrote it down. He tried to read it back. "Lesmar – Lesmarhag – Lesmarhaggowe!" he said, jubilantly.

"Close enough," said Walter.

"Never heard of the place," said the policeman. "Where's it near?"

"Glasgow," Walter replied. He'd considered saying Lanark but decided this man wouldn't know where that was, either.

"How many children did you say he had?" asked the policeman again.

"Six," replied Walter. "He has a wife and six children."

"Wife's name?" asked the policeman.

Walter was beginning to get exasperated with this man. Alright, so he had a job to do, but it looked like he didn't really want to be here.

"Mrs. Sarah McWilliam," replied Walter.

"Right, that's the main details down," said the policeman, "now, how exactly did this all happen?"

Walter was just about to start explaining when the door opened and Dr. Lomax came back into the room, followed by two men carrying a stretcher.

"The body's over there on the bed," said the doctor. "Take it back to my surgery so I can examine him properly to find out how he died."

Together, the men answered, "Yes, sir." They walked over to the bed and began to lift Robert's lifeless body on to the stretcher. Walter watched them as they did so. They were rough as they moved him and Walter was not impressed. "Hey, you!" he said, angrily, "mind how you lift that man's body!"

The two men stopped what they were doing and looked at Walter. The one closest to Walter said, "But he's dead!"

"So he might be," replied Walter, "but he's my friend, and I'll have you treat him wi' some decency!"

The other man turned to his partner and whispered, "Better do what he says – he's a Jock."

"Aye," said Walter, angrily, "so what if I am from Scotland? Do yous have a problem wi' that?"

Sheepishly, the two men apologised and they continued to move Robert's body onto the stretcher. They lifted the stretcher off the bed, manoeuvred out of the room and down the stairs. The doc-

349

tor turned to go. "I'm sorry it had to end like this Mr. Wilson," he said. The report will be sent to the coroner for the hearing."

The doctor left the room and closed the door behind him. The policeman sighed with relief. He didn't like dead bodies. There was something about them that made him shiver. "You can sit down now," said the policeman, thoughtfully, "over there on the bed."

Walter looked at him with disgust. "I'll stand, if it's all the same tae you," he said.

"Up to you," said the policeman. "Let's get back to the events of today. So, tell me, what happened at the Nag's Head?"

Sarah looked at Walter as he finished talking. She began to shake. "No! It cannae be!" she cried out, tears starting to run down her face. "I want my Robert! I want my Robert! He can't be dead! It's not true!"

Janet got down on her knees in front of Sarah and Sarah collapsed into her arms. Walter looked across at John and Mary, who were also crying, hugging each other.

Mary started to talk through her tears. "It's all my fault! I shouldnae ha' done it! If I'd no' been sae free and easy wi' everyone I'd no' be in this predicament. Da' would still be here if it wasnae for me! No! What have I done! Ma', I'm sorry!"

Sarah caught what Mary was saying and suddenly she realised that had it not been for her daughter's foolishness this would probably never have happened. She stood up and looked at Mary. "Sorry!" she shouted, "aye! You should be sorry! You're right. It is your fault!"

"No, ma'!" cried Mary. She got up and ran outside, crying hysterically. John followed her.

Janet stood up and held Sarah by the shoulders. "Sarah, I know this is a shock," she said. "It was a terrible shock for me when Walter came home. But don't blame Mary."

Sarah stopped crying and looked at Janet. "Don't blame Mary?" she said, angrily. "If it hadnae been for all her shenanigans he'd still be here. He wouldn't have had anything to defend! How can I not blame Mary?"

"Because," said Janet, trying to calm the situation, "for all she's done, she's still a child. She had no idea what she was doing would end like this. She was just testing you. All – "

"Testing?" said Sarah, incredulously, "aye, she was that, alright!" Sarah stopped for a moment and paused. "But, you're right," she added, after a few minutes. "She didnae realise how it would end. I must go tae her."

Janet let go of Sarah and she went outside to her children. Mary was sitting outside on the ground, in floods of tears, John by her side, trying to console her. Sarah picked up her gardening stool and sat it down next to Mary and perched on it. Sarah tried to lift Mary up so she could look at her. "Shush, Mary, it's alright," said Sarah. "I'm sorry."

"What're you sorry for, ma'?" asked Mary, trying not to cry. "It is all my fault. I killed him."

"Don't be so silly, girl," said Sarah, quietly. "You didnae kill him. He'd been drinking. He wasn't in his right mind."

"But the things they were saying," said Mary, now looking at her mother, "if I'd no' been so stupid, there'd have been nothing tae say."

Sarah shook her head and stroked Mary's hair off of her face. "No, Mary, no," Sarah began, starting to cry again. "If it hadnae been you there would've been something else, sometime or other. Someone would've upset him."

Mary got up on her knees and Sarah hugged her.

"Ma's right, Mary," began John. "You just feel like that now. You didnae kill him. He loved you. That's why he stood up for you."

Mary looked at her mother and saw such love in her eyes. "How can I make it up tae you, ma'?" she said.

"You can stop being such a – a – silly girl, and come back inside," replied Sarah. "We have got tae get through this – together. "

Mary stood up and she and John helped their mother up off the stool.

"Aye, ma', I know," said Mary. "But I do feel guilty."

As Sarah got to her feet she looked at Mary. "Aye, and you will – for a while," Sarah said. "But you'll get over it. It'll get better. Well, easier." She began to cry again. "I miss him!"

John and Mary propel Sarah back indoors to the waiting arms of Janet Wilson.

"Come on now, Sarah," said Janet, "sit yourself down." She put Sarah back on her chair and turned to Mary. "Will you get your ma' a cup o' tea?"

"Yes, Mrs. Wilson," Mary replied, drying her own eyes. "Would yous like one?" she asked Janet and Walter.

"Aye," said Janet, "that'd be grand."

Both Mary and John went to the kitchen end to make tea.

Sarah was calmer now. "So what happens now?" she asked.

"There's the inquest tae determine if anybody was responsible for Robert's death," said Walter.

"Well o' course they were. It's all that William Smith's fault!" said Sarah, eager to blame somebody.

"That's for the coroner tae decide, lass," said Walter.

"But what about his body?" asked Sarah. "When can I get him back?"

Walter shook his head. "I dinnae ken at this moment," he said. "I have tae go back tomorrow, so I'll find out what is tae happen, then. I shall be back on Saturday, this week. I'll probably no' go back after that."

Mary and John brought them all over a cup of tea each. There had been water on for a drink before Janet and Walter had arrived, so it hadn't taken long to make. Sarah, Janet and Walter drank their teas. Sarah felt much better afterwards. When they had finished Jane turned to Sarah. "Now will you be alright?" she asked. "We have tae go – Walter needs tae get some sleep afore he goes back tomorrow."

"Aye," said Sarah, now more composed. "Aye, we'll be fine. We'll manage."

They all stood up and walked over to the door. Sarah opened it and Janet gave her a hug. "Yous know where we are if yous need us," she said. Sarah nodded and they turned and began the walk back to the village.

The next few days passed by in a haze. The Days, the Carruthers and the Crossan families were upset to hear about Robert. They all got on well and had liked him. They all rallied round for Sarah and the children, offering to help out wherever they could.

The other children were told and all were distraught when they realised they wouldn't see their father again. Only Nathaniel, being so young, didn't really understand what it all meant.

Finally, the weekend came, and with it came Walter with further news. He got to the cottage on the Saturday, 2 October 1858. John was out in the garden and saw him coming. Sarah came out to meet him. As they walked inside Sarah asked, "So what do you have tae tell me?"

Walter sighed. "I have Robert's last week's wages," he said. "There's forty shillings, there." He handed the envelope with the money in to Sarah. "It's more than he would have got, only they gave extra on account of him dying." He paused to see how Sarah was coping with everything. She seemed to be doing fine.

"Thank you for that," she said. "Forty shillings? Is that it?" She sighed and shook her head. "It'll no' go very far."

Walter continued. "They had the inquest yesterday. We all had tae go."

"What did they say?" she asked. "Come, sit down and tell me. She turned to John, "John, get Walter some ale."

"Aye, ma'," he said. He went and poured Walter a glassful and brought it over to him. "Why, thank you, lad," said Walter. "Do you want some tea, ma'?" John asked.

"Aye," Sarah replied, "I would, son. Thanks."

As Walter sipped at his ale he continued. "Well, everybody told their part – pretty truthfully, actually. I thought William Smith wouldnae say why Robert got so angry, but he did. The coroner – Lawrence Holden – listened tae everything that was said. In the end he said Robert's death was 'misadventure'."

Sarah looked at him quizzically. "So does that mean I can have Robert's body back to bury him?"

Walter shifted in his seat. "Well, erm..." He struggled to get the words out. "Er, no. They've already buried him."

Sarah looked at him in shock. "Already buried him?" she said, slowly.

"Well, lass, they had tae," he replied, "it was almost five days!"

"But, I've no' been able to say goodbye tae him!" she said, burying her face in her hands. She began to cry.

John brought over Sarah her cup of tea and put it down beside her.

"Walter, what am I going tae do wi'out him?" Sarah asked him.

Walter put his glass down and turned to face Sarah. "Sarah," he began, "I've known you long enough. You're a strong woman. You've a good family – despite everything that's happened. You'll do just fine."

"But I miss him!" she cried.

"Do you want me tae fetch Janet up?" Walter asked.

"I dinnae want tae be any bother," Sarah said, her tears subsiding a bit.

Walter smiled. "Oh, you're nae bother, lass," he said. "I'll go fetch her just now."

John couldn't help but overhear what Walter had just said. He knew how hard all this had hit Walter as well as his own family. Walter was there with his mother giving her some comfort. "I'll go for you, Mr. Wilson," said John. "You sit there wi' my ma'."

Before Walter had a chance to say anything, John was gone. He was gone for about half an hour but when he returned he had Janet with him. Janet sat down with Sarah and Walter and they continued to talk.

"So when do I get the death certificate?" asked Sarah.

"No' for a while," replied Walter. "As I understand it, the Registrar will only issue it when he's got the full facts."

Sarah looked confused. "But the inquest is finished. He must have the full facts!"

Walter shook his head. "I dinnae understand the way it works in England!"

"Do you want tae get in touch wi' anybody?" asked Janet.

Sarah thought for a moment. "I ought to tell my sister," she replied. "We've always been very close."

"Well," said Janet, "you write your letter and I'll get it posted. Now, how's your Mary doing?"

Sarah looked sad. "She's in the other room. She doesnae come out much."

"Would you like me tae have a word wi' her?" asked Janet.

Sarah smiled. "Aye, if you would," she said. "And while you're doing that I can write a letter."

"I'll leave you two women tae it, now," said Walter. "I've delivered my news."

"Thank you so much Walter," replied Sarah, truly grateful, "for all you've done."

"Think nothing of it, Sarah," he added. "I'd like tae think if the tables were turned you'd do the same for me."

Walter stood up and hugged Sarah. As he did so, Sarah felt a bulge in his pocket and looked down. It was a newspaper. She looked at Walter. "Aye," he said, "it is a paper from England. "I bought it after the inquest, but when I read it I didnae think you'd want tae see it."

"Why?" Sarah asked.

"Cause they made a right pig's ear of it," he said, angrily. "That's why."

"Whatever do you mean?" she asked.

Walter tutted. "Well," he said, "you read it and you'll find out." He took the paper out of his pocket and turned to the page that contained the article. He handed it to Sarah who read it.

As Sarah stood there reading it she could not believe it. How could they not get any of the names right? And only four children?

"Who wrote this drivel?" she asked.

"I have no idea," replied Walter. "Now you can see why I wasnae sure that you'd want tae see it."

"Oh, I'm glad you did, right enough," replied Sarah. Now you can take it and do as you please wi' it!"

Janet smiled as she saw the fighting instinct of Sarah returning. She went into the bedroom to talk with Mary.

Walter said goodbye and Sarah thanked him again, closing the door behind him. She went and got paper and a pen and began to write a letter to her sister Mary.

Janet was in the bedroom with Mary for a while. When she came out she told Sarah that Mary would be fine. Janet told her that Mary was no longer sure she should take the job and John had told her he wanted to stay behind to make sure Sarah was alright.

Janet told Sarah that she must tell her children they have to get on with their lives. She pointed out that Sarah still had four children at home, and that Jane was perfectly old enough to help Sarah.

Sarah realised that what Janet said made sense and she promised to talk her two children out of giving up their lives. She gave the letter she had written to Janet for posting and Janet promised she would. They then said their goodbyes and Janet went back to the village.

Sarah knew what Janet had said made sense, and she decided she would go to her children and have it out with them. She went into the bedroom. John was sitting talking with Mary.

"Yous two," said Sarah. "A word."

John and Mary looked at their mother. "Yes, ma'," they both said, almost together.

Everything is going tae be fine," said Sarah. "I dinnae need tae have yous being mizzie for no' taking your jobs."

"I cannae leave you like this!" said John, earnestly.

"I dinnae want tae go now," said Mary, defiantly.

"Oh, but yous will go," said Sarah, confidently. "I dinnae want tae hear you blame me for no' getting on in the world because I held yous back. Yous will take your jobs."

With that, Sarah turned and walked out of the room and shut the door. She turned round and saw Jane standing in the doorway with the other children.

"What have you done?" she asked her mother.

"I've told John and Mary they have tae take these jobs," replied Sarah. "It'll be you and me taking on the world and your brothers and sister."

"Are you sure you know what you're doing?" Jane asked her mother.

"Do you no' think we're capable?" asked Sarah.

"I do, ma'," answered Jane. "I think you're the strongest person I've ever known."

The weekend passed slowly. Finally, Monday arrived and she headed up to the village to find out how she could get money to live on. She called in at the post office and Mary Scott explained the procedure to her. She would need to go to the Parochial Poor Offices, in Bankhouse, and explain her situation.

So, when she had finished there she left for Bankhouse, and went inside to talk to somebody. She found the offices and went to speak with the clerk.

"How do I claim for parish relief?" Sarah asked.

"What's your situation?" the clerk asked, in reply.

"My husband has just been killed, so I've no money and six mouths tae feed," answered Sarah.

"Do you have the death certificate wi' you?" he asked.

"It's no' come yet," she replied.

"It's no' come? Where did he die then?" he asked.

"He died in England. They've just had the inquest and I'm waiting on the certificate tae arrive," she answered.

"Well, you'll have tae wait until you get it," the clerk began, "but there's nae point you coming on a Monday, for the inspectors dinnae come here tae interview until Tuesdays."

"So, what do I do in the meantime?" asked Sarah.

"That's up tae you. There's nothing I can do – my hands are tied. Good day tae you." The clerk finished speaking and got back to his work. Sarah looked at him and realised there was nothing more she could do. She turned and walked out of the building.

Outside, she met Janet Wilson and explained what had happened. "Dinnae worry, Sarah," Janet said. "If worst comes tae worst we'll help yous out."

"I'll no' take charity," said Sarah, defiantly, "besides, I've still the 40 shillings Walter brought me. That'll keep me going until the certificate arrives."

"Well, if you're sure," answered Janet, "but remember the offer's there."

The two women parted and went their separate ways. For the rest of the week, Sarah tried to go on as if nothing had happened. She spent some time during her day reflecting on the man she would never see again, but she made sure nobody else saw her at her lowest. By the time the weekend came around she was beginning to spend less time reflecting.

On Saturday 9 October 1858 Jane and the younger children brought several letters back from the village when they went shopping. They came indoors and Jane saw her mother sitting in her rocking chair, thinking.

"Ma'," said Jane, "we've got some letters."

Sarah opened her eyes and looked at Jane. "Let me see them," said Sarah. Jane passed her one of the letters. Sarah looked at the handwriting on the envelope then she turned it over and opened it. She read it to herself, not wanting to embarrass herself by crying. The letter was from her father.

Wednesday, 6th October

My dearest daughter,

I was devastated when I got your letter. We all were. It's been a harsh few years. First we lost your mother, then Henry Wilson, shortly followed by your Agnes, and now poor Robert. I wish I could do something to help you. If it wasn't so far I'd come up there to be with you. As it is, I must just think of you. It was a dreadful end to his life, but just stay strong in the knowledge that he loved you.

Your dear father

Sarah shook her head as she read the letter. "Oh, da'," she mused. "I know you can't come!"

At that moment Mary came in from the village. She, too, has begun to come to terms with her father's death. She has been persuaded to believe that his death was not as a result of her actions, and put on a face to make people think that was true. More and more, Mary was looking forward to the birth of that little life growing inside her. She would soon come to know the responsibility of being a parent. As she came in through the door she heard her mother talking.

"Who were you talking to, ma'?" Mary asked.

Sarah smiled. "It's a letter from your granddad," Sarah replied. "I didnae realise you were near enough to hear! It's next Saturday you go off to Birkwood Farm, isn't it?"

"Aye, ma' – Saturday," replied Mary, hoping that Sarah would tell her she didn't need to go. "That's if you still want me tae go. If you need me here I can get in touch wi' them tae explain."

Sarah smiled. "Nay, lass," she began. "You go. I still have Jane, Sarah and David to help me with Nat and around the house. You and John must start your new lives. Before you know it, it'll be your time. You'll have to come back here to have the bairn, then as soon as you're back on your feet maybe you can go back to Birkwood Farm. I'll look after the bairn for you – you can come see him on your days off."

"Do you really think they'll let me do that?" Mary asked.

Sarah sighed. "If you prove yourself tae be a hard worker, they might just let you back," Sarah began. "I'm expecting you tae work the best you can for this farmer. You have tae show them how reliable you can be. Do you understand?"

"Aye, ma'," Mary continued, "and I will really do my best. Do you have any other letters?"

Sarah nodded. "Aye," she said, "there's this one I've just opened and another one here, not touched."

"Would you like me to read it for you?" Mary asked.

Sarah looked at her and smiled. "Aye, go on," she said.

Mary took the letter out of the envelope and she then opened the letter up. She read who it was from. "This one's from Auntie Mary.

Wednesday, 6th October

Dear Sarah,

Oh, what dreadful news! I am so sorry for you. You were so happy. If I could come again to visit I would, but I have to look after my hard earned money, now. It's just me and Thomas now – John decided he wanted to live with his grandparents, as I'm not his mother. Thomas and I are living with Joseph and his wife Elizabeth. We get on well enough. I am sure they will soon be wanting to start a family – I don't know if I shall stay there then.

I will keep you in my thoughts, my dear sister. Be strong. At least you have your children around you for support.

You ever loving sister,

Mary

Mary read the letter to her mother. "Who's the other one from?"

"Well, if I'm any judge of handwriting," replied Sarah, "it's from your Uncle Robert." She held the letter aloft then she told Jane "Go on – you open it!" She passed the letter to her younger daughter. Jane opened it. It was, indeed, a letter from Robert Foulkes.

"How did you know, ma'?" said Jane, astonished. "It is from Uncle Robert. He says,

> *Wednesday, 6th October*
>
> Dear Sarah,
>
> I can't believe that your Robert's dead. What a tragedy! Jane cried when I told her what was in your letter. We are both so sorry for you. You are so far away I don't know how we can help you.
>
> I hope you have enough money to live on. You will have to go to find out if you are entitled to any subsidy from the parish. Please let me know if you have any money problems that you can't cope with. I will see if I can find a way to help.
>
> You ever loving brother,
>
> Robert and Jane

Mary sighed. "Why don't any of them do more than just give their sympathy?" she asked. "You'd have thought at least Mary would have come up here!"

"Well, aye," answered Sarah, "I suppose she could, if she wasn't looking after her boy."

"Well, what about Robert and Jane?" Mary asked. "Wouldn't they like to come for a visit?"

"Well," Sarah began, "Robert and Jane have got a big family. Mary is raising her son on her own, without Henry. They have their own lives to lead." Sarah paused for a moment. "But, you're right, Mary – I'm useful enough when they want something." Sarah sighed. "Hmmph, but when I need them, it's a different matter! And where is that death certificate! If it's no' bad enough that they bury my Robert down there in England, I cannae do anything about getting parish relief without that damn piece of paper!"

Sarah sat back down again and started to cry. The trail of tears streamed down her face, but she did not sob this time.

CHAPTER 10

Loose ends

The next week passed by uneventfully. Would that death certificate never arrive? Sarah was angry but she wasn't sure who she was angry with most. She was angry with Robert for being so stupid as to die. But then again if it wasn't for Mary, maybe he would never have ended up in that predicament. But still, Mary was only a girl and didn't realise what might happen. Truth was, even Sarah could never have foreseen the events that followed.

Sarah was angry with the way that Robert's death had been dealt with. She had never even been able to say goodbye to her beloved husband. And she was still waiting for his death certificate to arrive.

By Saturday 16 October, though, despite having no death certificate, Sarah put on a brave face. This was the day Mary was to start her new job and Sarah was making her best efforts to keep cheerful so that Mary would go to work. Sarah doubted they would keep her on when her daughter's pregnancy reached its final stages, but that was a way off, yet.

Mary had packed a few things to take with her. She didn't have much, just a few clothes, but they wouldn't fit her for long. She took some sewing implements with her so she could adjust her clothes to fit as she grew. She stood there, in the main room of the cottage, with her mother, brothers and sisters around her.

"What are they going tae think o' me, ma'?" she asked.

"You'll do fine," said Sarah.

"I mean when I start tae show?" added Mary.

"Well," began Sarah, "they'll either keep you on or send you packing." Sarah looked at Mary. She could see her daughter was close to tears.

"Oh, for God's sake girl," said Sarah, "pull yourself together. What will be will be."

"I dinnae want tae go now," said Mary, starting to cry.

"It's no' like you'll be a million miles away, Mary," added Sarah. "You'll be able tae come visit from time tae time."

"Aye," said Mary, drying her eyes. "You're right. Well, I'll be off, then."

One by one her siblings said goodbye to her, then finally she went up to her mother and Sarah gave her a big hug. With that, she turned and walked out of the door, turned right and walked down the road. Her family watched her until she was out of sight. They all trooped indoors and Sarah looked at John.

"It'll be you, next week," she said.

John nodded. "Aye, ma'," he said.

Sarah began to adjust to life without Mary. In some ways, her not being there made life calmer. Much as she loved Mary, Sarah had to admit she had always worried about what she would do next.

Jane was proving to be a great help now that she was the eldest at home. She had already proved herself by taking the younger children to school for her mother. Every day on the way back from taking the children to school she called in at the post office to find out what letters had come, in the vain hope that her father's death certificate would finally materialise.

John had a much greater distance to travel. He had to catch a train at Lesmahagow station and travel as far as High Motherwell. From there he needed to change to a train on the Wishaw branch, which would take him to Wishaw, where he would then have to make his own way to Cambusnethan. Sarah was worried about him, but John made her realise that it was an easy journey and all would be well.

Finally, Saturday, 23 October came, and John was packed and all ready to go. Once again his family all gathered round him to say their farewells. He was eager to start his job, but he was worried for Sarah, coping for the first time without a grown man around the house.

"Will you stop fussing, John," said Sarah. "I will do fine. Have I not got four children here wi' me?"

"Aye, but I've been pretty much head o' the household since da' died," John added.

"Maybe so," replied Sarah, "but it's your time, now. Time for you tae put your mark on the world, and I'll no' be responsible for making you stay here."

"I'll walk a ways wi' you," said Jane. "I need tae go tae the post office tae get our mail, anyway."

"I'd like that," replied John. So he said goodbye to his other sister and brothers, then went up to Sarah and gave her a hug. "I'll be thinking o' yous," he said. "Be sure tae write me."

"Aye, son," replied Sarah, "I will."

He picked up his bag and went outside. "I'll be back soon," said Jane to her mother. Sarah nodded and Jane, too, went outside to walk alongside her brother.

Sarah set to doing the chores while she waited for Jane to return. Sarah and David were playing with Nathaniel, who was now 3 and a bit years old. Sarah fetched out the washing and made a start on that.

About three-quarters of an hour later Jane returned from the village. It was clear she had been running. "Ma'! Ma'!" she called. "It's come!"

Sarah stopped to look at it. She looked at it on both sides for a moment and then opened it. As she took it out of the envelope she didn't know whether to laugh or cry. She sat down to look at it.

"Three weeks! Three bloody weeks!" Sarah exclaimed.

"Why, ma'! Whatever is it?" asked Jane.

"It has taken –" Sarah peered at the writing on the paper, "– Mr. John Rawlinson three whole bloody weeks tae send me my husband's death certificate!"

"But, that's good, isn't it?" asked Jane.

"Well, it's good that he's sent it," replied Sarah, "but why did it have tae take so long?"

"So what must you do wi' it now?" asked Jane.

"I have tae go to the Parochial Board tae get relief," said Sarah. "I'll go Tuesday, as they're not open on Monday."

"So will they pay you?" asked Jane.

"I hope so!" said Sarah. "If not, then I havenae any idea as tae how we're going tae live."

Sarah almost wished the next few days away. Finally, Tuesday arrived and Sarah headed for Bankhouse, where the Parochial Poor Office was housed. Upon arrival she went inside to see the clerk.

"Good morning," said Sarah, politely to the clerk. "I came tae see you the other week tae claim but you told me I needed my husband's death certificate. Well, I have it now."

Sarah showed the clerk the death certificate she had received in the post. The clerk took it from Sarah and read it carefully.

"The Inspector's busy wi' somebody just now," he said. "If you'll sit down and wait he'll see you presently."

Sarah sat down. She was quiet for a moment then she looked at the clerk. "Can you tell me what happens, now?"

The clerk stopped writing in his ledger and looked at Sarah. "You'll have an interview wi' the Inspector," he said, "and then they'll come out for a home visit."

As he spoke the door to the office opened and the Reverend Allan MacNaughton came out. The clerk stood up and took the death certificate into the room. After a few minutes he came back outside. "You can go in now," he said. "The Inspector's free."

Sarah stood up and walked towards the open door. "Thank you," she said, as she walked into the room.

The room she found herself in was large with a large table behind which sat one man. He was in late middle-age, just turned 50. The sign in front of him stated that his name was the Reverend Thomas Burns. To the right of this table was another, smaller table, where a clerk sat taking notes about the meeting. Opposite the Reverend was a single chair. The Reverend motioned to Sarah that she should sit down. "Good morning, Mrs. McWilliam," he said, not looking up. "Please take a seat."

Sarah sat down as she was instructed. The Inspector looked up at last and looked at Sarah directly. He put the death certificate down on the desk. "Please explain the nature of your circumstances that has brought you here today," he said.

"Well, sir," Sarah began, "if you please, I live down at Auchtykirnal." The clerk began to write.

"How long have you lived there?" he interrupted.

"We came to live here in the summer of 1851, sir," she replied.

"Who is "we"?" the Reverend asked.

"Well," said Sarah, "when we came there was my husband, Robert, myself and my four children. The last two were born here."

"That makes six children altogether," said the Reverend. So, what is it you're asking for?"

"As you have the death certificate," Sarah began, "you can see that my husband died last month, leaving me with four mouths tae feed and no money coming in."

The Reverend looked puzzled. "Four children?" he asked. "Did you not just say you had six children?"

"Aye, sir," answered Sarah, "but the eldest two have moved away and are in service."

"I see," answered the Reverend. "Well, here is the death certificate back, and that will do for today. I will visit you tomorrow tae see your situation in more detail. You can go now." He gave the certificate to Sarah.

"Thank you sir," said Sarah, standing up and curtseying. She left the room and walked back out past the clerk, and into the street. Once out in the fresh air she stood still and took a deep breath. Then she turned and walked home. As she walked along she thought about the process that she would have to go through and began to cry, silently, just tears running down her face. The journey home seemed to last for ever, but finally, her cottage came into view. She was home. Once inside she began to sob.

Jane was in the bedroom but came out when she heard her mother cry. "Ma'," she said, "whatever is it?"

"Oh, Jane," said Sarah, trying to calm herself, "I hate this. I hate having tae ask for charity."

"Dinnae worry, ma'," said Jane, in an attempt to comfort her mother, "we'll get by."

Sarah did compose herself, ready for when the children returned from school, and for that evening, at least, things returned to normal.

Next morning, as expected, the Inspector arrived to visit. Once again it was the Reverend Thomas Burns. Sarah let him in, he took his coat and hat off and they sat down. Jane had just arrived back from taking the younger children to school. She made her excuses and left the room so that the Inspector and Sarah could talk.

"First," began the Reverend, "can we talk about how your husband came tae be in England when he died."

"Aye," replied Sarah. "He was working, sir. He couldn't get the same money locally."

"I see he died in a brawl at the local hostelry. Was he disposed tae fighting?"

"No, your honour," answered Sarah, "he'd just gone back after a weekend at home. One of his workmates was making fun of our eldest daughter."

"I see," said the Reverend. He made some more notes. "You said you moved here in 1851. Where were you before that?"

"We came up from Birkenhead," replied Sarah.

The Reverend looked quizzically at her. "So why did you come to Scotland?" he asked.

"My husband wanted to move back, closer to his roots," answered Sarah.

"So was he born in Lesmahagow? asked the Reverend. "I cannae find any record of him previously."

"No, sir," replied Sarah, "he came from Kirkmaiden, Wigtownshire, originally. We came here for the work."

"Ah," said the Reverend, "that explains it." He continued to write his notes. He then continued questioning Sarah. "Who is living at home wi' you now?"

"There's my daughter Jane – she's 13," said Sarah, "my daughter Sarah – she's 9, my son David – he's 7, and my youngest son Nathaniel – he's just 3."

"That's only four children," he said. "Where did you say the other two were?"

Sarah almost began to regret having done this, but she replied, "They're working away from home. My daughter Mary is living at Birkdale Farm as a servant, and my son John is working as a ploughboy in Cambusnethan for the owner of the Commercial Inn – who also has a small holding there."

He wrote this information down and then thought for a moment. "Are there any other children not living wi' you?"

Sarah wondered if she should say, but her honesty got the better of her. "Well, there's my son William – well, I say my son but he's really my husband's son by his first wife – I'm the only mother he's ever really known. He stayed behind in England when we left – he joined the army, and he's in India at the moment."

"Does he come home often?" the Reverend asked.

"Hah!" said Sarah, sarcastically, "He's never ever been here since we moved. He signed up afore we left and that was the last we saw of him. We had a letter from him, once or twice."

When he had noted that piece of information he looked at Sarah again. She was barely holding herself together.

"Some questions about you, Mrs. McWilliam, and we're nearly done," said the Reverend. "When were you born, and are you in good health?"

Sarah straightened up. She could feel she had begun to droop and she felt that was a sign of weakness. "I was born in 1813, and I am well enough. I have no ailments," she replied.

"Are you working?" he asked.

"No sir, I am not. I have four children living at home wi' me. I think that is work enough."

"Do you have any money for food at the moment?" he asked, almost knowing the answer before Sarah gave it.

"My husband's last wages came at the beginning of October," said Sarah. "I have been as careful as I could be, but it has all run out, which is why I came tae see you."

"Well," he said, "I can give you two shillings today. We have tae discuss your case on Sunday and you must come tae the Paro-

369

chial office at 10 o'clock, week Tuesday, tae see the board, who will give you their decision. I shall go now."

With that the Reverend stood up and put his coat back on. He took a purse out of his coat pocket and opened it. He took two shillings out of it and gave the money to Sarah. He put the purse away and picked his hat up.

"Thank you sir," said Sarah, relieved the interview was now over. She walked over to the door with him and opened it.

The Reverend said goodbye to Sarah, put his hat on and walked out of the door. She watched him walk up the road and then closed the door. She began to cry. Just tears, at first, but then she couldn't help herself and she began to sob.

Jane came out of the bedroom and held her mother.

"We'll be fine, ma'," she said. "I'll get a job. You can have my money tae live on."

"Oh, Jane, Jane, what am I tae do if they willnae gie me any money?" sobbed Sarah.

"Will you listen tae me?" demanded Jane. "I told you I'd get a job. Even if it's only taking in other people's laundry. We will not starve!"

Sarah stopped for a moment and looked at Jane, and suddenly smiled. Jane was confused. She looked at her mother quizzically.

"You just reminded me of something I said a few years back," said Sarah, more composed, now. "It was when your father was on strike. I took in washing tae do, then!" Sarah chuckled as she remembered how Agnes had offered to give them all her wages. "You're right, o' course, we willnae starve, but two shillings will have tae be spread thin tae last for nearly two weeks."

Once back at Bankhouse, Reverend Thomas Burns wrote up his entry in the Poor Roll Book. He knew pretty much what the result would be, but he had to wait on protocol. Besides, the Committee only met twice a month, so his notes would have to be precise.

Register of the Poor admitted on Roll C01/47/20:
Entry 142:
1858 Oct 26
Widow Sarah Foulkes or McWilliams

Residence:	Auchty Kirnal	
Country of birth:	England	
Date of visit to home:	Oct 27	
Condition:	Widow	
Age:	45	
Occupation:	None	
Wholly/partially disabled:	Able bodied	
Name/age of dependents:	Jane	13
	Sarah	9
	David	7
	Nathaniel	3

Other information:

Husband was a native of Kirkmaiden – had no residen-
tial settlement at time of his death, which took place
lately in England. Their son William is a soldier, presently in India; Mary, a servant; John, a farm servant

No of previous applications:	None
Result of application:	
Date:	Oct 26
How disposed by Inspector:	Relieved
How disposed by Board:	Entered in Record of
Disputed Settlements	

Sarah and Jane struggled to make ends meet for the next two weeks, but finally the appointed day arrived. Sarah returned to the Bankhouse on Tuesday 9 November for a 10 o'clock appointment. The clerk showed her into a different room and shut the door behind her.

She turned to look around the room. She had thought the other office was big but this one was much more grandiose. There was a long table at which were sat three men. On the left-hand side of this table was another desk for the clerk to make notes.

The clerk spoke, motioning to Sarah as he did so. "Come and sit down here in the chair, Mrs. McWilliam." Sarah did as she was bid. As she sat there she had time to read the name plates of the men in front of her. There was the local magistrate, John Stein, who was 57 years old, the local surgeon, Alexander Lindsay, a much younger man, 41 years old, and the Minister, 1st Charge, of the United Presbyterian Church in the village, Revd. Allan MacNaughton, the eldest of the three at 64 years old.

Sarah sat there, quietly, waiting to be spoken to. Finally, John Stein spoke. "Thank you for coming back tae see us. We had a good look at your case on Sunday and we've come tae a decision."

Sarah looked at them and smiled. Alexander Lindsay spoke next. "I'm afraid there's a problem wi' your claim. You see you've lived here only seven years. And your husband's no' from here, either."

"So, how long must I live here afore you'll gie me any relief?" Sarah asked.

Alexander Lindsay continued. "As a general rule, you have tae be born here tae get anything, but in your case, your husband came from Scotland, so you may be able tae get some relief from where he was born, which in your case, is Kirkmaiden."

Sarah's cool demeanour changed in an instant. "But I cannae get to Kirkmaiden! It took us about a day and a half the last time we went – and that was when Robert was alive. I have –"

The Reverend McNaughton interrupted her. "Calm down, Mrs. McWilliam. We're no' proposing that you go there. We shall help you draft a letter tae their parochial board. If you're successful what will happen is they will send money tae us and we shall pay it tae you."

"What if they refuse?" asked Sarah, panicking. "What then? You'll no' pay me, and they'll no' pay me – so what am I tae do?"

"You'll have tae be patient," answered John Stein, "as what relief we can gie you won't start until we hear back from Kirkmaiden. But what you'll get will be very basic, even if we can gie you relief."

The three men huddled together, whispering to each other. Then they went back to their proper places and looked at Sarah. Alexander Lindsay spoke. "If you wait outside we shall draft a letter for you tae sign. It'll then go in the post and you will hear from us when we get a reply."

"Thank you," said Sarah. She stood up and went out of the room, sitting down on one of the chairs in the corridor.

Minute book of the Parochial Board, Lesmahagow
C01/47/1
7 November 1858
The following cases were considered:
Widow McWilliams, The Meeting approve of this party
being refused by the Inspector

About fifteen minutes later, Sarah was called back into the room and a letter was laid in front of her. She read it thoroughly, nodding. She understood the text and was glad it was them who had written it. They used terms she would never have even thought of to use. She signed the letter and they gave her an addressed envelope – with a stamp on, for they knew she had no money – and told her to go directly to the Post Office and send it. She left the building and took the letter across the road to post it. Then she went home.

"How did it go, ma'?" asked Jane, when she got indoors.

373

"Oh, Jane," said Sarah, almost in tears, "what are we going tae do?"

Angrily, Jane replied, "What? They'll no' gie us anything?"

"We've no' lived here long enough," answered Sarah.

Jane put her hands on her hips and took an angry stance. "And how long do you have tae be here tae get it?"

"All your life, apparently," said a subdued Sarah. "But, there is a glimmer of hope," she added, "they've sent a letter tae Kirkmaiden parish tae see if they'll pay us."

"Why? Will they pay us, then?" Jane asked.

"That's where your da' was born," said Sarah, "so they may put us on their Poor Roll and send the money tae this parish. Then Lesmahagow will pay us the money."

"And what do we do in the meantime for food?" asked Jane.

Sarah looked at her daughter. "I have absolutely no idea."

Sarah sat still for a while, thinking about everything, then she stood up and started doing the chores.

Jane went up the village, a while later, to fetch the younger ones home and made a point of going to see Janet Wilson.

Next day, Wednesday 10 November, Janet Wilson came to visit. Jane was busy tidying up in the bedroom when Janet knocked at the door. Jane had been outside a few minutes earlier and saw Janet walking up, so she decided to stay out of Janet's way until she had spoken with her mother. Janet, in turn, made no mention that Jane had called in to see her the day before. Sarah told her how she had got on the day before and that the board would not pay her.

"So they'll no' gie you any money?" Janet asked, feigning surprise.

"They've written tae Kirkmaiden tae see if they'll gie me anything." Sarah paused. "Janet, what am I tae do?"

"I'll no' see you go hungry," said Janet. "Do you need anything at present?"

"Well, we've vegetables from our plot out back," said Sarah, "but there's only enough tae last to the end of the month. We've nothing else."

"Have yous no meat?" asked Janet.

"We cannae afford that," answered Sarah. "We'll get by on our vegetables."

"I'll hear o' no such thing!" said Janet, angrily. "What's your Jane doing?"

Sarah looked at Janet, bleakly. "But she's only thirteen. Nobody'll take her on yet – especially wi' Mary's track record."

"If you dinnae ask you'll never find out," said Janet, positively. "I shall go up the village and ask around. I will call in at the butcher's while I'm up there and see if he has any cheap cuts for yous."

"But –" Sarah tried to argue, but Janet would have none of it. "I'll get you some groceries, until yous get back on your feet, so you dinnae starve."

"I couldnae ask –" started Sarah.

"You're no' asking," said Janet, decisively. "I'm telling you! And, what about your John and Mary? Can they help you? Do they know what's been said?"

Sarah shook her head. "They'll come and see me the first Sunday in December – it's their first day off," she replied. "I shall tell them then."

"Make sure you do," said Janet, almost telling Sarah off. "I know you, Sarah – too well!"

Janet stayed with Sarah until after lunch. She had brought a meal with her, so they ate well for the first time in two weeks. Later, when Jane went to get the children from school, Janet walked back to the village with her. She told Jane to call in and see her on her way back from the school and Jane promised she would.

Janet had asked around to see if there was any work that Jane could do. Mary Scott in the Post Office would have nothing to do with her, but her brother, James Scott, the Grocer said he would give her a try. She could help out doing errands for him at first, and he would see how it went. She also went up to Kirkfieldbank, to see the butcher, William Halliday. He was middle-aged, but came from Galloway, so she thought he might have a soft spot when he heard the story.

Jane called in, as agreed, with the children. Janet was excited and straightway told her that the butcher would give them a bit of meat for Sundays. It wasn't likely to be a big cut of meat, but it would make Sunday a bit special for them. Janet also told Jane that James Scott would take her on in his shop. Janet told Jane to go to the Grocer's directly. Jane thanked her profusely and went immediately to the Grocer's. James was serving a customer when she got there, so she waited, quietly, outside, until he was finished. Jane put Sarah in charge of her brother whilst she went into the shop to find out more.

"Mr. Scott," said Jane, when she got inside the shop, "Janet Wilson told me you might have some work I could do."

James Scott looked at Jane. "Oh, you must be the McWIlliam girl. Aye, I have work you can do. It'll no' pay well, but it'll be something for your ma' tae help."

"That'd be such a help, Sir," replied Jane. "When would you like me tae start?"

"You can come in for a few hours tomorrow and I'll see what you can do," he answered. "I believe you take your family tae school, so on your way back from there come in and we'll get started."

"That sounds fine," answered Jane. "I'll see you tomorrow, then."

They said goodbye and Jane left the shop and took the younger ones home. She was so excited and so was Sarah when she told her the news.

It was just as well she did get the job. It only paid two shillings a week, but as Sarah heard nothing back from the Parochial Poor Office for three weeks, it was a godsend.

Sarah got up on Friday 3 December all fired up and raring to go. She had waited long enough. Surely Lesmahagow had heard back from Kirkmaiden by now?

It had been a while since Jane had seen her mother like this. "Ma', whatever's gotten into you today?" she asked.

"It's about time I went down tae the parish offices and got some answers," replied Sarah. "After yous have all gone I shall make my way up tae the village and go and wait there until I hear something."

"Good for you, ma'!" said Jane.

The younger children were all up and breakfasted. Thank goodness porridge was cheap. Jane took the children to school and then went to work. Over the last few days she had gotten used to working in the shop, and James Scott was pleased with the work she was doing.

Sarah got herself ready to go out and walked up to the village with Nathaniel. She went inside Bankhouse with the intention of telling the clerk she would stay until she was told what was happening. As it turned out she didn't have to wait long. Once inside the building she saw the Reverend McNaughton, so she walked up to him, bold as brass.

"Good morning, minister," she said, politely.

"Why, good morning tae you, Mrs. McWilliam," he relied. "How're you keeping?"

"I'd be keeping better if I knew I had money coming in," said Sarah, sharply.

The Reverend tried to appease Sarah. "I realise this must be frustrating for you, but there's —"

"Frustrating!" said Sarah in a loud voice. "You're bloody right I'm frustrated!"

The Reverend looked shocked. "Mrs. McWilliam — there's no need tae swear — and in God's presence!"

Sarah squared up to him. "I dinnae think the Lord will mind this once! When will you be getting a reply from Kirkmaiden?"

"It shouldnae be long now," he replied, cautiously. "As soon as we hear you'll be the first tae know. But if we dinnae hear anything by Wednesday we'll write them again."

"Hmph!" said Sarah. "I hope you hear before then, or you'll have some starved bodies tae bury!" She then turned and walked out of the offices in disgust.

Minute book of the Parochial Board:
C01/47/1 3 December 1858
The following cases were considered:
Widow McWilliams Prosecute
the claim against Kirkmaiden

(Interior, Sarah McWilliam's cottage at Auchtykirnal, late morning, Sunday 5 December 1858)

That Sunday John and Mary came to visit. The butcher had heard that Sarah's children were coming for dinner, so he sent her a small chicken. She made up the rest of the meal with the remaining few vegetables in her garden plot. John arrived early and Mary followed soon after. Mary could no longer hide the fact that she was with child – something she now regretted. Sarah dished up the meal and the family sat at the table.

"I cannae believe they've no' given you anything yet!" said John, angrily.

"It all takes time," replied Sarah. "They're having tae go through Kirkmaiden afore I can get anything."

"Well I think it's all wrong!" said Mary. "You've been here over seven years. It's not like you've just moved here!"

Sarah shook her head. "They dinnae look at it like that here," she replied. "Hopefully the money will start to come through soon."

"Well, dinnae you worry, ma'!" said John. "I've some money you can have."

Sarah looked hurt. "I wouldn't dream of taking your money, son," she replied.

John looked at Sarah. She could see he was determined she should accept his offer. He turned to Sarah and said, "Don't you dare refuse it. You've looked after me – us – ever since we were born. It's about time we started tae look after you, now!"

"Aye," joined in Mary, "and I'll give you some o' mine, too. You'll be fine, ma'."

Sarah sat there, tears welling up in her eyes. "I don't know what to say," she began.

"Then don't!" said John, defiantly.

"And I shall carry on at the Grocers until I can find a better job," added Jane.

Sarah gave in. She sat there, looking at her family and began to smile. Maybe everything would turn out for the better, after all.

But things were beginning to look up. Tuesday morning, 7 December 1858 Sarah was busy doing her housework and Nathaniel was playing when there was a knock at the door. Sarah answered it to find the Reverend Thomas Burns standing there. She invited him in and he sat down.

"So, what's this visit in aid of?" asked Sarah.

"We've heard back from Kirkmaiden," he said. "It's taken a while, but they've finally made a decision in your favour. They'll pay you four shillings a week until your circumstances change."

"Is that all?" Sarah asked. "Four shillings?"

"Aye," the Reverend replied. "That's a good amount, considering you've never lived there – and you're English."

"And when do I get paid?" Sarah asked.

"So you'll take it, then?" the Reverend asked.

"I've no' got a lot of choice, have I?"

The Reverend smiled. "The board will write tae them saying you'll accept it," he said, "and they'll start sending your money. As soon as we get it at the Board it will come tae you."

"So when will I get the money?" Sarah asked.

"It'll take about a week. Good day to you." The Reverend stood up and Sarah let him out. A short while later, Sarah and David arrived home from school – just the two of them now. Sarah was 9 years old now and her mother had decided she was old enough to go to school alone with her brother. Sarah could not believe her eyes – for the first time for a long time, her mother was happy.

"What is it ma'?" Sarah asked her mother. "Have you had some good news?"

"Aye, Sarah," her mother replied. "Some good and some bad, but it's mostly good. Kirkmaiden parish will be paying us Poor Relief, but we'll no' get it for about a week."

True to his word, The Reverend Thomas Burns arrived at Sarah's cottage the next Tuesday, 14 December. Sarah let him in.

He was smiling as she opened the door. "Morning, Mrs. McWilliam," he said, cheerily, as he came in. He walked over to a chair at the table and sat down.

"We've had the first money through from Kirkmaiden," he continued. "This is what they've sent tae cover from the first day you claimed up tae now – twenty shillings. It's more than you'll be getting weekly, mind." He put the money down on the table in front of Sarah.

"Praise the Lord!" she said. "I can buy some food, now. So, how often will I get this money?"

"Well," he said, "it should be sent every week, but as it has tae come from Kirkmaiden it may not be regular."

"And will you be bringing it to me, like this?" she asked.

The Reverend laughed. "Lord, no!" he said. "You'll have tae come to the offices for it. Every Tuesday."

Sarah nodded. Then a thought struck her. "And if it's not there when I come?"

"Then you'll have tae come back the next week," he replied. "I'll be going now."

He stood up and walked over to the door. Sarah opened the door and Reverend Thomas Burns walked off up the road to the village.

Sarah went back to the table and picked up the two ten shilling notes the Reverend had left her. It had been a long time since she had held twenty shillings in her hand, but she knew she must be careful with it. She made a list of the things she knew she needed and went up to the village to stock up. She kept four shillings back in case no money was forthcoming the next week, but the family ate well for the first time for a long time.

Hogmanay was not a joyful time this year. It was Sarah's first celebration without Robert and it made her miss him even more.

She stayed home and had a quiet time with her children. The money came in regularly enough, and Sarah spent the money wisely. The family didn't go without. Jane brought in her two shillings and gave it all to her mother.

The first week in January Sarah's money arrived late. It was only to be expected, really, what with the celebrations, but Sarah had kept that four shillings back for such an occasion as this. Another four weeks passed and Sarah was in the village after collecting her money on 1 February 1859, her usual Tuesday, when she saw Janet Wilson in the street. Janet came over to see Sarah for a chat.

"Janet! How are you?" asked Sarah.

"We're fine, Sarah," replied Janet. "And yourself?"

"Not so bad," replied Sarah. "I've just been for my money so I can get what I need."

"So it's coming through alright, then? asked Janet.

"Aye, pretty much," replied Sarah, nodding. "It's been there, mostly, when I've gone for it. What's your Walter doing these days?"

"He's found work in Glasgow," answered Janet. "He's said he'll no' go over the border again, so we're doing fine. How's your Mary keeping?"

"She's blooming," replied Sarah. "There's only about four months to go, now."

"What will she do wi' the bairn?" asked Janet.

"I shall look after it," said Sarah. "She can see it at weekends when she goes back tae work, for she'll have tae go tae work tae support the bairn."

"Do you think they'll take her back after she's had the bairn?" asked Janet.

Sarah shook her head. "We'll have tae wait and see," she answered.

"Well, I'll have tae be going now," said Janet, after a moment. "I'm glad tae see you're doing grand. Bye!"

"Bye, Janet!" said Sarah, and the two women went their separate ways.

Over the next few months things went on the same. Jane working for the Grocer, Little Sarah going with David on their own to school. On the Sundays when Mary came home Sarah could see the changes in her daughter. She wondered when the bairn would be born.

Finally, a week before the end of June Mary arrived home. It was late afternoon and everybody was there. Sarah was finishing off putting the washing away and Jane was helping her. Mary opened the door and walked inside. "They've sent me home, ma'," she said. "Said I cannae do the work now."

Sarah looked at her. "Well, I'm guessing it was getting too hard for you," she said. "It looks like that bairn will be here before the week's out, anyway."

Mary looked pleased. "Do you think so?" she asked, sighing with relief. "I'll be so glad when it's born. I'm so hot all the while."

"Get and sit down – take the weight off your feet," said Sarah. "Jane, go get your sister a drink o' water."

Jane did as her mother had asked and took it to her sister, now sitting down. Sarah, too, sat down, next to Mary. "You'll do just fine," said Sarah.

Five days later, Wednesday 29 June 1859, Mary was relaxing after dinner when she felt her first twinge. She pretended to ignore it but she knew it was time.

"Ma'," she said to Sarah, "I think it's starting."

"Well," replied Sarah, "you've a while tae go yet. Get yoursel' ready for a long night. In my experience, first babies take a long time tae come into the world."

As the evening wore on, slowly, the contractions became more regular. Mary didn't get a lot of sleep but she rested. Next morning Sarah got the other children up but left Mary to get what rest she could. It was a good job that Sarah had been a midwife because she couldn't afford to get one in. Sarah concentrated on Mary and the housework while Jane went to work. Sarah and David looked after Nathaniel for their mother.

The day wore on. By about 1 o'clock the contractions were coming fast and Sarah checked to see if Mary was ready. She wasn't quite there but by now, Mary just wanted it all to be over and done. "Be patient," was all Sarah would say.

Finally, at about 5 o'clock that afternoon, the baby was well on the way. Jane had come home early from work. James Scott knew her sister was in labour, and Jane didn't really have her mind on her work, so at 4 o'clock he sent her home for the day.

"I can see the baby's head, Mary," said Sarah. "Give it one more good push."

Mary did her best. She was sweating heavily – one of the hottest days of the year was not the best day to give birth. Sarah was glad Jane was home. She could help her mother, although being in the same room as somebody giving birth was not on her mind when she was on the way home.

Mary gave one big push and the baby's head crowned.

"It's coming," said Sarah. "Now don't push for a while."

Mary tried her best to oblige, but her urge to push was extreme.

"That's it," said Sarah, "now another couple of pushes and the baby will be out. Can you get ready with those scissors and string, Jane?"

"Aye ma'," replied Jane, "I have them, but I'm no' watching!"

"Well, as long as they're ready when I need them, lass," said Sarah, thinking back to her first time, helping her mother.

Mary gave a few more pushes, aided by loud screams, and finally the baby was born. As the head emerged the baby yelled.

"Well," said Sarah, "that's a good pair of lungs."

Once the baby was born Sarah got ready to cut the umbilicus.

"String, Jane," said Sarah. Jane passed her mother first one piece of string and then the other. Sarah carefully tied them round the cord in two places.

"Now the scissors," added Sarah. Jane passed her mother the scissors and Sarah cut the cord.

"Pass me that cloth over there," said Sarah. Jane was relieved to be able to turn her back for a moment. She got the cloth and passed it to her mother. Sarah took it and wiped down the excess liquid from the baby's face. She then passed the baby to Mary.

"Here you are, Mary," said Sarah. Sarah then turned to her other daughter. "Well done, Jane," she said, "you were a great help."

Mary lay there looking at her baby. "It's a boy! Oh, he's beautiful!" she said. "Thank you, ma'."

"What are you going tae call him?" Jane asked her sister.

"We must make a note o' the time. What is it, Jane?"

Jane went to look at the clock in the living room. She came back and wrote it down. "It's 5 o'clock, ma'," she said.

"Walter. Walter Brown," said Mary, nodding her head and smiling at the tiny baby in her arms. "That's what I'll call him."

"It'll have to be McWilliam, Mary," replied Sarah. "They'll not let you call him Walter Brown."

"Why not?" Mary asked. "Because you've no husband."

Mary sighed, angrily. "Fine, if I must. But I want him tae be known as Walter Brown. After his father!"

A short while later the final stage was over and Mary could now relax with her son. Sarah went into the other room to wash her hands and sit down. It had been a long few hours and she suddenly realised she was tired.

Mary's brothers and sisters all wanted to be near her. Jane had gotten over her squeamishness and wanted to hold baby Walter. Sarah sat in her chair and drank a cup of tea. As she sat there she looked up to the heavens. "Well, Robert," she said, "she's had it. He's a bonny wee thing, tae be sure!"

The next few weeks were hard for Mary. She wanted to be the best mother she could, but she had no idea. "How ever did you manage wi' me, ma?" she asked.

"I found out the hard way," Sarah replied.

On 19 July Mary took her baby to be registered. She knew what her mother had said, but she was determined to try to name her baby as she saw fit. She walked into the office and saw Duncan Campbell.

"Well, hello there," he said. "It's Mary, isn't it?"

"Aye, sir," she replied. "Mary McWilliam.

"Aye," he said, "I remember you from being at school." He looked at baby Walter. "So, you've come tae get him registered, then, I take it?"

"Aye, sir, I have."

He opened his birth register and began to write. "Now, what's the baby's name?" he asked.

"Walter Brown," Mary replied.

"Are you married then?" Duncan asked, "only I dinnae remember doing a wedding entry." Mary shook her head.

"So, it'll be Walter Brown McWilliam, then?" Duncan asked, to confirm.

"No, sir," answered Mary, "just Walter Brown."

"I'm afraid I cannae do that," said Duncan. "It will have to be either Walter McWilliam or Walter – middle name – Brown – McWilliam." He looked at Mary, waiting for her answer. Mary opted for Walter McWilliam. He wrote out the birth certificate as Sarah had predicted, and Mary went home with the job now done, but not happy with the result.

As the days passed, Mary became more adept at doing all the things she needed with the baby. She had no intention of working if she could avoid it. She loved being with Walter and wanted to spend as much time as she could with him.

Finally, Sarah and Jane's patience was wearing thin. "we cannae go on like this, Mary," said Sarah to her daughter one day. "We've two extra mouths to feed, and no extra money."

"So what do you want me to do then?" asked Mary. "Go for parish relief?"

"Well," said Sarah, "you could try asking Mary Day if you can help them."

So, later that day, Mary went round to the day's house and they told her she could use one of their winding machines to put silk on bobbins. They could only pay her a shilling a week, but at least it was money coming in. George Day brought the machine round and set it up in the bedroom.

And so, Mary became a pirn-winder. She hated it. True, it brought in some small amount of money, but it was not to Mary's liking. Eventually, Mary had had enough. She went to see if she could get poor relief. She had concluded that they had been resident much longer now, and she had a baby to support.

Late morning, Tuesday 22 November 1859, the Reverend Thomas Burns came to call again. Sarah knew how this was all going to end up but she stood by her daughter, anyway. Sarah let the Reverend in and took his coat and hat.

"Good morning, Mrs. McWilliam," said the Reverend. "So it's your daughter's claiming today, is it?"

"Aye, sir. She's recently had a baby," answered Sarah.

"I can see that," he replied. "Well, Mary, are you working?"

"Aye, sir," answered Mary, politely. "I help out on the small holding here, wi' the pirn winding."

"And how much do they pay you?" he asked, writing down her answers as he went along.

"I get a shilling a week, sir," answered Mary. "It's no' very much."

"Maybe so," said the Reverend, "but it's more than some get. Are you wholly or partially disabled?"

Indignantly, Mary replied, "I'm no' disabled. I've a five month old child tae look after."

"Aye," replied the Reverend, "as I suspected. He spent a few more minutes writing in his journal. "Well, for my part I shall have tae refuse your claim. But the final decision rests wi' the board. They'll meet on Sunday and you'll have their decision after that."

"So that's it?" asked Mary.

"I'm afraid so, Mary," replied the Reverend. "You just dinnae qualify. I'll be on my way, now."

He stood up and Sarah passed him his coat and hat. Sarah walked with him to the door and let him out. She shut the door and turned back to Mary. Mary looked at her mother.

"Do you think I'd have got something if I'd no' been working, ma'?" she asked.

Sarah shook her head. "I doubt it very much," she said. "They're all tight arsed buggers!"

Mary looked at her mother in shock. "Ma'! I've never heard you talk like that afore!" she said.

Sarah too, shook her head. "I've never had to live like this afore, girl!" she replied.

As the Reverend had expected, the board refused Mary's claim.

Register of the Poor admitted on Roll:
C01/47/20: Entry 189:

1859 Nov 22:	Mary McWilliam
Residence:	Auchty Kirnal
Country of birth:	England
Date of visit to home:	Nov 22
Condition:	Single
Age:	20
Occupation:	Farm servant & Pirn Winder
Average value of weekly earnings:	1 shilling
Wholly/partially disabled:	Burdened with infant child
Name/age of dependents:	Walter, 5 months
Other information:	

Father deceased; Mother a Pauper on the Roll of the Parish of Kirkmaiden – the Parish of her father Robert McWilliam's birth

No of previous applications:	None
Result of application:	
Date:	Nov 22
How disposed by Inspector:	Refused
How disposed by Board:	Refused
Grounds of refusal:	Able bodied and only one child

Life carried on much the same at Auchtykirnal. Sarah continued to receive her money from Kirkmaiden. She didn't get any more for having Mary and baby Walter at home, but Jane and Mary brought in a little more to help with food and other necessities.

Hogmanay came and went, but you wouldn't have known it in that household. Mary continued to spin for the Day family, Jane still worked at the Grocer's, but May was fast approaching, and with it came the Hiring Fair, on 8 May 1860. Both Jane and Mary went off with high hopes. Sarah stayed at home looking after baby Walter. She might have gotten Nathaniel off to school, but she was still looking after bairns.

Finally, Mary and Jane returned. Mary was jubilant and had a big grin on her face as she walked in through the door. Jane was still talking to Mary as they came inside. "I thought he was going tae hire you."

"Well, he didn't, but it doesnae matter now," replied Mary, "because I've been hired. Dinnae worry yoursel', though. You're too young yet. Come next fair you're sure tae find a good job. Meantime, you keep on wi' your job at the Grocer's. But, dinnae fall into the trap I did."

"I'm no' worried," replied Jane. Both the girls looked at Sarah. "Oh, hello, ma'," said Jane.

"Where's my Walter?" said Mary, almost ignoring her mother. "Oh there you are… Come tae your ma'!" Mary held out her arms and Walter crawled towards her. She picked him up and looked at her mother. "Was he alright?" she asked.

"He's fair wore me out," replied Sarah. "He's a canny wee thing, but he's fast."

Mary sat down with Sarah and put Walter on her lap.

"Well, how did you get on?" Sarah asked her girls.

Mary spoke for both of them. "I've been taken on at Greentowers Farm, just outside Lanark. They need a house servant. I start in four weeks. Jane didnae get a job, though. Maybe next time."

"Aye, well Jane's still young," replied Sarah. "She can stay on at the Grocer's. It might not pay much but it's something." Sarah looked at Walter, relieved that Mary was back. "That bairn o' yours is into everything now he's crawling! He moves sae fast!"

Walter began to wriggle and struggle but the more he struggled the tighter Mary held him. He started to cry.

"Let him down on the floor," said Sarah. "He just wants to crawl."

"But I want tae give him a cuddle, ma'," said Mary.

"Listen tae him!" said Sarah, getting annoyed. "He doesnae want one. Put him down!"

Reluctantly, Mary put Walter down on the floor and he stopped crying. He sat on the floor for a moment before going off to his toys.

The four weeks went by faster than Mary wanted and it was soon Saturday, 2 June. She no longer wanted to leave Walter, but she knew there was little else to be done. If she stayed at home with her son there would not be enough money to go round. At least working at the farm she could help out buying things for Walter. He was growing fast. At the end of the month Walter would be 1 year old.

Mary was all packed, ready to go. Sarah and her siblings were all there to say goodbye. Mary stood there, reluctant to leave. A tear rolled down her cheek.

"You'll be alright, lass," said her mother. "You've done this afore."

Mary nodded. "Aye, but I didnae have a bairn afore," she said. "It hurts tae leave him."

"I know it must," replied Sarah. "But you'll get tae see him at weekends, even if it's only for a few hours a week. You've had nearly the first year with him, so you've got tae know each other well. He's a good boy. He'll understand."

Jane picked Walter up. "We'll all help look after him for you," she said. "We'll tell him stories. You needn't worry, sis."

"Aye," replied Mary, "I know you're right." She held out her arms. "Let me have just one more hug." Jane passed Walter to Mary.

"Now, you be a good boy for your granny," Mary told him. She kissed him on the cheek and handed him back to Jane.

"Do you have everything you need?" asked Sarah.

"Aye, ma', I do," replied Mary. "Well, I suppose I'd best be going."

Mary picked up her bag and everybody gave her a hug. She opened the front door and walked out of the house, up the road to the village to get the coach to Lanark.

Mary settled in well but came home every other Sunday for a few hours as she'd agreed. Walter got used to not seeing his mother often after a while, but in the beginning there were tears on both sides. Eventually, Mary found it easier to come and go.

Things carried on much the same for a few months. Mary had plenty to do at the farm. Janet Muirhead, the farmer's wife had just had her first baby, so Mary was doing more chores than she had previously done in her employment at Birkwood Farm.

By October 1860 things had settled down. Walter was growing fast and Sarah was more able to cope now he was toddling. Jane and Sarah loved looking after their nephew and helped their mother whenever they could.

Sunday 14 October David didn't want to do anything. He got up that morning but wasn't hungry. He didn't want to play or do any schoolwork, either. Sarah put it down to him getting a cold. That night she packed him off to bed with a hot toddy.

During the night the household was awakened by David crying. Sarah got out of bed and lit a candle to see by.

"MA'!!!!!!!!!!!!!" David called out. Sarah walked over to David's bedside. "Coming Davy!" she said.

She went over to David's bed and touched him. He was burning up. This was no cold, Sarah decided. She knew this was worse than a cold but she wasn't sure what it was. She made a decision that if this was infectious she wasn't going to let the others get it.

"I dinnae feel very well, ma'," David whispered to Sarah.

"Aye, I can tell," said Sarah. "You're burning up, boy."

Jane was wide awake by now. "What's the matter wi' Davy, ma'?" she asked.

Sarah went over to Jane's bed. "He's got a fever," she said.

"I feel sick, ma'," said David.

Sarah ran into the other room and fetched a bucket for David, which she put beside his bed. "There's a bucket if you need it, son," she said. "Do you hurt anywhere?"

"I hurt everywhere, ma'," David replied.

Sarah began to think that David had the flu and she was afraid the others might catch it. She remembered how the flu had taken both children and adults, alike, when she had been in Birkenhead.

"I don't like the sound of this," she said. She turned to her other children. "I don't want you sleeping in this room while Davy's like this. Use the two beds in the other room. I'll stay here wi' Davy."

Jane and Sarah took their bedding into the other room and made up the beds. Jane would share with Sarah and Nathaniel would have the other bed. When she had finished Jane came back to see her mother. "Do you want us tae do anything else, ma'?" she asked.

"Aye," said Sarah. "You can help me move Walter's cot out from here. I don't want Mary coming home and finding her bairn sick wi' whatever Davy's got."

Walter thought it was a great adventure to be moved out from the bedroom. Nathaniel just wanted to go back to bed. Finally, all the other children had moved out from the bedroom.

Jane looked around her. "Where will you sleep, ma'?" she asked.

"I'll stay here," replied Sarah. "Somebody's got tae be here for him."

Two days later, David was not getting any better. In fact, he was clearly getting worse. He was beginning to develop lesions all over, as well as in his mouth and on his tongue. Sarah knew it wasn't the flu, but she wasn't sure what else it was. She had to make do the best she could because she couldn't afford to pay for the doctor. She remained constantly by her son's side.

Jane tried to help her mother to ease the strain but Sarah would have none of it. She told Jane to keep everybody out of the room and asked her to look after the others as best as she could. Jane said she would.

Sarah asked Jane to visit Janet Wilson and ask her what they should do. Jane promised she would, so that morning, when Sarah and Nathaniel left for school, Jane took Walter with her and went to see Janet.

Jane knocked at Janet Wilson's door and she opened it.

"Why Jane," said Janet, looking puzzled as to why Jane was there with the baby, "whatever is it?"

"Can I come in for a chat, Mrs. Wilson?" Jane asked.

"Of course you can," Janet replied. Jane went inside and explained the situation at home.

"You poor wee things," said Janet. "Dinnae worry yourselves. I shall get the doctor tae call."

"But we cannae afford tae pay him!" Jane replied, shocked.

"That's nae bother," replied Janet. "That's no' your concern."

"If you're sure about it all," said Jane, "but it's ma' I'm worried about. She's locked herself away wi' Davy and willnae let anybody in tae see her."

"That's just like her!" said Janet. "Now, how are yous coping wi' Walter?"

"It's hard looking after a bairn and the others," answered Jane. "Sarah tries tae help but she's still at school all day – as is Nathan, which means I'm home all alone wi' him."

"Well, I'll see what I can do tae help," replied Janet. "Now, away back home wi' yous," Janet said, "and I'll go visit the doctor." Jane asked Janet to let Mr. Scott know her situation, and that she'd be back working for him as soon as she could. Janet told her she would let him know.

So Jane took Walter back home. Sarah would still not leave David's side. Jane knocked on the bedroom door. "Ma', I spoke to Janet. She said she would send for the doctor tae come tae us."

"But I cannae afford to pay him!" replied Sarah from the other side of the door.

"Janet said for you not tae worry," replied Jane. "She said she was going for Dr. Currie straight away."

Sarah sighed. She hadn't wanted to get anybody else involved. "Is everybody alright?" she asked.

"We're all fine, ma'," replied Jane. "It's you I'm worried about."

"How's that bairn?" Sarah asked.

"Walter's fine. I've spoken wi' Janet and she said she'll see if somebody else can help."

As she stood there talking there came a knock at the door. "Oh, there's a knock at the door ma'," Jane told her mother. "It must be the doctor."

Jane went to the door and answered it. "Good day tae you, doctor," said Jane.

"I'm Dr. Currie, m'dear," he said. Dr. William Currie was just turned 40 years old and very smart. He carried a large doctor's bag with him. "Where's the patient?"

"My ma' shut herself away in the room wi' Davy, my brother," said Jane, pointing to the bedroom door. "I'll tell her you're here."

"Ma'," Jane called through the door, "the doctor's here. Shall I bring him in?"

"No, Jane," Sarah called out, "you stay there."

Jane opened the door and the doctor went into the bedroom.

"Mrs. McWilliam," the Doctor began, "Janet Wilson sent for me tae come. Before you say anything, Janet has told me she will pay my bill, so dinnae worry about it. Now let me see your boy."

Sarah looked exhausted as she stood up and moved away from her son's bedside. The doctor went over to him. He sat down beside the boy and put his bag down. He took out his stethoscope and examined him carefully. As he was doing this Sarah spoke to him.

"Thank you so much for coming, doctor. I'm so afraid for him. Is it the pox? I've never seen it afore, but those marks..." Sarah's words trailed off as she watched the doctor examine David.

The doctor looked at David closely under his clothes. He repacked his bag and stood up. He then turned to Sarah. "Aye, lass," he said, shaking his head. "Aye, lass, I'm afraid it is the pox. I see you took good precautions so the rest o' your family are safe."

"I wasnae sure what it was, so I thought to be careful," replied Sarah. "Is he going to be alright? Please say he will."

"I can see you're a knowledgeable woman," Dr. Currie replied, "so I'll no' beat about the bush. It looks like he's got a very bad case o' the smallpox. I think it's hit him very hard, and from the look o' these lesions it's one o' the worst type of pox. I cannae say he'll be alright. He may pull through, but there's more chance he'll no' beat it."

Sarah looked distraught. "Is there anything I can do to help him?" she asked.

"He's gong tae be much worse afore the week's out," the doctor said. "I can arrange for him tae go tae the Workhouse Hospital in Lanark if you want. He'll get good care there. But all you can do, in the meantime, is keep him comfortable. Gie him water, keep him cool. But there's one thing you must do – and that's try no' tae breathe in too much while you're near him. He's no' infectious just yet, but as soon as the rash starts tae appear you run the risk o' catching it yourself. Try tae keep your distance. Put some kind o' mask on if you can."

"What will they do for him in hospital?" she asked.

"They'll do no more than that," the doctor replied.

"Then I'll keep him here," Sarah said.

"Are you sure?" Dr. Currie asked, concerned that Sarah was trying to do too much.

Sarah nodded that she was sure. The doctor continued, "then I'll be on my way. I'll call back tomorrow tae see how he's doing. If you change your mind about hospital you can tell me when I come back."

"Thank you, doctor," said Sarah.

The doctor picked up his bag and left the room. As he shut the bedroom door Jane went over to him. "How is my brother?" she asked.

"It's no' good news," replied Dr. Currie. "I'm very sorry. I shall be back to visit again."

With that, Jane opened the door and let him out. She sat down in a chair, in a daze.

Janet called round later, at about the same time Sarah and Nathaniel got home from school. The doctor had called in to see Janet, as she had paid him so she knew as much as everybody else in the family.

"I'm so sorry tae hear about your David," she said, as Jane let her in. "I've been thinking about what you said about Walter being hard work."

"Oh, aye," said Jane, "and what can we do?"

"Well, I could help look after him a wee bit for you during the day-time," she said, "just so you can do a few chores."

"Oh, that'd be grand," replied Jane.

So, for the next few days Jane helped get everybody ready to go out, she took Walter to stay with Janet for a few hours while she did chores, little Sarah took Nathaniel to school and their mother spent the day with David. Dr. Currie called in every day to check on David's progress, but David didn't improve.

Finally, at 10 o'clock, on the night of 22 October, Sarah sent Jane to fetch the doctor back. She knew David's time was nigh and she didn't want to be alone. Dr. Currie arrived just before 11 o'clock and stayed by the boy's bedside until he died, at 25 minutes past 11 o'clock.

Sarah was exhausted. She had barely slept for the whole time that David had been sick. The doctor helped her make David look respectable and then he insisted Sarah leave the room and go out to be with the rest of her family.

They came out of the bedroom and Sarah sat down. As she did so, the doctor said, "I'm so sorry for you Sarah. But he's at rest now."

Sarah sat there, stony-faced for a moment, then tears began to trickle down her face. "I cannae believe I've lost him," she sobbed. "I wish there was something I could have done tae help him."

"No!" cried Jane, "he cannae be dead! I dinnae believe it!"

Sarah and Nathaniel woke up with the noise and baby Walter started to cry as his sleep was disturbed.

"What is it?" asked Nathaniel. "Where's Davy?" asked Sarah, on seeing that her mother was in the room.

Sarah tried to regain her composure. "I'm afraid your brother's dead. He died just afore half past 11 o'clock."

Sarah and Nathaniel could not believe it. Sarah started to cry but Nathaniel just sat there, in a daze.

"Now, Sarah," the doctor began, "you know we did everything we could for him. He had a very bad strain of the smallpox. We have tae keep an eye on you now for a couple of weeks – tae make sure you didnae get it. I shall call by in a couple of days tae see how you are. In the meantime, I want you tae stay indoors and away from the rest of your family as much as you can. I'll get in touch wi' the undertakers in the village tomorrow. Now you get some sleep."

Sarah nodded, almost like she was doing it involuntarily. "Yes, doctor. Thank you doctor."

Sarah stood up and went over to the door. She opened it and walked outside with the doctor. It was good to get a blast of fresh air after being cooped up for nearly a week. She watched the doctor disappear into the darkness, then she went back inside and closed the door. She leant on the door as a wave of sadness engulfed her. As she began to weep she slid down the door and sat at the foot of the door, sobbing.

Walter and Nathaniel sat listening to every last word their grandmother told them.

"Well, after that everything is pretty much as you know it," said Sarah. "In 1861 your Auntie Jane went tae live in as servant at Lawriemuir, wi' the family there. So there was just me, your Auntie Sarah, and you two boys *(pointing to Nathaniel and Walter)*. The place felt real big then, wi' just the four o' us. I'd not had less than five children in the place since we moved in."

Sarah chuckled, as she thought back to the feel of the cottage back then.

"About May time 1862," Sarah continued, pointing to Walter and Alexander, "your mother announced she was having another bairn. She never did tell me who Alexander's father was this time. I dinnae think she dared! She worked almost up tae her confinement, like she did wi' you, Walter, and then she came back home after Hogmanay tae have the bairn. I dinnae think she trusted anybody apart from me.

"Then there was your Auntie Jane. I could have done for her. After all she'd seen our Mary put us through, and what did she do? Only took up wi' William Campbell in the summer of 1863 – mind, at least he wasnae married – and got hersel' pregnant! Her William was born the 10th April 1864. Just like her sister, she came back here to have the bairn. Poor little beggar, though, he was a sickly thing. Didnae have much of a chance – he was only 9 month old when he died. Died in his sleep, he did."

Sarah paused as she thought of that wee feller.

"That was real sad. He was a happy little soul that night, when she put him tae bed. We thought he was getting stronger. She was beside herself the next morning when she went tae get him up. Just cold, he was. Just lying there, all limp and cold. She didnae see much of William Campbell after that. Mind, she's seeing another William, now – William Pate. I hope she behaves wi' this one!

"I just hope your Auntie Sarah learns from the mistakes her sisters have made. At present she's a servant at Corehouse Farm, just south o' Lanark. She's doing well there."

Walter jumped up and gave his granny a hug. "I love you, granny," he said. "I want tae stay here wi' you for ever!"

Sarah smiled at him. "Well, that'll be up tae your mother," she said, "when she finally decides tae settle down!"

Sarah leaned back into her chair. "Phew! Well, I fancy another brew. Do you want anything, boys?"

Nathaniel stood up. "You sit down, ma'," he said. "You deserve it, after your story-telling. I'll make you a cup o' tea."

Nathaniel went over to the kitchen end and started to make his mother a cup of tea.

THE END

All the main characters in this are real. The facts have come from my research over the last ten years. There are embellishments to fill the story out, but I have tried to show a snippet of how my family would have lived all those years ago. Walter McWilliam was my great grandfather. His life is another story.

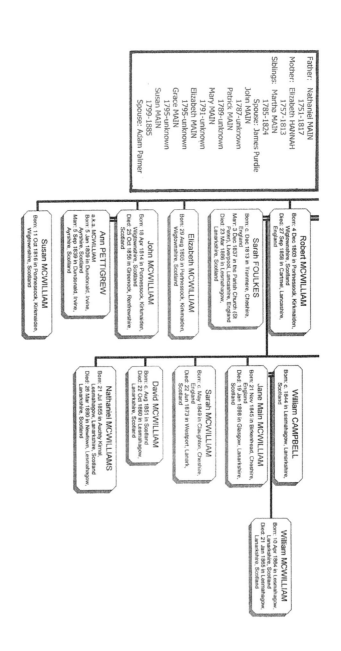

Father: Nathaniel MAIN
1751-1817
Mother: Elizabeth HANNAH
1757-1813
Siblings: Martha MAIN
1785-1824
Spouse: James Purdie
John MAIN
1787-unknown
Patrick MAIN
1789-unknown
Mary MAIN
1791-unknown
Elizabeth MAIN
1795-unknown
Grace MAIN
1795-unknown
Susan MAIN
1799-1885
Spouse: Adam Palmer

Robert MCWILLIAM
Born: 4 Dec 1803 in Portnessock, Kirkmaiden,
Wigtownshire, Scotland
Died: 27 Sep 1858 in Cartmel, Lancashire,
England

Sarah FOULKES
Born: c. Dec 1813 in Tranmere, Cheshire,
England
Marr: 3 Dec 1837 at the Parish Church (St
Peter), Liverpool, Lancashire, England
Died: 23 Mar 1886 in Lesmahagow,
Lanarkshire, Scotland

Elizabeth MCWILLIAM
Born: 29 Aug 1805 in Portnessock, Kirkmaiden,
Wigtownshire, Scotland

John MCWILLIAM
Born: 18 Apr 1814 in Portnessock, Kirkmaiden,
Wigtownshire, Scotland
Died: 25 Oct 1856 in Greenock, Renfrewshire,
Scotland

Ann PETTIGREW
a.k.a. MCWILLIAM
Born: 5 Jan 1809 in Dundonald, Irvine,
Ayrshire, Scotland
Marr: 5 Sep 1839 in Dundonald, Irvine,
Ayrshire, Scotland

Susan MCWILLIAM
Born: 11 Oct 1816 in Portnessock, Kirkmaiden,
Wigtownshire, Scotland

William CAMPBELL
Born: c. 1844 in Lesmahagow, Lanarkshire,
Scotland

Jane Main MCWILLIAM
Born: 21 Nov 1845 in Birkenhead, Cheshire,
England
Died: 19 Jan 1898 in Glasgow, Lanarkshire,
Scotland

Sarah MCWILLIAM
Born: c. May 1849 in Claughton, Cheshire,
England
Died: 22 Jun 1873 in Westport, Lanark,
Scotland

David MCWILLIAM
Born: c. Aug 1851 in Scotland
Died: 22 Oct 1860 in Lesmahagow,
Lanarkshire, Scotland

Nathaniel MCWILLIAMS
Born: 21 Jul 1855 in Auchty Kirnel,
Lesmahagow, Lanarkshire, Scotland
Died: 26 Mar 1890 in Newtown, Lesmahagow,
Lanarkshire, Scotland

William MCWILLIAM
Born: 10 Apr 1864 in Lesmahagow,
Lanarkshire, Scotland
Died: 21 Jan 1865 in Lesmahagow,
Lanarkshire, Scotland

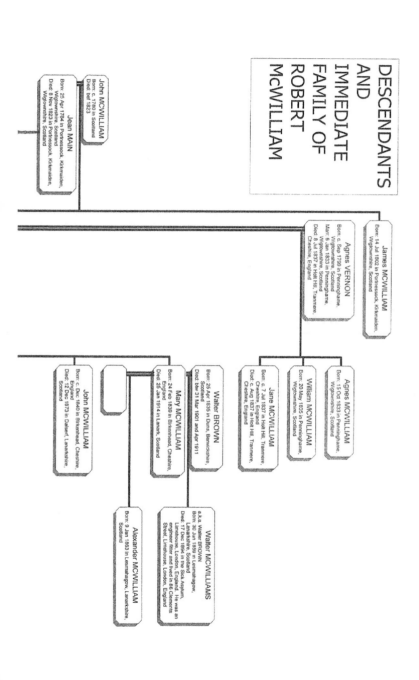

DESCENDANTS AND IMMEDIATE FAMILY OF ROBERT McWILLIAM

John MCWILLIAM
Born: c. 1780 in Scotland
Died: bef 1823

Jean MAIN
Born: 25 Apr 1784 in Portnessock, Kirkmaiden, Wigtownshire, Scotland
Died: 8 Nov 1823 in Portnessock, Kirkmaiden, Wigtownshire, Scotland

James MCWILLIAM
Born: 14 Jul 1802 in Portnessock, Kirkmaiden, Wigtownshire, Scotland

Agnes VERNON
Born: c. Sep 1799 in Penninghame, Wigtownshire, Scotland
Marr: 6 Jan 1823 in Penninghame, Wigtownshire, Scotland
Died: 8 Jul 1837 in Holt Hill, Tranmere, Cheshire, England

Agnes MCWILLIAM
Born: 15 Oct 1833 in Penninghame, Wigtownshire, Scotland

William MCWILLIAM
Born: 20 May 1835 in Penninghame, Scotland

Jane MCWILLIAM
Born: c. 7 Jul 1837 in Holt Hill, Tranmere, Cheshire, England
Died: c. Aug 1837 in Holt Hill, Tranmere, Cheshire, England

Walter BROWN
Born: 25 Apr 1835 in Duns, Berwickshire, Scotland
Died: btw 31 Mar 1901 and Apr 1911

Mary MCWILLIAM
Born: 24 Feb 1839 in Birkenhead, Cheshire, England
Died: 25 Jan 1914 in Lanark, Scotland

John MCWILLIAM
Born: c. Dec 1840 in Birkenhead, Cheshire, England
Died: 12 Dec 1873 in Dalserf, Lanarkshire, Scotland

Walter MCWILLIAMS
a.k.a. Walter BROWN
Born: 30 Jun 1859 in Lesmahagow, Lanarkshire, Scotland
Died: 17 Dec 1894 in the Sick Asylum, Limehouse, London, England. He was an engineer fitter and lived in 66 Clements Street, Limehouse, London, England

Alexander MCWILLIAM
Born: 9 Jan 1863 in Lesmahagow, Lanarkshire, Scotland

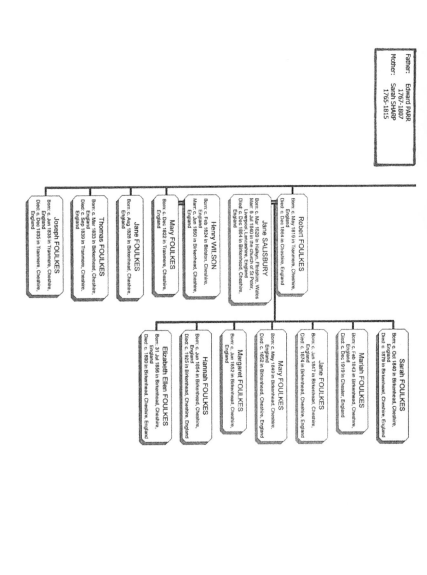

Father: Edward PARR
1767-1807

Mother: Sarah SHARP
1765-1815

Joseph FOULKES
Born: c. Jun 1835 in Tranmere, Cheshire, England
Died: c. Dec 1835 in Tranmere, Cheshire, England

Thomas FOULKES
Born: c. Mar 1833 in Birkenhead, Cheshire, England
Died: c. Sep 1839 in Tranmere, Cheshire, England

Jane FOULKES
Born: c. Aug 1828 in Birkenhead, Cheshire, England

Mary FOULKES
Born: c. Dec 1822 in Tranmere, Cheshire, England

Henry WILSON
Born: c. Feb 1824 in Bistion, Cheshire, England
Marr: c. Jun 1850 in Birkenhead, Cheshire, England

Jane SALISBURY
Born: c. Mar 1820 in Halkyn, Flintshire, Wales
Marr: 5 Jul 1840 in the church of St Peter, Liverpool, Lancashire, England
Died: c. Dec 1864 in Birkenhead, Cheshire, England

Robert FOULKES
Born: c. May 1819 in Tranmere, Cheshire, England
Died: c. Dec 1864 in Cheshire, England

Elizabeth Ellen FOULKES
Born: 31 Jul 1856 in Birkenhead, Cheshire, England
Died: c. 1950 in Birkenhead, Cheshire, England

Hannah FOULKES
Born: c. Jun 1854 in Birkenhead, Cheshire, England
Died: c. 1925 in Birkenhead, Cheshire, England

Margaret FOULKES
Born: c. Jun 1852 in Birkenhead, Cheshire, England

Mary FOULKES
Born: c. May 1849 in Birkenhead, Cheshire, England
Died: c. 1852 in Birkenhead, Cheshire, England

Jane FOULKES
Born: c. Jun 1847 in Birkenhead, Cheshire, England
Died: c. 1874 in Birkenhead, Cheshire, England

Mariah FOULKES
Born: c. Feb 1843 in Birkenhead, Cheshire, England
Died: c. Dec 1919 in Chester, England

Sarah FOULKES
Born: c. Oct 1840 in Birkenhead, Cheshire, England
Died: c. 1879 in Birkenhead, Cheshire, England

DESCENDANTS AND IMMEDIATE FAMILY OF THOMAS FOULKES

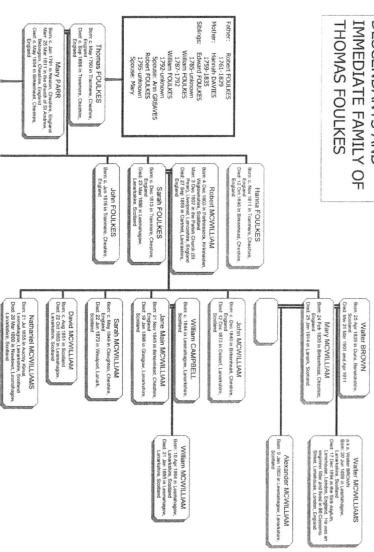

Father: Robert FOULKES
1761-1829

Mother: Hannah DAVIES
1759-1835

Siblings: Edward FOULKES
1785-unknown
William FOULKES
1787-1792
William FOULKES
1792-unknown
Spouse: Ann GREAVES
Robert FOULKES
1795-unknown
Spouse: Mary

Thomas FOULKES
Born: c. May 1790 in Tranmere, Cheshire, England
Marr: 25 Mar 1811 in the church of St Andrew, Bebington, Cheshire, England
Died: c. Sep 1866 in Tranmere, Cheshire, England

Mary PARR
Born: c. Jan 1791 in Neston, Cheshire, England
Died: c. May 1854 in Birkenhead, Cheshire, England

Hanna FOULKES
Born: c. Nov 1811 in Tranmere, Cheshire, England
Died: 12 Oct 1846 in Birkenhead, Cheshire, England

Robert MCWILLIAM
Born: 4 Dec 1803 in Porthsessock, Kirkmaiden, Wigtownshire, Scotland
Marr: 3 Dec 1837 in the Parish Church (St Peter), Liverpool, Lancashire, England
Died: 27 Sep 1858 in Cartmel, Lancashire, England

Sarah FOULKES
Born: c Dec 1813 in Tranmere, Cheshire, England
Died: 23 Mar 1886 in Lesmahagow, Lanarkshire, Scotland

John FOULKES
Born: c. Jun 1816 in Tranmere, Cheshire, England

Mary MCWILLIAM
Born: 24 Feb 1839 in Birkenhead, Cheshire, England
Died: 25 Jan 1914 in Larch, Scotland

Walter BROWN
Born: 25 Apr 1835 in Duns, Berwickshire, Scotland
Died: btw 31 Mar 1901 and Apr 1911

Walter MCWILLIAMS
a.k.a. Walter BROWN
Born: 30 Jun 1859 in Lesmahagow, Lanarkshire, Scotland
Died: 17 Dec 1894 in the Sick Asylum, Limehouse, London, England. He was an engineer fitter and lived in 88 Clements Street, Limehouse, London, England

Alexander MCWILLIAM
Born: 9 Jan 1863 in Lesmahagow, Lanarkshire, Scotland

John MCWILLIAM
Born: c. Dec 1840 in Birkenhead, Cheshire, England
Died: 12 Dec 1873 in Dalserf, Lanarkshire, Scotland

William CAMPBELL
Born: c. 1844 in Lanarkshire, Scotland

Jane Main MCWILLIAM
Born: 21 Nov 1845 in Birkenhead, Cheshire, England
Died: 19 Jan 1898 in Glasgow, Lanarkshire, Scotland

Sarah MCWILLIAM
Born: c. May 1849 in Claughton, Cheshire, England
Died: 22 Jun 1873 in Westport, Larark, Scotland

William MCWILLIAM
Born: 10 Apr 1854 in Lesmahagow, Lanarkshire, Scotland
Died: 21 Jan 1855 in Lesmahagow, Lanarkshire, Scotland

David MCWILLIAM
Born: c. Aug 1851 in Scotland
Died: 22 Oct 1860 in Lesmahagow, Lanarkshire, Scotland

Nathaniel MCWILLIAMS
Born: 21 Jul 1853 in Auchty Adnal, Lesmahagow, Lanarkshire, Scotland
Died: 26 Mar 1890 in Newtown, Lesmahagow, Lanarkshire, Scotland

Julie Isard-Brown was born in 1955 in
Northampton. She went to school at St. James VP
School and Northampton School for Girls. She is
married and has two grown-up daughters. She
works as accounts assistant at Corus Hotels Group,
Berkhamsted, Herts and lives in Croxley Green,
Herts. Her favourite activities are genealogy, acting
and attending conventions for Star Trek and Star
Gate. Through her passion for genealogy she has
reunited adoptees with their birth families. The
story 'The Mason's Wife' is her first book.
Julie is the youngest child of working class parents.
She was the first one in her family to get a Grammar
school education. She wanted to learn more about
her ancestry and after many years of research she
wrote her first book The Mason's Wife.

Ingram Content Group UK Ltd.
Milton Keynes UK
UKHW021120180423
420361UK00014B/965